THE SAME END

THE LAMB AND THE LION
BOOK THREE

GREGORY ASHE

H&B

The Same End

Published by Hodgkin & Blount
https://www.hodgkinandblount.com/
contact@hodgkinandblount.com

Published 2021
Printed in the United States of America

Trade Paperback ISBN: 978-1-63621-011-7
eBook ISBN: 978-1-63621-010-0

For that which befalleth the sons of men befalleth beasts; even one thing befalleth them: as the one dieth, so dieth the other.

Ecclesiastes 3:19

1

"I don't want to kill anything," Tean said into the phone as he unlocked the door and stepped into his apartment. "I'm already named for a murderer; that's bad enough. Besides, I haven't been hunting in twenty years, probably more."

His brother Amos sighed. "You don't have to kill anything. I'm not inviting you to go hunting."

Scipio, Tean's black Lab, bounded off the sofa, stretched, and then crashed into him. A wet nose found his hand, and Scipio did some happy whining to fully communicate how thrilled he was that Tean had returned. "You, Corom, Timothy, Seth, and Dad go hunting every Pioneer Day weekend."

"We go camping. And every year we invite you, and every year you refuse to go."

"Because you're not just going camping. You're going hunting."

"We go hiking. We cook potatoes in the Dutch oven. We try to find constellations. We eat s'mores and listen to Dad's dumb jokes. Like we did when we were kids."

"And you do some hunting."

On the other end of the call, Amos made an irritated noise that he suppressed quickly. "I'm just trying to get you to see the big picture. Yes, we go hunting."

"And fishing."

Another of those noises. "And fishing," Amos said; it sounded like he was gritting his teeth. "But you're missing the point. The point is that this year, we're not going camping."

"Hunting."

"Teancum, please!"

"Fine. What are you doing instead?"

"We're going to Vegas."

"Sin City? Bold choice. What does your wife think about that?"

"It was Bailey's idea, actually. She won some sort of KSL giveaway. Five tickets to Celine Dion. She's taking Mom and the sisters-in-law; Sara and Miriam opted out to give the other girls a chance to bond. They're even taking the kids for four days. We come back late on Pioneer Day."

"I hope you have a great time."

"And you know Bailey, so she called the hotel and talked them into reserving a block of rooms for all of us. It's an unbelievable rate."

Tean tried to repress a shudder. He'd once seen Bailey break down a Hobby Lobby clerk, leaving the poor man in tears, over a ten-cent price adjustment on a baby-Jesus-themed wreath. "Even better. I hope you all have a great time."

"A block of rooms for all of us, Tean. That includes you. Come on, please. This is a chance for us to bond, just the guys, while the girls do their thing."

Tean cradled the phone against his shoulder as he helped Scipio into his harness. "I've got too much work. A moose injured a hiker, we're still trying to figure out how bad the damage from the Beaver Mesa fire really is, and we've got to inspect close to fifteen thousand boats for invasive mussels on the hulls. I've got enough work for the rest of the year."

"Great. You're never going to catch up on it, so you might as well take a few days off and hang with your brothers."

"What about Jem?"

"I don't think even Bailey can get another free ticket to Celine." Doubtfully, Amos added, "Not this late."

Scipio led the way out of the apartment, and Tean pulled the door shut behind him. They went downstairs. "Do you want to try that again?"

"I was just joking."

"Jem isn't my wife. He's not even my boyfriend. He's my friend."

"Nobody else is bringing friends."

"Why can't I bring him?"

"You just said he's not even your boyfriend. He was unbelievably rude last time he came around, and he made everyone feel horrible—Mom cried, by the way. And I don't know why you feel like you need a bodyguard so you can attend family events. If you've got a problem with us, you can tell us yourself. We don't need your friend sticking his nose into our family business."

"He's not sticking his nose—"

"Does he even allow you to go places by yourself? Are you permitted to see your family on your own?"

"Goodbye, Amos."

They stopped at the first available stretch of grass so Scipio could relieve himself, and then they headed south. Salt Lake City was an oven in July, the dry heat baking the air. The whole city felt gritty with dust—they might not have precipitation again until the first snowfall—and where the sun danced on glass and stucco, it was so bright that Tean had to squint.

Everyone was looking for ways to beat the heat. He passed a kebab shop, its doors propped open, two fans humming to circulate air—and, as a bonus, blowing the smell of seared meat into the street, probably in the hopes of attracting customers. Scipio was definitely interested. A glitzy, upgraded hipster version of the old-fashioned ice-cream truck was parked at the next corner, and the line of people ran for half a block. Tean had no idea what mochi balls were, but if they were this popular, Jem had probably already tried them and fallen in love with them. Catty-corner, a pair of Latina girls were running an ancient shaved-ice machine, their only client a middle-aged woman who was digging through her purse while the kids threw murderous looks at the mochi truck.

Tean and Scipio were halfway to Liberty Park when his phone buzzed. It was Amos again. Tean dismissed the call. At the next crosswalk, it vibrated again. Cor, the next brother in line. Then, when they got under the shade of an elm, Timothy. At this rate, they'd burn through the immediate family before dinner, and then Tean would be ignoring calls from his ailing, elderly great-aunts until he put his head under the wheel of a mochi truck.

When Seth called, Tean answered and said, "What?"

"Oh. I didn't think you were going to answer, so I honestly wasn't ready."

"Goodbye, Seth."

"No, wait. Can I start with Amos is a jerk, and we're all sorry?"

"How often do you talk to each other? Is there a group chat I don't know about?"

"Yes, obviously. Except you do know about it. It's on that app you refuse to download. I've sent you ten invites."

"I'm not going to Vegas."

"Please?"

"I'm not going."

"Ok. That's fine. I mean, we'll miss you, but that's fine." Someone had set up sprinklers in one of the open fields of the park, and kids were darting through the spray, laughing, shrieking, slipping, coming up muddy and grinning. "Would you at least think about it, though?"

"You know that you guys do this with everything? You invite me, invite me, invite me, and you don't want me there, but then I'm the bad guy if I don't go."

A diesel dump truck rumbled past, the engine so loud that it obliterated other sounds.

"Do you really feel that way?"

"Never mind. I'm tired. I've got a lot going on." When they got to the fenced section of the park, Tean knelt to unhook the leash from the harness. He opened the gate and let Scipio race inside. "Thanks for the invitation, but I'm not going to be able to make it."

"You know what?" Seth said.

Tean shook his head and didn't answer.

"Your friend was right about a lot of stuff. But you're not giving us a chance to make it better."

"Right. Got it. It's my fault again."

"Don't do that. You know this was Dad's idea, right? This is all about you. Just like every conversation we have in this family is about you. He's told everyone who would listen that he wants you there."

"Dad's freaking out because I stopped writing Mom blank checks," Tean said.

"Jeez, Tean, I get it! Dad's an asshole! Quit letting him screw up your relationship with people who love you."

At the other end of the fenced area, Scipio was playing tag with a Pomeranian. The Lab would get as close as he dared, and when the Pomeranian whirled around, Scipio would shoot off in the other direction.

Tean started to laugh. Then Seth started to laugh too.

"I honestly don't know if I've ever heard you use a bad word before," Tean said.

"Well, it's not the first time."

Tean sat on a bench; the back was hot from the sun, and he rested his elbows on his knees, watching Scipio play. "So, what? Everybody resents me because I'm the black sheep and you have to talk about me and think about me and pray about me?"

"You are an extremely frustrating person sometimes. Did you know that? If this is what you put Jem through, somebody honestly ought to give that man a medal."

"You should hear him when I make him wash the dishes. You'd think he was the victim of a war crime." Then Tean's face heated. "We're just friends, you know."

"Why?"

"What?"

"He's crazy about you; that's obvious. He stood up for you. Heck, you dragged him to a family party, and he didn't run away screaming. You should probably jump straight to marrying him."

"It's complicated."

"Is it because of Ammon?" Seth sounded hesitant. "Just so you know, well, everybody knows. More or less."

"It's complicated. That's all."

"That's your way of saying you don't want to talk about it."

"Seth, if I'm being totally up front, I don't think I can talk about it. Not with you, anyway."

Scipio had taken up position near the fence and was barking at joggers.

"I'm really sorry to hear that," Seth said.

"I'll think about Vegas," Tean said. "I need to go. Please don't make Great-aunt Gilda call me."

The call ended in taut silence.

After collecting Scipio, Tean headed back to the apartment. The line for the mochi truck was longer. The Latina girls had packed up, maybe to try their luck somewhere else. Tean considered stopping at the kebab shop, but then he remembered he had a brick of tofu and a few cloves of garlic at home, and he figured he could make something out of that.

As he neared the apartment building, he heard Mrs. Wish screaming.

"Stop it right this minute! I absolutely will not tolerate this behavior. You are both gentlemen, and you will behave—no, Senator Borah, don't you dare, I will not—" And then more screams.

His neighbor was an older woman in a housedress printed with sailboats, her white hair up in a bun. She was currently trying to wrangle three of the Irreconcilables. The cats' leashes had gotten tangled, and two of them—Senator Poindexter, a Siamese, and Senator William Borah, a Bengal—were hissing at each other, lunging, trying to fight. The third cat, Senator Frank B. Bandegee, a domestic shorthair with a white patch on her chest, was pulling in the opposite direction. Mrs. Wish was yanking on the tangled leashes and screaming.

Tean secured Scipio's leash to the trunk of a short-needled pine, and the Lab flopped onto his stomach, obviously curious to see how Tean sorted this out. Tean got his leg between the fighting cats, clapped his hands loudly a few times, and when Senator Poindexter retreated and hissed at him, Tean took the leashes from Mrs. Wish's hands. He untangled Senator Poindexter's, passed it to Mrs. Wish, and said, "Take him back to the apartment, please."

"No, no, we're going to work this out. They just need more time together."

"That's only going to make things worse. Take him back, please."

"I really think they'll be the best of friends if they'd just—"

Senator William Borah hissed and lunged again, and Mrs. Wish let out a shriek. She stumbled back, dragging Senator Poindexter with her, only barely managing to keep her balance.

"I am very disappointed," she announced, straightening the housedress. "I am very disappointed in all of you."

Still untangling Senator William Borah and Senator Frank B. Bandegee, Tean had the suspicion that he was included in that statement. Mrs. Wish trundled back to the apartment. Tean retrieved Scipio. The Lab had watched the proceedings with disinterest, but when Senator Borah got within range, he bent and sniffed at the Bengal.

"Leave him alone," Tean said, using the leashes to force the animals apart.

Scipio sneezed. He was still eyeing Senator Borah.

"I know," Tean said. "This is why we don't have cats."

On his way back to the apartment, he got a text from Ammon: *Want to grab dinner?* Tean dismissed the message without replying.

By the time he made it upstairs, Mrs. Wish had gotten Senator Poindexter inside her apartment, and she stood in the hallway with her hands on her hips.

"This is absolutely unacceptable behavior, Senator William Borah," she said. "I will not stand for it." To Tean, she said, "I'm sorry you had to see that, Dr. Leon. I thought we'd reached a détente, but it seems they're determined to act like little boys instead of gentlemen."

"Mrs. Wish, they're not acting like boys or men. They're acting like cats. Unneutered cats. And if I had to guess, I'd say Senator Frank B. Bandegee is in estrus. This is why you should have all of the Irreconcilables fixed; you're not going to be able to socialize them out of this. It's instinct."

"Well, I should hope not."

"I'm sorry, but it is. You can't fight nature."

"Senator Frank B. Bandegee is an excellent young lady, but the boys have other choices, and I'm sure they can find a way to—"

"It's not about choices, Mrs. Wish. And it's not about logic or reason. You've got two males who are fighting over a mate. That's not going to end well; you need to take care of this, even though I know you don't like your options."

Mrs. Wish frowned, the lines around her mouth deepening. Then she shook her head. "We'll just continue to go on walks. They'll work things out between them."

Sighing, Tean passed over the leashes. Then he led Scipio to their apartment. As he was heading inside, he got another text, this one from Jem. It was a GIF of a woman eating an enormous bowl of pasta, which was Jem's way of asking if Tean wanted to get dinner. Tean dismissed that message too.

Tean shook his head, already thinking about Mrs. Wish again as he helped Scipio out of his harness. He wasn't sure why so many people fooled themselves into thinking that if they ignored a problem, it would eventually go away.

2

"Hold on," Jem said into the phone. "This might be them."

"I don't care," Tinajas said. Keys clicked on her end of the call. "I'm hanging up now."

"Just hold on." Eyeing the white Mercedes GLE through the window, Jem decided these were the people he'd been waiting for. "It's them, but they're not getting out of the car for some reason."

"I don't care. Really. I do not care at all. I have a rich, fulfilling life that has nothing to do with you."

"Really? It sounds boring. Wait, wait, I think they're arguing."

"Again: do not care. You called me at work to bother me—"

"I called you at work to harass you."

"—and complain about how bored you are—"

"Well, I like to keep you updated."

More clicking from Tinajas's end of the call. "—in spite of me repeatedly telling you not to bother me at work. Great. Consider me officially updated. Goodbye, Jem. Sell a house, make lots of money, and pay me back the five hundred dollars I loaned you."

"Loaned me? I thought that was a birthday present."

"It wasn't. It was a loan. Which is what I told you when I gave you the money and made you sign an IOU to pay me back."

"I thought that was my birthday card."

"Really? You thought you were signing your own birthday card?"

Sensing that he might have spun things out a little too far, Jem said, "This guy looks really douchey. He keeps checking his sunglasses lanyard."

"Goodbye, Jem."

"And the wife is way too young for him. Oh, maybe she's a mistress?"

"Sell a house. Pay me my money."

"She looks like she's got fake boobs."

"Do not call me at work ever again," Tinajas said and disconnected.

From inside the house, which was currently for sale, Jem took one last look at his prospective clients. They were definitely arguing. He made a quick tour of the ground floor—everything was in order, but it felt creepy to stand at the window, watching them—and settled himself in the kitchen. He checked his phone. He sent Tean a GIF of a woman eating pasta. He considered doing this showing with an accent. Maybe Swedish. Or—or he could pretend to keep getting lost. That was a new one. He could walk straight into a closet and pretend to be completely baffled that it wasn't the butler's pantry or whatever these fucking jackals wanted. He was willing to do anything, at this point, that made the game even the tiniest bit less boring.

It had been different at the beginning. When he hadn't known what he was doing, when he'd been figuring everything out. Everything had been painstakingly slow because it was still so hard for him to read. First, making a fake license. Then making fake business cards. Then making a fake website. Then making contact with other agents, pitching himself as a client broker, which he was incredibly proud of himself for having invented. Utah was in the midst of the biggest housing boom in its history. New houses were going up all over the state, but construction couldn't keep up with demand. More importantly, the new houses were often an hour or two away from Salt Lake, which meant houses that were closer in were going for unimaginable sums. And Jem had figured out how to get a nice little cut of that business.

When the knock came at the door, he sent Tean a GIF he had made of Scipio wagging his tail, and then he went and answered.

"Hello," he said, showtime grin, already shaking hands. "Jake Brimhall. Jake Brimhall. Nice to meet you both, you must be Sam and Diane."

The man was fifty, too tan, and the sunglasses lanyard was just the tip of the iceberg. Not golf, Jem decided after a moment. Boating. The woman was probably skating close to thirty, too tan, and the boobs were definitely fake. Dancer, Jem decided after a moment. Former cheerleader.

"No," the man said. "Dwayne and Leslie Rae."

Leslie Rae gave Jem a limp flutter of her fingertips and a dead-eyed smile.

"God, of course. Sorry. I've got Sam and Diane a little later. Then Jerry and Elaine. And Ross and Rachel. It just doesn't stop, you know? Come in, come in. God, look at you, you guys belong here. Have you seen the neighbors? You're going to fit right in."

"I don't know about that," Dwayne said, hands on his hips. "This place has sure seen better days."

Leslie Rae looked like she was trying to pop her gum, only she didn't have any gum at the moment.

Jem walked them through the house.

"A/C needs to be replaced," Dwayne said, fanning the warm air.

"Don't worry, it's only five years old," Jem said with an easygoing smile. "I just turned it on when I got here, that's all."

Upstairs, Dwayne pointed at a cracked window.

"Two words," Jem said, holding up two fingers to drive the point home. "Home warranty. You make sure the seller writes it into the contract, and then you get that taken care of first thing."

In the basement, Dwayne kicked the furnace, apparently under the impression that this was the homebuyer equivalent of kicking the tires on a car. The hollow boom echoed back from bare cement.

"Doesn't sound good," Dwayne said, frowning.

Jem nodded. "You know what? I've got an agent in mind. If you want me to put you in touch, you just say the word. He'll make sure you get a few grand off the price to cover that furnace."

Back in the kitchen, Dwayne flipped the lights on and off. "Bulb's burned out."

"I've got one in the car," Jem said. "I'll swap it out after you go."

Dwayne opened his mouth.

"Dwayne, Leslie Rae, now's the time to make a decision. I've got Homer and Marge coming in twenty minutes, and I need to know if you want me to make things happen for you."

That was the magic phrase, *make things happen*. It could mean anything. It meant whatever people like Dwayne and Leslie Rae wanted it to mean. They'd already paid two hundred dollars for pre-screened access to elite homes, a back network of agents managed by a client broker. At least, that's what Jem had said they were paying for. He didn't even know what it meant himself, but people like Dwayne and Leslie Rae ate it up.

Dwayne and Leslie Rae glanced at each other. Leslie Rae made that gum popping movement with her mouth again. Dwayne started to nod.

Then Leslie Rae said, "What do you even do?"

Jem smiled and raised his eyebrows. "I'm a client broker." It was the tone that sold it, sounding slightly embarrassed that he had to explain.

"But what do you do? That's what I was asking Dwayne the whole way over. What does he do? And Dwayne couldn't tell me."

"I told you," Dwayne said, coloring under his tan. "He's a client broker. He pre-screens. He's got a back network of agents."

Jem nodded, shrugged, spread his hands.

"Isn't that what a normal real estate agent does?" Leslie Rae said. Her mouth popped invisible gum again.

He'd made a mistake, Jem realized. He'd miscalculated. He'd been so focused on Dwayne kicking the goddamn furnace that he might have overplayed his hand.

He laughed. "In a normal world," Jem said. "Five years ago, ten, maybe. But that's just not the way things happen anymore. You want a house?" He snapped his fingers. "It's gone before you even find it. If you're using a normal agent, I mean. You've got to get one step ahead of the game. You've got to pre-buy. You've got to beat the market curve, anticipate, outfox. Dwayne knows what I mean."

"I told her about pre-buying," Dwayne said, shooting a look at Leslie Rae. "I couldn't think of the word, but that's what I was telling you about."

For a moment, Leslie Rae looked like she might argue. Then she shrugged.

Jem could have left it there. Another two hundred in cash. But his blood was pounding, and he felt awake and alive for the first time in months, having to think on his feet, having to riff. Riffing was what he did best. And now he was riffing again, the words spilling out of him.

"I don't want to overstep," he said. "But I've got to warn you, this place is going to go fast. I think it might go today, if I'm being totally honest."

Dwayne shifted his weight. "We'd have to have that furnace looked at."

"Absolutely. And you should, you absolutely should." Jem hesitated. He let the moment hang, and then he lowered his voice. "Look, I shouldn't do this, but the owner is a friend of the family. Practically family; I call them my aunt and uncle. He and my dad were on the high council together for thirty years, and he was the stake patriarch when I got my patriarchal blessing. He and his wife were on their third mission to Georgia—that's the country, not the state—when the cancer came back." Jem shook his head. "We haven't given up on a miracle, but that's about what it's going to take."

"Jeez," Dwayne said.

"I'm sorry to hear that," Leslie Rae said in the vocal equivalent of ordering at a drive-thru.

"Normally, as a client broker, I'm supposed to hand you off to an agent at this point, but—Uncle Dan and Aunt Roseanne, they need money bad. They'd be willing to consider selling without an agent to save the commission." Jem shook his head. "I can't even believe I'm telling you this, but they'd be willing to take half what the house is worth, just to get the cash in their hands."

"I thought homes were selling too fast these days," Leslie Rae said. "I thought that's why we needed a client broker."

"Homes are going fast. Agents, banks, and wire transfers, they're still taking their sweet time."

"What's the catch?" Dwayne said, narrowing his eyes. It furrowed his too-tan face like an old baseball mitt.

"If they don't make a mortgage payment today, the bank repossesses the house. It's got to be cash, and if I'm totally honest—it's got to be cash because it's a gray area, if you get what I mean."

"There it is," Dwayne trumpeted. "There's the other shoe. Did you hear it drop?"

Jem shrugged. "It is what it is. I thought maybe—well, it could have worked out for everybody: you get a house that instantly doubles in value, Uncle Dan gets his chemo. But you're right. I'm not really comfortable with it either. I'm sorry I brought it up."

Dwayne was breathing a little faster. He was tapping the kitchen counter. "Now let's just think about this for a minute."

"It seems pretty awful," Leslie Rae said. "That's what I think about it. Giving them half what they deserve just because they need it now."

"If they didn't need it so badly," Jem said, and then he stopped, as though unable to go on.

"Well, you heard him, didn't you?" Dwayne gestured at Jem. "You heard how bad they need it. We're doing them a favor. How low do you think they'll go?"

"Dwayne Mapes, can you even hear yourself?"

"I'm not made of cash, and this is a business transaction. I want to do these people a solid turn, but it's business first. How low will they go?"

"This house came in at four twenty-five," Jem said. "They've got to have two hundred thousand by the end of the month. Goll', I'm getting sick just talking about this. I don't know, I don't think—"

"Young man, listen up. You're feeling sick because you're thinking about all the money they'd be leaving on the table. That's a young man's way of looking at things. That's a healthy man's way of looking at it. Where's your Uncle Dave—"

"Dan," Leslie Rae said.

"Where's your Uncle Dan going to be if he holds out for the full value?"

"Dwayne Mapes, you are sleeping on the couch tonight."

"Let the men talk, please. Well, sir?"

"I know," Jem said. "I know. And I get it. But it still makes me sick. I shouldn't have said anything."

"You're thinking about it all wrong. You're doing them a favor. You're saving your uncle's life. That's how you ought to be seeing this."

Jem shook his head.

"What are we talking with that outstanding mortgage payment? Sixteen hundred? Two thousand?"

"Jeez, no," Jem said with a laugh. "Five-oh-five. They bought this place twenty-five years ago. It wasn't worth anything back then."

Dwayne practically licked his chops. "Well, that's nothing. We can handle that."

"But it's got to be cash. This is a real fine line, and if it makes you uncomfortable at all, knowing you're walking it, I'd rather not put you through that."

"You ought to be thanking us, young man. And your uncle ought to be thanking you. This is a square deal all around, and I'd say the Lord put us in each other's path. Now, I'm going to get that cash. What I need from you is for you to talk to Uncle Don—"

"Dan," Leslie Rae said, "Dan, it's like you don't even listen."

"Talk to that Uncle Dan and get things in order for me."

"Done," Jem said. "Should I cancel my other showings? Frick, I feel like I'm making a huge mistake."

"Son, you tell those people this place is as good as sold."

He walked them to the door. Leslie Rae stopped to measure the opening into the living room and said, "It's like they built this place for ants."

When they stepped outside, Jem moved to the window. He held his phone to his ear and waved. The closest ATM was five blocks away, and if he had to judge by the gleam in Dwayne's eye, Jem thought the greedy old lech would sell a kidney to get that five hundred in cash. Once they were out of sight, Jem scrolled through GIFs until he found one of Scrooge McDuck swimming in gold coins. He sent it to Tinajas.

She sent back a middle-finger emoji.

3

Tean stacked the boxes from The Pie. Then he set them side by side. Then he stacked them again. Scipio leaned into him, his muzzle poking up over the counter, drawn by the smell of tomato sauce, hot cheese, and a variety of cured meats. Tean kneed the Lab gently away from the pizzas and offered him, instead, a rawhide-substitute treat. Scipio took it gingerly and then dropped it on the floor, fixing Tean with a look of pure disgust.

Tean didn't have time to soothe the dog. He straightened the plates and forks and knives and napkins. Did anybody need forks and knives with pizza? He put out spoons too, just in case. He checked the Bristlecone, which was on ice, the glass beaded with condensation. He thought Jem liked brown ale. He thought Ammon liked brown ale. He had put a single bottle of cider for himself in the ice, but then he'd thought maybe that was too much, and he'd put the whole pack of cider in a bottom cabinet behind a roll of trash bags.

Scipio had his muzzle on the counter again.

"Right," Tean said. "Xanax."

But he'd only taken two steps toward the bedroom—he now kept the bottle hidden, although he wasn't convinced he could successfully hide anything if Jem really wanted to find it—when someone knocked at the door.

Scipio lunged toward the noise, barking.

Tean followed, and when he opened the door, he smiled and said, "Come in."

Ammon Young, childhood friend, former lover, and one of the immense complications in Tean's life, stepped into the apartment. Scipio backed up a few steps, his whole body stiff, growling. Ammon gave an embarrassed grin, rubbed a hand through blond hair that was starting to thin, and said, "Hi. And hi, Scipio."

"Ignore him, he's—oh. Hi."

Ammon's hug lasted a moment too long for it to be a simple, friendly hug. When he released Tean, his smile looked more like the one Tean remembered from high school. "I didn't even try to kiss you."

"I noticed."

"How's that for progress?"

"Well, you did have to point it out."

Ammon's grin got bigger, but instead of answering, he squatted and said to Scipio, "Come on, I'm your buddy. Can I give him a treat?"

"You can try. He looked at me like I was insulting his family honor when I gave him one earlier. Here, see if he wants one of these."

Taking a small, liver-flavored treat from the pouch that Tean held out, Ammon said, "Skip, Skip, let's have a treat. I'm your friend." He held out the treat, and Scipio forgot to growl as he leaned forward to sniff the offering. He accepted it grudgingly and then turned and dropped it on the linoleum.

"Hey!"

"I know, that's what he did to me too."

Scipio slunk over to the couch and curled up on a cushion.

"I thought he wasn't allowed on the furniture."

Tean was saved from having to explain by the door opening. Jem stopped in the doorway. He'd gotten his hair cut again, and the hard side part was perfect as always. He had broad shoulders and a muscular build that the jacket and trousers couldn't hide. Ammon was bigger; if Tean were being fair, Ammon was probably better looking all around, with more classically handsome features. Over the last few months, he'd regained the gym-toned body that had filled Tean's fantasies as a teenager and his bed as a younger man. But Jem was Jem.

Scipio charged across the room. The Lab didn't notice how Jem flinched, and he crashed into Jem's legs at full speed. By then, Jem had recovered, and he was crouching to rub Scipio's ears. Scipio was whining with excitement, licking Jem's face, crashing into him so many times that he finally managed to knock Jem on his butt. Tean was trying to get the dog to back up, and he didn't notice until too late that Ammon had put an arm around him.

"Fuh, fuh, he put his nose in my mouth. Tean, why are there treats on the floor?" Jem snatched up the liver one and held it out; Scipio took it and swallowed it. When Jem collected the rawhide substitute, Scipio took it out of his hand before Jem even had a chance to offer it. The Lab carried it over to the couch and curled up again, gnawing on his treat.

"I'm sorry," Tean said, and Ammon held on a little too tightly before Tean managed to get free. "I swear we've been working on staying." He gave Jem his hand and helped him up. "Are you ok?"

"I know what a dog's nose tastes like. No, I'm not ok."

"I'll put him in the bedroom."

"It's too late. I can never un-know what a dog's nose tastes like." Then Jem's gaze slid past Tean to Ammon. "And I think I misunderstood your message, so I'll come back another day."

"You didn't misunderstand. We're going to have dinner. Together. You're both my friends, and you need to be able to spend five minutes in a room together."

"Five minutes," Ammon said. "Starting now."

"You said we were having pizza," Jem said. "You didn't say we were also having a torrential douche."

"I want to point out that he started it."

"You started it by being you and having your dumb face—"

"Ok," Tean said.

"Calling me names," Ammon said. "Really mature."

"I can be mature," Jem said. "You haven't even seen me try to be mature."

"Ok, that's enough," Tean said.

"If it's too much to have a civilized dinner with friends—"

"You're not my friend. Tean is my friend. My best friend."

"Just a normal friend," Tean said. "And I really think—"

"Best friend? I've known Tean for more than twenty years. You haven't even known him for twenty months."

"Ok!" Tean slapped the counter. "That's enough."

Scipio looked up from his treat long enough to woof once.

Jem was staring back defiantly. Ammon was studying his sneakers.

"I'm tired of the pissing matches. I don't want to date you." He pointed at Ammon. "I don't want to date you." He pointed at Jem. "I've had just about enough of all the men in my life. Eat your damn pizza, and if you can't be decent human beings, go home."

"Nickel in the swear jar," Jem whispered. Then, to Ammon, "It's our Disney World fund."

"Sorry," Ammon muttered.

"Don't tell me," Tean shouted. With a little more control, he added, "Also, I'm sorry I'm still shouting."

"I'm sorry, Jem. And Tean, I'm sorry too."

"Well, now I have to say I'm sorry or I look like an asshole," Jem said. "So I guess I'm sorry."

Tean covered his face.

"But if you had to pick one of us," Jem said. "Like, a desert-island type of situation. Just in theory."

"Oh my gosh."

"It would really speed things along if you could just tell us."

"Neither of you. I would pick the moldy skeleton in the shipwreck."

"He's already in a relationship with the mermaid statue thingy on the front of the boat."

"It would probably be a ship," Ammon said. "Not a boat." When Tean and Jem both looked at him, he raised his hands and said, "I'm trying to be helpful."

"Then I'd swim out into the ocean. That would be better than this conversation. I would throw away my Julia-Child brand shark repellant, and I would swim straight into a garbage current, and I'd paddle until I ran out of strength. And then I'd drown. And my bloated corpse would float there until a shark came along and ripped me apart."

Ammon made a face and reached for a beer.

"What about your guts and stuff, though?" Jem said. "You didn't talk about your guts."

"They'd get sucked up in a ship's engine, obviously." Tean considered it for a moment. "Some kind of gull might get my eyeballs."

"Ok," Ammon said, and the Bristlecone hissed as he opened it. "Let's talk about something else."

"But your bones would probably jam a ship's propeller, right?" Jem said. "And then a Carnival cruise ship would be stuck adrift for months on the garbage current. And they'd eventually have to start eating each other. And then they'd get smeared in the news as the Cannibal cruise lines."

"New topic, please," Ammon said and took a swig of beer.

"There'd definitely be some executive suicides," Tean said, his eyes narrowed in thought. "And a trickle-down effect. Maybe huge swaths of coastal regions shut down because the cruise industry has collapsed. Are you happy? You just shattered Port-au-Prince's economy because the two of you had to measure your, um. You know."

"All right. There. You got it out of your system." Ammon opened a box, and steam and the aroma of garlic and sausage wafted up. "Can we eat now?"

"Cocks," Jem said.

Ammon choked on pizza.

"He was talking about our cocks," Jem said.

"I wasn't talking—you two were the ones—" Tean jerked a slice of pizza free, slapped it onto a plate, and shoved it at Jem. "Eat. And be quiet."

For a few blessed moments, the only sounds were chewing, beer caps pinging against the counter, and Scipio's drool dripping. Jem kept sneaking the Lab pieces of sausage when he thought Tean wasn't looking, and Ammon kept taking long drinks of Bristlecone.

"I thought you were Mormon," Jem said.

"Don't—" Tean began.

"No, it's fine." Ammon held out the brown-glass bottle, eyeing it, and then he shrugged. "I spent a long time convincing myself I could have everything I wanted. Turns out, I can't. So I'm picking the things I want the most and trying to be honest about it, which is what normal, healthy people do. Or so I understand."

"God, I wouldn't have any idea," Jem said. "It sounds awful, though."

The laugh must have caught Ammon by surprise because suds burst out of his nose, and then he staggered to the sink, coughing and wiping his face while Tean patted him on the back. Then he got him a wet cloth, and Ammon wiped his face, still chuckling. Jem was letting Scipio lick invisible traces of sauce from between his fingers, and he was wearing a small smile.

"I haven't seen you laugh that hard since you convinced Clyde Kerry that he got his girlfriend pregnant by letting her wear his 501s."

"Oh my God," Ammon said, squeezing his eyes shut. "I was such a dick in high school."

"In high school?" Jem murmured.

"What was that?" Tean said.

"That was a private conversation with Scipio. I was telling him about . . . something."

Tean fixed him with a glare. Jem smiled and stroked Scipio's ears.

"You're not going to tell me you were a saint in high school, are you?" Ammon said.

"Jem probably doesn't want to talk about—"

Waving Tean to silence, Jem said, "I was in juvie. We had classes. Kind of. A lot of workbooks, which, well, I could make fuck-all sense out of. You were supposed to get a GED or high-school equivalency diploma if you finished everything."

"You don't have a high-school degree?"

"Ammon!"

"It's a question, Tean. If you want us to be friends, fine. But if I can't even ask him a question, we might as well go back to measuring our cocks."

Tean groaned.

"No, no degree." Jem played with Scipio's scruff. "And in case Tean hasn't told you, I can't read either."

"He can read. You can read."

"He didn't tell me that. He doesn't tell me anything about you, just so you know."

"He didn't tell you how much better I am at sex?"

"That's not what—I never—"

Ammon's hand settled on his shoulder, and he squeezed once. "He's just messing with me." Then, to Jem, "God, you really know how to wind him up, don't you?"

"It's too easy."

"I just want to point out," Tean said, "that Jem Berger is the one who got drunk and called me last weekend to make a series of indecent proposals, and so if anyone is easy, it's him."

"I wasn't drunk. I was high. And I put a lot of thought into those ideas."

Ammon gave a tiny half-shake of his head, and he was smiling as he turned to Tean. "Do you want to watch Daniel's baseball game with me tomorrow?"

"Wow. Is—are you sure?"

"Is Lucy going to be there? Is that what you were going to ask?"

"I think it's a fair question."

"It's completely fair. Yes, she will be. But you're my friend, and I can ask my friends to do stuff with me."

"He's my best friend," Jem put in.

"Casual, you-had-high-school-shop-together-and-didn't-see-each-other-again-until-your-twentieth-high-school-anniversary level of friends," Tean said, unable to look away from Ammon's eyes. "I can't, Ammon. It means a lot to me that you'd ask, and I'd love to go another time, but I can't."

"Another time," Ammon said. "Sure."

"He's got a date."

The only change was a slight furrow between Ammon's eyebrows.

"Well," Tean said, his face heating. "Yes, actually. Maybe Jem could go with you."

"No!" they both shouted at the same time.

"I'm sure he's got better things to do," Ammon said.

"I do." Jem nodded vigorously. "I've got to pick lint out of my crotch hair."

Ammon didn't seem to hear him; his gaze was fixed on Tean, and the struggle on his face was painful to watch. Finally, with what seemed like remarkable control, he said, "Am I allowed to ask questions?"

"Half a question," Jem said. "And you have to say it backwards."

"Will you stop it? You can ask questions. I might not answer them."

"Did you meet him on Prowler?"

"Yes."

"What's his name?"

"I'm not going to answer that."

"Name his?" Jem suggested in what he obviously thought was a helpful tone.

"Where are you going?" Ammon asked.

"Going you?"

"Enough," Tean snapped. "I'm not answering that one either."

"I'm not being nosy for kicks and giggles," Ammon said. "Online dating isn't necessarily safe."

"He's right," Jem said. "You should borrow his diaphragm. And his asshole-bleaching kit. Ammon, be a pal and lend him your asshole-bleaching kit, please?"

Tean leaned against the counter. He glanced at the lower cabinet where he'd hidden the cider. He rarely wanted to be drunk, but the thought was a parachute right then. "Fireflies—"

"No," Jem groaned, dropping his head onto the table. "You made him start with the firefly thing again."

"Please don't tell me this is more animal trivia," Ammon said. "I'm being serious right now."

"I'm being serious too. Fireflies of the species *Photuris* prey on fireflies of the species *Photinus*. The females mimic the light signals of *Photinus* fireflies. When they show up to mate, instead of sex, they get murdered. And eaten."

"Great. Right now, I don't want to talk about fireflies. I want to talk about you being safe."

"Put a condom on a banana," Jem said. "Show him how to do it."

"And it's not just interspecies violence." Tean grabbed a Bristlecone. "Open this, please? Sexual cannibalism is rife in the animal world. Chinese mantises. Black widow spiders. Some animals kill their sexual partner before consummating the act. Some consume them during sex."

"It's like having a sandwich in bed," Jem said. "Like on *Seinfeld*."

When Ammon handed back the open Bristlecone, he said, "Fine. We'll do this the little-kid way. What are you going to do when a praying mantis tries to eat you after sex?"

"I'll probably pretend to have a heart attack."

At the table, Jem choked on something and managed to wheeze, "Please record this."

"That's not going to stop a crazy person from killing you."

"It worked when I went to Try-angles. This guy kept trying to buy me a drink, and he wouldn't take no for an answer, so I pretended to fall asleep."

Jem's eyes were huge and bright. He was biting his lip. Ammon covered his face with two big hands.

"It's a proven tactic," Tean said, trying to square his shoulders. "Female dragonflies fake sudden death to avoid male advances."

"Never stop," Jem breathed.

"Stop what?"

"Any of this."

"You don't have to stop," Ammon said, "but if we could press pause for a minute. I'm going to ask you again: what's his name, and where are you going?"

"I don't—"

"I'm your friend, right? And we've been working up to this. You've gotten more comfortable telling me when you have dates—"

"I don't know about that," Tean murmured.

"—and now we're taking the next step as friends. You're not going to go out with a stranger without providing some basic information in case something happens to you. You could have a stroke. You could get hit by a car. You could get mugged. And nobody would know where you'd been."

Tean closed his eyes. Then, after letting out a slow breath, he said, "Ammon, please don't make me regret trusting you."

"If we're going to figure out how to be friends again, we have to start somewhere."

"His name's Ragnar."

"Oh my God," Jem said.

"For fuck's sake," Ammon said. Then, almost immediately, "Sorry."

"See? This is why I didn't tell you."

"No, no. I'm sorry. It won't happen again. And where are you guys going?"

"Stanza."

Ammon's eyebrows went up. "A little pricey for a first date, don't you think?"

"Yeah, well," Tean pulled on his collar, "I finally have disposable money for the first time in my life, and I want to spend some of it on myself."

"Buy some sex toys," Jem said. "Some really scary ones."

"Will you be quiet for five seconds?"

"What is a scary sex toy?" Tean said. "No, please, don't answer that."

"Too late—"

"Thank you for trusting me," Ammon said. He downed the rest of his beer and met Tean's eyes. "Will you tell me if you go home with him? I'm not asking for details. I just want to know if I should come down and take care of Scipio."

Scipio raised his head at the sound of his name, his expression wary as he studied Ammon.

"That seems like too much."

"If we're friends—"

"No, Ammon. I don't feel comfortable talking to you about that yet."

Something Tean couldn't describe flitted across Ammon's face. Then he nodded. "Thanks for being honest about your feelings. I appreciate that you respect me enough to do that."

Jem pretended to throw up into his beer bottle.

"Enough," Tean said.

Jem continued the gagging noises.

Tean pegged him with a crumpled-up napkin, and Jem slumped sideways on the table, dead.

"Now," Jem said, "can I please ask one question?"

"No."

"Ammon got to ask questions."

"Ammon isn't going out of his way to make my life more difficult."

"I think I should get a turn. I want to ask a question."

"Fine, jeez, before I lose my mind."

"I want you to be completely, devastatingly honest: does Ragnar have a better beard than me?"

4

The next day was Wednesday. Jem took two clients on showings of high-priced homes. One was a gay couple with a wide age gap, and the older man cornered Jem in the bathroom and put his hand between Jem's legs, his whole face wrinkling when he winked. After that, Jem had given them a song and dance about insider information, a fault in the house's foundation, that their agent could use to chop the asking price almost in half. He even offered to put them in touch with a structural engineer who could fix it for pennies on the dollar, for an immediate return on their investment. The old gay counted out a thousand dollars on the front porch, licking his lips. His partner was in the car playing a Nintendo DS.

After paying Tinajas her money, Jem still had a nice chunk of cash from the last two days' work. He was already starting to think about the next game; it was important to keep moving, and while the client broker thing had been fun, something in his gut told him he was running out of time. Better to come up with something new. He liked it best when the people he took were thieves and assholes; for some reason, the mental voice that had started to sound a lot like Tean gave him less grief when he pulled one over on those types. Maybe a collections broker. He liked the sound of that. Hardly anybody even knew what a broker was, and he could spin the idea a lot of different ways.

He parked the Kawasaki a block south of Tean's Central City apartment. He got street tacos from a cart, and then he stood in line at a mochi truck. The day was hotter than hell, the air shimmering over the asphalt, but in an hour, maybe less, it would be bearable. Once the sun went down, the temperature dropped significantly, and most evenings the mountain breeze made things almost pleasant. He ate his mochi on the curb outside a Sinclair, in a growing pool of shade, licking the melted ice cream that had run down the inside of his wrist.

When Tean came out of his parking lot driving the white Ford, Jem got on his Kawasaki. He started counting. He hadn't gotten to thirty before Ammon pulled out in a silver Chevy Impala.

Busted, motherfucker.

Jem kick-started the bike and followed. True to his word, Tean headed to Stanza, a restaurant and wine bar only a few blocks north of his apartment. It was close enough to walk, and the fact that Tean was driving suggested he thought he—or they—might be going somewhere else after. Jem could picture it: they were laughing over wine, they were laughing over their food, they were laughing as they talked about grad school and books and science. Ragnar was probably some brilliant geneticist splicing pufferfish DNA into pomegranate seeds or something like that. And he'd be a Viking sex god too, of course. And after all that wine and all that laughing, after both of them being oh-so-impressed at how smart the other one was, Ragnar would ask if Tean wanted to keep talking, and the doc would do that thing where he tried not to smile and pushed his glasses back up his nose. Jem gunned the bike to make it through a yellow.

That was a mistake. The Kawasaki didn't exactly roar, but it was loud, and Jem spotted movement inside Ammon's car. Maybe it was nothing. Or maybe the detective was checking the mirror, seeing who was behind him. Sure enough, when Tean turned into Stanza's tiny parking lot, Ammon slowed the silver Impala.

Jem swore under his breath. He wasn't ready to break cover yet, but his heart hammered against his ribs. Sweat soaked his hair under the helmet. Then, after another agonizing moment, someone honked, and Ammon started forward again. Jem let out the knot of air in his chest. He rolled forward. As he pulled even with Stanza, he coasted and risked a glance. Tean was standing in front of the wine bar, staring at him. Jem kept his cool, barely, and continued coasting. He trusted the helmet and the lack of context to keep Tean from recognizing him. When the doc looked away, Jem accelerated slowly.

He went to Whiskers, a gay bar near the Marmalade District, and ordered a Campfire whiskey. He drank. He got cruised twice. The first was a Latino guy in a tight white shirt that displayed some very nice muscles. His coloring made Jem think of Tean, though, and Jem put down two more Campfires after the encounter. The second guy was blond, skinny, and had a beard. Way too bushy and wild for his build. He said something about coding, and Jem just nodded and drank more. It was the beard. Ragnar probably had a beard.

They fucked in the blond's SUV, the seats down in back. When the blond tried to work a finger inside Jem, Jem laughed and flipped the blond on his back. He shook his head and said, "I don't think so."

The blond moaned and touched himself, and Jem figured that meant he was ok with the switch.

After, while Jem tied the laces on his ROOS, the blond asked for his number.

Jem kept laughing about it, laughing on the dark streets, laughing when he squinted against the brightness of the traffic lights, laughing when he made a bad turn and the rear tire skidded, laughing every time it popped back into his head, until he got to the little brick bungalow in Federal Heights. He retrieved the key from the lockbox on the door and let himself inside. Even drunk, he navigated the bulky old furniture without turning on the lights. When he got to the back of the house, when he was sure the blackout curtains that he'd hung were closed, he hit the light switch in the bedroom.

A bed with a sagging mattress. A closet with mirrored doors. A vanity table that had been painted white poorly, with drips and streaks frozen in the satin gloss. From the top of the dresser, a teddy bear in a tuxedo, with top hat and cane, oversaw the proceedings. Jem stripped. The house was old enough that the only bathroom was in the hall. He washed up; in the morning, he'd wipe out the sink and tub just in case. The house had been on the market for three weeks, almost a record with how fast homes were moving, but so far nobody wanted to deal with an as-is home being sold by out-of-state relatives who had no interest in clearing out the junk.

Stretched out on the bed, he closed his eyes, but the Campfire made his mouth taste like smoke, made his mouth taste like the blond, and then he opened his eyes and grabbed his phone—he had the vague idea of jerking off, just to get to sleep.

Instead, he saw a missed call and voicemail from Brigitte Fitzpatrick. She must have called when he'd had the blond's ankles behind the headrests; there's an image for mommy dearest. She'd sent a text as well, but reading was too much work in general, and definitely too much work when he was wasted. He played the voicemail.

Her voice was brittle; that was the first thing he'd noticed when they met the first time. It wasn't the voice he remembered from childhood. "Jeremiah." She cleared her throat. "Hello, Jeremiah, this is your—this is Brigitte. I hope I'm not bothering you. I'm sure you're very busy." A nervous titter. "I just wanted to see if everything was ok. Gerald says you haven't cashed any of the checks."

"No duh," Jem told the phone. "Because I don't fucking need you, and I definitely don't need Gerald and his fucking Wells Fargo account."

"—wondering if you're getting them, that's all. And I—I wanted to make sure everything is all right. Gerald says he thinks it would be all right for you to come meet your—meet the children. If you're still interested, that is. We're having a party on Pioneer Day."

"Right," Jem told the phone. "Right."

"Once we've got everything hammered out, I'll send you the details. I know Gerald would love to meet you as well."

"Right," Jem told the phone, and then he threw it across the room.

Brigitte was still talking in her thin, high voice.

On the wall, above where the phone had fallen, vinyl letters spelled out FAMILIES ARE FOREVER.

5

On Thursday after work, Tean invited Ammon to take Scipio on a walk with him. When Ammon met them downstairs, Scipio did his usual growling and whuffing. Tean barely noticed.

"What happened to your face?"

Ammon touched a faint bruise along his jawline. "A few months ago, I would have lied to you about this, but I'm trying really hard to be honest. This was some father-son bonding time."

"Ammon, oh my gosh. Your father hit you? What happened?"

"We hugged. We went fishing. He bought me a chocolate malt."

Tean stared.

Tapping the bruise again, Ammon cut his eyes to the left and shrugged. "Don't make me talk about it."

Tean scrambled for what to say and settled on: "I've never heard you be a smart aleck before."

"One night of trying to be Jem's friend."

Tean's grin grew slowly.

"Let's walk," Ammon said, "before you remember you don't like me."

"I like you," Tean said.

Ammon squeezed his arm, laughed, and shook his head.

The late July sun ricocheted off the glass, turning the streets into shooting galleries, the light blinding no matter how Tean squinted. They kept to the shaded side of the street, where the cement wouldn't burn Scipio's paws. It was a relief to get to Liberty Park, the grass still lush from daily watering, the cottonwoods offering a canopy against the sun. The smell of the pond on the south side of the park filled the air; two girls were chasing the ducks toward the water and then running away, screaming, when the ducks turned on them.

"I don't think it's going anywhere," Tean said. "With Ragnar, I mean. I don't know if that matters to you or not, but I figured I'd tell you."

Ammon was silent for the next ten yards. Then he said, "It matters to me. I thought you knew how much this mattered to me."

"I don't want us to be pressured, though. I want to figure out how to be friends again first. We did everything wrong the first time, and if there is something real between us, I want it to have a solid foundation."

"I know, Tean. You've told me. At length. And I've told you that I'll do whatever you want me to do because I want you in my life, however you'll have me."

Tean opened his mouth.

"Nope," Ammon said. "We're not going to do this all over again. A hundred times, give or take, is enough. Tell me why it wasn't a love connection."

"Gosh, I can't even imagine what Jem would say if he heard that."

"Quit stalling."

"I don't know. Things seemed like they were fine. We had a good time. He laughed a few times when I wasn't telling a joke, but that almost always happens, so it didn't seem like a big deal. He said he wanted to see me again. But he hasn't answered any of my messages since."

"It's probably because you're undatable."

"Ammon!"

"Sorry, it's the truth. You're too smart, hot, and good for all those guys. They know you're out of their league. You're just going to have to settle for me. You're out of my league too, of course, but I'm willing to make the sacrifice because I'm crazy about you."

"Scipio, make him stop. Attack. Bite. Kill."

Tail wagging furiously, Scipio was too busy trying to sniff out whatever was hiding under a cracked slab of sidewalk.

"Traitor," Tean said.

"If I'm honest," Ammon began.

"No more pretending to insult me while secretly hitting on me. We're not there yet, and I don't like feeling rushed."

"I was going to say, I think you're reading too much into a few dates. You're a great guy. If they can't see that, it's their loss, and you're better off without them. You've got to give it some time before you can call it quits."

"If I don't get sexually cannibalized before then."

Ammon grimaced. "Right. I forgot."

They completed their loop of the park. A cat got too close, and Scipio barked wildly at it. When the cat came closer, Scipio backed up until he crashed into Tean's knees, his whole body shaking. By the time they'd gone another fifteen yards, Scipio was prancing again and lunging at squirrels.

"How was Daniel's game?" Tean asked.

Ammon made a noncommittal noise.

"Is it ok for me to ask about stuff like that? You invited me, so I thought maybe I was allowed, but—but I wasn't sure."

"Tean, you can talk to me about anything. It wasn't great. I mean, I sat on the topmost bleacher, and I wore a hat and sunglasses because the poor kid can't even stand to look at me. He's going through a really bad time, probably the worst time in his life, and I'm making it harder. Lucy caught him hoarding pills. He bought a shirt that says I HATE FAGS, God knows where. And then I look at his cell phone data, and he's visiting myshirtlessboyfriend.com every afternoon. I don't know what to do."

"I know I was part of that. I don't know if there's anything I can do to make it better, but if there is, I want you to tell me."

"Part of what? Me being gay and closeted?"

"No, the rest of it."

"Me cheating on my wife, lying to my family, picking up anonymous guys and risking my relationships and my career? That part?" Ammon rubbed a hand over his cropped blond hair. "Tean, you were the first guy I was ever willing to be myself with. That means everything to me. And I blew it because I wasn't brave enough to take a risk with you. I'd be lying if I told you Lucy and the kids don't have some really hard feelings toward you, but the truth is, I made those choices because I'm a sex addict and because I'm a coward. The nights it wasn't you, it was someone else. You mean the world to me, but you weren't the cause. And you definitely weren't the problem."

"You're too hard on yourself."

"If I am," Ammon said, his eyes crinkling at the edges, "it's been a long time coming."

They walked the rest of the way home in silence.

"Come over," Tean said. "Let me take a look at your face and see if there's anything I can do."

"They're bruises. Unless you've got a magic potion up your sleeve, you can't do anything except give them time." His eyes were very blue then, catching the light. "All I'm doing these days is giving things time to heal, it seems."

"Come over anyway," Tean said. "I'll make dinner."

Something that might have been a smile twitched at the corner of Ammon's mouth, but before he could answer, his phone buzzed. He answered: "Young. Yes. Ok, I'm on my way." He listened to a longer stretch of information, swore, and hammered his fist against the apartment's bulletin board. It rattled. A shower of thumbtacks hit the ground, and flyers, now released from the board, fluttered down. One was for HEAL YOURSELF WITH TAHITIAN NONI JUICE - CANCER, DIABETES, HEART DISEASE.

When Ammon disconnected, Tean said, "What happened?"

"It's a murder. The killer ran into traffic and got hit by a car while trying to escape; I've got to go. Do you know where Jem is?"

"What? Why?"

"Do you know, Tean?"

"No. He doesn't like to tell me—no, I don't know. I can find him, though."

"Collar him. Then call me."

"Why?"

"Because the killer has been asking for Jem Berger since they put him in the ambulance."

6

Jem sat in the hospital lobby, waiting. Tean's phone call had made him drive across town to the University of Utah Hospital, where a uniformed officer had finally tracked him down and told him to sit and wait. Tean had showed up a while later, but since neither man knew anything, all they could do was sit in silence. At first, the lobby was busy, an early evening rush of men and women leaving work to go home, and another crowd arriving for visiting hours before going home themselves.

Hours passed. By then, the summer sky was purple, twilight softening the valley in every direction, and the lobby was almost empty. A white lady with frizzy hair was scrubbing makeup off her face with a wipe, examining herself in a compact mirror, tugging up her blouse as though trying to compensate for the plunging neckline. An older black man was reading *The Economist* and chewing piece after piece of Juicy Fruit gum. A pair of white boys, both in sagging jeans and too-big t-shirts, sulked in chairs at the far end of the lobby, obviously feeling very put upon.

"Mr. Berger?"

The officer was young, her face fresh, and she smiled as she motioned for Jem to follow her. When Tean stood, she shook her head.

"I need to go with him," Tean said.

"I'm sorry, but only Mr. Berger."

"I want to talk to Detective Young."

"No," Jem said. "It's fine."

"It's not fine." Tean grabbed his arm, his voice dropping to a whisper. "You have no idea what you're walking into. You have no idea who wants to talk to you. This is weird, and I don't want you doing it on your own."

"Tean, it's fine. It's a hospital. It's going to be fine." Jem slowly pried the doc's fingers loose. "You didn't have to come.

"Of course I had to come. The whole thing is so strange that it's making me sick to my stomach." Turning to the young officer, he said, "If Detective Young allows me to—"

Sighing, Jem took Tean by the shoulders, turned him back toward the lobby, and gave him a gentle push. "Go home, please. Give Scipio extra treats for me."

"I'm not going home. I'm going to wait here until I know they're not trying to do something to you."

"Like probe me anally," Jem said.

"Like—no, not like that. What in the world is wrong with you?"

"Come on," Jem said to the officer, whose name tag said Marina. "That one will keep him busy for a while."

They rode the elevator up. Muzak played over hidden speakers. It sounded like a jazzy, synthesized rendering of "The Piano Man." Officer Marina clasped her hands, her eyes locked on the digital display.

"What's this guy's name?" Jem asked. "Who are we going to see?"

"You'll have to talk to Detective Young about that."

"I thought he wouldn't be allowed any visitors until he was processed into the jail."

"You'll have to talk to Detective Young about that too."

"Why's he still here?"

Nothing this time, just a polite smile.

"Does Detective Young always have the same stick up his ass, or does he rotate the sticks daily?"

A slightly bigger smile.

When they got off the elevator, Officer Marina steered them to the right, and they followed a long hallway. At the end of it, Ammon and his partner, Kat, sat in tubular chairs. Ammon looked like someone had given him a love tap, with faint bruising along his jaw. Jem found himself humming the theme song for *The Price is Right*. Kat glared at Jem.

"Did your perp do that to you?" Jem said to Ammon.

"What? Oh, no. Thank you, Officer Marina. Give us a minute, would you?"

"Who do I send the ice-cream cake to?" Jem asked as Officer Marina retreated. "Do they like pistachio-flavored ice cream? Do they like fudge cookie layers?"

"I told you this was a mistake," Ammon said to Kat.

Kat just grunted.

"So who the fuck did you drag me up here to see?" Jem's eyes shot to the closed door. "What's this all about?"

"A suspect in a murder, for a start."

"Doesn't this guy have some sort of rights?" Jem asked. "Even a couple of stormtroopers like you two ought to remember that. Or is this some weird legal limbo that you're going to use to cornhole him? If you think I'm going to help you screw him over, you're in a for a surprise." He smiled. "And it's not an ice-cream cake."

"Deal with him," Kat said, standing. She began to pace a short stretch of vinyl tile. "Before I run out of patience."

"Mr. Hidalgo has been arrested and charged with murder. He knows his rights. He's choosing to waive his right to have an attorney present for this conversation with you."

"Why isn't he in jail? Why aren't we having this conversation in an interview room, the whole thing recorded?"

"We are going to record it, dumbass," Kat said. "I'm going to record the whole thing."

"Mr. Hidalgo is staying overnight because he has some internal bleeding. He's not doped up on painkillers, before you try to accuse us of anything. They gave him extra-strength Tylenol; that's it."

"And you want me to get him to confess? Fuck both of you pigs."

"Jesus Christ." Kat stopped pacing long enough to put her hands on her hips. "What's wrong with him?"

"I watch a lot of TV," Jem said.

"We want you to talk to him," Ammon said. "He's been asking for you since they picked him up off the asphalt. Figure out what he wants. If he confesses, well, that's great. If not, no big deal. This is an open-and-shut case."

Jem eyed him. "Bullshit."

"Think what you want."

"I think that's bullshit. If it were an open-and-shut case, you wouldn't be bothering with this. You've got something hinky, and you want me to flush it out for you."

"Are you going to talk to him or not?" Kat said.

"I don't know any Mr. Hidalgo."

"He knows you."

"Fuck, fine. Let's get this over with."

Kat opened the door and went inside. Jem followed. He was two steps into the room when he stopped.

"Motherfucker," he said, breaking the word in half. "No fucking way."

Jem had met the man in the bed over ten years before. Antonio Hidalgo—although Jem had always just thought of him as Antonio. He had the same coarse hair, although now it was bleached orange, and he'd ditched the textured cut that Jem had once compared to a crinkle-cut french fry. That comparison had gotten Jem a busted nose. Antonio had put on some pounds since Decker, and he'd gotten tattoo sleeves—roses twined around pistols, skulls, a ROSA inside a flaming heart, a character that looked like the Joker from the *Batman* movies.

For a moment, Jem was back in Decker, back in the dorm, with Blake and Antonio pinning him to the bunk. Antonio had been the one to yank the jumpsuit down, forcing it below Jem's waist. The air had been cold. The bunk's steel frame, cold. Jem, cold, shaking so hard his teeth chattered. And the hands holding him were hot. Tanner's knee between his legs, forcing them apart, hot.

"Fuck you," Jem said, "you fucking son of a bitch. If these cops weren't here, I'd kill you myself. I'm out of here."

"Hold on," Ammon said, trying to grab his arm.

Jem shoved him and kept going.

"Jem, wait," Antonio said, his voice hoarse.

Jem caught the door and flung it open.

"It's Andi," Antonio shouted.

Jem took a step.

"Andi Fontella."

Jem hesitated. He looked back.

"Tanner did this to her, not me. Come on. Please. Please, man."

Ammon had recovered from his stumble, and now his gaze darted back and forth between Jem and Antonio.

"Fuck you," Jem said. "They think they can sew you up in this? Good. I hope you fucking rot. And I hope you get a big old fucker as your bunkmate."

He charged out into the hallway. He tried to take deep breaths as he headed for the elevator, but the air had a medicinal smell, and it made him sick. He curled shaking hands into fists. He slipped on something, a wet patch on the vinyl tiles, and went down hard. His knee exploded with pain, and suddenly he wanted to cry. Tears flooded his eyes. He concentrated on the throbbing in his knee. Anything to keep him out of Decker, out of the past.

A hand caught his elbow and helped him stand. "That looked like a nasty fall," Ammon said, his voice surprisingly neutral. "Do you want to sit down?"

Shaking him off, Jem said, "You knew."

Ammon's face was expressionless.

"You knew, you piece of shit."

"We looked him up. When I saw Decker, I thought maybe that's why he was asking for you. That's all."

"And you didn't say anything."

"It looks like I was right not to."

"Fuck you." Jem took a limping step toward the elevator.

"Why'd he ask for you?"

"I don't know. You're the fucking detective; figure it out."

"I'm asking you to think. Be smart about this. Why'd he ask for you? He could have asked for a lawyer. He could have said nothing. He could have told us whatever he seems to want to tell you. But he asked for you, and that doesn't make any sense because whatever history you two have, it's doesn't look like you're his white knight." Ammon hesitated. "Is he an ex?"

"Jesus, you'd love that."

"It's a legitimate question considering what I just saw in there."

"No, he's not an ex. He's a miserable, cowardly turd who made my life hell. And whatever he wants, I'm not giving it to him."

"Who's Tanner?"

"He was their little ringleader. Even worse than old crinkle-cut in there, if you can believe that."

"And you don't want to know why Antonio is willing to send him up for this? You don't want to know why he's turning on his buddy? You don't want to know why he thinks you're the one who will believe him?"

Jem jabbed the down button.

"This is your chance to get back at those pieces of shit."

"I can handle that on my own, thanks."

"It doesn't feel good to know that this guy needs you? Is desperate for you to help him? That doesn't feel even a tiny bit good?"

"What would feel good, ass-lips, is a bottle of oxy and an icepack." Jem jabbed the down button again. "Stop talking to me."

"If Antonio's right, and if Tanner's responsible for this, are you going to be able to sleep at night knowing he's still out there? Knowing he'll do this again to someone?"

"Find him, then. Stop him. That's your job."

"I can't do anything if Antonio won't talk to me."

Whirling away from the elevator doors, Jem faced Ammon. He limped forward, still favoring his knee, and drilled a finger into Ammon's chest. Ammon rocked back, but he didn't give ground.

"I know you," Jem said. "I know who you are. I know this is what you do. You get inside people's heads, and you fuck with them until they don't know up from down. You do it professionally. You do it personally. You're not going to do it to me."

Ammon's grin was small and hard. He caught Jem's wrist, his grip crushing, and leaned in. His breath was warm on the side of Jem's face. "I'll dole it out in little scraps here and there. Holding back just enough until he thinks he's weaseling it out of me. I'll start with little things. I'll start to say something and then stop. I'll pull a long face, and when he asks, I'll say, 'No, no, it's nothing. Just something with Jem.' He'll go crazy digging because he's so protective of you. And then, a few days later, 'I'm just dealing with a lot of stuff at work, stuff I thought I was going to get some help with.' And I'll go on and on like that until he's finally talked himself into seeing you for what you are: a conniving little shit who only cares about himself, who let a murderer walk free."

Something beeped down the hall. At the nurse's station, two women burst into laughter.

"Let go of me," Jem said.

"Oh my gosh," one of the women was saying, still laughing. "You're wicked!"

"Let go of me," Jem said again.

Ammon's grip relaxed, and Jem twisted free.

"Well?" Ammon said.

"Why do you even want him? Why can't you just leave us alone?"

"Because he's mine."

"He's going to figure you out one day. You can't mindfuck him forever."

The smile was only in Ammon's eyes now, but it was vicious.

"Fine," Jem said. "Let's see what this piece of shit wants from me."

7

Antonio had raised the back of the bed while Jem had been gone. Now he was propped up, the fluorescent lights revealing the scrapes and road rash on the side of his face. He was very light skinned, and at Decker, he'd had a roadmap of freckles across his whole body. Most of those looked like they'd faded with age, but they might have just been hidden by the abrasions.

"What?" Jem said, dropping into a tubular chair.

"Not so fast." Kat pulled out her phone and tapped it a few times. "Let's do the formalities."

With the video recording, Kat and Ammon walked Antonio through several versions of the same thing: his acknowledgment that he understood his rights, was not under duress or medication, and was choosing to waive his right to an attorney for this conversation. At some invisible signal, both cops seemed to decide enough was enough, and Ammon nodded at Jem.

"Spit it out," Jem said.

"Hey, man." Antonio's eyes skated over Jem and dropped to the linoleum again. "How's it going?"

"No. I didn't come here to do the good-times roundup. Tell me whatever you want to tell me, and then I'm leaving."

"Yeah. Tough. You know, the way we did you, that was messed up—"

"Keep going, and I'll walk out that door again."

"Ok, ok. Jeez. Look, I didn't do this. What they're saying I did. Tanner did it."

"The big, bad wolf. I've heard this one before. 'It's all Tanner's fault. Tanner made me do it.'"

"No, man." Antonio shot up in bed, wincing, but held himself upright. "I loved Andi. I wouldn't have hurt her. Never." His eyes filled with tears, and he sagged back against the bed, wiping them away. "You got any tissues or anything? I'm gonna bawl like a bitch in a minute."

Ammon ducked out of the room.

"How'd you know Andi?" Jem asked.

"She's my girl." Antonio hesitated. "Andi said she knew you in a group home. In Tooele."

"Foster home. And how the fuck did I become your topic of conversation?"

"I told her I'd been in Decker. I told her everything." Antonio had the grace to blush. "Almost everything. She said she knew a kid that got sent there. That's all."

The hum of machinery was a white noise that made it hard for Jem to think. He remembered Andi: blond, too thin, all knees and elbows. She'd been Benny's age, and they'd overlapped at LouElla's home in Tooele for less than a year.

"What about Tanner?"

"He got her, you know? Fuck, I am so fucking stupid, and I let this happen. When I get out of here, I'm gonna kill that son of a bitch, you know?"

"You still haven't given me anything, and I'm getting bored with this. Andi's dead. That's too bad. I wish it'd been you instead. Fuck off and die, Antonio."

"No, no, no, man. Please. Can you be cool? I'm at a fucking nine, and you're fucking with my brain. I can't even think right because you're so in my head." Antonio took a few deep breaths. "I'd been doing a job with Tanner. I didn't like it; Andi didn't like it neither. She wanted me to go straight. Blake and I, we both wanted to go straight. Blake says he's going to meet a nice guy after this, clean up his act."

"Jesus. Blake's gay? Give me a break."

"He is. He's really messed up about it, but he is, and he wants to get out of this life, you know? Me too. Andi's helping me." He smiled, and it lasted an instant before it shattered. "Anyway, Tanner's thing was wack, so I decided to call it quits. I came back up to Salt Lake. Then Tanner started calling. I didn't want to see him; you know how he gets when someone tries to say no. But he told me things were cool between us, and . . . and I wanted it to be true." Antonio licked his lips. "So I believed him. He said he wanted to pay me for the time I'd put in. Fuck, man, I wanted to believe that too. I thought he meant later, but Tanner drove all the way back that night. I was low-key freaking out, you know? But things seemed chill. We smoked a few j's. We had some drinks. Everybody was having a good time. We were partying. Like we do, you know? And we did some shit that must have been bad. It was heavy, really heavy, and we were all messed up. Tanner started putting his hands on Andi. I told him no. Tanner didn't listen, though. You know how he gets."

Jem knew: the feel of a warm hand around his neck, the cold air whispering over his bare skin.

"Andi tried to pull away. He grabbed her, hard. She slapped him, and he let go. I was on my feet. Tanner was playing with this toy gun he liked, and he shot her. It wasn't going to kill her or nothing, but she started screaming because it hurt. Tanner liked that."

Yes, Jem thought. Yes, Tanner had always liked it when he could get you to make a noise.

"What kind of toy gun?" Jem asked. "What does that even mean?"

"It's not a toy, but it's not a real gun either. It shot these needles."

"Where'd he get it?"

"I don't know."

"Why'd he have it?"

"I don't know."

"Bullshit."

"I don't know where he got it," Antonio said, staring defiantly at Jem.

"But you know why he had it."

"He liked it. Liked shooting things with those needles. He found a jackrabbit with a hurt leg and shot it up really bad, and the poor thing wouldn't die. He made me bash its head in with a rock." Antonio sniffled, and a tear slipped free before he could wipe it away.

Jem laughed. "You're unbelievable."

"It was a rabbit, man. He tortured it!"

Hands on his shoulders, forcing him onto the scratchy polyester bedding. Hands between his knees. A hand around his neck, so he could only take reedy breaths, so that he was dizzy, his panicked body burning through oxygen. The sudden explosion of pain.

"He shot her," Jem said hoarsely. "And?"

"And she started screaming, like I said. I wasn't even thinking. I went for Tanner with my bare hands. Nobody was going to do that to Andi. He shoved me, and I went down. I had this nice little Sig on the table, and he grabbed it and shot Andi because she was coming toward him. I—" Antonio's voice broke. "I ran. He was going to kill me too, man, and there was nothing I could do about Andi."

"So you left her to die alone. That's some genuine, storybook love."

"Can't you make him be nice to me?" Antonio looked at Kat. "I'm not saying anything if you can't make him be nice to me."

"When you were sixteen," Jem said, "and nothing more than a human-sized waste of DNA, you couldn't bluff your way through a game of Go Fish. Don't try to learn now. Here's what I think. I think they've got a gun that has your prints on it. I think they've got your girlfriend full of bullets that have your prints on them. They've got drugs in the apartment, signs of a struggle, and you trying to run. Why the fuck should anybody believe Tanner was involved?"

"Because he was, man. You know how he be. He's . . . he's scary. If he wants something, he takes it. If he wants to put his dick in something, he's going to do it. He's a pussy hound, and he's a mean one. That's what gets him off, hurting people. You know that. And if he wants to hurt somebody, he's going to have fun while he does. I knew he'd try to put this on me. As soon as I ran, I knew. And I knew you'd tell them what he's like, tell them he did this. I never would have done nothing to Andi. I loved Andi, man. She was my girl."

"If you're telling the truth, they'll figure it out. If not, I hope they stick you in a hole for the rest of your life."

When Jem stood, Antonio lunged upright again, his face twisted with pain. "I heard about you. I heard about Benny. I heard about what you did for that lady who got eaten up by an alligator. People talk about that shit. You can do that for me now. You can prove I didn't do this."

"Maybe," Jem said. "But I won't. Like I told you: fuck off and die, Antonio."

"Jem, please! Please, man! Do it for Andi."

Jem turned away.

"He's with Blake. The two of them, together. They're down in Moab. They've got this thing with drugs. Lots of money. Tanner met a girl at a club, and she hooked him up."

"What's her name?"

"I don't know. He just wanted us down there for backup, you know?"

"What's his plan?"

"I don't know. I swear to God, he didn't tell us anything."

"You're fucking useless." Jem headed for the door. "And this all sounds like bullshit."

"Hold on," Ammon said quietly.

Jem kept walking.

"They're staying at this place, the Pinyon-Pine Lodge. Jem, if you let me carry this one, he's going to do it again. He's going to keep doing it, just like he did you, just like he wanted to do Andi. He's going to keep—"

Then Jem was out in the hallway, moving toward the elevator. Quick steps. The blackness at the edge of his vision was threatening to wash in like the surf.

"Jem," Ammon said at his shoulder.

"If you touch me, I swear to God I don't know what I'll do."

"I just want you to come back so we can—"

Miraculously, the elevator dinged as soon as Jem touched the button, and the doors slid open. He stepped into the car and jammed buttons on the panel, not caring where he went. Anywhere but here.

"Do whatever you want. Tell Tean. Arrest me. Shoot me in the back of the head. But I'm not talking to him again. Figure this out yourself."

8

Tean was at work Friday morning when the call came. He thought it might be Jem; he had waited for Jem in the hospital lobby for almost an hour the night before, and then he had tried calling, but Jem hadn't answered. Finally he had gone home, slept poorly, and woke worried.

"Please hold for Dr. Castorena," a nasally young man's voice said.

"No," Tean said.

The silence on the other end of the call was punctured by a panicked, "You have to!"

"I'm going to hang up very slowly. She'd better hurry."

Two seconds later, a woman's husky voice came on the phone. "Jeez, I'm sorry, really. I've told him a million times not to do that."

"It's fine."

"He's shaking, the poor thing. I don't know if anyone has ever said no to him before."

"There's always a first."

Utah's state medical examiner had a deep laugh. "Can I ask you to consult on an autopsy today? It won't take long. I really only have two questions."

"I'm very busy today. I've got to deal with BassGate."

"Do I dare ask?"

"Two guys who were caught cheating in a bass fishing competition at Lake Powell. It hit local news; it should have been a citation and a fine, but they want to make a federal case out of it. You'd think the DWR was conspiring with them."

"Sounds like it's going to take months to unravel."

"Frick, please don't say that. If I have to respond to one more bureaucrat who wants to know what I'm doing about this situation, I'm going to lose my mind."

"I really don't want to drag you away from important business."

"You're the devil," Tean said. "I'm getting in the truck right now."

The Office of the Medical Examiner was located in Taylorsville, a straight shot down the I-215 beltway from the DWR offices. Like so much of new construction in Utah, the ME's office was glass and steel and desert-toned paints. The exact same design could have been used for a dentist's office. Or for an Arctic Circle. Or for a spa.

After signing in at the lobby, Tean asked around until he learned that Elvira was still in the autopsy lab. He put on disposable PPE in the locker room and headed into the lab. It was a clean, brightly lit space with an abundance of equipment—some of it looking extremely high tech, and other pieces that were oldies but goodies: saws, shears, forceps, rolling tables, autopsy tables, and so on. Elvira was standing over one of the autopsy tables, where a young woman's body lay naked. Even from a distance, Tean could see the damage done from multiple gunshot wounds to the chest. At least four, he counted. The Y-incision showed that her chest and abdomen had already been opened, although the cavities were closed up again—whether out of respect for Tean's supposed sensibilities or for some other reason, he wasn't sure.

Raising her head, Elvira motioned for him to join her. "Alexandria Fontella, twenty-six years old. You can see cause of death for yourself, and this is clearly a homicide. The toxicology report won't be back for days, probably weeks, but from what I saw at the scene, I won't be surprised if she has a cocktail of drugs in her bloodstream. They were smoking meth for sure, and I'll wager a paycheck it was cut with something nasty." Elvira shook her head, staring down at the girl from behind the face shield. "The whole thing is a mess."

"I don't see any sign of bite marks. I don't see any sign of animal involvement at all, in fact. What am I missing? Why am I here?"

Castorena retrieved a tray from one of the rolling tables. On it lay a slim length of metal about eight millimeters long. She let Tean take the tray and offered a pair of forceps. He used them to pick up the piece of metal. One end was clearly broken. The metal was hollow, like a tube.

"This is the broken tip of a needle."

"Ding ding ding."

"You didn't need me to tell you that."

"I spotted that on the x-ray; it was embedded in a rib. The rest of the needle is gone, and I'm guessing it won't be recovered at the scene."

"It would take a significant amount of force to drive a needle into the bone like that. Do you think she was stabbed?"

"What if I told you that there's inflammation in the surrounding tissue, similar to what you'd see after a penicillin injection, and that a preliminary series of tests revealed porcine antigens on the recovered tip of the needle?"

Tean's eyebrows went up. "That sounds like ZonaStat."

"What makes you say that?"

"Well, a couple of things. ZonaStat is the name for an injectable contraceptive. It's a vaccine, technically, although it's not a permanent contraceptive. A glycoprotein, porcine zona pellucida, is extracted from pig ovaries. It's accompanied by an adjuvant. It's used to control wild animal populations in different formulations. ZonaStat-D for deer. ZonaStat-H for horses. And, the reason my mind jumped immediately to ZonaStat is that it's administered with a dart syringe and a CO2 injection rifle—they have to shoot the animal from a distance because wild deer and mustangs aren't going to let you walk up and poke them." Tean frowned. "What I don't understand is why a human would be injected with this kind of immunocontraceptive. I honestly haven't even heard about something like that; there are much, much safer contraceptives for humans."

"Could a CO2 rifle produce the force to lodge the needle in bone?"

"I don't know. Probably. Especially at close range." Tean hesitated. "You think someone used a dart syringe as a weapon? I don't see a needle mark—is it on her back?"

"I think one of these gunshot wounds was intended to cover up the needle mark."

Tean played through the sequence of events. "Someone shoots this girl with the dart. Then she's killed. The needle mark is strange and likely to be noticed, so the killer retrieves the dart, not knowing that the needle's tip has broken off and is lodged in a piece of bone. Then the killer attempts to hide the wound by shooting another bullet at the needle mark."

"Something like that."

"Gosh."

"Do your conservation officers use ZonaStat?"

"No. We don't currently have an excess population of deer. But it's possible that the Bureau of Land Management does. They manage the wild horse herds, and I know they've struggled to keep the herds from getting too big."

"The BLM is in charge of the herds?"

"The BLM is in charge of almost twenty-three million acres of public land in Utah. Over forty percent of the state is administered federally. That includes the herds and a whole lot else."

"I didn't know that."

"Then you haven't talked to a hunter or angler recently. Nine times out of ten, they'll spit it out in the first five minutes. They're usually not happy about it."

"Are there any of those herds near Salt Lake City?"

"Yes, actually. There's one in Tooele—the Onaqui herd."

They talked for a few more minutes, but the conversation died quickly, and Tean excused himself. As he drove back to the DWR offices, though, he kept turning it over in his head. He tried Jem's phone again, and it went to voicemail. Tean left another to go with all the ones from the night before.

9

It was easy to break into Antonio's apartment—a garden unit in a run-down building of yellow brick. Tinajas had provided the address after a quick search on the motor vehicle registry. Jem parked the Kawasaki in back, an asphalt lot broken up by weeds, some of them growing knee-high. A privacy fence screened him from the abandoned video rental store to the north, the Kroger to the east, and the shoebox-sized pharmacist to the south. A few cars were scattered through the lot, domestic sedans mostly, one boxy Saturn that looked like it had come out of a kid's Lego set. Where two sides of the privacy fence met, someone had piled music stands, their black paint long since flaked away, a dried snake of rust showing the path of runoff the last time it had rained.

He walked the exterior hallway once, ignored the apartment's door, which was taped shut with yellow and black lines of DO NOT CROSS, and made a circuit of the building. No police on site. Alone in the back lot, Jem hunkered down, worked the tip of the barrette he carried between the window and the frame, and turned the latch. The window opened inwards; with some wiggling, Jem got it free of the frame completely, and then he dropped inside.

Antonio's bedroom was filthy. A pile of basketball jerseys. A pile of basketball shorts. Sneakers formed a crumbling pyramid, with a lone Adidas Ultraboost Uncaged sliding down from the top. A pizza box dark with grease stood open on a child-sized dresser, a few strands of cheese fossilized inside. On the bed, the sheets looked like they hadn't been changed in years. Jem regretted not bringing disposable gloves; this was the kind of place you could get tetanus just by looking around.

The bedroom door opened onto the main living area, which held a cream-colored sofa spotted with stains and a Barcalounger that must have been thirty years old, the upholstery torn in places, a fat tongue of yellow foam sticking out. It was obvious that the police had taken a great deal of the room's contents, probably anything and everything that might possibly hold DNA evidence, trace evidence, or fingerprints. A lone numbered marker, 37, had been forgotten behind the Barcalounger, where a tech had collected something. Blood spatter stained a triangle of carpet and a four-foot section of wall.

Jem moved into the kitchen. An ancient Amana refrigerator stood at one end; at the other, an electric range held the gravelly remains of food crusted under the burners. Jem used a paper towel to open cabinets: Froot Loops, unopened Red Bulls, powdered strawberry-lemonade drink mix, moldy hot dog buns, cans of Progresso soup. Antonio loved chicken and wild rice; maybe some clever attorney could spin that to show a wholesome side to the accused murderer.

On one side of the refrigerator, a magnet for Magna U-Choose Auto Parts and Salvage held a strip of photos, the kind that you got in a booth. Four photos. Black and white. Antonio in a flat-billed Jazz cap. A blond girl on his lap—Andi, all grown up, the ghost of the girl Jem had known peering out through her eyes. She made a funny face. She made a pouty face. She kissed Antonio on the cheek. She arched her back, breasts out, obviously trying for a smoldering gaze. Antonio in love. Antonio in love. Antonio in love. Antonio in love. The way he looked at her, that's how Jem knew. He'd seen the same dumb look on his own face once or twice. When he rode shotgun in a white Ford. When he passed a mirror in one particular Central City apartment.

Love wasn't the same as innocence; Jem knew that. He still took the strip of photos. In the back lot, he propped it at an angle on one of the music stands, so that air could flow around it more easily, and rolled the wheel on a Bic. A yellow flame sprang up, and he ran it back and forth along the edge until the paper caught. It burned for a few seconds before the breeze fluttered the paper, lifted it, and carried it over the privacy fence. A tiny red bird with burning red wings.

He was getting back on his bike when his phone buzzed. It was Brigitte; he sent mommy dearest to voicemail, waited, and played the message.

"Jeremiah, dear." That brittle voice. "Gerald and I would love to have you over on Pioneer Day. You could meet the children. Would you like that?" She rambled on for almost a minute with the details and finished with, "Gerald really does want to know about the checks, sweetheart. He just needs to know if you're getting them. Call me?"

Jem deleted the message.

The phone buzzed again, and he considered tossing it in the pile of music stands, but he checked the screen instead. On the fifth buzz, he accepted the call and held it to his ear, silent.

"Could you please call me back?" Tean said. "I'm really worried."

"Or I could talk to you now."

"Oh, I thought I got your voicemail again. Where are you? Are you ok?"

"I'm at the mall."

"City Creek?"

"No, the South Jordan one."

"Why?"

"They have a better pog collection."

"I don't know what that means. Scipio, no, I just cleaned the glass."

Ferocious barking in the background made Jem's pulse shoot up. "Did he see a squirrel?"

"Of course. Jem, are you ok?"

"Why wouldn't I be?"

"Because you got dragged into a police interview at the hospital last night, and you haven't been answering my calls."

"I'm sorry. Things just got busy."

"Will you come over tonight? I'll make those miniature apple pies you like."

"That was an accident. You were trying to make miniature quiches."

"But I remember how to do it."

"I've got some stuff to take care of."

"No Ammon. I promise I won't try to make you be friends. Tonight."

A minivan with one tire that was extremely low limped into the lot. The side doors slid open, and children poured out, screaming. It was like a clown car. Jem lost count at six because they were all milling around, and they all looked the same with bowl-cut hair and overbites.

"I could probably eat something before I get back to work."

"Scipio and I are just hanging out. Come over whenever you want."

After disconnecting, Jem made himself wait ten minutes; looking desperate never helped anyone. Then he left the rug-rat horde in the parking lot—there was still no sign of the minivan's driver, and two of the rug rats were trying to fence with music stands, not quite strong enough to swing them easily—and drove to the closest CVS. He bought one of each of the theater-size boxes of candy, except Good & Plenty, because black licorice was a sin against God. Then he bought a pint of vanilla ice cream and a second pint of something that was called Peanut Butter Apocalypse NOW WITH MORE BROWNIE CHUNKS. He made sure it had been a full half hour before he drove to Tean's apartment.

Scipio shot off the couch toward him, barking once and then whining with excitement. He hit Jem at the knees with approximately the same force as an icebreaker, and then he kept nosing into him, spinning around, crying a little and then slamming his body into Jem. Tean kept taking nervous half-steps toward them, but Jem waved him off and crouched to pet Scipio—well, as best he could with a bag in each hand.

At some point, Scipio seemed to decide Tean wasn't excited enough because he ran across the linoleum and crashed into Tean before running back to Jem.

"Yes, ok, I saw. He's here. I know, it's very exciting."

"You're not convincing at all," Jem said, heeling off his ROOS. "At least Scipio likes me."

"I like you too. I like you a healthy, normal amount. The same way I like my fingernails. Or roasted cabbage."

"More," Jem said. "Because of my animal magnetism."

"You've got one of those nose hairs again."

"God damn it." Jem said, but he smiled as he passed over the bag of goodies. "Put this away, please."

While Jem took care of the offending nose hair in the bathroom, Tean called out, "This is a lot of candy for someone without dental insurance."

"It's not for me, dummy. It's for you."

"I don't like candy."

"Jesus, I wish sometimes you could hear yourself, actually hear what you sound like."

"Peanut Butter Apocalypse? That looks . . . good."

Another smile broke out, and Jem was glad he was in the bathroom and didn't have to hide it. "Keep going."

"Vanilla!"

Leaving the bathroom, Jem said, "I don't know why you like vanilla so much. It doesn't taste like anything."

"It tastes like vanilla."

"Fine, but that's like the flavor equivalent of Elmer's glue."

"You know those aren't real brownie pieces in there? They're just some sort of weird processed product they call brownies."

"I can't hear you," Jem said, putting his hands over his ears.

"Let's go get dinner."

"I'm having two Big Macs tonight."

"Let's go somewhere new."

Jem groaned and fell forward onto the kitchen counter. "Please don't do this."

"We agreed that you'd try some new things."

"I like trying new things. I love trying new things. I tried the McRib when it first came out, and I cried when they took it away. You're the one that survives on a pinto bean, boiled for twelve hours, with a single grain of non-iodized table salt on top."

"Jem—"

"Non-iodized because the iodine would give it too much flavor."

"Yes, I got that. Jem, I know you don't like reading the menus and not knowing what—"

"That's not why."

"Well, it sure seems like it because every time I suggest a new place that has a menu with pictures, you're happy to try it, but when we went to that French place—"

"That wasn't my fault. The waiter was snooty. And I don't know why it's such a big fucking deal that I read a fucking menu. I can't even read fucking *Dick and Jane Pushed the Widow Down the Well*. Why does reading a menu matter so fucking much?"

After a moment, Tean ran his hand over the short hair on the back of Jem's head. Jem made a noise.

"Don't worry, I won't mess up the line in your hair."

"It's called a part." The doc's hand continued to move lightly, scratching, playing with the buzzed hair, and Jem said, "Ok, sorry about that. I'm back. It's all under control."

"Doesn't have to be under control. You're allowed to be frustrated. And Scipio has decided that when you yell it's a game, so he's very interested right now. He's trying to give you a rope."

"I thought you were just happy to see me."

Tean laughed quietly.

And then Jem told him. Not all of it. Not the specifics of what had happened at Decker, just enough to sketch out the relationship. And not the way Ammon had acted when it had just been the two of them. But knowing Andi at LouElla's, and his conversation with Antonio, and his search of the apartment. Then he sat up, took the theater-size boxes of candy out of the bag, and lined them up on the counter. He opened each one as he went.

"Why did you burn the pictures?"

"I hate him." Jem shrugged. "If he killed her, then the pictures didn't mean anything. If he loved her, well, that fuckstick didn't deserve her. He definitely didn't deserve to be happy. So I burned them."

Tean was silent for a long time. When he spoke, his voice was cautious. "Manufacturing and/or transporting drugs in southern Utah makes some sense. There's a lot of open land, and not a lot of people. Relatively empty highways. It's also close to the borders of three other states. That part of the story seems plausible, at least."

"Now the other shoe, please."

"I'm going to skip over the part where I tell you that you shouldn't have broken into a crime scene."

"Gee, thanks."

"And skip over the part where I tell you that the fact that Antonio might have genuinely loved Andi doesn't have any bearing on whether he killed her or not. The reality is that people and animals kill all the time, for all sorts of reasons. Do you know what the most murderous species is?"

"Humans."

"Only if you include malice aforethought as part of the definition. If you take that out, and if you just think about murder as conspecific killings, I mean, killing members of the same species—"

"I know what conspecific means, Tean. I've been your friend for almost a year. Sometimes you say conspecific in your sleep."

Tean's face flooded with red.

"When we used to boink," Jem added.

"Please don't ever—"

"Glasses."

Tean caught them at the last second, pushing the frame (still wrapped with electrical tape) back up his nose. His light brown skin looked like it had been set on fire.

"Try these," Jem said, shaking out candy from the first box.

"I thought we were going to dinner."

"We are. This is part of your ongoing education. If I have to go to some shitty five-star restaurant tonight and read some fucking menu in some fucking calligraphy shit, you have to do some learning too. Put it in your mouth. Oh my God, I honestly didn't think you could blush any harder."

Tean must have decided there were no productive responses because he shoved the candy in his mouth. He made a face. "Waxy. And why is it so crunchy?"

"Because they're Nestle Crunch bites. And because crunchy is good."

"Bleh. Crunchy is not good. Crunchy makes me think I'm chewing up tiny mouse bones."

"Dear God, how did I get myself into this mess. No, don't answer that. Now these."

Another face.

"Even worse?" Jem said.

"Well, they're not crunchy."

"Dodged that bullet."

"But they're sour."

"Only at the beginning. Then they're sweet. They're Sour Patch Kids."

"That's even worse. Why would you want it to change to sweet? And why would they make them anthropomorphic?"

"I'm sorry it's not a single, shriveled grape that's been mashed together with a drop of something that came out of a bee's butt under a cold, moonless sky."

"I think a shriveled grape is called a raisin. And honey doesn't come out of a bee's butt, not exactly. And I don't know why the moon would make any difference."

Jem sighed. This was going to be harder than he'd thought.

Four boxes later, when Tean was spitting out pieces of mini Charleston Chews, Jem said, "I can't believe I'm going to say this, but I think I'm going to do it."

"You know I'll help you with the menu. And the reason it's important is because you need to keep trying new types of texts, new levels of difficulty, and—"

"Not the menu. Andi deserves—deserved better than what she got, I guess. And I want to know if Antonio is telling the truth. I'm going to try to find Tanner."

"Ok."

"That's all?"

Tean's dark eyes were very big and very soft behind the broken glasses. "I think this is a big part of your life that's unresolved. I think it makes sense that you'd want to know, one way or the other, if these guys have killed someone. Can I be honest, though?"

"All the time, unfortunately. Sometimes brutally."

"I'm worried that you've got a different motivation, maybe one that you're not even fully aware of."

Ruffling Scipio's ears, Jem said, "Revenge?"

Tean nodded.

"Oh, I'm fully aware. If I catch any of those three in a dark alley, I'm going to put them down. Hard. And then I'm going to cut off their dicks and turn them into festive earrings. Because they have tiny dicks."

A tiny smile tugged at Tean's mouth and then was gone. "And you're not worried that wanting revenge will skew how you interpret things? You're looking for a way to punish these guys. You don't want to tell me what they did to you, and that's fine, but I can tell it was bad. You're not worried that will affect how you think?"

"Not really." Jem popped some Nestle Crunch bites in his mouth and, around them, said, "Two reasons: first, if Antonio is full of shit and I can prove it, then he'll still go down for murder. That'll make me almost as happy as watching Tanner go down. It's win-win. And second, because you'll be there to keep me from making any mistakes."

Tean's jaw sagged. The glasses were hanging off the tip of his nose, and Jem gently settled them in place again.

"What? Was it supposed to be a surprise? All this pussyfooting around, asking me if I'm worried, blah, blah, blah. Obviously you're going to help me; you're my best friend."

"Normal friend."

"You'd give up your life for me."

"I'd give up my Saturday afternoon for you. But not to move anything heavy. And not a good Saturday, like when there was a traffic accident I could watch on TV."

"God, what I would give for five minutes inside your brain."

Tean grimaced. "I did get a call today. The ME asked me to consult on Alexandria Fontella's autopsy."

It took a moment. "Andi's?"

Tean nodded, and then he told Jem the rest of it.

When he'd finished, Jem said, "Antonio mentioned the dart-gun thing. He said Tanner liked to use it to torture people. Holy fucking shit. He was telling the truth."

"He told the truth about one detail," Tean said. "That doesn't mean he told the truth completely. And unfortunately, the dart syringe doesn't really narrow anything down. There are herds of wild horses all over the state, and the BLM has offices and supplies in several locations. We're not really any closer to pinning down where Tanner might have gotten the weapon or the syringe with ZonaStat-H."

"What about Moab?"

"The BLM has a herd-management area on the west side of Canyonlands. Or there's the Onion Creek HMA, which is east of Moab."

"You just happen to know where all the herd-management areas are near Moab?"

"No, I looked up all the HMAs in the state after the autopsy. I was actually focused on Tooele, because it's close to Salt Lake, but it sounds like that's not where we should start. There's a BLM office in Moab too."

"I guess I'm going to Moab."

"We're."

Jem smiled, and it felt like the first real one in over a day. "Thank you."

"We'll have to take Scipio; I can't find someone to watch him this late."

"You could come down tomorrow."

"And let you go by yourself tonight?" Tean shook his head. "Nice try. You've got some clean clothes here from the last time you crashed on the couch. Pack those and your emergency comb. I'm going to get a bag together, and then we can go."

As Tean headed toward his bedroom, Jem said, "Tean? Seriously. Thank you."

"What are casual acquaintances for? Oh, and you're really going to have to up your candy game. If that's the best you can find, I really don't understand why you like it so much."

"Noted."

"I remember when I was a kid my grandma used to have these little pink and white ones."

"Oh God. No."

"They tasted like licorice. Wait, why are you covering your face?"

"Go away before I die of grief."

10

The drive took a little over three and a half hours. Scipio slept in the back seat as they followed US-6 to US-191, which carried them out of the shrub-steppe along the Wasatch Front, across the mountains, south and east onto the desert plateau that stretched across Colorado, New Mexico, Arizona, and Utah. Jem had never been here before, although he'd seen pictures of southern Utah. Pictures of Arches National Park. Pictures of Canyonlands. Hard stone scoured clean by wind and time. Orange rock in bizarre, twisted formations. On the drive, though, with darkness settling in, his only impression was of a vast emptiness and the crowded stars overhead. A lone service station broke the horizon, a blaze of sodium-vapor lighting like a spotlight on a stage.

"Maybe we should fill up with gas," Jem said as they got closer.

"We've got three-quarters of a tank."

"Maybe we should get water."

"Are you thirsty?"

"Not now, but I will be when we run out of gas and we stagger for a hundred miles with nothing but tumbleweed and rattlesnakes for company, and eventually we die in each other's arms in a best-friend hug, and the vultures pick our bones clean, and the desert polishes them until they're so bright they hurt your eyes to look at them."

Tean shifted in his seat, glancing over, his eyes bright. "What about sunburn?"

"Christ, the sunburn. You'll be fine, you miserable son of a bitch, but I'm going to fry. I'm going to get those horrible, third-degree burns where your skin cracks and oozes and they have to do skin grafts."

"If you survive."

"If I survive, which I won't. You, on the other hand, will probably find some kind of desert cow and drink its blood and have a nice base tan when someone eventually finds you and rescues you."

"You probably won't believe me, but in some areas, they actually do run cattle down here. In the winter. Not as much anymore because economies of scale make it less profitable, but there are a few holdouts." After a slow breath, he added, "Not that I don't appreciate this detailed imagining of our gruesome deaths, but that's normally my thing. Could you explain what prompted it?"

"I don't like this—all this space. I don't like being out here. And I don't like deserts or sand hogs or things that want to bite me and pump me full of poison."

"What is a sand hog?"

"I don't know. You're the vet; figure it out!"

"Ok, so, a couple of things. First, just so you know, that way is east. It's where the sun comes up."

"I know how to find east."

"And if somehow you got stranded out here, you could go east and follow one of those ravines until it took you to the Green River. And then you'd have water. And you could eat sedge and sego lilies so you wouldn't die."

Jem crossed his arms. "Ok."

"Or you could go to the Flying J that's coming up."

Jem grunted.

"Is this real or fake? I can't tell."

"It's both, dummy. I'm nervous. I've never been somewhere this dark, and there are too many stars. I don't like being in the middle of nowhere. I don't like not knowing how to take care of myself. And yes, I know you'll take care of me, and that's actually even more fucking terrifying, believe it or not. Not because I don't trust you, but because—God, I don't even know. So just let me borrow a page from your book and imagine disasters until I'm safely back in range of a cell tower."

They drove for two more miles before Tean said, "If it helps, you can also think about scorpions."

Jem groaned and slid down in his seat.

The Pinyon-Pine Lodge was a two-story, ramshackle building located east of Moab, far enough out on US-128 that the city lights were lost. The siding was rough-hewn logs with adobe chinking, although the windows were relatively modern and satellite dish receivers dotted the roof. Lights blazed behind curtains, and silhouettes showed the lodge was busy—this was tourist season for Arches and Canyonlands, as well as the less well visited La Sal Mountains. Pinyon pines and juniper trees studded the grounds, but instead of the brush and scrub that Jem had seen on the drive, a neatly tended, vibrantly green lawn wrapped around the hotel and ran all the way down to the Colorado, which was ruffled with starlight and easily visible from the parking lot. Money to burn, maybe. Or, more likely, just Mormons and their obsession with perfect lawns.

They got out, and it only took some minor coaxing to convince Scipio to stay in the cool, dark car with the windows down. The air was even dryer than Jem had expected, and he smelled the red-rock dust that coated the curb, the asphalt, and a few of the cars. The river made background noise. Music was playing on the patio behind the lodge, accompanied by the clink of glasses and silverware and laughter. A guy stumbled into view, bent at the waist, and puked. Two guys came after him, both of them bellowing laughs, and caught his shoulders when he looked like he was about to fall.

"Maybe that's how they keep the grass so green," Jem said.

"This is ridiculous," Tean said, hands on his hips as he looked around. "We might as well be staying at a Marriot."

"That sounds great. Let's stay at a Marriot. In Salt Lake. With room service. In fact, let's go now."

"This was your idea."

"I know. That's how you can tell it was stupid."

Tean started for the building, and Jem went after him.

Inside, the lodge continued its pseudo-Western theme. More exposed wood on the walls, glossy with some kind of sealant. Pine floorboards that had been sanded until they were white. To the right, just off the reception area, an antler chandelier hung over a dining room, the tables and chairs all knotty pine, the napkins—from what Jem could judge at a distance—blue chambray.

"Just like the cowboys," Jem said.

"What?"

"Nothing."

"What now?"

"Now we find out if Tanner and Blake are really staying here."

"How?"

"God, I have no idea. I should have thought about that."

The expression on the doc's face was worth it.

"Glasses," Jem whispered as he passed Tean, slapping his butt as he went.

The glasses fell straight off Tean's face.

While the doc squatted to pick them up, Jem headed for the reception desk. Riffing like this was what he did best—and, if he were honest, what he enjoyed most. He took his time crossing the room, sizing up the kid on the other side of the counter. Eighteen. Maybe a very young-looking twenty. Hair dyed black and worn long. Lots of split ends. Black-painted fingernails. He was wearing a green polo with an embroidered brown logo: a tree, and words running around it in a circle. The outfit was complete with a pair of khaki-colored chinos that Tean was going to drool over. Polo and chinos, Jem thought. But what this kid really wanted to wear was a cloak.

"Hi," Jem said, with the game-show smile. "How's it going?"

"Welcome to the Pinyon-Pine Lodge," the kid mumbled to the computer screen, the words running together, "where your dream vacation is our destination how may I help you?"

"Sweet hair," Jem said.

The kid threw him the horns without looking up.

"We're meeting up with some buddies," Jem said with a grin. "Bachelor party." He looked around the reception lobby. "This place is tight. Could we get our keys?"

"What's the name of your party?"

Strike one, Jem thought. "I don't know what name they put it under. They said they were going to be the only bachelor party here this weekend."

The kid leveled a dead-eyed stare at him.

"How about Blake Bigney?" Jem said. "Or Tanner Kimball?"

The kid typed a few times. He made a face. He typed some more. He made the same face. He might have been doing some quick mental math about how much his pancake makeup was going to cost him this month.

"Have you worked here long?" Jem asked.

The kid's mouth twisted.

"I don't mean anything by that," Jem said. "I didn't mean you seem like you're new."

"My parents own this dump."

"Oh. So you grew up here? Pretty cool."

"It sucks." Footsteps moved nearby, and a woman with 90s bangs and a royal-blue cocktail dress, complete with shoulder pads, poked her head into the room.

"Russell, is everything ok?"

"Yes, Mom."

Mom retreated.

Then, to Jem, Russell said, "I'm sorry, neither of those guests has anyone else listed in their party."

Bingo bango bongo, Jem wanted to say. Instead, he smiled. "Damn it. They're so fucking dumb. Can I run up there and get them? They'll come down and tell you."

"I can't give out guest information, sir."

"I don't want any guest information. I just want to ask them to come down here."

The kid shook his head, the split ends of his hair swaying. "I can't give out their room numbers."

Jem pretended to check his phone. "God, I don't have any service. Could you call their room?"

Frowning, Russell seemed to consider this. Then he shrugged. "Which room?"

"Let's try Blake."

After punching in the elaborate code of 90232, the kid passed the phone over to Jem. He listened to it ring. He imagined Blake answering. The call cut off without connecting.

"Do you want to try again?" the kid asked.

"What about Tanner?"

Another uncrackable cipher: 90234. When Russell passed the phone to Jem, Jem's hands were sweaty. Hey, fuckface, how's it hanging? Maybe that would be a good opening line. God, it was an inferno inside this place. The ringing went on and on and disconnected.

"No luck," Jem said. "Are you sure I can't run up there and knock?"

"I'm sorry, sir."

By this point, Tean had joined him at the counter. Jem threw him a quick look; Tean was studying him openly, his bushy eyebrows drawn together.

"We might have to book our own room," Jem said.

"That's fine." The bushy eyebrows made a fuzzy vee. "Are you fine?"

"Great," Jem said. "Fantastic." He turned to the kid. "Could I walk back to the patio? I saw some of our friends out there. I can get the name and find out how they booked the rooms."

"We're really not supposed to—"

"I'll be super fast." Jem smiled. He thought about the black fingernail polish, the dyed hair, the sullen resentment. His smile got bigger. "Hey, you're really lucky to live out here, you know? The beauty of nature. Feeling one with the universe. I bet you can feel God's hand sheltering you every day, just pouring blessing into your life. I just thought of that right now: you're so lucky. I hope you realize that."

"This place?" The kid sneered. "This place is the asshole of nowhere. And God is a fucking joke. Life is a fucking joke. People are just pieces in a machine. Existence is meaningless, and—"

From the other room, in a lilting voice: "Russell, did you do the toilet check at nine?"

"Yes, God, Mom." To Jem, in a slightly quieter voice, "And when the Earth is consumed with a dark and unquenchable hellfire sent by the Dark Lord—"

"Did you finish folding those napkins?"

"Jeez, will you stop crawling up my butt? Yes, I folded them. Why can't you treat me like a grownup?"

"Language!"

Leaning over the counter, the kid added in a whisper, "And when the Dark Lord's eternal flames burn all the meaningless shit out of people's lives, only those who have sworn the Blood Pact will survive, in a realm of pain and terror and—"

"Did you replace the urinal cakes?"

"Mom!"

"I'm just going to check on my friends," Jem said. "Tean, take it away."

"Russell," from the other room in that singsong voice, "pull up your pants. I can see your undies."

"Hail, Satan," Russell whispered fiercely to Jem.

Tean, eyes bright, stepped up to the counter. "You know, that's a very interesting point about an infernal conflagration consuming the world. But have you ever thought that maybe the sheer pointlessness of existence is because the universe is itself meaningless, rather than because a diabolical power hasn't yet purified everything with a dark, refining fire?"

"Um," Russell said.

Jem grinned as he jogged into the dining room and waved at Mom.

The last thing he caught behind him was Tean saying, "Let me tell you about Camus."

Inside the dining room, the guests were mostly middle-age and older, enjoying dinner and drinks as couples or in small groups. A wall of French doors opened onto the patio, where a younger crowd, mostly guys, was laughing and drinking. Something with a good beat was playing. After a quick glance, Jem ignored them; Blake and Tanner probably enjoyed a party as much as the next guy, but this was a crowd of friends, and they looked like the nerdy-with-too-much-money type. Probably tech guys from Utah and California, probably reassuring themselves of their manliness with a weekend drinking beer in a lodge in southern Utah. Not Blake and Tanner's crowd—not unless things had changed drastically.

As Jem had hoped, a service hallway at the back of the dining room connected with a narrow set of stairs. He passed a young woman in the same Pinyon-Pine Lodge polo that Russell had been wearing. She slowed, giving Jem a strange look, and he just smiled and trotted past her. He emerged on the second floor, let the service door swing shut behind him, and began checking rooms.

Probably because the lodge had been built in stages, the numbering of the rooms wasn't exactly intuitive. Jem made his way up and down the first hall, where the rooms ran from 299 all the way down to 240. No 232 or 234. He followed the landing, which looked down on a lounge on the main floor. Voices floated up.

"—yes, Satan's unholy fires are an ok reason to believe that life is purposeless and nothing we can do means anything," Tean was saying, "but consider Heidegger's proposition about *Dasein* and temporality, which really offers a fuller framework for the absolute meaninglessness of the universe—"

"I think my mom's calling me."

"I didn't hear anything. Now, *Dasein* is interesting in Heidegger, but what's even more interesting is his idea of death as a possibility."

"Ok, Mom. Yes, I'm coming right now!"

For some reason, the next branch of the hallway was numbered 2200 to 2266, which didn't make any sense to Jem. He passed an older couple, the man leaning heavily on a cane, the woman in a wig that would have made Dolly proud. The man tipped his Stetson at Jem, and the woman flashed a hand covered in silver and turquoise. He took the next branch and saw that the numbers started at 201A, which he wasn't sure meant anything, and finally found 232 and 234.

This must have been one of the original sections of the lodge; the floorboards were warped and cracked in places, the light fixtures were tarnished, and the exposed joists overhead were rough-hewn. The doors were solid pine, and the locks were ancient. Jem could have breathed on one and it would have opened. He knocked at 232 and listened. Nothing. He knocked at 234. Nothing.

He let himself into 232 first. Blake was a pig, his shit everywhere, but Jem didn't find anything more interesting than a bag of what he thought was oxy. He left it in the mesh liner of the suitcase. On the dresser, held open by the TV's remote control, lay a pamphlet for the Onion Creek Wild Horses—SEE THEM IN THE WILD. He took a picture with his phone. He tried 234 next. Tanner wasn't exactly going to pass a barrack inspection, but the room wasn't a complete disaster. The only thing interesting was a stack of papers. The wall of text stopped him cold, but he made himself slow down and decipher the key words in a few of the titles: survey, assay, uranium, carnotite. The mine was called Nueva Vida. He took pictures of these papers too.

Time was up. He let himself out, made sure both doors were locked, and went downstairs. When he got back to reception, Tean was gone. Jem found him in the parking lot, walking Scipio along one of the grassy berms. Scipio was inspecting a juniper and sneezing every three seconds.

"I booked a room," Tean said. "They accommodate animals, and it sounded better than trying to drive back tonight. Was that the right thing to do?"

"I don't know." Jem told him what he'd found, passing over his phone with the pictures.

"Is this their cover? Tourists who might be interested in mining rights?" Tean frowned as he swiped through the images. Then he stopped on a picture that showed him against an outcropping of gray, lichen-stained stone, with an intensely blue sky behind him. He was looking off at something else, just a hint of a smile. He looked young and alive and beautiful.

"Is that me?"

"Duh."

"That doesn't look like me."

"Of course it does."

"When did you take it?"

"After you watched that crow try to murder me."

Tean blinked several times. "You threw a rock at it, and crows have phenomenal facial recognition and memory. They're not above revenge, and besides, you brought it on yourself."

"It was trying to get a rabbit!"

"Wait, you took this picture when we hiked Bridal Veil?"

"Yes, Jesus, will you let it go?"

"I don't remember you taking any pictures of me."

"That's because whenever I say I want a picture with you—or a picture of you—you make that face."

"I don't make a face." Tean hesitated. "What face?"

Grabbing the phone, Jem said, "Go find a mirror. You're making it right now. Can we please drive out to this mine and check it out?"

"Why would they be there?"

"I don't know."

Tean frowned. "What's going on?"

"I don't know. I feel weird. Something is weird, and I don't like it, and I don't know why they left those papers out unless they wanted someone to see them and know what they're pretending to be interested in."

"That sounds like a trap."

Jem hesitated. He remembered Decker: an overheard conversation, the laundry room, the white-hot hope burning in his chest, and then the shadows waiting for him. His mouth was dry when he said, "Maybe. Can we just drive out there and see?"

"If it's a trap—"

"If it even looks like there's a possibility of that, we'll turn around."

"Jem—"

"Please."

Nodding slowly, Tean led the way to the truck, and they used the lodge's Wi-Fi to pull up a map to the Nueva Vida mine. They drove east on US-128 again. Without service on their phones, they had to rely on road signs and markers, gauging their progress against the downloaded map. Tean finally turned off at the BLM route marker, following a dirt road into the black box of a canyon. Clouds of dust billowed up, filling the truck, and Scipio began to sneeze again. The truck trundled over the rutted ground, and the only sounds were the creaking of the suspension and loose rocks crunching under the tires.

The mine looked abandoned. Old rail tracks led into the pitch-black opening. There was no sign of life, and in the dark, even with their phones as flashlights, it was impossible to tell if other vehicles had been up here recently.

"Do you feel any better?" Tean asked.

Jem shook his head.

"Do you want to look around some more?"

Jem shook his head.

"Maybe they're in Moab. We could drive past the BLM office. If they've been stealing equipment like the dart syringes and the injection rifle, we might be able to learn something."

"Where are the horses?"

"What?"

"The Onion Creek HMA. The flyer in Blake's room."

Tean was quiet for a long moment. "East. But I don't see why they would—"

"The injection rifle. The flyer. The horses. Please?"

Tean guided the truck back to the highway, and they went east again. The mesas and broken buttes on their right. The Colorado an albino, starlight snake on their left. They turned off on another of the BLM roads. Two miles later, at the mouth of a slot canyon to the south, moonlight glittered on glass.

"Stop," Jem said.

Tean stopped the truck. They left Scipio there and jogged down the loose shale, slipping, trying to catch their balance. Jem grabbed a scrubby brush to balance himself and swore as thorns punctured his hand, but he waved Tean off when the doc tried to make his way over. When they reached the flat, sunbaked ground at the bottom of the slope, they could move faster. The night was bright enough that the scrub and thistles and tumbleweeds threw shadows.

When they got closer, Jem's suspicions were confirmed: it was a car parked less than a hundred yards from the slot canyon. They went to the car first. It was a Camaro, only a year or two old. It couldn't have been there long—someone would have noticed and called it in—but the hood was cool to the touch. Jem used the hem of his shirt to open the door. He smelled weed and a Hawaiian Punch air freshener hanging from the rearview mirror. He was reaching for the glove compartment when Tean called his name.

When Jem turned, he was surprised to see the doc at the mouth of the canyon, kneeling next to a shadowed bulk. It wasn't until Jem got closer that he realized it was a horse. It had to be one of the wild ones because it was so thin its ribs were showing. It was dead; its chest was still, and several dark wounds marked its neck and side.

"She's still warm," Tean said, his voice tight in a way Jem had only heard a handful of times before. "Someone shot her."

The moonlight made the bloodstains black against the cracked earth. Something clacked deeper down the slot, and Jem turned to look.

"No," Tean said.

"I'm just going to take a look."

"Jem, no. Someone shot this mare. There's an abandoned car. For all we know, the shooter is still here. Let's go back and call the sheriff and the BLM rangers."

Another sound came, like rocks striking together. The echoes made it hard to judge distance, but it couldn't be far. Jem pulled out his phone, switched on the flashlight, and started forward.

Swearing, Tean came after him.

The canyon floor sloped up, and after a hundred yards, the brittle, crumbling texture of soil underfoot changed. Jem panned the light across the ground and saw red rock that had been washed clean. He moved more slowly, trying to keep from making noise, but the narrow walls of the canyon seemed to give back every sound: his sneakers scuffing stone, his breathing, even his heartbeat, although he knew that had to be his imagination. Tean, of course, made no noise at all. When Jem glanced back, he was just a ghostlight bobbing along behind him.

The noise came again, and Jem was sure this time that it was close. Breathing, too. At first, he took it for the distorted echo of his own exhalations, but after another thirty yards, he was convinced: something else was here, something breathing wildly. On the verge of panic. He slowed enough that Tean caught up. When he looked over, the doc was just a shadow against the steep red walls. Tean shook his head.

Jem moved forward again. The canyon jagged left, and when they came around the corner, the slot opened into a fork. Where the two paths met, floodwaters had converged for thousands of years, and a slightly wider section opened up. Wide enough for more of the night's weak light to filter down. Wide enough for a scraggly juniper.

The tree flinched, branches snapping, hard berries raining down, and Jem scrambled back. His heart pounded in his chest. Tean put a hand on his back; with his other hand, the doc forced Jem's light down. When Jem opened his mouth, Tean shook his head again.

As Jem's eyes adjusted to the darkness, he saw what Tean must have already understood. A foal was caught in the juniper's gnarled branches. Jem could see only the back legs. One of the hooves came down hard, clipping against the red rock, and the sound echoed up the slot.

Then Jem saw a body. It lay ten yards past the juniper, past the foal, and even in the weak light filtered by the canyon's high walls, Jem knew the man—woman?—was dead. He could smell it now, the smell of ruptured bowels and body cavities, a smell that had sent the foal into a panic. He took a step forward.

Tean caught his arm, and the doc's grip was iron.

"I'll be—"

"No." Tean pointed past Jem, farther up the righthand fork. After what felt like an eternity of watching, Jem saw something move.

"Someone's waiting for us."

"It's not a person," Tean whispered. "It's another mare. She's not going to leave her foal."

"Well if it's just a horse—"

Tean's grip tightened, yanking Jem back a step. "I said no. If you get between her and her foal, she'll lose her mind. She could kill you."

"She's a horse; I think I'll be ok."

"She probably weighs close to a thousand pounds, and most of that is muscle and bone. She'll be terrified for her young, and she just needs to hit you once."

"Can't you talk to her?"

"I'm a trained professional, not Dr. Doolittle. Let's go. We'll call this in, and they'll get a team out here. They can tranq the mare, get the foal loose, and take things from there."

"I'm not leaving."

"Jem—"

"I'm not. If it's Tanner, I want to know." He swallowed against the sudden tightness in his throat. "I know I'm acting weird. I know I'm not making any sense."

Tean said nothing.

When Jem tried to peel Tean's hand away, Tean shook him by the arm. "Stop. Just stop."

"I'm not—"

"I know you're not. You're driving me crazy right now. Stay put until I tell you it's safe."

And then, before Jem could say anything, Tean gave another savage yank, propelling Jem toward the canyon wall. The doc slipped forward into the night, pocketing his phone as he went. He was speaking quietly, calmly, words that Jem couldn't hear but that he knew were probably nonsense. The juniper thrashed again. The falling berries sounded like a hailstorm. When a breeze rolled down the canyon, it washed away the dead body's stink, and Jem smelled horse, something he thought of as sweat and lather and terror.

By then, Tean had reached the tree. He was still talking in that calm tone. Based on cues that Jem couldn't perceive, Tean moved forward by inches. The whole process dragged on and on until it felt like hours. Then, with a suddenness that made Jem startle, Tean grabbed one of the juniper's branches and pulled. Wood crackled, and the foal burst out of the tree. Tean flew backward and landed on his ass. The clatter of hooves filled the slot as the foal raced to rejoin its mother, and then both horses streaked away, becoming shadows, then vanishing.

Tean was already picking himself up by the time Jem reached him.

"Are you ok?" Jem said.

"I'm fine," Tean said, dusting himself off. "I just got a little too close."

Jem caught the glasses before they fell, resettling them on Tean's nose.

"Thanks."

"Are you hurt?"

Tean shook his head.

"Did that mean horse hurt your bummy?" Tean met Jem's eyes but didn't answer. After a moment, heat filled Jem's face, and he looked away. "I'm sorry. I just need some sleep; I feel like I'm going out of my mind."

To Jem's surprise, Tean found his hand and squeezed, and Jem had to blink to clear his eyes. He pulled free after a moment and trotted up to where the canyon widened. Taking out his phone, he squatted for a better look. The stink of death was thick, and a few flies, untroubled by the darkness, buzzed and flew up from the body. A white man, average height, still relatively young. Dark hair. Aside from that, it was hard to tell. He had been trampled to death, dozens of hooves crushing him underfoot. His face was destroyed. His body too. Blood had soaked the thin t-shirt, and in places, broken bones poked through his clothing.

They walked back to the truck. Jem retrieved a pair of disposable gloves. He checked the registration in the Camaro's glovebox: Tanner Kimball. He closed the car and headed up the slot canyon again while Tean stayed behind with Scipio. He lifted the dead man a few inches and worked the wallet out of his back pocket. Even in the filtered moonlight, he recognized Tanner's name and picture on the driver's license. More than five hundred dollars in cash. Visas and Mastercards in different names—Jem took those. Gas receipts from the last few days, stations up and down US-6 and US-191, the roads between here and Salt Lake. Jem replaced everything except the credit cards and returned the wallet to the dead man's pocket. He walked back to the truck.

Tean and Scipio were sitting in the Ford's bed, the dog's head in Tean's lap as Tean stroked his ears.

"That's not Tanner," Jem said. "But someone sure wants us to think it is."

11

They had to drive back to Moab before they got a signal, and by then, it made more sense to head directly to the police station to file their report. After that, everything became a jumble. They spent an hour answering the same questions over and over again; when they weren't answering questions, they were sitting on a bench just outside the holding cells, in case they hadn't gotten the message. The woman who did most of the questioning, Tebbs, was middle aged, Native American, no nonsense, her salt-and-pepper hair in a butch cut. A younger man took over after a while, introducing himself as Chief Nobles. In his office, framed pictures hung on the wall: a blond wife and two blond kids; a boat on what Tean thought was Lake Powell; a house that might have come out of *LDS Living*.

An hour later, the Grand County sheriff showed up. Sheriff McEneany, nervous and pale, looked all of twelve years old and probably still didn't need to shave. His belt buckle proclaimed him the 2017 Silver Star Rodeo Champion. He asked them a few questions and stood around, thumbs in his Sam Browne belt like he'd just cracked the case. Nobles and Tebbs didn't exactly roll their eyes at each other, but their vicarious embarrassment was so intense that Tean found himself trying to find somewhere else to look.

After that, they had to drive back to the canyon. Scipio stayed with Tebbs; the last thing Tean saw when he glanced back was Scipio already on his back, Tebbs laughing under her breath while she scratched his belly. When they got to the canyon, they walked Nobles and McEneany back to the body. McEneany and Nobles looked at the body and then moved a dozen yards away to confer in low voices. McEneany shook his head vehemently at whatever Nobles was saying.

"Trouble in paradise," Jem whispered.

Tean agreed, although he couldn't figure out the reason for it.

When the two law-enforcement officers came back, Nobles called Highway Patrol while McEneany called the BLM office. Then there was more waiting. The highway patrol cruiser arrived first, lights and sirens, the whole production. The trooper introduced himself as Haggerty. He was Native American, young, and his haircut reminded Tean of Jem's. Haggerty studied Tean and Jem just long enough that when he finally moved on, Jem whispered, "Ping, ping, ping. That's the sound of my gaydar exploding."

"Be quiet," Tean said, mostly because he didn't think he had a gaydar.

When the BLM ranger arrived, he was driving an upgraded Jeep, and he made a big show of veering off the road, rumbling down the shale, and driving up to the mouth of the canyon. He walked past Jem and Tean without a word; Tean heard one of the other men address him as Jager.

"Asshole," Jem said.

"Does he not understand this is a crime scene?" Tean said.

McEneany seemed to take this as a cue to assert himself because his little bantam chest puffed up and he shouted, "Keep it down, please."

"This is what I'm talking about," Jem muttered. "Assholes."

All the same questions again. All the same answers. One problem, Tean understood, was that their story was so strange that it was suspicious: Antonio's request cobbled together with the ZonaStat-H needle at the autopsy, driving down, finding the body hundreds of yards down a slot canyon that was miles deep on BLM land. At night. But another problem was that they didn't make very good suspects, either: they had taken their discovery directly to the police.

Haggerty, McEneany, and Nobles had moved off for another conversation, McEneany shaking his head vigorously again, when Jager came over to Jem and Tean and said, "Up."

"Excuse me?" Jem said.

Tean was already standing.

"Get your asses up." He had to be on the hard side of forty, his dark hair thin and messy, his cheeks heavy with stubble. "Do you have a hard time hearing, son?"

"Jem, please."

Jem got up, although he made a big show about taking his time. He'd barely gotten to his feet when Jager seized him by the arm, grabbed Tean too, and steered them toward the Jeep. Jem still hadn't caught his footing, and he stumbled a few times, kicking rocks ahead of them.

"Hey!" McEneany was puffing up again. "Hey, what's going on?"

Jager kept walking.

"Special Agent Jager." That was Haggerty. The trooper's voice was a whipcrack. "Why does it look like you're about to put two men who haven't been detained in your vehicle?"

Jager shoved Jem and Tean, releasing them so that they stumbled forward, and spun back.

"I thought maybe we ought to have this discussion without these two listening to every word. That might be hard for the fucking pinup boys of the local yokel brigade to understand, but if you haven't figured it out, these two are our primary suspects."

That, Tean understood quickly, had been a mistake. McEneany looked at Nobles. Nobles looked at Haggerty. State and local boys versus the lone fed.

"Let's think about that for just a minute," Haggerty said.

"I don't need a glorified park ranger telling me how to do my job," McEneany squeaked.

"Special Agent Jager," Nobles said, "I think you've jumped the gun."

"If I've got bears stealing picnic baskets," McEneany said, "I'll call BLM. Otherwise, I don't need jack spit from you fellows."

"I'm going to save you boys a lot of trouble," Jager said. "It's a murder on federal land. That's a federal crime. We'll take it from here." Over his shoulder, he said, "Get in the back of the Jeep." When neither Tean nor Jem moved, he barked, "Get in the fucking Jeep."

Tean took a step, but Jem caught his arm, shaking his head.

"I'd say it's not clear what happened." Haggerty's voice sounded calm, but it still had that whip-crack energy underneath it. "We've got a dead man who looks like he might have been trampled to death. Murder, well, that's for the state's medical examiner to decide."

The only light came from the headlights of the parked vehicles. It caught Jager on one side, painting his throat, the bulge of stubble when he swallowed. "I'm talking worst-case scenario here. We'll get these boys settled and have a lengthy conversation."

"No," Haggerty said. "I don't think so."

It took longer than that, but that was the beginning of the end. Tean and Jem ended up back at the police station in Moab, a two-story building of brick that looked bleached by the sodium lamps. The hours blurred together. Questions. No more questions. Burnt coffee. The droning of a Coke machine. Questions. No more questions. A phone ringing shrilly. Shift change, men and women coming on duty, most of them giving Jem and Tean long, considering looks. Scipio slept through most of it, his head on Tean's Keens, snoring. Judging by the crumbs on his whiskers, Tebbs had given him some treats.

"Thank Jesus nobody decided we need these," Jem said, whacking the cuffs attached to the bench. The cuffs spun away, jangling when they hit one of the metal supports bracketed to the wall.

Questions. More questions. No more questions. The world became unreal; exhaustion, mental and physical, caught up with Tean. He couldn't seem to focus his eyes. He felt himself drifting, not quite able to sleep because Jem's knee kept bouncing; the blond man seemed restless, verging on jittery. A headache had started behind Tean's eyes, and somehow, even that felt unreal.

And then, suddenly, they were free to go.

"Are we supposed to stay in town?" Tean asked Tebbs as she walked them to the door.

Jem snorted. Scipio sneezed.

"We've got your contact information. If we need to follow up, we will. Thank you both for your help."

And with that, they emerged into the mid-morning light, Tean blinking against the sudden brightness. The day was already hot, the air smelled like dust and frying doughnuts, and down the street, kids at a card table hawked arrowheads, fishing lures, and diamondback rattles. Even from a distance, Tean had his doubts about the rattles, which had a plastic shine. A banner hung across the street announcing THANK YOU PIONEERS - FIREWORKS AT 9. A second, smaller banner hung below that said FIREWORKS

RESTRICTIONS STILL IN EFFECT. From the streetlights hung a parade of American flags.

They drove back to the Pinyon-Pine Lodge, and Tean paid for a second night, which seemed unjust since they hadn't gotten to use their first night. The pet-friendly rooms were in a separate wing at the back of the ramshackle structure, probably to better contain possible outbreaks and infestations—fleas were always a risk in pet-friendly accommodations. Tean normally gave each place a thorough inspection; today, he barely had the energy to get Scipio food and water. Jem mumbled something about checking something and slipped out of the room before Tean could ask any questions. Tean collapsed on the bed and slept.

He woke to Scipio's barking. Groaning, Tean could make out the Lab standing stiff-legged on Jem's empty bed. Then a knock came at the door, and Tean realized that's what had startled the Lab. The clock told him that it was barely past noon; he had slept less than two hours. His eyes were grainy as he kicked his way free of the covers. Jem had gotten himself locked out, of course. He'd left without a key, and the door had automatically locked behind him, and now he was knocking hard enough to wake the dead—which was more or less how Tean felt.

"Ok, ok, will you please calm down?" he asked as he opened the door.

Ammon stood there, his face pale except for red spots in his cheeks, his eyes fever bright.

"No," he said, his chest heaving. "I will not fucking calm down."

And then he took Tean's head in his hands and kissed him.

12

Tean pulled back from the kiss, but Ammon wouldn't let him go. They stumbled into the room together. Ammon kicked the door shut behind him. Tean caught Ammon's wrists, trying to pull his hands away, but Ammon just kept moving until Tean bumped up against the wall. His fingers bit into Tean's scalp. His body, so much bigger than Tean's, pinned him against the rough log paneling.

When Ammon drew back, Tean said, "Stop, stop it." But he wasn't pulling on Ammon's wrists anymore.

Ammon leaned in to kiss him again.

"Stop."

Ammon hesitated and drew back. Scipio was still barking wildly.

"Let go of me. Skip, enough. Ammon, I said let go."

Scipio quieted, lay down on Jem's bed, and still somehow managed to look ready to leap into action if Ammon made a wrong move. Ammon's grip loosened, and he pulled his hands away, taking time to smooth Tean's hair before releasing him completely.

"What in the world is wrong with you? Are you completely out of your mind? I told you that I don't want—"

"Listen to me." Ammon didn't shout. He didn't even raise his voice. "Do you know what happened to me today?"

"No. Why are you down here? Did Antonio—"

"I went into work to catch up on a few things. Some moron had taken a message from the Grand County Sheriff's Department. It was sitting on my desk, one of those carbon-paper slips. 'Dead body. Wildlife vet.' That's all. Do you have any idea what that did to me?"

Tean's lips felt bruised from the kisses. He could still taste Ammon in his mouth, and the big man was still close enough that

Tean was aware of his body heat. "I'm sorry; I don't know why they did that."

"It was an accident. A dumb mistake. Kat and I were halfway here before I got hold of someone in the sheriff's office, although that's probably mostly because of all the dead zones we had to drive through. After that, at least I could breathe."

"Ammon—"

"I'm not done. The thought of losing you, that destroyed me. I'm still shaking. Look." He held out a hand that was visibly trembling. "I'm tired of this. I'm tired of pretending we can go back to the beginning and build things up from scratch. You still have feelings for me, I know you do. And what I feel for you, I can't even put it into words. You're everything to me."

"I don't know what you want me to say. I told you that I want to be friends—"

"I moved into your building to be close to you."

"You're confusing physical closeness with emotional closeness. They're not the same thing."

"One is a starting place for the other. I know you're scared that I'm going to hurt you again. And you're right to be scared; I've treated you horribly. You're the most important person in my life, and I've hurt you more than I've hurt anyone else. But being scared isn't a way to move forward with your life. I'm not going to sit around and pretend to be ok while you go out with other guys, and every once in a while you and I pop popcorn and watch those weird YouTube videos of earthquakes."

"Earthquake-related building collapses," Tean corrected. He put a hand on Ammon's chest and tried to force him back, but Ammon didn't budge. "I'm sorry you feel that way, but I've told you how I feel, and I—"

Ammon knocked his hand away with enough force that the blow actually hurt. Then Ammon stepped in, crushing Tean against the wall again, and kissed him. It was slow. It was surprisingly gentle. And it was passionate, Ammon's hand coming up to clutch Tean's hair, his knee between Tean's legs.

"That's how you feel," Ammon whispered as he pulled back. "You know it, and I know it. If you want to punish me, I'll take it. I know my sex addiction has seriously affected our relationship, and I'm willing to pay whatever price I need to pay to make things right.

But I'm done with the lying. You need to be honest with yourself about what you want."

When he stepped back, giving Tean space, Scipio was on his feet again, growling.

"It's ok," Tean said, one hand cradling his aching wrist. "Scipio, it's ok."

"What's all the racket?" Jem called from the hall. "Did you guys get out the Cheez Whiz without me—oh." He stopped in the doorway. "How the living fuck?"

"It's a long story," Tean said.

At the same time, Ammon said, "Kat and I are down here to figure out who has jurisdiction over this cluster. If Antonio's telling the truth, and it seems more and more like he might be, then this has bearing on our murder, and we want looped in."

"Great," Jem said. "Go play cops and robbers. We're exhausted. We need to sleep. In our hotel room. Together."

"Jem," Tean said.

Ammon wore a crooked little smile. "Right. And here I thought maybe you'd want an update on that body you found last night."

"What?" Jem said. "You already heard something? I thought that's why you came down here, to get information."

"Right," Tean said, trying to keep his voice even. "I thought that's why you came down here."

Ammon ignored him, but Jem flashed him a look.

"On the drive, I got in touch with the sheriff, who wanted to tell me everything he could. Poor kid. Is he as young as he looks?"

"Younger," Jem said.

"How the hell did that happen?" Ammon shook his head. "Never mind. I'll get us a table at the restaurant. You guys clean up." The crooked smile was back. "In your hotel room. Together."

13

They showered, dressed, and walked Scipio. It was almost one, and the day was so hot that the air shimmered with it. The sun came down so intensely that Jem found himself squinting. He'd lived in Utah his whole life, but this part of the world was new to him, and he was surprised to find his throat and nose painfully dry. Part of his discomfort, he thought, might also have something to do with the constant, low-grade headache he was feeling. While Tean was looking in the other direction, Jem popped another of the pills; he'd scored them from a trucker a few weeks back, and he wasn't sure what they were, but they kept him awake and working. That's all he needed for the moment.

"I'm going to get a nosebleed," he said as they made another loop under the scanty shade of the pinyon pines. The grass and the shade were the only place it was safe to walk the Lab, and Scipio was having a grand time investigating every inch of ground.

"Possibly."

"I'm going to have one of those nosebleed hemorrhages and die from it."

Tean was staring out at the horizon, where the ribbon of highway curled into blue sky. He made a vague noise of agreement.

"Did you know a million Midwesterners die from desert nosebleeds every year? They drive all the way out here with three kids shrieking in the back of the station wagon. They open the door. Step out. Boom. And the coolest part is that the blood boils away on the pavement before they hit the ground."

"I didn't know that," Tean mumbled.

"Of course, the real problem is the bodies. Sand hogs can smell the blood. *Porcus arizonicus*. You can't keep them away. And they've got those big tusks. Of course, they're nothing compared to those desert bugs that pop your eyeballs and suck out your brain, um, *Moabus brainius* I think."

"What?" Tean blinked. "What are you talking about? *Moabus*—that's not a real thing."

"Huh. I thought I read about it in one of those tourist pamphlets in the lodge."

"Gosh, that reminds me. We didn't bring your workbooks."

"Oh, dang. I'm so sad. I cannot believe we did that."

"I hear the sarcasm, and I'm ignoring it. We're going to find some time to practice today." A massive yawn made his jaw crack. "I completely spaced out. Come on, let's take Scipio back to the room, and we'll go get something to eat. Ammon's waiting."

"What's going on with you?"

"I'm just tired."

Teancum Leon was many things; one of them was a terrible liar.

When they got to the restaurant, the lunch rush was almost over. A family of seven occupied a large table at the back of the room, near the French doors that opened onto the patio, and a young couple in what appeared to be Ralph Lauren hiking gear sat at a two-top, but otherwise the only occupant was the Salt Lake City detective. Ammon already had a Coke, and he was tapping at his phone. He looked up long enough to wave, pulled out the chair next to him, and went back to his phone.

"Thanks," Jem said, moving for the seat Ammon had indicated.

"Don't antagonize him," Tean said, steering Jem toward a different chair. "Is everything ok?"

Ammon grunted and kept tapping.

A girl, probably no older than sixteen, stopped at the table long enough to hand out menus and ask about drinks.

"A beer," Jem said. "No, better yet, a whiskey."

"I'm sorry, sir. This is a family restaurant."

"Some families drink beer," Jem said.

The girl's face said she didn't believe this.

"He'll have a Coke," Tean said. "I'll have water."

"Make sure you squeeze the water extra hard," Jem said, "to get out any flavor that might have accidentally seeped into it."

"Ignore him."

"And no ice. And make sure you don't hold the cup too long or carry it too close to your body or look at it with your eyes. You don't want anything to change that water from room temperature."

"Did you know," Tean said, "that, just in terms of numbers, humans don't rank in even the top thirty of the most murderous mammals?" He fixed Jem with a glare. "We've got a lot of catching up to do."

"Not this stuff again," Ammon muttered, still typing. "Could you drop it with the weirdo act?"

Red glowed in Tean's face, and he looked down at his lap.

"Ok, then." The girl's smile was too wide as she backed away. "Just the Coke and the water."

"Done," Ammon said, pocketing the phone and flashing Tean a smile. "Sorry about that. Kind of an evolving situation."

"Why do you want to help us?" Jem said as he opened the menu. Pure text. Dense text. Tiny text. He flipped it closed. "Normally all you do is frown and complain and talk about how hard your life is when we do your job."

"Jem!"

"No, it's fine, he's got a right to ask. The simple answer is that you're already involved. You got Antonio to open up about a lead, and you followed that lead here. I don't like the thought of either of you being in danger, but I'd be stupid not to get any information I possibly can out of you. If that means sharing, well, I'm ok with that."

"Jem, this would be a good time to, you know." Tean tapped the menu.

Jem kept his gaze on Ammon. "So this isn't about helping us find Tanner. This is about giving us the absolute bare minimum of information you can in exchange for us telling you everything we know."

"Well, that's one of the things we need to figure out—if the remains recovered last night belong to Tanner Kimball."

"They don't. That was not Tanner. He's not dead."

"Interesting. His ID was found—"

"His ID doesn't mean shit."

The words rang out in the restaurant; half-log pine paneling apparently had excellent acoustics.

"Let's order," Tean said. "Jem—"

"I'm just getting a burger." He shoved the menu away from him.

"This would really be a good opportunity to—"

"No. I'm fine." Jem's face was warm. "I know what I want."

Tean nodded, but Ammon spoke first. "We could take turns reading the menu. Would that help?"

It was like being doused in gasoline and touched with a match.

"Ammon," Tean said quietly, "I appreciate that you're trying to help, but I'm not sure now is a good time for you to get involved."

"I'm sorry."

"It's fine; I know you were trying to help."

"No, that's a great idea," Jem said, grabbing the menu blindly and opening it against the tabletop. "Let's do that."

"Will you take a breath? He didn't mean anything by it."

Maybe. Ammon's face was smooth, maybe faintly worried, a crease between his eyebrows like he realized his mistake. But his eyes, his eyes were a whole other story.

Jem smoothed the menu with the heel of his hand. "Sou—sou—sou—"

"Southwest," Ammon prompted.

Jem threw the menu. He meant—he thought he meant—to toss it. Instead, it flew across the table. It struck Tean in the chest and fell into his lap. Shooting to his feet, Jem knocked back the chair. He caught it before it could fall.

"Ammon, just stop. Jem, he didn't mean anything—will you come back here?"

"I need to use the restroom."

Jem didn't look back. He couldn't find a restroom, so he had to settle for the business center, which was a cubbyhole on the main floor that held a single, ancient PC, an inkjet printer covered with a fine layer of dust, and a thick braid of cables that looked perfect for making a noose. Jem figured that would be as good a way to go as any. He shut the door, leaned against it, and pressed his hands against his eyes.

It shouldn't have mattered; his whole life had been like this. But it was Tean sitting across the table, with that familiar mixture of worry and hope on his face. And it was Ammon pulling out the chair. And it was another sleepless night, and the pills, and Tanner and Antonio and Blake, and all those times in Decker.

A soft knock came at the door.

Jem wiped his face and cleared his throat. "I just need to finish printing my pornography."

"Oh." Then, "Can I help?"

"Are you a printing machine disguised as a human?"

"No."

"Then you can't help. I'll see you back at the table."

"I could three-hole punch it and put it in a binder. Or I could laminate it. Or I could collate it."

One last check, face dry, no snot bubbles, nothing to do for red eyes or the color in his cheeks. Jem stepped away from the door and opened it.

"I'm sorry," Tean said. His hair was wilder than ever, which meant he'd been pushing it back with his hands, and his glasses were on the tip of his nose. "I shouldn't have said anything; I knew it wasn't the right time, but I had reading on my brain, and I didn't think about what I was doing, putting you on the spot like that. That was very stupid of me. And I'm sorry about Ammon too. I know you won't believe me, but he was honestly trying to help. He's not—he's not very sensitive sometimes, but his heart is in the right place."

"Jesus God," Jem said, and he was surprised to find himself smiling as he slid the glasses back up Tean's nose. "Are you even real?"

"Yes, but unfortunately, I am not a disguised pornography machine."

A boy who must have been twelve or thirteen was passing by. He froze, and his face turned red, and then he sprinted away.

"You know he's going to be googling pornography machine for the next five years, right?"

Tean sighed. "I know."

They went back to the table, where a mound of nachos waited. Ammon was back on his phone, tapping madly, but when they sat, he looked up.

"Hey, man, I'm really sorry—"

"No big deal," Jem said, dishing himself nachos, refusing to meet Ammon's look. "Don't sweat it."

The girl came back. They ordered—Jem went with a burger, which was almost universally safe—and he plowed through the nachos. Tean ate four chips, but he scraped away the cheese and meat and beans first.

"Is it Mardi Gras?" Jem asked.

"What?"

"Give me that," he grumbled, piling the discarded deliciousness onto his own plate.

Then the rest of their food came, and Jem was pleased to find that the burger was above average. After his first bite, he said, "Are we going to talk about Tanner or not?"

Ammon finished another of the seemingly endless string of texts and put away his phone. He had some sort of salad, and he forked lettuce and chicken as he said, "Well, as I told you, right now the assumption they're working on is that this is Tanner Kimball."

"It's not."

"I understand that's what you think. But you have to look at it from their perspective: a state ID was found with the remains, and a car registered to him was at the scene, and he's close enough in height, weight, and coloring that it could be him. That goes a fair distance. The remains were severely damaged—"

"We know," Jem said through a mouthful of burger. "We found them."

"—which makes visual identification impossible. The damage to the face in particular was extensive, so a dental record match seems unlikely at this point. They may be able to get usable fingerprints from the remains, but that's not going to be a straightforward process either—they'll have to try to remove the skin, which was damaged as well. Obviously the best bet would be DNA; they've sealed Blake and Tanner's rooms at the lodge and collected their belongings, so they should be able to find a sample for comparison, but the reality is that that kind of test won't be completed for months, and then only if we beg, plead, and kick down doors. So that's the long way of telling you that they're using the limited information they have and proceeding on an assumption."

"They're wrong: it's not Tanner."

"How do you know?"

"I know."

Ammon moved lettuce around with his fork and threw a sidelong look at Tean.

"If Jem says it's not Tanner," Tean said, "I believe him. Do you think it's Blake's body?"

"Maybe," Jem said. "Blake and Tanner were similar enough. They were both white, and they had the same kind of coloring—dark hair, dark eyes."

"Apparently establishing identity with evidence doesn't matter," Ammon said. "You've got an expert who's already made up his mind."

"I'm not saying it was Blake." Jem ran his hand over the table. "It could be someone else; I really don't know."

"But you know the dead man isn't Tanner," Ammon said.

"It's not. It's not him."

"Ok," Tean said. "Let's all take a breath."

Ammon's expression was sour, and his eyes slid away.

"Doesn't it seem strange to you," Jem said, "that the damage to the body was so extensive? Doesn't it seem convenient that you can't identify the remains visually?"

"He was trampled by a herd of wild horses," Ammon said, gesturing to Tean as though asking for backup. "It's not like they were wearing ballet slippers when they went over him."

"Why was he out there? Why drive his car out near a herd of wild horses, park by a slot canyon, go in on foot, and then randomly get run down and trampled to death?"

A strange look crossed Tean's face, but before Jem could ask what it meant, Ammon was talking again.

"Well, I don't think his plan was to get trampled to death," Ammon said. "And I don't know why he was out there. It's not what most people would do, but I don't think it's that unusual either. The BLM has problems every year with people going off designated roads—"

"In a Camaro?"

"—and getting too close to the herds. And I want to remind you that I'm on your side: I think the whole thing is fishy. But I've learned the hard way that sometimes things are weird just because they're weird. We need more information before we can make a decision here."

"Hold on," Tean said. "You think he's right?"

"I think it's a possibility," Ammon said grudgingly. "The two men do look alike. A car registered to Blake Bigney was still in the lodge's parking lot; they've towed it, and the techs will go over it."

Eyebrows shooting up, Jem said, "He didn't take Blake's car?"

"No." Then, after some sort of internal struggling faintly visible on his face, Ammon added, "And there have been no reported stolen vehicles. No missing people either, for that matter."

"He's still in the area."

"We don't know that."

"Holy shit," Jem breathed, "Tanner's still here."

"What information do we have?" Tean asked.

"Hardly anything. The deputy medical examiner isn't willing to shoulder this one, so all he would say is that the most likely cause of death probably, going out on a limb without a full and properly executed autopsy, might have been, could be blunt force trauma to the head."

"Gee," Jem said. "And he got a college degree and everything."

"Elvira is an excellent forensic pathologist," Tean said, frowning, "but I'm not sure even she'll be able to tell exactly what killed this man. If she can, it'll take time, maybe a lot. The reality is that, for the moment, we have to leave at least three possibilities open: homicide, suicide, and accident."

"He accidentally put his head under a herd of horses," Jem said. When Ammon opened his mouth, Jem added, "That was a joke."

"He could have decided to conduct his own personal tour of Onion Creek and the herd," Ammon said. "Some white trash idiot is out there shooting a gun, and it startles the herd and forces them into a stampede. He gets trampled."

"I said it was a joke."

"Even in that scenario," Tean said, "we're looking for someone sadistic. One of the horses was killed; I'm sure several others were wounded. It takes a certain kind of person to shoot at a wild animal like that, especially when we're not talking about hunting. Have they recovered the bullets from the dead horse?"

Ammon's hand stopped, the Coke halfway to his mouth, and he said, "I'll check on that."

"Suicide seems unlikely for the same reason. It's entirely possible that someone jumped from the canyon's rim, intending to kill himself. Under other conditions, a stampede up the slot canyon could have just been bad luck, although it's an unnatural direction for panicked horses to go. But the gunshot wounds to the horses make the coincidence much less likely."

"But not impossible," Ammon said.

Tean looked like he wanted to argue, but then he shrugged. "Not impossible. As you said, it could have been someone who was shooting the horses for fun, spooked them, and intentionally or not drove them toward the slot. Did they estimate time of death?"

"You should have seen the deputy ME try to hotfoot it on that one. His best guess under these unusual circumstances, blah blah blah, is that he'd been dead for more than twenty-four hours. He suggested Wednesday or Thursday, so, again, first-class forensics."

"At this rate, they should be hiring out-of-work veterinarians," Jem said. "Tean could do a better job than whoever this jerkoff is."

"No," Tean said, "I couldn't. I'm a vet, not a pathologist."

"Frankly," Ammon said, "they'd do better hiring you, Jem. You're a better investigator than anybody in the sheriff's department, from what I can tell."

Jem had no idea how to respond to that. He settled for: "We haven't talked about the thing that makes this not an accident or a suicide. That dead guy has Tanner's car and Tanner's ID. Antonio claimed Tanner killed his girlfriend on Thursday and sent us down here to look for him. He told us Tanner was wrapped up in something with drugs. Then we get down here, and it looks like Tanner has met a tragic end, although we conveniently can't identify the body. There's no way that's a coincidence."

"Except it could be," Ammon said. "I'm sorry, but it could. There's a lot of weird ways to die in this part of the world, and people keep finding new ones. Tean, tell him."

"That's true," Tean said slowly, his eyes darting to Jem and then back to Ammon. "But I think the point here is that we don't lose anything by treating it as a murder and, possibly, as a way for Tanner to fake his own death in order to avoid prosecution for Andi's death. Jem doesn't think that was Tanner in the canyon; that's good enough for me. If we decide to wait on cause of death, positive ID, all of that, we're going to lose weeks. Maybe months."

"Not necessarily. Once the jurisdictional pissing contest is over, law enforcement will get to work. You'd be surprised how many times there's a witness, or someone heard something, or an obvious answer works itself out when the investigation really gets going."

"Yep," Jem said. "I'd be extremely surprised."

"Look, this was fine, talking this out," Ammon said. "And I appreciate your input. You're both smart, and you've made good points that need to be considered. I'm going to take those points and communicate them to the police chief and the sheriff. But I'm not even in the running for who's going to carry this case. The best thing you two can do is step back and let the professionals handle it."

"Do you think the sheriff can handle a case like this?" Tean asked. "Because of his age, I mean."

"Do not try to change the subject."

"I'm just asking—"

"I know what you're asking. I've known you since you were a scrawny kid without any hair under his arms, and I know what you're doing."

To Jem's surprise, Tean smiled. "Ok, fair. I heard what you said about staying out of this."

"And?"

"And I'm acknowledging it. I appreciate your concern. It means a lot to me."

"Not good enough."

Tean nodded. He scraped the tines of the fork across his plate, set the fork down, and asked, "Are you going to answer my question?"

Ammon stood, pushing back his chair so that the legs squeaked across the polished pine boards. He took out his wallet and began counting out bills.

"Ammon," Tean said.

"For fuck's sake, Teancum. What I went through today, that doesn't mean anything to you?"

"I'm sorry that—"

"Don't talk. I can't fucking listen to you right now."

He threw the money on the table and left.

"He's such a—"

"Don't!" The word was savagely sharp. Tean covered his face with his hands and repeated more softly, "Don't."

They finished the meal in silence. Well, Jem finished both their meals in silence. Tean sat with his head in his hands. After the girl had cleared the table, Jem paid with cash. Touching Tean's arm, he said, "You can either sit here and feel awful, or you can come back to the room and feel awful while Scipio licks your ear."

"What did you find in their rooms today?"

"I didn't—" The look on Tean's face made him stop. "Nothing, unfortunately. The police were still there, dusting for prints, looking incredibly proud of themselves. How did you know?"

"Because you're you."

"I'm not sure if that's a good thing or a bad thing."

"It's a bad thing. Ninety percent bad, ten percent McDonald's. Eighty-five percent bad, ten percent McDonald's, five percent sweet. Seven percent sweet. Seven-point-five." Tean scowled. "I need a piece of paper. There's something in there about Vanilla Ice too, but I think that requires differential calculus to figure out."

"Tean," Jem said, words slipping out from under him like he was trying to cross an ice floe. "I can do this by myself. You know, if it's too much with Ammon and—"

"God damn it."

"Swear jar," Jem whispered.

"Of course you can't do it by yourself." Tean pushed back from the table. He headed past Jem and out of the restaurant.

"Where are you going?"

"To feel awful and have a dog lick my ear!"

The hostess near the front was staring at Tean, her eyes wide.

"It's not a sex thing," Jem told her. "Um, I don't think, anyway."

Up ahead, Tean muttered, "Oh my gosh," and walked faster.

14

A couple of hours later, Tean's original plan of self-pity and Scipio's commiseration hadn't panned out. Scipio had been much more interested in climbing all over Jem, and Tean had only managed a few minutes of outrage before he fell asleep.

When he woke, the sun had shifted, and Jem was awake again too—if he'd slept at all. The blond man's eyes were glued to the TV, which was playing some sort of cartoon with giant robots. Tean made his way to the bathroom, washed up, and then returned to the bed. Scipio immediately crawled onto his lap, crushing his thighs. In less than thirty seconds, the Lab's whole body was shaking with the force of his snores. The smell of sun-hot dog and commercial bath soap filled the small room.

"How do you find a murderer?" Tean asked.

"We found Benny's murderer by looking for people who had a reason to want him dead." Something happened on TV, and Jem scooted to the edge of the mattress. An explosion. Jem flinched, turning slightly as though to shield himself. This was how he watched TV, and Tean never got tired of observing. It was field research. A single-subject study of a man who had never been allowed to be a boy. Over his shoulder, Jem added, "And by trying to figure out where he'd been in the days before he got killed."

"And we found Joy's killer by doing the same thing. So how do we find Tanner?"

Jem flinched and twisted again.

"Jem?"

"Huh?" He leaned sideways a few inches, his attention still riveted to the screen. "Um." He jumped slightly. "Same way."

"How much longer in your show?"

Jem didn't answer.

Sighing, Tean pulled out his phone and did some light informational reading. He lost track of time and came back to the sound of his name.

"Earth to Tean, hello?"

"Sorry." When Tean glanced up, the TV was off, and Jem was smiling. "How long have you been trying to get my attention?"

"I only said your name a couple of times. What were you reading?"

"It's stupid," Tean said, dropping the phone. "Let's talk about—"

"I love stupid. What were you reading?"

"It's so dumb. Please let's drop it."

"I just watched a show about giant robots that turn into an even bigger robot. Please don't make me feel like I'm on my own here."

"Why would they turn into a bigger robot? Why wouldn't they just start as the big robot? Why do they need to turn into anything?"

"Nope," Jem said, sitting cross-legged on the bed. "You're not getting out of it that easily."

Tean hesitated. Then he said, "If you have to know—"

"I do."

"—and if you're going to insist—"

"I am."

"—and if you're fine with ignoring all my attempts to avoid talking about this—"

"Totally, perfectly fine with it."

"—then I was reading the Darwin Awards."

"That sounds very science-y."

"It's not, actually. It's, um, kind of a guilty pleasure."

"Is it science porn?"

"No."

"Is it any kind of porn?"

"No."

"Is it about any size robot turning into another size robot?"

"Not even close."

"Then you're really going to have to help me out here."

"It's about, well, people who die in awful ways that are tied to being stupid. The name comes from Darwin's idea of natural selection, with less well adapted individuals and species being passed over, in terms of their evolutionary success, in favor of better adapted ones."

Jem blinked. "What?"

"And I know it's elitist, and it makes fun of people who might have been very smart but made one very bad choice, and it celebrates a power dynamic that we should be trying to eliminate from our society, but . . ."

Arms loose around his knees, Jem looked like he could wait all day.

"But sometimes it's just really interesting. And bizarre. And funny. And I know it's weird, and everybody hates when I talk about this kind of stuff, and that's all I'm going to say about it."

"One example."

"It's too weird."

"Quit saying that. Give me one example. Your favorite one."

"I don't have a favorite."

"Oh my God, you are being really difficult right now. Do you understand that?"

"Fine. If I had to pick one that I find gross and incredible and funny—"

"Which you do."

"—then I would say this one from the 19th century. His name was Gouverneur Morris, and he was a pretty important person at the time. He's one of the Founding Fathers, actually—he signed the Articles of Confederation and the Constitution. He died in 1816 from an infection." In a rush, Tean finished, "From using a whalebone to try to clear a blockage from his urethra."

Jem's eyes widened. "It is porn."

"It's not porn!"

"It is. It's sounding porn. Historical sounding porn. And it's megadark."

"Ok, can we please talk about—"

"I love it."

"What?"

"I love it. You find the coolest shit. And you know all these amazing, unbelievable facts. About everything, pretty much. And you're the smartest human alive, even if you're not smart enough yet to understand why big robots turning into a giant robot is actually incredibly fucking awesome. Why are you embarrassed about any of that? Except the robot part, I mean. You should be embarrassed about that."

"People don't like hearing about that stuff."

"Trust me: some people like it. I'm at the top of that list."

"Ok. Well, let's talk about—"

"Who?"

"What?"

"Who doesn't like it? You don't get self-conscious like this normally. When we were in line at that ice cream place a couple of weeks ago, you spent the entire wait explaining to that little girl why her cat couldn't enjoy ice cream."

"She was interested!"

"Sweet Jesus, is this about Ammon? Is this because he told you to cut it out at lunch?"

"No."

Jem raised two blond eyebrows.

"Ok." The word exploded out. "My parents hate it. My siblings hate it. Hannah pretends it's not happening, and when she can't, she hates it. And yeah, it . . . it sucks when Ammon says stuff like that because I am weird, and I know I'm weird, but it's nice when I can forget about it for a little while."

Leaning back, Jem propped himself on one elbow, his face unreadable. Then he said, "Ammon wouldn't know cool or fun or interesting or smart or awesome or a good time, not even if someone was sounding the fuck out of him with a whalebone."

Tean burst out laughing. He laughed so hard that he woke Scipio, who snorted, raised his head, looked around, and fixed Tean with a look of infinite disappointment. That just made Tean laugh harder. He laughed until tears ran down his face. And when he'd finally recovered, he was lying on his side, looking at Jem stretched out on the other bed, at the indecipherable smile on the blond man's face.

The list formed without Tean even trying: Jem knew how to cut a deck of cards like a magician; Jem knew how to cook a surprisingly good spaghetti and meatballs; Jem knew how to fix Tean's hair so it looked like a real human haircut; Jem knew how to talk to anyone—old men about cars or horses or fishing, old women about their flowerbeds or church or, in one memorable case, about bull riding, kids about toys and cartoons, teenagers about clothes and shoes and

Instagram; he knew how close to sit next to Tean without making him uncomfortable; he knew when to be quiet and when Tean wanted to talk, even if Tean didn't know what to say; he knew how to make Tean laugh.

And then Tean thought of Ammon: *You need to be honest with yourself about what you want.*

"What's going on under all that scarecrow hair?"

"I'm just thinking about how great you are."

"Well, yeah. And you're great too. That's why we're best friends."

"Normal friends," Tean said, and he had to focus to keep his fingers extended, to keep himself from clutching Scipio's fur as he ran his hand down the Lab's flank. "Regular, ordinary, everyday friends."

"With soulmate-level intimacy and dedication."

"No. The same level of intimacy I have with the people who shrink-wrap my bulk underwear orders."

"God, you make it sound so sexy."

"Which happens to be the exact same level of intimacy that I have with that woman who drives the street sweeper past my building on the last Friday of every month."

"Stop, stop." Jem flopped onto his back, plucking at his shirt, fanning himself. "You're getting me all hot and bothered."

"Which is perfectly equivalent to the level of intimacy I experienced with that raccoon that got stuck in the dumpster last week."

"Hold on, hold on. The one that was wearing the onesie when we finally got him out?"

"He wasn't wearing a onesie. It was wrapped around him."

"That bastard! He told me I was the only man for him! I'm going to kill that cheating son of a bitch."

This, Tean thought, smiling into the pillow. This was what some lucky guy, some other lucky guy, was going to get to do for the rest of his life. When he looked over again, Jem was on his back, arms behind his head, staring up at the ceiling.

"Do you want to tell me now?" Tean asked quietly. "Whatever it is that's going on with you?"

"He was a C-. Used his claws too much. And don't get me started on his technique giving head."

"Jem."

In profile, Jem's face revealed the tension in his jaw more clearly.

"Ok," Tean said. "You don't have to. But I just want to help."

"Don't worry about it." Jem's jaw cracked when he opened his mouth again. "I can handle this. I've got it completely under control."

Except we're here, Tean wanted to say. Except you're not sleeping. Except there's something in your eyes, and I don't know how to help you stop hurting.

"Jem, there's nothing wrong with needing help—"

"I just want to find Andi's killer," he said, swinging his feet off the bed. He headed into the bathroom. "And then I never want to think about these people again."

15

Jem peed, washed his hands, and dried them on a towel. Then he stood there, listening. The only sound was Scipio snoring. Then voices up the hall, little kids, one of them screaming, "It's not fair, it's not fair, give it back." Jem hung the towel on its ring and let himself out of the bathroom.

"Back to your original question," he said as he lowered himself to sit next to the overnight bag he'd packed. "How do we find Tanner?"

"How would you find him?" Tean asked; the Lab still had him pinned to the bed.

Digging through the clothes and tools he'd brought—what little he'd been able to assemble on the spur of the moment—Jem said, "Well, most of my normal options are out."

"Because he might be dead?"

"He's not dead. No, because of this weird situation. Normally, I'd start with his last known location."

"Here, I guess. The lodge."

"Right. And I'd ask around, figure out who had interacted with him. Maybe he's got a buddy who picks up night shifts here. Maybe there's a girl he always buys drinks. That's out because the police are doing the exact same thing. They're going to be all over this place for a day or two, which also puts a hitch in the next thing I'd normally do."

Tean sighed and ran fingers through the Lab's fur. "Dig through the trash."

"More or less." Jem pulled out a wide leather belt with a buckle the size of his fist. He set it on the floor next to the bed, and the buckle thunked against the boards. "Although you don't have to say it like I'm the human equivalent of your sex raccoon."

"You've already tried to get into their rooms, and I think you're right that the police will have taken anything, including the trash, that seems relevant. I guess we can hope they slip up and overlook something, but it seems like a bad idea to hope for incompetent law enforcement."

"I don't think you'll have to hope very hard. When I walked past the rooms earlier, one of them was covered in fingerprint powder. We might as well have Barney Fife up there. Thank God Ammon is on the case; I'm sure he'll get the whole thing sorted out."

"I'm going to let that slide because you haven't had McDonald's in almost a day, and you're probably in withdrawal."

Jem tried to hide his smile as he continued to search the bag. "Anyway, if the trash was a bust, I might try breaking into his house or office. Credit card statements, phone records, bills, anything from his bank. I'd talk to the neighbors if I thought it was safe, although that's hard to pull without them warning off the guy. But that's all a bust; we don't even know where he lived."

"You could ask Tinajas."

"That's actually a really good idea. Why didn't I think of that?"

"Withdrawal. Jesus Christ!" Tean leaned forward to rub the spot on his calf where Jem had slapped him with the belt, and Scipio snuffled and scrambled off his lap. "That stung."

"Swear jar," Jem said with what he considered his angelic smile.

"Defend your master," Tean said, nudging Scipio. "Bite. Attack. Maim. Kill."

Scipio rolled onto his back, and with a sigh, Tean scratched his belly.

When Jem placed the call, Tinajas answered on the third ring: "Fuck off."

"Good morning to you too."

"It's not morning. It's late afternoon, you debauched cuntmonger. Now leave me alone so I can enjoy this fucking drip of a four-year-old's birthday party." Her voice changed as she spoke to someone nearby. "No, Martha, I will not watch my language. Go fuck yourself on a railroad spike." To Jem again, "Hold on, we're singing happy birthday."

Jem held the phone away from his ear and told Tean, "They're singing happy birthday." A chorus of voices was barely audible from the phone's speakers.

"She's at a four-year-old's party?"

"Well, she might now technically be five. It wasn't clear if that was her age before she blew out the candles or after."

Tean blinked several times. "You realize that it's not actually blowing out the candles that makes you a year older, right?"

But Tinajas was talking again, so Jem said, "I'll explain the science behind it later," and held the phone to his ear.

"It's not a question of science," Tean muttered.

"—so I'm going to hang up now," Tinajas finished.

"No, wait, I need help."

"I know. If you'd been listening, you would have heard the first part of that sentence where I said, 'I don't care if you need help, I'm spending time with my family, so I'm going to hang up now.' Now I've said it twice, and I'm wasting time talking to you in the foyer. If you made me miss the chocolate cake, I'm going to borrow Martha's railroad spike and shove it so far up you that your vet will be able to pull it out of your throat."

"He actually probably could do that. He's very good."

"Goodbye, Jem."

"No, no, no. Tanner Kimball. Can you find his address for me?"

"Hold on. Guillo, I swear to Jesus Christ himself that if you don't get back into the kitchen with that plate, I will whip your ass so you can't sit for a week. I've got to go; this place is a madhouse. I think I saw Dionica letting the dog eat cake out of her mouth."

"What about Tanner?"

"I can't get it for you until Monday. I'm not going to work just to get you an address."

"Tin, please, I really need it!"

"Dionica, you're mashing frosting into his fur!"

The call disconnected.

"Well, so much for that," Jem said. When he glanced up, he was surprised to see Tean on the phone.

"No, Amos, I didn't promise to meet you at the hotel. I didn't say anything like that. I said I would think about it. Well, I don't care what Seth told you. I'm telling you right now that I never promised to go on this trip. I'll pay for the room. That's not the point, Amos; I said I'd pay you back." He listened, knees pulled to his chest, free hand pushing back his wild, bushy hair. "That's not fair. You can't say this trip was all about me when you're only there because Bailey got free tickets to—no, don't put Cor on the line. I don't want to talk to anybody. Hi, Cor. I'm going to hang up now. No, I'm not going to have this conversation with you. I do care. I appreciate that. No, I don't want that." His forehead dropped to his knees. "Look, I said now is not a good—ok, ok, I understand, and that means a lot to me, and I love you guys too, but I—"

The doc looked up, surprise on his face when Jem took his hand and worked the phone free of his grip. Jem made a crackling noise that he hoped passed for static, disconnected the call, and powered down the phone.

"That probably crossed a line," Jem said, "and you can borrow a page out of Tinajas's book and whip my ass with this belt if you want."

Tean hid his face against his knees, and his shoulders moved once. Not a sob, but maybe a very tense exhalation. Jem squeezed the back of his neck. A soft hiss in the ducts said the AC had kicked on again.

"You'd probably like it," Tean finally said, lifting his head. His eyes were red but dry.

Jem nodded. "Probably. Want to tell me what that was about?"

So Tean told him. "And, of course, now the whole story is that I promised to go, and they booked me a room, and how could I change plans like this, and the whole weekend is about me and rebuilding our relationship as brothers, and—and it's a bunch of crap. They feel bad because you shamed them in May, and now they think they can bully me into a weekend—which they're also spending with their wives, by the way—and pretend everything's ok."

Jem's hand was still on the back of Tean's neck; it was a minor miracle the doc hadn't shook him off, hadn't squirmed away or found another escape. He scratched lightly at the warm skin. "And if they're telling the truth?"

"I never told them I'm going, and I never asked them to book—"

Tightening his grip, Jem gave a little shake that made the glasses slide to the end of Tean's nose. He caught them with his other hand and pushed them back up, and then he shook Tean again.

"Ok, ok, stop it. You're going to give me the adult-equivalent of shaken-baby syndrome."

"Wouldn't that just be shaken-adult syndrome?"

"I don't want to give them this. They're always—they're always dragging me around like this, always doing things so that they look perfect and I look like the problem. I'm tired of it. And, if I'm being totally honest, I like that they feel bad. I want them to feel bad for a while."

"All right. Fuck 'em. Let them feel terrible."

"Well, I don't want them to feel terrible."

"Nope, that's what we're going with. Awful. Horrible. The human shit-stains on the universe's nice white panties. We want them to feel ten times worse than they ever made you feel."

"They're my family. I don't want—jeez, I honestly don't want them to feel whatever you just described. I'm not even sure I understood what you just described, but I don't want that."

"Of course you don't. You're a good guy, and you're hurt and upset, and you don't like people bullying you into things. Sometimes you don't even like people mildly suggesting you try new things."

"If I wanted to try Mexican fusion, I'd go to a Mexican-fusion restaurant, Jem. I don't need you mucking up my recipes."

"Yes, I learned my lesson. I want to apologize again for my revolutionary idea that we should put cheddar cheese on our nachos and use tortilla chips instead of mushy plantains. Anyway, what I'm trying to say is that even though you don't like how they went about this, they're still your family, and you still care about them, and maybe you should give them a chance."

"Hold on. You hate my family."

"Yes, God. I want to push Hugh or Lou or whatever his name is into one of those machines that make slices of American cheese. A million little plastic-wrapped slices of Hugh. But the point is that they're not my family. They're your family. And you're the one they're trying to make things right with."

"Possibly. Or it's just more of their usual games."

"My recommendation? Leave your phone off until you decide. They seem annoyingly persistent, like someone else I know."

Jem whuffed when the doc's elbow caught him in the gut. The noise drew Scipio's attention, and when Jem fell onto his bed, trying to get his wind back, the Lab bounded onto the mattress next to him.

Apparently Scipio's primary first-aid strategy was licking every inch of Jem's face.

"Stop, stop, stop," Jem said, getting a pillow over his face. "Tean, it's slimy and sticky at the same time. How is that possible?"

"Saliva's actually very interesting. It—"

"No, stop, I'm already dying of boredom. Jesus Christ, that was my shin!"

"Oops," Tean said.

Pulling the pillow away, Jem tried to use it to run interference. Scipio must have thought it was a game because he got a mouthful of pillow and started tugging and growling. The familiar panic started in Jem's chest, and he released the pillow. Scipio stumbled back, caught himself at the edge of the bed, and then carried the pillow forward to nudge Jem with it.

"Scipio, come here," Tean said.

"No, he's fine. I just don't want to play that game." Jem glanced over at Tean. "I think I know what we need to do next."

Tean raised an eyebrow.

"The first question we need to answer is why Tanner wanted to fake his own death. Then we need to know what he was involved in. The drugs, I mean. If we can do that, we can figure out why he's still in the area and what he's going to do next. And if we can figure out what he's going to do next, we can catch the son of a bitch and prove he killed Andi. And that he killed Blake, I guess, or whoever was in that canyon."

"Maybe, Jem. Catching him isn't the same as proving he killed Andi."

"But it's the first step."

After a long moment, Tean nodded.

"If I wanted to find someone, I'd learn everything about them that I could. Where they went, what they did, who they spent time with. From their diet to their sleep schedule to their favorite sex positions. Literally every detail I could find, just in case it helped down the road."

Tean was wearing a curious expression, but he nodded.

"I'm starting to realize that, aside from Decker, I don't know anything about Tanner. I don't know what his home life was like before Decker. I don't know what happened to him after he left. I never tried to find him; I wanted to, but at the same time, I didn't.

Maybe that's where we need to start: figure out who he is, who he really is." He raised his chin. "But I can't do it on my own. It's going to take me too long, and I'll—I'll get frustrated and give up if I try to do it myself."

Tean nodded again. "Let's work on it together. It'll be good—"

Jem groaned.

"—practice."

16

They read on their phones until dinner, taking one break in the early evening to walk Scipio and let him run and play at a local dog park. The swath of thick grass looked impossible against the red-rock walls to the east. At this hour, with the sun falling toward the horizon, the shadows were lengthening, and the light took on the same colors as the rock: orange and red, fire and gold. It haloed the leaves on a line of cottonwoods and turned them into living torches, the leaves translucently green and strung on a web of fire. Where it touched rock and stone, the colors deepened, red becoming a shade of brick, orange like hammered copper, until the sun's angle shifted and shadow swallowed a few more inches. Even the river's muddy-orange waters caught the light, the riffles outlined in slick white needlework. Tean breathed the desert air, clean, sweet with the smell of the Colorado and salt cedar.

Jem stayed outside the fenced area, reading, while Tean kept one eye on Scipio—the Lab was sprinting up and down the length of the park with a Golden Retriever—and read too. Tean had done the initial search for any materials related to Tanner Kimball, and he'd been surprised by the abundance of results. He'd split the reading up as best he could, sending shorter, more manageable articles about Tanner's life after the juvenile correction facility to Jem's phone. Tean saved the longer, more difficult pieces about Tanner's pre-Decker life for himself. After the park, with Scipio half-snoozing in the back seat, they went back to the lodge. They left Scipio with fresh food and water—the Lab was already napping, paws twisting the sheets as he twitched—and grabbed dinner in the restaurant.

They got a table at the back. The room was crowded tonight, young couples, young families, older couples, older families. A lone woman in Merrells and cargo pants, her hair held back in a kerchief, reminded Tean of Hannah. At the table next to Tean and Jem, a red-faced man was trying to tell a story—something about a stretch of the Colorado he had rafted that day. He was bellowing to be heard over his family's fragmented conversation. He wore a blond toupee that he kept having to settle back into place.

"For fuck's sake," Jem muttered, glancing over at the man before turning back to his phone. "Put a bullet between my eyes if I ever tell you I want to track down my dad."

"Are you ok?"

It looked like it took serious effort for Jem to tear his gaze away from the screen. He set the phone down and glanced at Tean before his eyes skated away. "Tanner was a real piece of shit. Is a real piece of shit."

"He is. He really is." Tean hesitated. "What did you learn about his life after Decker?"

"Not much. Hardly anything, really. He's got a LinkedIn page that describes him as an entrepreneur, venture capitalist, and micro-finance ally, whatever the fuck that means. He claims he worked at some of the top tech companies in the valley. He's got a Facebook page and an Instagram that are locked down, but his profile pictures show him climbing mountains and hiking and being a ski bum. You know, in case you couldn't figure out on your own that he's loaded. I think it's mostly horseshit; he's not as good at this as me."

Tean nodded. "Did you know he had assault charges on his record? That's why he ended up in Decker."

"Big surprise," Jem said.

"What does that mean?"

Jem shook his head, the slightest hint of a flush coming up as he scratched his beard. "He's a piece of shit." His gaze cut away again. "That's all. If he's done anything like that since, it hasn't made the papers. The *Daily Herald* had a stub about him passing bad checks, but that was almost ten years ago. Shit. What a waste of time."

"I don't think it was, actually."

"If you say it was good practice, I'm going to hulk out and smash this table."

"Hi!" The young man had an enormous smile, and his waiter's apron was covered in buttons. It took Tean a moment to realize that all the buttons were mementos from state and national parks. "How are you guys doing tonight?"

"Well, you just eavesdropped on me threatening to smash a table," Jem said. "How do you think I'm doing?"

"He's not doing great," Tean said.

For a moment, the young man's expression was frozen in a blank smile. Then he started up again. "You guys down here to do some camping?"

"We're literally staying in a hotel," Jem said. "What do you think?"

"He's grumpy," Tean said. "Don't let him bother you."

The young man laughed. "I bet you guys are going to do some great hiking, right? The hiking is great down here. It's great."

"Did you hear that, Tean? It's great. Everything's great."

Again that blank, frozen expression. Then more smiling. "You guys are in luck tonight because we've got our killer cowboy beans on the fire. We only make them once a week, and we always sell out."

"Did the cowboy beans kill someone?"

"Stop it," Tean whispered.

"Or do they have a killer cowboy in them?"

Tean kicked him under the table.

After another of those mini-reboots, the young man whipped out a pad and a pen and said, "What can I get you to drink? What about a couple of lime rickeys after a long, hot day in the saddle?"

"Do the lime rickeys have gin in them?"

Apparently, that was the funniest joke the young man had ever heard.

"Who is this kid?" Jem said, craning his neck to look around. "Are we on *Candid Camera*?"

"He'll have a Coke."

"A beer."

"And I'll have a water."

"A whiskey."

"I've got a Coke and whiskey, oops, I mean a water. Gee, you jokers have got me all turned around. I'll be right back."

"Shoot me," Jem said as the young man trotted away. "Or put me down humanely like I'm a lame horse."

"Ok, now you really have to tell me what's up. Why are you being mean to that kid? Usually I'm the one who's mean."

"Oh, please. You couldn't be mean to a waiter if your life depended on it. I'm angry because—I don't know. I just hate this. I hate all of it. I hate what he did to Andi, and I hate having to learn about everything else he did."

"Like the assaults," Tean said softly.

"All of it." Jem massaged a spot between his eyes.

"But you got upset when I mentioned the assaults."

"Will you cut it out with that?"

"A Coke and a water. Sorry, fellas, no whiskey today. And I brought you a lime rickey to try, just for funsies."

Still massaging the spot on his forehead, Jem mouthed, *Just for funsies.*

"Stop it," Tean whispered again.

They ordered their food—after all the questions, Jem ended up getting the killer cowboy beans—and then Jem tried to send the young man away with the promise that Tean would be perfectly satisfied with a few flakes of oatmeal dusted with the crumbs from a rice cracker. The red-faced man at the table next to them had really gotten into it, pounding his fist on the table, shouting about his raft, while a bird-like woman kept patting his arm and saying, "Everyone listen to Harold, everyone please listen to Harold."

"So it's another dead end," Jem said, massaging his temples now. "The research, I mean. I guess we'll have to wait until Tinajas can give us something on Monday."

"I'm not sure it's a dead end. And I don't think it was wasted. In fact, I think I learned a lot about Tanner. He comes from a well-off family, apparently a devoted family. Reading carefully, I think they made problems go away several times before he was finally prosecuted."

Jem's hands froze. The question was on his face, but he said nothing.

"Had you heard something like that before?"

After a moment, Jem gave a tiny shake of his head.

"Well, it's obvious that Tanner has some sort of personality disorder, although therapists and psychiatrists won't give an official personality disorder diagnosis until a child reaches the age of eighteen. The behavioral problems come through pretty clearly in the profile pieces that were written around the assaults—the second time he was charged, the *Tribune* and the *Deseret News* both dug deeply into his life, and they cobbled together a pretty detailed account of his childhood highlights: bullying, destruction of property, fighting. There's one story that seems particularly relevant. According to the *Tribune* article, in eighth grade, Tanner tricked a girl into letting him come over when her parents weren't home. She was a good girl, not the kind to have a boy over without her parents knowing. Tanner pretended to be gay, if you can believe that—used her gay best friend as a kind of Trojan horse to get him inside. As soon as Tanner was inside, he assaulted the girl. When the gay best friend objected, Tanner turned on him too. He managed to get on top of the boy, held him down, and tried to cut off his ear with a pair of pinking shears. In eighth grade."

"And he didn't get in trouble? Nothing?"

"It doesn't seem like it."

"It sounds like what happened with Andi. A party, a girl rejects him, he freaks out, someone gets hurt."

"That seems to be a pattern, yes."

Jem grunted.

"There's more than just that one incident. He splashed gasoline on a neighbor's car and lit it on fire, but the accelerant burned out without doing more than cosmetic damage. He—" Tean swallowed. "This one is not pleasant. He stole a nail gun from a construction site. Over the next year, a neighbor who took in strays reported multiple dead animals, their bodies full of nails."

"He likes hurting things. Animals. People." Jem's voice was planed flat, empty of emotion. "He takes his time doing it. If he can fuck with your head while doing it, that's just icing on the cake."

"And it sounds like what happened with Andi, right? The dart syringe. He likes his toys, just like Antonio told us."

"This isn't telling us anything I didn't already know. I knew he was a sadistic prick. I knew he liked hurting people."

"But it's more than that. These are patterns of behavior that confirm Antonio's story, which is important. And they tell us that Tanner got away with this kind of behavior for a lot longer than most people. He never got charged with anything until he was sixteen and had his first assault charge, and he walked away from that one. The girl showed signs of sexual violence, but whoever assaulted her had used a condom, and Tanner ended up producing an alibi: a party with friends. People didn't even talk about this other stuff until the second assault charge, and that's only because the second girl was lucky enough to have one of those nanny cameras that caught the whole thing. That's what he went to Decker for. That's what his family couldn't buy his way out of."

"Ok, so now we know Mommy and Daddy tried to keep him out of trouble, and we know he's exactly the kind of monster I already knew he was. Great. Big revelations."

Tean sat back in his seat. The hub of voices washed over him, a surf of white noise that in a strange way made it easier to concentrate. Opposite, Jem was still hunched over the table, head in his hands. No killer cowboy beans yet. No rice-cracker crumbs.

Tean stood and pulled his chair around the table.

"What are you doing?"

"Sitting on this side of the table."

"Well, don't."

"Why not?"

"Because it's annoying."

"Maybe I want to share your killer cowboy beans when they come."

"No. You can't. You'll get all farty and gross."

"Did you know that plant lectins in undercooked beans can actually cause food poisoning? In theory, if you're already in a compromised state, they could kill you."

"Another thing to look forward to."

"Jem."

Jem groaned. "Now what?"

"We don't have to do this if it's too hard."

"What does that mean?"

"It means I can't do this on my own. It was your idea to try to learn about Tanner. That's what we've been doing. Now you've completely shut down, and I'm trying my best here, but I don't know how to see what you would see."

"What, Tean? What is there to see? He's a monster. I knew that one; check it off the list. He gets away with it. I knew that one too; double check. And he's got this perfect, amazing life now. Wow, things worked out for Tanner again. What a fucking shock."

"I don't understand. We're here because you wanted to do this; if you changed your mind, then let's go home. If this is too much for you, which I think—"

"I don't want to hear what you think. Just shut up for a while."

The waiter came back with their food. He had a strip of masking tape on the apron now, with Randy written in black marker. "You guys," he said, laughing as he set down their food. "I didn't even tell you my name was Randy. I can't believe how wack I am today."

Tean tossed his salad with a fork, distributing the vegetables, picking out the fried chicken tenders and setting them on a plate, ignoring the orange dressing that had come on the side. He ate a few of the cherry tomatoes, which were surprisingly good. The lettuce was crisp and cool.

"Oh my God," Jem said through gritted teeth. "I'm sorry, ok, but please don't punish me like this."

"Like what?"

"Put the goddamn dressing on the salad."

"What?"

"I'm sorry. I'm really, really sorry. But please don't make me watch you pick out all the good fried chicken, completely ignore the spicy southwest dressing, and rabbit-munch your lettuce. Please. I made a mistake, but I'm a good person at heart, and this is cruel and unusual."

Tean set down his fork.

Jem offered an uncertain smile. "I'm sorry?"

With a shrug, Tean pushed the chicken tenders toward Jem. Jem broke off a piece and dipped it in the dressing. Tean went back to his salad.

"Tean, please, I'm—"

"It's fine. Let's forget it; I don't want to talk about it."

He forked another cherry tomato.

"No," Jem said. "I will not stand by and witness this travesty of a meal."

"Will you please—"

Jem took the fork from Tean's hand, grabbed the knife from where it rested on the table, and cut up the chicken tenders. After placing them back in the bowl, he picked up the dressing.

"I don't like—"

"Teancum Leon, if I don't know what you like and do not like after months of watching you abuse food, I never will. I know you think you don't like dressing. But really you don't like a lot of dressing. And I'm adding the perfect amount, and you're going to like it, and then maybe you won't hate me." He tossed the salad, forked lettuce, tomato, chicken, and crispy tortilla strips, and passed the fork to Tean. "Now I won't feel like I stood idly by during the salad equivalent of an airplane crash."

Tean accepted the fork and put the food in his mouth.

Jem raised an eyebrow.

"It's good."

Jem shrugged.

"And I don't hate you."

Jem tried another of those hesitant smiles.

"But can you please tell me what's going on with you?"

Jem clutched the table so hard that his knuckles popped out against his skin, blanching from the pressure. Then he relaxed and said, "I think you'll like the cowboy beans too."

"Ok," Tean said with a sigh. "When you're ready."

They ate in quiet for a while. The family at the table next to them left in a herd, with Harold still trumpeting something about his rafting experience—something to do with an air pump. The silence was comfortable enough, or it would have been if Tean hadn't worried about what it was hiding.

Skittish animals, Tean thought. Wild things. A foal caught in a juniper tree. You couldn't move too fast, and you couldn't always come straight on. Slow, from the side. A tiny smile crossed his face. Too hard, too direct, and you could end up like poor Gouverneur Morris, trying to solve things with a whalebone.

"You know what I really want to understand?" Tean said casually. "Why were Blake and Tanner staying here? At the lodge, I mean. I'll be curious to know what Ammon thinks."

"What Ammon thinks?"

"Yeah, I think he could really provide some insight."

"You've got to be fucking kidding me."

"He's a cop. He knows stuff like that."

"Give me a break." He glanced around as though seeing the lodge for the first time. "This isn't exactly the kind of place drug dealers would stay. Too many families. Too much traffic. Too many good citizens."

"Maybe they just really liked the lodge."

"Maybe." Jem hemmed. "I'm not sure that's the right question, though. The right question is where were they partying while they were here? Those guys didn't come down here to play tiddlywinks with Brother and Sister Johnson from Beaver, Utah." Jem's gaze came up, his eyes clear and fixed on Tean. "Oh, before I forget: I called Ragnar on your phone and left a message saying you were desperately in love with him and needed his magic dick to make you feel better."

"You did what?"

With an explosive grin, Jem shook his head. "Nah. I just wanted to test your outraged voice."

"I hate you."

"Yeah, that's good. Like that."

"No, I really hate you. Scipio and I are going to sleep in the truck tonight. No, scratch that. You're sleeping in the truck tonight."

"Let's go back to the room. We're going to find where Blake and Tanner have been spending their free time. You're going to need your outraged voice."

17

In their hotel room, Jem sat on his bed and dealt out the credit cards in two rows. Six cards: four Visas, two Mastercards. Joseph Mendez, Joseph Mendez, Chandler Nash-Moore, Destiny Briones, Wendy Cowling, Wendy Cowling. Scipio came over, nosed at Chandler Nash-Moore, and nudged the Visa off the bed.

Scooping up the card, Tean said, "I don't think the credit card companies will issue a statement unless we can provide an address, a date of birth, some sort of identifying information."

"Probably not." Jem hesitated, and then he slid one of the Wendy Cowling cards forward. Then he slid it back. "I need you to help me with this part. Which of these cards are premium?"

"What do you mean? They're credit cards."

"Right, but even credit cards have tiers. I've never had one, well, not one of my own, so I haven't bothered to dig into it too deeply, but you can sometimes tell by the materials. This black one is thicker, see?" He touched one of Wendy Cowling's again. "And someone clearly took more time to design it." He looked up. "What?"

Tean shook his head. "I know I promised not to try to push you into things, not to try to fix your life, because it doesn't need fixing. But can I give a brief plea that you will reconsider college? I know you don't believe how smart you are, but Jem, please."

"I noticed a few tiny details. And no talking about college until I can read *Dick and Jane Go to a Sex Dungeon* all on my own. Research, please."

After a few minutes of tapping, Tean said, "The one you pointed to, the black one. And the shiny blue Visa. No, behind that one. They're the premier cards."

Jem moved them to the top. The Visa had been issued to Chandler Nash-Moore, and the Mastercard to Wendy Cowling. He glanced around. "Did you see a local directory? Something like that?"

Tean grabbed a faux-vinyl portfolio from the desk and passed it over.

"Watch and learn," Jem said with one of those rare, genuine smiles that fully revealed his crooked front teeth. He dialed a number, held the phone to his ear, and said, "Yes, hello, I need to speak to someone who can help me with a fraudulent credit card charge. Yes. That's fine, thank you." To Tean, he mouthed, *Manager*. "Yes, Chandler Nash-Moore. Can you look up transactions by card number? Let me give you mine." He read off the number. "I'll hold." To Tean, he mouthed, *I'm holding*.

"Yes, I got that part."

Jem flipped him the bird. "Yes, thank you Ms. Fluitt. You're sure? Perfect. Thank you so much." He disconnected the call. "One restaurant down. One hundred million to go."

"Wait, that actually worked?"

"Of course. Nobody's suspicious when you want to give them your credit card number. Let's split these up."

"This isn't really my thing."

"Too bad." Jem flashed another smile. "It'll be good practice. We'll make a morally bankrupt homosexual out of you yet."

"That's not—"

"With a feather boa. And high heels. If they kick up dust about this, you can tell them that the card was lost and you're trying to collect receipts to prove to the bank the times and dates of the charges you claim were fraudulent. Oh, and use *67 to make sure your number is blocked, so they can't see who called."

"Wouldn't the bank already have that transaction information? And wouldn't the bank's fraud department handle this?"

"Of course. But that's the thing about bureaucracy: they make you do crazy-ass things that nobody understands, so nobody will question you."

They split up the list, working through the restaurants. Tean surprised himself by having a good time doing it, and the rush of success when he finally got a hit—a roadhouse up US-128—made him grin and squeeze Scipio in a hug that made the Lab squirm free and lick Tean's hair.

"Good fucking job," Jem said, slapping his knee. "Now write down the info and keep working."

The real pleasure, though, was watching Jem. He wasn't just good. He was unbelievably good. He changed voices without seeming to think about it. He made jokes. He laughed. He flirted. He said weird, unreal things that somehow people seemed to swallow: "This is a neo-capitalist bank, sir, and if you'll remember the Reagan doctrine, you'll understand a proto-receipt reprint policy." And then, with one of those real grins to Tean, mouthing, *What the fuck am I saying?*

Tean just shook his head and placed the next call.

After a while, it wasn't as fun, but it remained surprisingly easy. They finished bars and restaurants and moved on to hotels, starting with the priciest ones in the area. Tean was talking to an uppity young man at a place called Tafone when things got strange.

"I'm so sorry, Mr. Chandler-Nash. I cannot believe something like this happened. Please hold for a moment."

On the other bed, Scipio was licking a combination of Jem's ear and the cell phone, and Jem was trying not to giggle as he said, "No, no, that's just my pet peacock, Balthasar. Balthasar, present colors!"

Tean waved frantically, and when Jem, still giggling, disconnected, Tean placed his call on speakerphone.

When someone came back on the line, it was a different voice, deeper, older, more self-assured. In one of Jem's movies, Tean thought, he would have been the snooty maître d' whom the wild and crazy kids outsmarted.

"Mr. Chandler-Nash, this is Adrian. I'm deeply, deeply sorry to hear about the possibility of fraudulent charges. First, I'll admit that we've been worried after you stopped coming in. Are you all right?"

"Well," Jem whispered, "are you?"

"Yes," Tean said. "I'm fine. An emergency. I had to leave town."

Jem pointed at Scipio, who was washing the undercarriage. "Tell him about Balthasar," Jem whispered.

Tean waved furiously for silence.

"I can assure you that we haven't placed any charges since the initial hold, Mr. Chandler-Nash."

Jem was making a rolling motion, and Tean had no idea what that meant, so he asked, "Not even incidentals?"

"No, sir. Absolutely not. Any incidentals will be charged to the villa," a note of doubt crept into Adrian's voice, "the same way you charged your drinks and meals to the villa."

Jem drew his hand across his throat in a *cut-it-off* gesture, and Tean said, "I'm sorry, of course. I've been swamped with paperwork trying to get this resolved. Thank you so much for your help."

"Sir, if the card has been compromised, would you like to provide us with a new one so that we can—"

Jem reached across and disconnected the call.

"Holy cow," Tean said.

"Holy shit," Jem said. "Try it with me: holy shit."

"Why were they renting a villa at Tafone but staying here?"

"My guess," Jem said as he hopped off the bed, "is that they're putting up their party friends there. Someone they want to impress. Or keep happy."

"Whoever Tanner's working on with this drug thing?"

"Maybe. I think that's a good possibility. Let's find out."

They used the lodge's Wi-Fi to preload the directions out of Moab and south on US-191 to The Tafone, which from its website appeared to be a boutique hotel with satellite villas available for rent, everything a whitish-brown stucco with oxidized-green metalwork and brightly colored azulejos. After giving Scipio another run at the dog park, they headed to the Ford.

They drove west first until they hit Moab, then south along the town's main thoroughfare. It was evening, the sun balanced on rimrock, the day's heat already fading. The tourists were out in force, crowding the city's narrow sidewalks, jamming the streets, laughing and drinking and eating on shaded patios. One woman was carrying a giant insulated mug that said MAMMY'S DESERT SUNSET; her t-shirt was covered with an oversized icon of a battery, only instead of the usual bars that showed the level of energy, it showed a half of a margarita glass. DANGER DANGER LOW-BOOZE BITCH MODE ACTIVATED.

"Good Lord," Tean muttered.

"Please, please, please buy me that shirt for my birthday."

"You just had your birthday."

"Tean, please. I am not joking with you right now."

And then they were past Moab, past the tourists, past the spilled drinks and the vomit and the middle-aged men who insisted on wearing body-shaping swim shirts. On their left, civilization trickled away from the city: a tin barn with a bullseye painted on the corrugated roof; frame houses behind windbreaks of singleleaf pinyon and yellowpine, bulldozers and dump trucks butting up to an excavation that marked where more homes were being put in. A strand of power lines ran south like a garrote.

On their right, though, red-rock mesas glowed in the evening light. Juniper and pinyon pine, of course, because this was their country, the leaves dusty and brown, the branches gnarled. But also prickly pear, dagger-bladed yucca, fishhook cacti, blackbrush. Russian thistle, looking meaner than hell. The slender cane stems of ocotillo, the flowers long gone. Even determined little tufts of matchweed along the shoulder of the freeway. Already as the desert cooled, life was emerging to prowl the narrow band of hours when the temperature was tolerable. A jackrabbit huddled behind a straggly clump of sand sage. Something moved higher up the mesa, disturbing a clump of Spanish bayonet on one of the narrow ledges. Some sort of rodent, Tean guessed. A rattlesnake's dinner.

The Tafone looked a little harder used in person than it had in the pictures. In places, the white-brown stucco had crumbled away, exposing the metal laths underneath. The oxidized green of the metalwork showed trails and drips of reddish-brown rust. A blacktop road led southwest away from the main building, which served as the hotel proper, toward several free-standing villas. More stucco. More red-tile roofs.

Five villas, to be exact, arranged in a half-circle, with the Tafone's main building just far enough to offer the illusion of privacy. Tean and Jem parked the Ford, got out, and walked. Three of the villas were empty; the red-orange dust on the patio furniture and the silent fountains made it clear that the hotel wasn't wasting extra resources keeping empty units in sparkling condition.

That left two villas: the one on the north end of the half-circle, and the one on the south. Tean and Jem went north first. Some sort of Mercedes SUV was parked alongside an Audi in the circular drive. Lights showed in the windows. When Jem stepped off the drive, heading for the side of the house, Tean whispered, "Watch out for rattlesnakes."

"What?"

"Rattlesnakes. Places like this, with food waste and garbage, attract rodents, and rodents attract snakes. Just keep your eyes open, that's all. Well, and your ears."

"Just keep my eyes open?"

"And your ears."

"What the hell kind of place is this?"

"It's a desert."

"A desert with rattlesnakes," Jem whispered furiously. "You took me to a desert with snakes?"

"Well, pretty much every—"

"Great, Tean. This is just perfect. We're in snake country. Now I have to be on high alert. The minute I let my guard down, I'm toast. One day I'm going to be innocently taking a whiz—"

Tean blinked "Can you do it guiltily?"

"—and a rattlesnake is going to bite me right on the tip of my dick—"

"That seems very unlikely."

"—and not in a good way!"

"There's a good way?"

Jem let out a high-pitched noise. "I cannot do this with you right now. This is why people invented axes and backhoes and nuclear bombs: so we wouldn't have to get our dicks bitten off by snakes."

"Jem—"

"No, I can't. I cannot do this with you. Just—just be quiet. We're trying to sneak around, if that's not too much to ask."

It didn't seem like a good time to point out who was making most of the noise, so Tean laid a finger over his lips and nodded. With another of those suppressed, high-pitched noises, Jem led the way. They were halfway around the villa when a chorus of voices reached them.

"London, don't chase your sister with a squirt gun! Not in the house, you two, not in the house! Bill, will you try telling them?"

"Have another drink, Charisse?"

"God, Daddy, I will. I really will."

"And see if the ball-and-chain wants one too."

"I didn't realize she'd reached the legal drinking age, Daddy."

"Be nice to your new stepmother, please."

Jem waved toward the front of the house, and they reversed course.

"No way," Jem said when they were walking back down the drive. "That's too many moving parts, and you don't want to bring friends and family along for something like this—they're the ones who might point out that it's a risky investment, or they might want to double check your numbers, that kind of thing."

"I'd like to take this opportunity to explain that out of the approximately seven to eight thousand venomous snakebites every year in the United States, only five are fatal on average."

Jem glanced over. "God, you're glowing. Spit out the part you're excited about."

"Those fatal ones are usually attributed to diamondback rattlesnakes."

"I hate this place. I hate everything."

"Think of it this way: you're six times more likely to die from a lightning strike, eight times more likely to die from a heavy TV falling on you—"

"Jesus Christ, are we cartoon characters now?"

"—fourteen times more likely to die from falling out of a tree, and ninety-five times more likely to die falling off a ladder."

"Ladders, the silent killer. Oh God, your face. Just tell me already."

"No, it's not important."

"You're literally going to explode if you don't get to tell me."

"It's just that worldwide—"

Jem groaned as they headed toward the southern villa.

"—an estimated 138,000 people die each year from snake bites, and there are around three times that number of amputations and permanent disabilities, which, you know, just is another example of global inequity and the incredible privilege that Americans enjoy compared to many developing countries."

"Do you feel better?"

"If anything, I feel worse."

"But feeling worse makes you feel a little better, right?"

Tean was silent for another ten feet. Then he said, "I don't know how to answer that without sounding tremendously screwed up."

Laughing, Jem slung an arm around his shoulders, his body warm in contrast to the desert's cooling air.

The southern villa's windows were dark, but the blinds were raised and the curtains pulled back. The sun had slipped behind the tall red cliffs, but a haze of blue light still illuminated the desert. It was enough to see inside the shadowed rooms: a pair of high heels abandoned next to a plush sofa; cut-glass tumblers, one with a smudge of lipstick, on the wet bar; through the French doors that opened onto the back patio, Tean could see a matching set of roller bags next to the dining table. Pink. If he had to guess, the same color as the lipstick on the tumbler. He took a picture of the luggage tags.

"Keep an eye out for snakes," Jem said quietly, squatting by the French doors. He pulled on a pair of disposable gloves, passed a second pair to Tean, and drew a slim piece of metal from one pocket. He worked it between the doors. "Of both the two-legged and four-legged varieties, please."

"There's no variety of snake that has any number of legs. That's part of what makes them snakes."

"That's a sophistical answer," Jem said, and then he grunted and twisted, and one of the French doors popped open. "And you know I can't stand sophisticals." Then he grinned up at Tean. "I bought a word-of-the-day calendar, but I'm only on January 2nd."

Tean waited.

"Ok, I stole it," Jem said. "But only because the clerk was a dick and kept looking at me like I was going to steal something."

"Not that it matters at this point, but you also used sophistical wrong."

"You're being very phenomenological." He grinned. "January 1st."

"Please stop talking," Tean said, "before I have to turn us both in to the police."

They moved quickly through the darkened villa. In the mini-kitchen and dining area at the back, they found a collection of high-end alcohol, mostly gin and vodka, and the remains of a charcuterie board in the fridge. Jem grabbed a cracker, scooped something that looked like pâté, and popped it in his mouth. When Tean looked at him, Jem's face got angelically innocent.

"I'm hungry," he whispered.

"You know what that was?"

"Salty crackery goodness with some other salty mushy goodness."

"It was—"

"Don't tell me."

"—pâté, which is a forcemeat, which means it's ground up and possibly pureed."

"I said don't tell me."

"It definitely contains liver." Tean brightened. "Kind of like Scipio's treats."

Jem made spitting noises and wiped his tongue against the back of his hand. "God damn it, Tean. It tasted good! Why'd you have to ruin it?"

"I just thought you should know."

"Come here, I want to show you something. It's at the top of a ladder."

Aside from the abandoned heels, the living room was empty of anything interesting—the décor, which highlighted a knockoff Navajo blanket hanging on the wall and a plastic longhorn bull skull decoupaged with torn-up French postage stamps (some kind of irony? idiocy?), made Tean eager to move on to the next room.

The villa had three bedrooms, each with an attached bath. The first looked unused, and in the bathroom, the fixtures were spotless. The next bedroom had a leather duffel sitting on an armchair. A man's button-down shirt was draped over the back of the chair, and oxblood brogues sat near the closet door.

They went to the third bedroom. It was empty of personal possessions, but more of the lipstick marked tissues in the bathroom wastebasket.

"Do you want this room or the other one?" Jem asked.

"You're better at weaseling and ferreting and rooting around. Maybe you should take the room with all the stuff."

"If you take this room, you also have to search the luggage in the kitchen."

Tean made a face.

"You'll have to pick through a lady's unmentionables."

"Jeez, um. I'll search the guy's room."

Tean tried not to walk faster as he left.

"Bras," Jem called after him.

"Shut up."

"Panties!"

This time, Tean did walk faster. In the man's bedroom, though, he slowed down. He searched the leather duffel first. Clean clothes—boutique t-shirts, preppy shorts, a pair of stretchy joggers. Dirty clothes, noticeably dressier, were wadded up at the bottom of the bag. After months of listening to Jem talk about clothes, getting dragged around stores by Jem, being forced to try on clothes by Jem, and having to look at pictures of clothes Jem wanted to buy (which often included fluorescent colors, asymmetrical geometric shapes, and acid washes), Tean knew he was looking at several hundred dollars' worth of clothing. A dopp kit held even more toiletries than Jem used, and Tean took several pictures, mostly as ideas for gifts.

The bed, the nightstands, the dresser, and the closet offered nothing. The bathroom backed up to the third bedroom, and on the other side of the thin wall, Tean could hear Jem searching, which seemed to involve a lot of grunting—apparently moving heavy furniture was part of the protocol. Tean checked the shower, the vanity, and the mirrored medicine cabinet. Nothing.

He was reaching to turn off the light when he saw the dusting of paint flakes on the vanity's backsplash. Tean hesitated. And then the part of himself that had woken up after meeting Jem Berger—the part that Jem had called, at various times, devious, a criminal mastermind, and a morally bankrupt homosexual—made him walk back to the mirrored medicine cabinet. He opened it, swung the door back and forth, and ran his fingers around it. At the bottom of the stainless steel unit, he touched a raw edge of wallboard.

Grabbing the mirrored cabinet, he drew a breath to steady himself. Then he pulled. The cabinet slid from the wall, exposing a hollow space in the framing. On the other side of the framing, a second piece of wallboard divided the bathroom from the third bedroom. Jem was still moving around, making those same noises of strained effort. Someone had opened a hole in the wall at about eye level—and, judging by how the paper had split and the gypsum dust had fallen, Tean thought the hole had been made from inside the third bedroom—and when Tean leaned forward, he could see easily into the room.

"What in the world are you doing?"

Jem lay spread-eagle on the bed. At the sound of Tean's voice, he tried to sit up, pulling the mattress with him for a few inches. He was tied down, Tean realized. The restraints ran under the mattress, which was why it moved when Jem tried to sit up.

"Don't come in here," Jem shouted.

"Jem, what the heck happened?"

"Don't come in. I'm—I'm naked."

"No, you're not. I can see you." As Tean settled the cabinet back into the wall, he shouted, "Hold on!"

"Fine, you can come in," Jem was saying as Tean came down the hallway. "But you have to keep your eyes closed and not look at me.

When Tean stepped into the bedroom, he spotted the decorative wooden wall ornament that hid the peephole. Then he took in the rest of the scene. "Explain."

"I said don't look at me!"

"Why did you handcuff yourself to a bed? And more importantly, how? And even more importantly, just to make sure I understand, why?"

"First of all, they're not regular handcuffs. They're sex handcuffs. So the correct question is, how did I sex-handcuff myself to the bed?"

"Jem!"

"I didn't mean to! I found the cuffs, and I tried one on. No big deal, I can pick the locks on these things with a paperclip. But I wanted to see how they were connected, so I reached across the bed and . . . got stuck."

"You can't accidentally put a handcuff on yourself."

"Yes, you can. Probably. But in my defense, that's not what happened." He shook his left hand. The paracord that he wore as a bracelet had gotten caught in the handcuff's chain. "I'm stuck."

"This is like when Scipio tried to go behind the couch for a treat."

"Never mind," Jem said, lying back and closing his eyes. "Just let me die here. I'll become a desert skeleton, that's fine."

"Not coincidentally," Tean said as he sat on the mattress, taking Jem's arm: warm, the ripple of veins, and by some great injustice in the universe, even his forearm had serious muscle development, "it was a liver-flavored treat. I'm starting to see a pattern. Also, if you're lucky, you might end up being mummified instead of skeletonizing. You know, because of the dry heat."

"Yeah," Jem said, "if I'm lucky."

After a few false starts, Tean found the tangle and worked it free. He squeezed Jem's arm, and Jem rolled upright, grabbed a paperclip from one pocket, and began twisting it in the lock.

Then, at the front of the villa, a door opened, and footsteps moved inside.

18

"Shit," Jem whispered.

"Hurry," Tean whispered back.

"Shit, shit, shit."

In the villa's living room, a woman was speaking. "It has nothing to do with my ass."

A man answered: "Keep telling yourself that. The fact that you can't get one man in your bed suggests otherwise. You've got a blank scorecard after how many at-bats?"

"Please don't embarrass yourself by using sports metaphors. Nobody's interested in your ponytailed ass either, in case you didn't notice."

"Jesus, you are really being a bitch tonight."

"Fuck you."

"Yeah, fuck me."

Jem was still working on the cuff.

"I thought it was easy," Tean whispered.

"It should have been," Jem whispered. "These are the real deal. I've almost—there." The cuff opened, and Jem carefully lowered the cuff and chain to the floor. "Window."

But as Tean took his first step, the man's voice said, "Someone's been in here."

"Of course someone's been in here. The beds don't make themselves."

"The light's on in my room."

"It was probably the maid; she forgot to turn it off."

Tean was trying to get the window open—it had all kinds of locks and safety measures, and he couldn't seem to get them all disengaged at the same time. He shot a panicked look over his shoulder, and he was surprised to see Jem catch his attention. The blond man mouthed, *Trust me*. Then he called out, "We didn't have any mints for the pillows."

"What the fuck? Kalista, call the police." The voice changed, directed down the hall. "Stay the fuck back there. Whoever you are, stay the fuck back there or I will fuck you up."

"If you could hold off on calling the police," Jem said, "we're here to talk about Tanner Kimball. We're about to save you a lot of pain, possibly your lives."

Silence from the other room. Then the woman—Kalista, presumably—said, "No, I'm sorry, I hit the emergency contact on my phone by accident. Thank you. Yes, I'm very sorry."

"Kalista," the man said.

"I'm curious," she said.

"Who are you?" the man called down the hall. Then, to Kalista, "This is stupid; call the police."

"That would be even stupider." Toward the bedroom at the end of the hall, she said, "What do you mean, you want to talk about Tanner?"

"That's pretty much exactly what I mean," Jem said. "We've got information about Tanner Kimball, Blake Bigney, and Antonio Hidalgo. We'll be happy to share it with you. We'd also like to get some information in return."

"There's nothing to talk about," the man snapped. "So you can get the hell out of here and thank God that we didn't have the police drag you off to jail."

"Why don't we sit down and talk about it?" Jem said. "My business partner's here with me. He's also my best friend. Why don't we come out there and do this a little more reasonably?"

"Just, you know, for the record," Tean said, "we're not really best friends. And we're definitely not business partners. We're more like cousins, and he's the one who gloms on to you at family reunions and won't give you five minutes of peace and quiet."

"Really?" Jem murmured. "Right now?"

"I honestly don't know why I do anything anymore. You broke my brain."

"What the actual hell?" the man said.

Sweat slid down Tean's spine in the silence that followed.

Kalista laughed. Then she said, "Come out with your hands where we can see them. Nick's a decent shot, and I'm better, so don't do anything stupid."

When Tean took a step toward the door, Jem actually groaned, caught his arm, and dragged him back. "Jesus, will you please get some common sense?"

Tean was trying to figure out what that meant as Jem took the lead and headed down the hall.

They kept their hands out and visible as they moved into the living room, and a tiny knot of tension loosened when Tean saw that neither the man nor the woman held a weapon. The man was slight and short, with long, dark hair gathered in a knot at his nape. He had exaggeratedly dark eyes and red lips; it took Tean a moment to realize he was wearing makeup, and it took Tean another moment to process the shirt with its stiff, standing collar of pink lace. The woman was taller, built solidly across the shoulders and hips, her hair barely long enough for the clip that held it back from her face. She was wearing a red dress that Tean, with the knowledge that had been imposed on him recently, guessed had cost a lot of money. Her makeup was less obvious than the man's, but Tean thought that might just be gender bias.

"Hi," Jem said. "Sorry about this. Sorry we had to meet like this. Jem," he pointed to himself. "Tean." More pointing. "And honestly, I'm sorry about the reverse housekeeping scenario."

"Reverse housekeeping?" Nick waved the phone at them. "This is trespassing, breaking and entering, stealing."

"Nope. Just plain old reverse housekeeping: we mess up the beds, we put the towels on the floor, we leave a tip for you on the nightstand."

"What the actual hell?" Nick said.

"I don't know," Kalista said, "but for the first time in a solid month I'm not bored. Go get us something to drink."

"Get it yourself, bitch."

"Go." Kalista shoved the smaller man.

He flounced off, hips swishing so quickly in such tight pants that the friction looked like it could start a fire. At the opening to the kitchen, he stopped, glanced over his shoulder, and made a disgusted noise before flouncing away again. Both hands were flopping with all the exaggerated movement.

"Well," Kalista said, smiling as she lowered herself into a chair. "Go on. Explain."

Jem dropped onto the couch, pulling Tean down next to him.

"We're—" Tean began.

"—representatives of an interested party," Jem cut in. "Can we leave it at that for now?"

"For now," Kalista said, her lips curving in something that should have been, but didn't quite reach, a smile.

Nick sashayed back into the room. He tossed a cut-glass tumbler at Kalista without warning. She caught it, smirked, and leaned back in her seat.

"Tean was a professional catcher for the Utah nine-and-under Bumblebees," Jem said, "but I forgot my mitt."

"Does he always make jokes?" Nick asked Tean as he handed each of them a glass.

"It's not his fault," Tean said. "He got toxoplasmosis from eating cat litter."

Jem shoved him so hard he almost fell off the couch.

Nick's façade cracked, and a smile slipped out. He splashed gin over the ice in their glasses and then sat on the arm of Kalista's chair and poured some for her as well. He didn't have a glass, and when he noticed Tean's gaze, he said, "Seventeen months sober."

"Good for you," Tean said. "That's very impressive."

"It was that or die," Nick said. "It's not as impressive when you think of it like that."

Tean didn't know how to answer that; he sipped the gin, realized gin was not one of the alcohols he liked, and set the glass on the coffee table.

"You still haven't told us why you're here," Kalista said. "I think you're running out of time."

"Am I correct," Jem said, "in understanding that you might have some sort of business arrangement worked out with Tanner?"

Kalista gave a one-shouldered shrug.

"Well, you might be interested to know that he's wanted for at least two murders and is currently in hiding. He's radioactive right now; if he gets anywhere close to you, you're going to get burned."

"Son of a bitch," Nick muttered.

Kalista gave Nick a long look and then turned to Jem. "And you're telling us because you and your . . . interested party, you just wanted to help us out of the goodness of your heart?"

"No," Jem said with an embarrassed smile and a shrug. "I want to kill Tanner Kimball. And I'd like to do it without stepping on your toes."

"Why?" Nick said, smoothing the hair over his ears. "What did he do to you?"

Jem's smile just got bigger. "Not only is Tanner a hot potato, the kind you don't want to handle right now, he's also a backstabbing son of a bitch. If you keep him involved, he's going to put a bullet in the back of your heads and walk off with . . . whatever business you're conducting."

"So you say," Kalista said. "Unless I put a bullet in his head first."

"This was just a friendly warning," Jem said. "Tanner isn't someone you should—"

She made a chopping noise, the gesture so vicious that some of her hair came loose from the clip. "You two need to leave now."

"If you could help us track down Tanner, I could make sure he doesn't complicate your business—"

"I said go!" The words were a shout.

Jem threw a helpless glance at Tean.

"I want to show you something," Tean said, standing. "Can you give me two minutes and then make your decision? After you see this, I think you'll want to cooperate."

Again, Kalista's face went blank. Some sort of internal calculation, Tean decided. Something that belied the spoiled princess routine. Then she nodded.

"Go into your bathroom, please," Tean said to Nick. To Kalista, "Go into your bedroom."

"I don't like the idea of—" Nick began.

"We'll stay right here," Jem said.

Nick and Kalista exchanged a glance. They must have reached a decision because they headed down the hallway.

"Ok," Nick called back.

"Grab the medicine cabinet and pull," Tean shouted.

From the back of the villa came a thump. "Holy shit!"

"Nick, are you ok?"

"I'm flat on my ass because I pulled too hard. Yes, I'm fine. What the actual, ever-living fuck?"

"Kalista," Jem called, "check between the mattress and the box spring."

A moment later: "What the fuck is this?"

"Kalista, you're not going to believe this?"

"What the fuck is this? Is this some kind of joke, Nick?"

"Kalista, shut the fuck up and look at the wall."

Tean knew when she understood; she screamed.

When Nick and Kalista came back, Kalista kept saying, "Call the police, call the police."

This time, Nick was the cool one. He perched on the arm of the empty chair, Kalista pacing in front of him, and studied Jem and Tean. "Ok," he said, "tell us all of it."

"You've heard pretty much all of it," Jem said. "Tanner and his friends are nasty pieces of work."

"Did any of the three attempt to initiate sexual encounters?" Tean asked.

"That motherfucking son of a bitch," Kalista screamed. She grabbed her tumbler and hurled it. It struck the wall and shattered.

"I wish, honey. I caught Tanner checking out my ass a couple of times, and I gave him a few winks, but he didn't bite." Nick waved a floppy hand. "Blake's a major homo, but he's so closeted I'd need a bulldozer to get him out of there. And Antonio was always talking about his girl."

"What the fuck is that in there?" Kalista pointed to the bedroom at the end of the hall. "What the fuck is that?"

"I think you know what," Jem said. "If things went the way Tanner wanted, he would have had a little fun before running off with your money. Taking some pictures of you through that peephole would have been the least of it, I think."

"But it's Nick's bathroom."

"If things had gone differently, I think Blake would have suddenly become very interested in Nick. They would have hit it off quickly. Or, if that didn't work, Blake and Antonio would have taken Nick out of the equation."

"That son of a bitch." Her nails bit into the arm of the chair. "I'm going to kill him!"

"When was the last time you saw Tanner?" Jem asked. "Do you know where he might be hiding?"

"Get out. I want you to get out."

"When did you see him?"

"Nick, make them get out!"

"When?"

"Wednesday! Wednesday! The three of them were in an argument and pretending like they weren't. They left; Tanner called Thursday to tell us he was taking care of something, and he said he'd be back in time for the deal. Now get the fuck out!"

Jem rose, and Tean led the way to the door.

Nick followed them outside; from within the villa came the sound of glass breaking mixed with Kalista's shrieks.

"At least she didn't get hurt," Jem said. "She ought to be grateful."

"Please," Nick said, sniffing. "She's pissy because she doesn't like having her toys taken away. She thought she was going to have fun with Tanner."

A thunderous crash made Tean think of a heavy piece of furniture being overturned.

"That's going to be hell when they charge your credit card for the damage," Jem said.

"Tanner paid," Nick said with a grin. "He insisted after Kalista told him she was scared her ex might track her down. He and his friends insisted on staying somewhere else, just so we didn't draw attention."

"Gee, what a guy."

"Could I talk to you?" Nick said to Jem.

"We're talking right now."

Nick's eyes cut toward Tean. "In private?"

"No," Tean said.

"It's fine," Jem said.

Tean tried to catch Jem's eyes, but Jem was examining Nick openly, his expression frank and interested as his gaze swept up and down the smaller man.

"Go on," Jem said. "Shoo."

"Shoo?"

"That's right. Shoo."

Tean didn't stomp on his way to the truck, but his steps were very loud.

He watched the shadows of insects moving against artificial lights. He watched nightjars swooping for their evening meal. He thought about all the things he was going to tell Jem: scorpions and coral snakes and harvester ants and camel spiders. Somehow he ended up looking straight at the villa, at the cement walk where Jem and Nick were silhouettes. Nick stretched up, and for a moment it looked like he was going to kiss Jem, and then he dropped back onto his heels, laughing. He held Jem's hand for a moment, and then he headed into the villa.

When Jem reached the truck, he had a bemused grin that looked annoyingly self-satisfied. He glanced at Tean, stopped, and raised his eyebrows. "What?"

"Nothing."

"Your face isn't saying nothing."

"I'm saying nothing. My mouth is saying nothing."

"You're allowed to go on dates, but I can't talk to a cute guy?"

"You are a real jerk sometimes, Jem," Tean said, and he climbed into the truck and slammed the door.

19

They drove north on US-191 toward Moab. The city was an oasis of artificial light, a haze just visible above the striated cliffs ahead of them that were dissolving into the gloom.

Jem tried to keep his voice even. "Ok, explain how I'm a jerk."

Tean tightened his grip on the steering wheel; any tighter, Jem thought, and he was going to rip it off the column. And then probably beat Jem to death with it.

"So you're giving me the silent treatment?"

"No. I just don't want to talk about this."

"You don't want to explain why you're mad at me? What about all that stuff about feeling your feelings and—"

"I am feeling them!"

When the shout died out, the only sound was the hum of the tires.

"You and I agreed we were better as friends," Jem said.

"I told you I don't want to talk about this."

"Too bad. I am your friend. I've tried to be a good one, or as good as I can be. I don't understand why I'm a jerk just for talking to a cute—"

"Quit saying that. That's not what it is."

"Oh, really?"

"Really. I don't care about that."

"Uh huh."

Tean shifted in his seat, sitting up straighter, still throttling the steering wheel. "You can date whoever you want. Talk to whoever you want. Kiss whoever you want."

"Fuck whoever I want?"

In the pale radiance of the dash, Tean's blush was visible. "But I don't like being told to 'shoo' just so you can hit on someone during an interview as part of—of whatever we're doing here."

"You almost called it a case."

"It's not a case. It's just us doing something that we shouldn't be doing. And don't change the subject."

Night had leeched the colors from the stone. The bands of red and orange and grayish green were gone, everything stripped down to shades of gray except the yellow stripes illuminated by the headlights. The smell of sagebrush and pine resin, the smell of the steppes, was mixed with the dry, dusty air of the desert plateau. For someone who loved the city, Jem was uncomfortably aware, he had a surprisingly strong reaction to that combination of scents. He reached over and put his hand on the back of Tean's neck.

Tean jerked, trying to throw him off.

"Stop it. Jesus, now I know where Scipio gets it from. Like father, like son."

Tean didn't exactly gnash his teeth, but the clicking sound was suspiciously familiar.

"I said stop it, God damn it." Jem tightened his grip long enough to give a few gentle shakes, and then he relaxed his fingers, his thumb stroking the side of Tean's neck. "I'm sorry, all right?"

"Fine."

"I was just trying to be funny; I didn't mean anything by it."

The doc hunched lower; the muscles and tendons in his neck were stiff.

"Well, yell at me or something. Feel your feelings so we can go back to being best friends."

"Is he your type?"

Jem burst out laughing. "What?"

"You heard me."

Jem couldn't have explained why he did what he did next. He slouched in the seat, his knees spreading, taking up as much room as he could. He scratched lightly at the back of Tean's neck. "I wouldn't exactly say I have a type, but, sure. He's cute."

They must have gone a quarter mile, the tires whining beneath them, Tean coiling tighter and tighter before he said, "He's probably got hemorrhoids."

This time, Jem caught the laugh before it could escape. "What?"

"Did you see how he walked? He's definitely got hemorrhoids."

"I think he just walks that way."

"Of course he does. He walks that way because he's got bulging veins in his rectum."

"Sweet Jesus." Jem cleared his throat. "The good news is that there's a lot of anecdotal evidence that anal sex helps with hemorrhoids. Pushes them back into place. So, you know, I'm basically a physician. A trained medical professional. Administering a life-saving procedure."

"Perfect. So he's not just your type, but you're going to have sex with him, hemorrhoids and all, regardless of however many STIs he has floating around in his system. And crabs. He's probably got crabs. And now you have them, but you should have thought of that before having sex with him."

"Well, I was going to ask your blessing first. And a lotion—I think they've got a lotion for that."

Jem's breath exploded in a whoosh as Tean slammed a fist into his belly. Croaking for air, Jem managed: "Glasses."

With one finger, Tean shoved the glasses back into place. "And his hair."

"Can't breathe."

"His hair is stupid."

Jem tugged on the doc's wild, pushed-back hair. "His hair, huh?"

"You can't even see his ears. For all you know, he's one of those people who have had their ears surgically altered to look like elves."

"I like elves. Elves are sexy. And you've got to admire someone who would commit to something like that."

Tean made a noise that was uncannily like a steam whistle.

"I know," Jem said. "He's perfect."

"Fine. His swollen rectal veins and his crabs and his lopped-off ears don't bother you. Whatever. I don't care. But he's still part of the case."

Squeezing Tean's neck, Jem said, "A little credit, please? Do you really think I'm going to let some guy lead me around by my dick? I'm disappointed. And, actually, kind of hurt. If he wants to hit on me, great. That's one more opportunity for me to talk to him. Think of it as pumping him for information instead of, you know, just pumping him."

Tean actually had the decency to blush even harder.

"You know, like, pumping him."

"Yes, I get it."

"A hand job. My hand on his dick. Sliding up and down, squeezing. That's what I'm comparing it to."

"Oh my gosh."

"That kind of pumping."

"Jem, I'm sorry for doubting you, but please, please, please stop talking right now."

Laughing, Jem scratched the doc's neck and let him drive. Night had closed in. On their left, the desert and the red-rock cliffs and the cacti and the scrub had all vanished. On their right, scattered lights revealed homes, a pole shed with aluminum siding, a gas station. Ahead of them, Moab was coming into focus, the haze of light sharpening into discrete points.

"Do you think he knows where Tanner's hiding?" Jem asked.

"Please do not make me talk to you about a boy."

"Dummy," Jem said, shaking him again. "This is about finding Tanner. Do you think they know where he's hiding?"

Tean frowned. "I don't know why they would. He wouldn't have wanted them to be able to track him down, and they seemed genuinely upset."

"Maybe they were lying."

"Maybe. Do you think they were lying?"

Jem shrugged. "I don't know. It's safer to assume everyone is lying until we know otherwise."

"I don't think—" Tean cut off and cocked his head. "I don't know. I didn't like them. Either of them, actually. And not just because, you know."

"They're drug dealers, and you're jealous of your best friend getting some dong?"

"He's probably got one of those STIs that make your penis have a yellowish-white discharge."

Jem pretended to throw up into the footwell.

"What about the argument?" Tean said.

"Yeah." Jem hooked his fingers behind Tean's collar, playing with the cotton. "I was thinking about that too. Tanner, Blake, and Antonio are ready for this deal to go down. Blake and Antonio are having second thoughts. Then something happens on Wednesday, and according to Kalista and Nick, they get in a big fight. Thursday,

Antonio and Tanner are back in Salt Lake, and Tanner kills Andi. Antonio gets arrested, Blake's dead in a canyon, and Tanner vanishes."

They had reached the outskirts of Moab. Tean signaled to turn left, and he followed a side street, flipped around, and parked in front of a prefabricated building with a cracked foundation. The streetlights were spaced wide here, and Tean had chosen a dark spot.

"Why are we skulking?" Jem asked.

Tean let out a sigh. "We've run down everything we could on what Tanner was doing in Moab, but we still don't know where he might be hiding. That's why we need a new angle."

"What new angle?"

"We're going to break into a federal government building and, in all likelihood, be arrested, convicted, imprisoned, and probably murdered by our cellmates because we refuse to join their prison gangs on ethical grounds."

"I want you to focus on the very short interim," Jem said, "between imprisonment and being murdered because I have this gut feeling you're going to get a job in the prison laundry, and I know how much you love doing laundry."

Tean stared at him.

"You've got to look on the bright side," Jem informed him. "Now, where are we breaking into?"

20

Jem followed Tean toward the low building of brown stone. Security lights illuminated the parking lot and the entrance; a sign announced that this was the Bureau of Land Management - Moab Field Office. The only vehicle in the parking lot was a brand-new Silverado. It had a luxury trim package, with chrome bumpers and a chrome front grille, alloy wheels, and tinted windows. Jem was pretty sure if he got close enough, he'd see leather upholstery.

"Tanner gave us another lead without meaning to," Tean said. They stood in a patch of deeper shadow cast by a line of poplars. "The weapon. The injection rifle he used to shoot Andi. He could have gotten an injection rifle pretty easily, but the immunocontraceptive in the dart syringe, that's made and sold by the Science and Conservation Center in Montana. You can't just buy it in PetSmart."

"This is the stuff they use to keep horses from getting knocked up?"

"Right. I've been thinking a lot about Tanner shooting Andi with that gun because it's so strange. We know Tanner liked causing pain. The injection rifle probably appealed to his sadism because he could hurt people and animals with it, but the injuries wouldn't be fatal. It's entirely possible that Tanner saw someone using one of the injection rifles down here and that's where he got the idea. He could have ordered one. For that matter, he could have walked into a veterinary supply store, a farm supply store, or even a sporting goods store and bought one over the counter. But what he couldn't do is get his hands on ZonaStat-H. Not unless he stole it. And the only people using it in this part of the world are BLM staff who are trying to control the mustang population."

"So he stole it from the BLM."

"He had to have."

Jem considered him for a moment, the way Tean stared at the building with his bushy eyebrows drawn together. "Spit it out."

"What?"

"The rest of it, spit it out."

"Jager was weird."

"The BLM guy?"

"Right. He's a special agent; he's supposed to investigate federal crimes that occur on federal land. The fact that he would want to talk to us after we found that body definitely makes sense, but . . ."

"But it was freaky as fuck."

"Yes. I couldn't even tell you why, but it was weird. He was weird."

"Trust your gut."

After a moment, Tean nodded.

"Now," Jem said, "as a budding criminal mastermind, do you have a plan?"

"Yes."

"Let's hear it."

"You get us inside, and we search Jager's office and the secured storerooms."

"That's not a plan. That's a wish."

"Does it help if I tell you it's an order?"

Grinning, Jem said, "Do you want to be the sneaky snake or the goody gopher?"

"Please don't tell me that's a sex game."

"Hold on."

"Jem—"

"No, I just need to savor this moment. That was the best thing you've ever said to me. I never want to forget this."

"Jem!"

"No, it's not a sex game. Yet. I'm talking about our plan. Sneaky snake and goody gopher team up to get inside the BLM. Just like in nature. In the real world."

"First of all, in the real world, snakes and gophers don't team up. Snakes eat gophers."

"That's a kind of teamwork. They're both doing their part." Tean opened his mouth, and Jem hurried to say, "See that truck? You're going to knock on the front door of the BLM building until the security guard comes to talk to you. Then you're going to tell him that you were walking by when you saw someone hit that truck with their car."

"Someone randomly drove into a parking lot at this hour, ran into that truck, and drove away."

"Yep."

"Nobody's going to believe that."

"He's a security guard who spent more than I make in a year on a truck, Tean. He's going to believe it. Make your face right."

"What does that mean?"

"Simultaneously outraged and unbearably pleased with yourself. Like the time you caught me borrowing sugar packets from McDonald's and you went back to pay the manager for them."

"You weren't borrowing them; you were stealing them. Borrowing implies you were going to give them back."

"Not necessarily. I never gave you back that ugly hat I borrowed."

"It's called a fedora. And I bought it because you told me I needed something stylish in my wardrobe. And that's a perfect example of stealing."

"Well," Jem said, "I did you a favor. Get into place, goody gopher. Keep him talking as long as you can, and when he goes back inside, walk around back."

Tean's mouth opened in an indignant O as Jem jogged away.

The BLM building had all the charm and verve and architectural panache of every government-designed structure, which was to say, in Jem's opinion it was only slightly uglier than a cardboard box. A used one. That had already been broken down for the recycling bin. The building's simple outline didn't offer any convenient nooks or crannies for Jem to hide in, so he settled for taking up position at the corner of the building. He gauged the distance to the door as fifteen feet. He crouched and tightened the laces on his ROOS.

Tean approached the door, but instead of knocking, he rang a doorbell. It sounded inside the BLM building. After a moment, Tean jabbed the button again. The guard, when he arrived, was a young guy, and he matched the mental profile Jem had started to assemble. He had his thumbs in his belt, obviously wanting to draw attention to the holstered gun, and he was sun-brown, a diet of beer and fast food already catching up with him. He said something through the glass.

"I saw a hit-and-run," Tean shouted back, pointing over his shoulder, movements and words exaggerated. "Somebody ran into that truck."

Inside the building, the guard bellowed something that sounded like "What the hell?"

"Do you know who owns that truck?" Tean said.

The guard's answer was to push open the door and run out into the parking lot.

Jem had worried that his own footsteps might be too loud, but the guard was making more than enough noise. As soon as the guard had gotten past Tean, Jem sprinted toward the door. Tean didn't look at him, but he did catch the BLM door and give it an extra shove before taking off after the guard. That extra push kept the door open just long enough for Jem to grab it before it swung shut. He slipped inside, the door locking as it closed behind him. Out by the Silverado, the guard was shouting questions. The last thing from Tean that Jem heard was, "I didn't get a very good look at them, but they were definitely teenagers. Hooligans, I mean. And I think they'd been drinking."

Rolling his eyes, Jem jogged across the lobby. It was your standard setup: molded plastic chairs, end tables covered with outdated magazines, a pile of Trident wrappers, a melamine reception desk with a plastic nameplate that said SURESH. A camera watched everything, and Jem resisted the urge to give it a wave. He knew—and Tean must have known—that they had no chance of doing this without getting feature roles in that night's production of the BLM security camera variety hour, but if it ever went to court, there was no point in antagonizing people.

The shouting in the parking lot had subsided by the time Jem followed the hallway behind the reception desk. A door stood open on his right. A copy of *Bucks and Does* lay open on a vinyl rolling chair, and either lady deer had changed a lot since the last time Jem had seen one, or the security guard was enjoying the company of his right hand during the shift. A camera showed a rotating selection of views from outside and inside the building, and Jem stayed long enough to watch until they repeated. Most of the cameras were placed outside; the few that were inside occupied access points, which meant the only tricky part would be getting out of the building without being noticed. The solution was probably going to be very simple, something along the lines of run like hell.

Ahead he spotted a staff kitchen and lunchroom; the refrigerator was making a grinding, clanking noise that made Jem think Karen and Debbie were going to come in on Monday and find their tuna salad had gone over. Two more doors opened off the hall: one to a conference room that smelled like Fritos (or maybe like feet; Jem couldn't decide), and the other locked, with a plaque that said Director. He left that for later, although he doubted they'd have time.

A second hallway branched off, cutting across the width of the building. Bathrooms, a janitorial supply closet with bleach fumes that made Jem's eyes sting—and a mop that fell and cracked him across the face—several shared offices, and then an unmarked door that was locked. Bingo, bango, bongo. He left it for the moment and kept going; he passed several more workspaces, these divided up by cubicles, and then, at the end of the hall, another office with a plaque that said SPECIAL AGENT JAGER. A crash-bar door opened onto a dark swatch of asphalt; Jem leaned into it with his hip, and cool, desert air and the smell of motor oil washed over him.

A shadow came toward him, and Jem reached for the pocket containing the paracord with the hex nut.

"Jesus, Tean," he whispered. "Give a guy a heart attack."

"He was crying," Tean snapped. "I wouldn't have done it if I'd known it was going to upset him that much."

"His truck didn't actually get hit by another car."

"He doesn't know that." When Tean tried to squeeze past Jem, he stopped. "What happened to your face?"

"Nothing."

"No, there's definitely swelling. Stop it. Don't you dare try to pull away from me." Somehow, by that point, Tean had Jem's head in both hands. For somebody who was always trying to squirm away from hugs, back-scratches, best-friend-completely-nonsexual cuddling, and anything even close to resembling physical affection, the doc seemed completely untroubled by Jem bucking and trying to twist his head free. "Gosh, you're so darn fractious. You make petting Senator Poindexter look easy."

"I know that's a cat and not your willy, but you should still try to be more careful how you phrase things."

"Who hit you?"

"There was a second guard. I had to take care of him. Don't worry; I think he'll live. If you can call it living."

Tean was quiet for a moment. In the relatively weak light of the hall, his eyes were black, and the heat of his hands made Jem flush. Pine, sage, the dusty smell of high-plains grasses and all the wild, open spaces. How many people had ever cared if Jem had gotten hurt? How many people had ever held his head like this? How many had ever worried about him, fussed over him, held on and refused to let go, even though something feral in Jem raised its hackles whenever another person tried to take care of him? How many people had ever called him fractious and said it like it was half-wonderful and half-maddening? For that matter, what the hell did fractious even mean?

Jem did it without knowing he was going to do it. He turned his head and kissed the heel of Tean's hand.

Tean yanked his hands away and held them at his side, fists clenched.

Explanations unspooled in Jem's head: that was just a friend thing, that was just because you're such a nice guy, a laugh, a smirk, God, you make it too easy. He couldn't crack open his jaw.

Instead, Tean spoke first, his voice tight, with a tremor he must have been trying to hide. "The guard was calling his mom when I left, but he won't be out there forever."

"Ok," Jem said.

Tean stepped inside, and Jem let the door swing shut. He pointed to Jager's office and they kept moving. In his hurry, he grabbed the wrong door, and the mop clipped him across the side of the face again.

"God damn it," he whispered.

"A second guard," Tean said drily.

Shoving the mop back into the closet, Jem pointed a finger at Tean. "Not another word."

Tean mimed zipping his lips. But his eyes were full of something Jem didn't want to read, even if he could, so he closed the closet door and went to work picking the lock on the next one.

"Really?" Tean asked after a moment. "You're going to be able to pick that?"

"This lock is one step up from the privacy locks that people have on their bathroom doors."

"For the closet where they keep guns and ammo?"

"Let's not jump to any conclusions. It's the only locked door besides the director's, though, and this is the BLM Moab Field Office, not Fort Knox. Although if we find any of those gold blocks, I get to keep them."

"Bullion."

"Bullion yourself. I called them."

"No, that's what the blocks—"

The door swung open, and Jem stood and followed Tean into the room. Tean found a light switch, and exposed bulbs flared to life. It was a storeroom, as Jem had guessed. And it looked like the BLM wasn't particular about what they stored. The air smelled a little bit like the barns that Jem had been inside of—something like grass or hay, and a nauseating chemical smell, but without the accompanying animal stink. He saw a few spare tires, a spool of braided fishing line, two aluminum jerrycans—something sloshed inside when he kicked one—and boxes, bags, crates, and more. A wire cage at the back partitioned the room, and on the other side of the cage, he could see banker's boxes, tactical vests, rifles, shotguns, and boxes and boxes of ammunition. Tean was already picking a path through the maze, so Jem moved to examine the cage.

A heavy padlock hung on the gate, and when Jem checked the construction—as much of it as he could reach, anyway—it all seemed solid.

"There's no way I can get through this. Not with the tools I have."

Tean was examining something and didn't look over, but he waved for Jem to join him. When Jem reached him, he saw why: a black metal cabinet against one wall held two of the injection rifles, CO2 cartridges, and boxes of darts.

"Do I need to worry about fingerprints?" Tean asked.

"Well, they've already got both of us on camera, so I'm not sure it matters."

"Perfect," Tean muttered as he began opening boxes. "I'm going to get sodomized to death by Biggie and have my skull used to make toilet wine because we got caught on camera."

"First of all, I silenced our only witness."

"Don't say the mop."

"The mop. Second, I'm going out on a limb here and assuming Biggie is your cellmate."

Tean was shuffling boxes, checking each one in turn.

"And third," Jem said, "if they make the wine in your skull, isn't it technically skull wine and not toilet wine?"

"Go do something productive," Tean said. "Go fight that mop. Best two out of three."

"You are very mean to me sometimes."

With a long exhalation, Tean removed a dart from the final box and held it up. "Notice anything?"

"Are you going to stab me with it if I point out that you keep caressing the tip? Before you do, glasses."

Tean caught them just as they reached the tip of his nose. As he pushed them back up, he said, "These are all single-use darts, which fits what I saw at the medical examiner's office. The construction is plastic, and the tip of the dart, which is technically a needle, is thinner and cheaper than reusable ones. That's why it broke off when it caught up against Andi's rib."

"Ok. And?"

"And do you see a refrigerated unit where the immunocontraceptive is kept before it's placed in the dart syringe?"

Jem shook his head. "The only refrigerator I saw was in the staff kitchen, and it's on its last legs. Macey and Kacey are going to be furious when they get here and find out their schmears have gone bad over the weekend."

"This is Moab, Utah. Nobody is schmearing anything on anything. Oh my gosh, please don't say anything because I just heard it." Tean took a deep breath while Jem fought a grin. "My point is that wherever they keep the immunocontraceptive, it's not here, but there were traces of it in the needle lodged in Andi's body."

"So either Tanner committed two separate thefts—one to get the rifle and darts, and another to get this immune stuff—or he committed one, but he stole a gun and darts that already had the drug in them. It has to be the second one. Tanner's not above stealing, and he'd steal from two separate locations if he had to. But there's no reason he would care about the drug. My guess is that he saw someone using one of these things, got a micro-boner for it, and took it right then. At least some of the remaining darts had the drug already in them, and that's how one of them ended up in Andi."

Tean nodded. "Now let's get the heck out of here, please."

"One more thing."

"We're not checking the fridge for schmears."

"No, Jager's office."

"No."

"A quick look."

"No, I'm putting my foot down. Jem, wait up, I'm putting my foot down."

Jem tested the handle on Jager's office door; unlocked. He let them in. The door had a large window set into the upper half, so instead of risking the overhead lights, Jem turned on the flashlight on his phone. After a moment, Tean followed his example.

The office consisted of a desk, two filing cabinets, and a tiny window. A ceramic tray full of succulents sat next to the window. Jem had Tean help him rock the filing cabinets back and forth, moving them a few inches out from the wall, and then Tean held each cabinet at an angle while Jem lay on his back and messed with the lock, which ran vertically through the frame. It only took him a couple of minutes to get each one opened, and then he put Tean to work examining the contents while he searched the desk.

Tean found something first, letting out a low noise that made Jem look over. When Tean beckoned, Jem joined him. They stared at the small revolver at the back of the filing cabinet drawer. Its grip was decorated with a stylized American flag, and a silver chain was wrapped around the barrel. Jem worked the chain loose, but before he could examine it, Tean spoke.

"Why does he have a revolver in a filing cabinet?"

"That," Jem said, "is a drop gun."

"A what?"

"A drop gun. It's stolen, or he took it from another criminal, so there's no way to trace it back to him. Special Agent Jager shoots whoever he wants to shoot, and then he drops that gun next to the guy, gets the victim's prints on it, and presto chango, now it's a justified use of force."

Tean was silent for a long moment. "That's horrifying."

Jem squeezed his shoulder before he remembered the awkward kiss, but Tean didn't react. Then Jem went back to the desk. He took everything out of the drawer before removing it to check the underside.

He was so focused on his search that he noticed the movement in the hallway too late. The door flew open, and Jager was there, his thin, dark hair messier than ever, the stubble on his face thicker than Jem remembered, verging on a genuine beard. He came into the room with two hard strides and kicked Jem in the head.

The world shattered into white. Jem would have fallen, but he slumped against the desk, and it kept him upright. The hissing white static in his vision cleared slowly. The side of his head, his cheek, and his neck was warm and wet. Tean was saying something, and it must have been important because he sounded furious. Jem tried to focus on the words. Was it about the kiss? Was Tean really that angry about the kiss?

Then a hand grabbed Jem by the hair, hauling him up. Jem moved with the hand, scrambling to support himself against the pain in his scalp, and then something sharp and cold settled against his neck.

"Since when do cops carry knives?" Jem mumbled.

"Jem," Tean said, "are you ok?" Jem was still trying to focus his eyes, but he knew he wasn't seeing right because Tean was holding a gun. "Let him go and get the fuck out of our way."

Jem tried to remind him about the swear jar, but whoever was clutching his hair—Jager—gave a vicious jerk, and Jem let out a moan.

"Let him go! I'll do it. I swear to God I'll do it."

"Nice try, buddy," Jager said, sounding almost amused. "You've got three things going against you, though. First, you're a fag. Second, you've had plenty of time to do it already, and if you haven't done it by now, you're not gonna do it." Jager yanked on Jem's hair again. "Come on. We're going for a ride, the three of us."

"I'll put a bullet right through your head."

"Jesus, buddy, even for a cocksucker you're stupid. The third thing, and this is a big one: gun's not loaded. Now come on. We'll do this nice and easy and fast."

The gun bucked in Tean's hand. The muzzle flash made Jem squint, and then the clap of the gunshot deafened him. The bullet missed—or maybe Tean had intended to shoot the wall. Jem felt the knife at his throat, a tugging heat where it cut, and then he was free.

He turned to face Jager, hand diving into his pocket, and he pulled out the barrette with its sharpened clip. He stabbed Jager twice in the belly before the other man could react, and then he grabbed Jager's wrist and beat his hand against the doorjamb, once, twice. Jager dropped the knife, and Jem kicked it under the desk.

"Tean, come on," Jem shouted, shoving Jager down onto the linoleum.

Tean stumbled after him. He was still carrying the revolver. In his haste, he caught the desk drawer with his leg, and he stumbled and hopped around it. Jager was trying to get his gun free from its holster; blood made dark patches on his BLM polo.

"Come on, come on, come on," Jem shouted.

As soon as Tean reached him, Jem grabbed his arm and dragged him toward the exit. Jem waited for the shot. He saw Jager's hand on the gun, struggling with the holster snap.

Then they plunged out into the cold, the night, the desert, the smell of gasoline and motor oil, the sound of the poplars as a breeze kicked up. They ran.

21

Tean drove down Moab's main street at ten under the speed limit, vaguely aware of cars and trucks whipping past in the opposite direction. The intensity of the artificial lighting was blinding, and he was shaking so hard that he had to white-knuckle the steering wheel with one hand to keep from falling apart. Jem touched his arm, and he flinched and made a noise.

"I'm going to take this," Jem said quietly, his fingers warm where they wrapped around Tean's hand, slowly loosening his grip on the revolver. The blood on the side of his face looked black. "That's it, just let me take it. You did so good. You did amazing. But I need you to let go now. You can just let go and relax." Tean's fingers spasmed and released, and Jem slid the gun free. "That was so good. You're doing really wonderfully. Pull into that gas station."

"I'm fine," Tean mumbled, but he eased into the Maverik's lot, where they floated in a cloud of sodium light. He stopped the truck and put his hands over his eyes. When Jem pulled him into a hug, he didn't fight it, and after a while, he stopped shaking.

Then, tapping Jem's arm, he wiped his face and said, "I can't believe I fell apart like that. I'm sorry. I've—I've been in situations like that. The canyon with Ruth. The trailer, when Phil attacked us. That abandoned building with Leroy. I'm sorry. I'm sorry. I'm—"

Jem cupped his face. "How about you stop for just a second? Don't say anything. Practice your usual Tean form of communication." A smile softened the words.

Tean nodded. The heat of Jem's hand on his face. The smell of his hand, of whatever soap he'd used last, of his skin. He closed his eyes and saw Jem slumped against the desk, saw blood running down his face, saw himself as though he were standing outside his body, saw himself like a statue, the gun pointed at Jager, doing nothing as Jager grabbed Jem and put a knife to his throat.

"I froze," Tean whispered.

"It's ok. I know how you feel about guns and killing. You were in a terrible situation."

Tean shook his head.

"It's ok," Jem repeated. "You got us out of there. Focus on that; that's what matters."

Tean couldn't find the words, but what he wanted to say, what he needed to say, was that Jem had it all backwards. Tean wasn't shaking because he was scared. He wasn't in shock. He didn't need reassurances or comfort, although he couldn't pull away from Jem's touch. Looking down the barrel at Jager, he hadn't felt the wavering sickness that he remembered from his one and only time turkey hunting with his grandfather. He hadn't felt anything but the desire to kill this man who had hurt Jem. To murder him. And the feeling was still burning its way through him, scaring Tean with how much it made him want to hurt another living creature.

"Enough," Jem said, patting Tean's cheek. "Wherever you've gone, get back here with me."

Exhaling again, Tean nodded. When he looked over, he said, "You're bleeding."

"I'm fine."

"No, you're not. Look in the mirror."

"Oh. Damn. I liked this shirt."

Tean got out of the truck, retrieved his gear bag, and came around to the passenger side. He opened Jem's door. The sodium lights flooding the gas station's pad made it easy for Tean to examine Jem, although Jem whined and squirmed and batted at Tean's hands.

Clicking off the penlight, Tean said, "I don't think you have a concussion, but you need a doctor—"

"You're a doctor."

"—a doctor for people to make sure."

"Pass."

"No, no passing, not with that cut on your neck and that laceration on your head. Jeez, that guy must have been wearing steel-toed boots. We're lucky he didn't kick you any harder."

"It felt plenty hard."

"I'll look up a hospital—"

"I said pass."

"No.

"You can't tell me no." A smirk pulled at one side of Jem's mouth. "My body, my choice."

"I'm deciding this. I'm the one who's worried about you. I'm the one who—who had to watch something horrible happen to you. I'm the one who can't sleep at night because I don't know where you are or if you've got a roof or if you're safe or if I'm going to see you again, and I am sick as fuck of feeling like this all the time. And shooting that gun made me feel very macho, so I'm yelling, but it's starting to wear off and I'm a little embarrassed, but I'm not backing down."

Jem's face was blank. "I'm not going to a hospital or a doctor-in-a-box or whatever you—"

"Stop talking."

"Don't—"

"I said stop."

Red spots bloomed in Jem's cheeks, and he clenched his jaw. Tean ignored the death look. He made Jem move around to sit on the truck's tailgate, where the light was better. Then he opened the gear bag again, taking out antiseptic wipes. He cleaned the cut on Jem's neck first, and then he administered lidocaine, grabbing Jem's head when Jem winced and tried to pull away.

"Don't move," Tean snapped. "I need both hands for this next part, and I don't want you walking around with crooked stitching on your throat."

"Like Frankenstein's monster."

"I said stop talking." Tean did the sutures carefully, taking his time with the needle and forceps. Cars roared past the gas station lot, but Tean had parked far enough back that they didn't have to worry about the dust. A Dodge Ram pulled up to the pumps, its lights sweeping across Jem and Tean, picking out the copper and red and even a few strands of silver in Jem's beard. Jem was very pale and, Tean noticed now, shaking.

"Does it hurt? The lidocaine should have helped."

"No." The word was tiny and whispered.

"Are you scared of needles?"

"No."

"Then what?"

Jem's gaze was fixed over Tean's shoulder, his lips white with pressure.

"There," Tean said, snipping the excess thread on the last suture. He dressed the wound. "I'm going to do the laceration now." He waited for the argument, watching the tremors in Jem's hands.

But Jem just gave a jerky nod.

Tean repeated the process; Jager's boot had torn open the skin on the side of Jem's head, and the wound was ugly and wide but not deep. Tean did the best he could and dressed the wound. He disposed of the waste in a biohazard bag, cleaned the suturing kit as best he could—although everything needed to be sterilized—and packed the gear bag again. Jem was still sitting on the tailgate, so Tean helped him stand and walked him around to the passenger seat, where he offered a clean—albeit plain—t-shirt that he kept in the truck for field work.

"How's the pain?"

Jem shook his head once as he stripped out of his bloody tee.

"Are you angry at me?"

Another shake of his head.

"I shouldn't have yelled at you, and I shouldn't have forced you to let me treat those wounds. I'm sorry. I was feeling really overwhelmed. I took it out on you because I didn't want to feel powerless anymore."

"I liked it," Jem said, tugging on the clean shirt. He rested his head on the seat, a smile flitting across his face. "You should do that whole yell-at-me, take-charge thing more often. Very butch. I'm just mad you wouldn't give me a Frankenstein scar."

"Jem—"

"I need a minute."

The smell of diesel exhaust floated past Tean. He counted to sixty, but Jem had his eyes closed.

When Jem spoke, his voice was flat, as though he had ratcheted it down as tightly as he could. "It's hard for me. Scary."

After a moment, Tean asked, "What?"

"All of it." His eyes squeezed even more tightly shut. "Not being able to do it myself."

Tean thought, for a moment, what Jem's childhood must have been like: an ever-shrinking circle of the things he could control; the fear and helplessness as he was uprooted and passed from home to home again and again. The gesture came out of nowhere: a lock of hair had fallen out of Jem's part, and Tean brushed it into place. He yanked his hand back when he realized what he'd done. Jem's eyes opened to slits.

"You don't have to do everything yourself," Tean said. "You can let other people help sometimes."

Jem's smile was hard and lopsided. Behind Tean, the bell on the Maverik convenience store jangled. Teenage voices carried, bouncing off the cement pad, just laughter and strings of swear words.

"Time to go," Jem said quietly.

So they left.

As Tean merged into traffic, he said, "I'll get you your own room at the lodge so Scipio won't bother you."

"I honestly don't know if it's safe to go back to the lodge. We should probably get Scipio and go."

"You don't think—Jager wouldn't—" But both times, the sentences caught in Tean's throat.

"He's dirty," Jem said. "The knife is a dead giveaway; a cop ever pulls a knife on you, you know something is fucked up. He was going to kill both of us tonight, Tean. He was going to drag us out to the middle of nowhere and cut our throats, and honestly, he could probably do it so nobody would ever find us."

Tean nodded. "That's . . . that's a very good point. But why would he help Tanner fake his own death?"

"I don't know."

"Do you think maybe it's a mix-up?"

"The way he acted made it seem more serious than a misunderstanding."

"No, that's not what I meant. Jager obviously has something he's willing to hide, and he's willing to kill to hide it. But maybe it's unrelated to whatever happened with Blake and Tanner and Antonio."

"No way."

"I know that logically it makes more sense for everything to be connected, but the world isn't necessarily logical. It's entirely possible we stumbled onto two separate things."

"Nope. First, because Jager acted so fucking weird that night at the canyon."

"That could have been—"

"And second, because he had Blake's necklace wrapped around that drop gun." Jem motioned, and Tean pulled the chain out of his pocket and passed it over. Jem let it dangle from his fingers, silver glittering in the ebb and flow of headlights. "This is Blake's. Why the hell does he have Blake's necklace? And why keep it at his office?"

"It's a silver cross. A lot of people—"

"Blake wore this in Decker. It's his; I know it's his. And it has his initials on the back. BB."

They turned on US-128. On the left, the Colorado was a black snake, glittering under cliffs of red sandstone, their tops lost in darkness. On their right, the headlights picked out ephedra and bitterbrush, a tumbleweed rocking where it was caught on sharp yucca leaves, the dart and flutter of small black shapes. Bats, Tean guessed, dining on the insects along the river.

"We need to call Ammon."

Jem sighed.

"I know you don't like him—"

"Fuck that. You know I hate him, but that's not the point. He's a cop."

"And?"

"And cops protect cops."

"Jager isn't—"

"You know what I mean. First, Ammon's going to ask if we're sure, absolutely sure, about what happened. Then he's going to try to convince us that it was a misunderstanding. Then he's going to suggest there's another explanation. And then, if we somehow muck our way through all his bullshit, he's going to tell us that he can't help us because we've got illegally obtained evidence and it's worthless. That's how the system works, Tean. The guys like Ammon, they've got the whole thing rigged."

"That's not fair to Ammon. It's not his fault that the court systems have evolved laws on evidence. And this isn't even about Ammon; this is about Jager."

"Same fucking difference," Jem muttered.

"You don't have to like him, although it would sure make my life a hell of a lot easier, but I'm not going to just sit here and listen while you claim he's part of some batshit brotherhood-of-cops conspiracy."

The air whipping through the windows filled the space between them.

"Keep it up," Jem finally said.

"I will keep it up!" Tean swallowed and slid his hands along the steering wheel. "Keep what up?"

"Keep filling up our swear jar, please. I'd like to go to Disney World this year. And I'm not saying there's a conspiracy. I'm just telling you, that's the system."

Tean opened his mouth.

"Call him," Jem said. "See for yourself."

Placing the call, Tean said, "You stay out of this. Don't bait him."

Jem crossed his heart.

On the eighth ring, Ammon answered. "Sweetheart, I'm sorry—"

"Sweetheart," Jem said.

Tean flashed him a look.

"—but I'm still trying to work out this nightmare. We've been going all day, and honestly, I don't think we've resolved anything. Can I call you when I'm going to the lodge? I'd like to see you tonight before I go to bed."

"Excuse me?" Jem said.

Tean shushed him. Viciously. Into the phone, he said, "Something happened, and you need to know about it." Then he told him about Kalista, Nick, and Jager.

As Tean talked, Ammon's breathing changed: short, clipped, rapid. When Tean finished, Ammon said, "Are you the stupidest fucking man alive? Are you? Answer that question, please, because I need to know so I can decide exactly how the fuck I'm supposed to handle you."

"Well?" Jem whispered. "Are you?"

Tean let go of the wheel long enough to pinch Jem's leg, and Jem howled. Over Jem's cry, Tean said, "I know you're upset—"

"You don't know the first goddamn thing, Tean. That's the whole problem. When I get done here, you and I are going to have a talk. A very long talk. And I'm going to explain things to you so that you understand perfectly fucking clearly why this is never going to happen again."

"Don't talk to me like that," Tean said.

"How am I supposed to talk to you when you won't listen to me when I talk any other way?"

"I'm calling to tell you about a dirty cop, and you want to lecture me on—"

After a deep breath, Ammon sounded slightly more in control. Or slightly less insane with rage. "Give me a break. This is more of the Hardy Boys bullshit that Jem is always dragging you into. Jager's not dirty; he's been in that field office for fifteen years, and nobody's ever had a problem with him. You were going through his stuff; he probably thought he was being robbed. This sounds like a really awful misunderstanding, but that's not the same thing as a dirty cop."

Jem had the decency to stare out the window so Tean didn't have to watch him gloat, and Tean was surprised to find his face hot, his eyes stinging, as the conversation unrolled exactly the way Jem had predicted.

"It doesn't matter," Ammon finally said. "You broke in there. You let Jem talk you into this dumbshit move—"

"It was my idea."

"That's even worse! And because you did, now what might be a key piece of evidence is absolutely worthless in court."

"You wouldn't have found it anyway. You weren't even looking at Jager."

"This isn't about me. This is about you taking stupid risks, putting yourself in danger, all to impress Jem because he's a bad boy and you've still got a crush on him."

"I'm not having this conversation with you again."

"It's juvenile, Tean. Grow up. He's irresponsible, he's dangerous, and he's going to get you hurt. Whatever fetish you've got—"

Tean disconnected the call. And then, breathing heavily, he hurled the phone onto the dash. It made a cracking noise when it struck the windshield, and then it slid to the other side of the cab, where Jem caught it before it could fall to the floor. Tean barely noticed. He focused all his attention on the circles carved out by the headlights. Grama grew in straggly clumps along the shoulder of the road. Curlicues of tamarisk spilled inky-black over the stars reflected in the Colorado. Stunted willows etched the river like glass. He put his head out the window and smelled red-rock dust, mud, juniper.

"Leather," Jem said.

For almost a full minute, Tean struggled not to respond. Then he said, "What?"

"It's a leather fetish. You want me in leather boots, a leather codpiece, leather nipple, um, pasties, leather collar, leather hat. Because I'm a bad boy. And you've got a hard-on for bad boys."

"Do you have any idea how awful leather is?" Tean said. "I'm not just talking about the animals that are slaughtered to manufacture it. I'm talking about the environmental impact."

"I don't," Jem said, "but I think you should tell me. In fact, I think you should yell at me about leather all the way back to the lodge."

"We're not going back to the lodge." Tean dropped his foot on the accelerator, and they shot up US-128. "We're going to Onion Creek. We're going to look at where the stampede happened because the whole thing was wrong, and I should have noticed it earlier."

"Please tell me you're doing this to spite Ammon."

"Of course not. I'm doing this because two people have been killed and they deserve justice."

Jem nodded.

"Spiting Ammon is just this incredibly fucking satisfying extra."

"Swear jar."

"Don't get me off topic. The first problem with the leather industry is chromium-saturated wastewater."

"You realize I was just saying that stuff about yelling about leather to help you feel better."

"I don't care. You have to listen, so be quiet." Tean took a deep breath. "But toxic runoff and contaminated waterways are the obvious problem."

"Of course. Obvious."

"Very few people consider the environmental damage that is a precondition to leather production."

"But you do."

"Deforestation, for example."

Tean got so caught up in the explanation that he forgot about Ammon. He barely noticed when Jem leaned over to push his glasses back into place, but he didn't miss—couldn't miss—when Jem rested a hand on his nape, the touch warm and strong and solid.

22

Onion Creek came out of the sandstone bluffs, a silver scribble running down to the Colorado. The starry sky showed the silhouette of rimrock: a ring of larger formations—the Towers to the north, the Titan farther east, Fisher Mesa to the south—but also pinnacles, hoodoos, balanced stones like goblin heads. At night, with the weak light giving just enough clarity to make out those shapes, the valley—with its improbable name of Richardson Amphitheater—was a surreal place, a wax world twisted into nightmarish shapes. When Tean got out of the truck, a coyote was howling.

"God, this place is a fucking trip," Jem said. "Next time, I get to pick where we go on our bromance date."

"This isn't a date."

"Anything's a date if it's two people who want to pork."

"Excuse me?"

"Or if they just want to be super best friends," Jem added hurriedly.

Tean grabbed his gear bag, two high-powered flashlights, and several disposable gloves. He also grabbed bottled water.

"We need to get you a daypack," Tean said, handing Jem one of the bottles of water.

"I'll carry your bag."

"No, it's fine."

But Jem was already pulling it off Tean and slinging it over his own shoulder. "You've had a bad night. And I've made it worse. Let me do something nice for you."

"Oh. Thanks. Although you were the one who got kicked in the head."

"But I have a very thick skull. Besides, I want to dig through your bag and steal any good meds." Jem flashed a huge smile, the real one that showed his crooked front teeth. "Kidding."

"Not funny."

"Too soon?"

"Not funny on general principle."

They left the Ford on the BLM road, scrambling down the rocky shoulder until they reached the flat pan of the valley. Tufts of panic grass whispered against Tean's khakis; when Jem's leg caught on a Russian thistle, the crackle of dry vegetation exploded in the valley's stillness. The sound echoed back, somehow even louder, and the name amphitheater no longer seemed quite as silly.

"What about snakes?"

"What about them?"

Jem kicked a chunk of rock off into a shadowy clump of sage; something darted out—a kangaroo rat, or maybe a packrat—and Jem jumped.

Catching Jem's arm, Tean steadied him and fought a smile.

"Do not laugh."

"Never." Tean cleared his throat. "As the desert gets cooler at night, most of the snakes become less active."

"Less? Less isn't the same as 'dead and will never move or rattle or bite me again.'"

"Well, very few of them are active by day during the summer, and their activity level at night depends on the temperature, how quickly they can feed, that kind of thing."

"So I'm supposed to hope that these snakes have full tummies and they won't bother me?"

"Well, mostly you're supposed to pay attention, look, listen, and stop moving if you spot one. They don't want to have anything to do with you."

Jem mumbled something, and the words *snake* and *my dick* were the only part Tean could make out. Tean laughed quietly and released his arm.

"I didn't say let go," Jem growled.

When Tean took his arm again, Jem moved closer, a whiff of antiseptic floating with him. He remembered Jem's pallor, the way he shook when Tean touched him. Another broken place. Another door that Jem had nailed shut because it hurt too much to open—even though life had a way of opening those doors again and again.

They found the slot canyon easily, and Tean scowled as he played the flashlight back and forth. "Those morons ruined the scene."

"Almost like they meant to," Jem said.

Tean frowned.

"I'm not saying they did," Jem said. "But if they didn't, they ought to hand in their badges and start setting pins at a bowling alley." Adjusting the weight of the gear bag, he said, "What did you mean, this was all wrong?"

"Two things," Tean said. "The first thing I should have realized—the first thing anybody should have realized—is that a herd of horses is unlikely to stampede into a narrow space like a slot canyon. They stampede because they're in a panic, and panicked animals are trying to get away from whatever they perceive as a threat. A lot of stampedes do happen at night, and the causes can seem insignificant—something as trivial as a tumbleweed can get a herd panicked and running. But stampeding animals wouldn't ordinarily choose to run into a cramped space."

"So somebody forced them up the canyon."

"I think so. Cowboys can turn stampedes—they'll do it to keep a herd from running straight into a river, for example, or off a cliff. And some Native Americans tribes would steer buffalo stampedes off of buffalo jumps, so they could harvest the animals after they fell to their death."

"How do they do it?"

"Well, now they typically use a loud noise. Pistols are still common. The key is to turn the leaders of the stampede; the rest of the herd will follow."

"So," Jem said, "if they could force the leaders of the stampede into the mouth of the canyon, the rest of the herd would go too."

"In theory."

Jem seemed to think about this for a moment. "It sounds dangerous."

"It is. I mean, you're either on a horse or, in some cases, on an ATV. You're trying to direct a terrified animal that's capable of crushing you, and another fifty or hundred other animals—more, in a lot of cases—right behind it."

"So we're talking about someone who knows what he's doing."

"I think so."

"It wasn't Tanner, then. Not that part"

"No, I don't think so either."

Jem's blond eyebrows arched. "Why do you say that?"

"Because this required two people. What was your reason?"

"Because I knew him, and he was a massive tool who didn't like animals." Jem scanned the valley and the slot canyon again. "Two people. One to start the stampede and keep them moving this direction, and another to turn them into the canyon."

"Minimum. A larger team would be ideal, but when you're covering up a murder and faking a death, you probably want to reduce the number of people involved."

"Jager."

"We don't know that."

Those blond eyebrows went up again.

Tean sighed. "Yes, probably Jager. He's worked for the BLM for decades. Even if he's only an indifferent rider, with all that experience, he'd probably be able to manage something like this."

"But they weren't just firing into the air to scare the horses. They were shooting them."

Tean nodded.

"That was Tanner," Jem said. "The sick little fuck would have gotten off on something like that."

"So we're back to the same question: why would Jager help Tanner?"

"Greed or fear." Jem glanced around again, his gaze moving more slowly as he panned the flashlight. "God, you weren't kidding. It looks like they had a tractor pull out here. There's no way we're going to be able to find anything, not after they trampled everything."

"Actually, that was the second thing."

"What?"

Tean cleared his throat. "Well, the stampede obviously started somewhere else. That's the other thing I should have realized. We need to see where it got started."

"How do you know this kind of stuff?"

"How do you know that saying Reagonomics and proto-receipts and who knows what else will convince someone to give you info about credit card transactions?"

His grin was incandescent. "Because I'm a scumbag. You, on the other hand, are brilliant."

"I've just spent a lot of time reading things most people don't read."

Jem's eyes were fixed on him, so intense even by moonlight that Tean had to look away.

Tean cleared his throat and said, "It'll be more difficult at night, but I think it's worth a shot."

"And you're easy on the eyes. Have I mentioned that?"

"From here on out, we need to be quiet so we don't startle any animals."

Tean started away from the canyon, his steps tracing a half-circle as he covered the ground near the red-rock cliffs. Jem kept pace, the gear bag making a soft thunking noise against his hip. The smell of Onion Creek blew toward them from farther up the valley: mud, and a note of heavy-metal bitterness that Tean didn't miss.

"You might be the gentlest person I've ever met," Jem said, his voice barely louder than their steps scuffing across the alkali hardpan. "I don't want you to think I don't trust you. It's not about you; my brain knows I can count on you. Let you help me. It's just hard. I don't know how to say it. It's—it's terrifying, actually."

"I shot a door," Tean said. "And one time I clubbed a guy with your dirty sock. I'm not that gentle."

"It was a clean sock. And that door had it coming." Jem let out a breath slowly. "I didn't say thank you. That's what I'm trying to say. And I'm sorry."

Tean shrugged. "What is a casual acquaintance for?"

"Platonic soulmate, you mean."

"The relationship equivalent of two mismatched socks tumbling together in a dryer."

"Did you know you've got a cute butt?"

Stumbling, Tean would have fallen except Jem caught his arm. "Now would be a good time for those ball gags I saw you researching on your phone."

Jem's face darkened, the change visible even in the weak light. "I was—that was—" He coughed, spat, and said, "A friend asked me, you know, to give my opinion." Then he leveled a finger at Tean. "And I just want you to admit one good thing about yourself. Say, 'I have a perky butt.' Say it."

"Jem—"

"No, I want to hear you say it. 'I, Teanemic Mahogany Leon, have a butt as perky as cherries jubilee.' Or say you're smart. Or you're kind. Or you're funny, but like a black hole."

"Jem—"

"Say it, or we're going to have a fight. A real one."

"Jem, in the first place, I have absolutely no idea what you're talking about. More importantly, the stampede came this way." He gestured at the hundred-yard span ahead of them, where brush and scrub had been trampled and broken. "Come on."

They followed the trail of destruction. It crossed a shallow wash of sand and loose rocks, and it ended at a narrow stream. Tean played his flashlight over the churned mud and the accumulation of tracks.

"They came here to drink. See how some of the tracks are baked into the ground? This was a place they visited frequently. This is where they were startled into a stampede."

"Is that Onion Creek?" Jem asked.

Tean shook his head. "Onion Creek isn't potable. Too many toxic things leach into the water from deposits in the ground. Arsenic and sulfur, I think, although I might be remembering that wrong. This is a tributary, and it must be clean enough that the horses are willing to drink from it."

"He was here. Tanner, I mean."

"I think so. Close enough to see the herd, definitely."

"No, look: tire tracks."

Tean raked the light at an oblique angle. Near the stream's bank, where the soil was soft, a tire had left clear impressions. Jem took several pictures.

"Let's see what else the fucker left," Jem said.

They stuck together for the search; Jem groused whenever Tean let go of his arm, and Tean didn't mind working a spiral pattern together. It didn't take long before Jem called out and pointed to a flash of brass. A rifle casing. Jem photographed it, and they moved on. They found another. And then another. And then they found a cigarette butt, the white paper glowing when the flashlight's beam skimmed across it.

"Careless," Tean said.

"Or intentional," Jem said.

Tean moved back toward the stream, trying to gauge if Tanner—or whoever the shooter was—had gotten any closer to the herd while firing. Jem, with a strange look on his face, moved off into the darkness, his flashlight bobbing from side to side. His disappearance barely registered until he called Tean's name, his voice sharp.

Tean picked a path through the scrub in the direction of Jem's call. He stopped when he smelled putrefaction, and then he hurried.

Jem was standing at the lip of a ravine, where the ground dropped away into darkness. At the edge of the flashlight's reach lay a dead man, his body bloated, the skin split and slipping. A white man with dark hair.

"Is that—"

"Blake. That's Blake." Rage choked the words. "So who the fuck did we find back in that canyon?"

23

"Either you get in your truck," Ammon said, "or you go to jail."

Jem was too tired to care why Chief Nobles, Sheriff McEneany, and Trooper Haggerty didn't want to talk to them again after the first round of interviews. Jem was also too focused on Jager to give the issue much thought. The BLM special agent stood off by himself, just within the ring of floodlights that had been set up to illuminate the scene. The only indication Jager gave of their encounter earlier was the way he carried himself, his posture slightly off, favoring the two stab wounds Jem had delivered with the sharpened tip of the barrette. Jem barely heard what Ammon was saying; his attention was fixed on Jager, willing the agent to try something—anything—again.

"Come on," Tean said, tugging on Jem's sleeve. "Before you start growling."

Jem let Tean lead him back to the truck, and when the doc wasn't looking, he swallowed two more of the pills he'd bought off that trucker. They drove to the lodge, where Scipio, fully rested, decided now was the perfect time to play. They indulged him for as long as they could, letting the Lab run on the lodge's impossibly green grass—mostly, he inspected sticks and marked the trunks of the pinyon pines. The Colorado murmured at the edge of the lodge's electric lighting, and then it spread a blanket of currents and spangled eddies, the stars caught up in deadfalls and bobbing in the riffles. Jem started out of a doze at the touch of Tean's hand, and his first thought was that sometimes people woke from nightmares and spells with a kiss.

"I don't think you've slept in three days. Let's get you to bed."

He came close to sleep. He went to a white-walled place where hands grabbed him, held him, where he'd run and they caught him every time. When Jem jerked up from the pillow, the stitches pulled, and a headache throbbed to life. Scipio was standing on his back, all four paws firmly planted, barking.

"Oh my actual fuck," Jem moaned, pulling the pillow over his head.

"Down," Tean was saying, obviously trying to keep his voice low. "Scipio, down."

Jem tried to roll over, but Scipio was surprisingly heavy, and the Lab didn't have any trouble adjusting his balance to stay directly on top of Jem when Jem shifted.

"Oh my actual ever-fucking fuck."

"I'm sorry," Tean whispered. "Ammon called, and Scipio went crazy."

"Is he part mountain goat?"

"Why would Ammon be part mountain goat?"

Jem packed the pillow down more tightly over his ears.

"Oh," Tean said after a moment. "Scipio. Right."

"Please kill me."

"Go back to sleep. Scipio, down. Right now."

With a whine, Scipio turned in a circle, all four paws finding new pressure points on Jem's back. Something popped ominously, but it felt surprisingly good. Then the dog dropped down, his body stretched out across Jem's. A warm, wet spot formed between Jem's shoulder blades, and then the snoring started.

"He, um, might be asleep."

"Go away. Go back to vet school for twenty years."

This time, Jem drifted, his mind racing while his body tried to crash. When he came back, his neck was wet. He tried to push the dog's head away.

"Oh my God, oh my God, that's my neck! Stop cleaning my neck."

The Lab settled for a long last swipe of his tongue, and then he heaved his weight off Jem and moved to the end of the bed. Jem pulled the pillow from his head and looked around. The room was empty, and Tean's bed was made.

"Where's your dad?" Jem asked the Lab. "Did he go off to find his daddy?"

Scipio answered with a languorous stretch, inviting Jem to scratch his belly. After a moment, Jem obliged. The bathroom door opened, and Tean stepped out, naked except for a white towel wrapped around his waist. Jem didn't move except for the slow, lazy stroke of his hand over Scipio's flank.

What did Tean see when he looked in the mirror? Jem wasn't sure. Not reality, that was obvious. Too many years of Ammon, too many years of bad first dates, too many years of his family. Maybe it went deeper. Jem considered the doc. Wiry dark hair in a stripe down the center of his brown chest. The taut lines of his hips, his ribs, his throat. He still hadn't seen Jem yet, his attention fixed on the bundle of dirty clothes that he'd dropped when he came out of the bathroom. He stooped to pick them up, twisting at the torso, exposing the long, lean curve of his spine. Second grade was hazy for Jem, but he remembered they'd written Valentine's poems—dedicated to their moms, of course. *I think you're pretty like a book.* Jem had forgotten the rest of it.

"Oh," Tean said, red flooding his face. "I'm sorry, I thought you were still asleep."

"I don't mind."

Tean blushed harder, grabbing clean clothes and heading back into the bathroom. When he emerged again, he was dressed, his hair sticking up in wild clumps.

Jem patted the bed. "Either Scipio gets to fix your hair, or I do."

"I choose Scipio."

"Don't you fucking dare. Grab the pomade and a comb from my bag."

"Twenty-seven combs to choose from. How will I ever decide?"

Tean was so pleased with that joke that he was still smiling when he came over with a comb and the pomade, and that meant Jem was smiling too. To Jem's surprise, Tean sat on the floor, his back against the bed. Jem moved to sit with his legs straddling the doc. He ran his fingers through wet hair. Then he warmed a small bit of pomade between his hands and worked it through the dark strands. He took the comb next. Rigid at first, Tean relaxed by degrees until his cheek rested against Jem's knee.

"You're really good at this. Have you ever thought about being a barber?"

"Still trying to fix my life?" Jem kept his voice light as he teased out a snarl with the comb.

"No. Trying to find a way to keep you in mine."

Jem had absolutely no idea what to say to that, no idea how to tease out that snarl of a statement, so he worked in silence for a few minutes.

"You should let me fix your hair before you go on dates," Jem said. "You're a sex machine no matter what, but the hair would be a nice touch."

The silence that followed was even longer, and when it broke, Tean's voice was so quiet Jem had to lean forward to hear him.

"Jem, what am I supposed to do to help you?"

"What do you mean?"

"I don't know. You were making noises last night, and I was going to check on you, but Scipio beat me to it. It—it scared me, how you sounded."

"I'm fine." He ran the comb through Tean's hair one last time and squeezed his shoulder. "You're all set."

"I really don't think you are fine. I want to help—"

"What did Ammon call about?"

The silence was a rebuke that made Jem's face heat, but he didn't back down. After a moment, Tean answered, "He told us not to leave the lodge until we hear from him again."

"I think you and Scipio should go home."

"You're kidding."

"No. You've got work tomorrow, and anyway, this is dangerous. Tanner has killed three people now. It's time for you to go home. I'll be back in Salt Lake in a day or two."

"You don't have a car."

"I'll figure something out."

"You want to stay here so you can kill Tanner."

"I want to find him because he's a murderer, and he ought to pay for that."

Tean still rested against Jem's knee, his body warm where it pressed up to Jem's. "You want to be the one to make him pay, though."

"I don't know what you want me to say," Jem said. "You don't like lying." Jem traced the line of Tean's neck. "Go home. Tonight. Scipio is sick of this hotel room; he told me."

Through the window came the sound of outraged shrieks, a boy's laughter, a man bellowing, "Lincoln, give your sister back her tampon!"

"No," Tean said.

"She might need it," Jem said.

"I'm not going back. I've got plenty of personal time, and we'll figure out something better for Scipio. I bet they've got doggie daycare around here." His voice steadied. "I'm not leaving until you're ready to go."

"That means a lot to me. Nobody in my whole life would do that for me except you. And Tinajas, I guess, but she'd bitch about it so much that I'd rather do it on my own. But you're going home tonight. That's what's safe."

"No."

"You're going—"

"Don't say it again," Tean said. Quiet. Firm. Even. Jem had heard him use that voice when he'd talked to the foal caught in the juniper.

"You realize this was actually easier when I just lied to you all the time and slurped your bone—ah! Jesus Christ, how the hell did you learn how to do that? You actually broke my leg." Jem massaged his thigh, where Tean had driven his knuckle into a nerve, the whole leg gone to pins and needles.

"I've got four brothers, dummy." Tean stood, pushing his glasses back into place. "Now, tell me what we're going to do about Blake?"

"Well, not much, considering he's dead."

"Our initial theory doesn't make sense anymore. We'd assumed that Tanner had killed Andi, come back to Moab, and faked his own death by murdering Blake and disfiguring the remains. Now, it's easy to see why there are some problems with that theory. First, we found Blake, and he's definitely dead, but he's not the one Tanner left in the canyon."

"So who is? That's what I don't get. According to Ammon, they don't have any tourists missing. Nobody local has disappeared. We don't have any candidates for our third dead guy."

"Either there's nobody to report him missing—he was traveling alone, for example—or nobody's noticed he's missing. In that case, he could be a local, a loner without a network of people who would quickly notice his absence. Or he's here because of Tanner, Blake, and

Antonio. That seems to be the best option, but we haven't had any signs that a fourth person was involved."

Jem shook his head. "I honestly have no idea. It could be any of those things. It could be something totally obvious that we're overlooking."

Tean's phone buzzed; he pulled it out of his pocket and made a face.

"Ammon?"

Dismissing the call, Tean said, "Timmy. Apparently, brother number three got tapped this time to try to emotionally blackmail me into a fun weekend."

"I really wish you could hear yourself sometimes."

"I hear myself perfectly fine." The phone buzzed again, and Tean looked like he might dismiss the call again. Then his face changed.

"Ah," Jem said. "This time it's Ammon."

"What does that mean?"

"Glasses," Jem said.

Tean caught them as they slid off his nose. He answered the call, putting the phone to his ear, and angled his body away from Jem.

Scipio sat up at the sound of the voice on the other end of the call. His body vibrated with a growl that was barely audible.

"You and me both," Jem murmured.

With a harumphing noise, Scipio flopped onto his side, kicking at the blankets until he had satisfied some hidden doggy need.

"I hear what you're saying. I'm trying to validate what you're saying. Yes, I'm telling you that I hear you. Ammon, I'm really trying to understand where you're coming from, but if I have to say the words 'I hear what you're saying' one more time, and you don't listen to me when I say them, I'm going to throw my phone into the Colorado." A long silence. "Yes. I understood you the first three times. I don't—" Tean cut off, pulled the phone away, and stared at it. "He hung up."

"Did he want to know how to do a wash and set?"

"He kept saying 'Don't use this as an excuse to get into any more trouble.' I don't know why he suddenly felt the need to call me and say that. He delivered the same message about fifty times last night and again this morning." The phone buzzed again almost immediately, and Tean glanced at it. "Unknown number."

Jem's phone buzzed at the same time. He didn't recognize the number on the screen. They answered at the same time.

"Son." Jem recognized McEneany's chipmunk voice. "This is the sheriff speaking. I want to make it perfectly clear that your vacation in Grand County is at an end. I want you and your friend out of here so fast your feet don't have time to touch the ground. Understand?"

"Got it."

"Don't make this anything more than it has to be, son."

This kid, Jem thought. This kid who wasn't even old enough to shave. But what he said was, "Abso-tutely."

McEneany disconnected with a grunt that was probably supposed to be masculine.

On the other bed, Tean was saying, "I understand, Chief. Yes, we'll leave right away." When he put down the phone, he said, "Nobles."

Something prickled in Jem's gut. He glanced over, surprised to see that it was barely nine o'clock. "Something happened. Everybody wants us to leave because something happened."

"What?"

"Something else happened. That's why they're all freaking out." Jem opened his phone's browser and felt the familiar wave of helplessness threaten to capsize him. "You do it. Look for what happened."

"No. You can do it."

"Tean, this isn't the time for grammar lessons."

"First of all, I would absolutely love to have grammar lessons with you, but that's not the same thing as reading practice."

Whatever the noise was called that Jem was making in his throat, it woke Scipio.

"Ok, ok," Tean said. "I'll look at Salt Lake news. You look at Moab."

It was the first headline, and it wasn't hard for Jem to understand. He recognized the picture: the stucco villa, the cliffs banded in red and orange. HOTEL SHOOTING. "Someone attacked Kalista and Nick. I think, anyway. There was a shooting at their hotel."

"And I think I know who it was," Tean said, turning his phone toward Jem. The headline said MURDER SUSPECT ESCAPES.

Antonio's picture stared back at him.

24

They found an independent doggy daycare; a woman named Martha ran it out of her house. She was middle-aged and wearing a leather corset, her hair electric blue and shorter than Jem's. Her two fat old hounds shuffled around, crooning with delight as they met Scipio. As soon as Scipio was off the harness, he sprinted in circles, teasing the hounds, trying to get them to chase him. The hounds did some more delighted howling, but they seemed content to let Scipio handle the running side of things.

"But what if they're mean to him?" Jem said as they drove away.

"What?"

"What if they bully him?"

Tean blinked several times. "Martha will separate them."

"I didn't raise my goddog to be a coward. If they bully him, Scipio isn't going to roll over."

"That might be literally what he does. He's a cupcake."

"What if they don't play with him? What if they don't include him in their doggy games?"

"I'm sorry, I need you to help me out. What is going on right now?"

"Jesus fucking Christ, Tean. You are the worst dog dad I have ever met."

After that, they drove past the Tafone, with its crumbling stucco and its red-tile roof. A Grand County Sheriff's Department jeep was parked across the access road leading back to the villas, so Jem motioned for Tean to keep driving. A quarter-mile down the highway, they flipped around and came back. Jem squinted, trying to make out the villa where Kalista and Nick had been staying. If anything was happening back there, he couldn't tell.

"What the fuck was Antonio doing?"

"That's one good question," Tean said, eyes fixed on the road as they headed back toward Moab. "A couple more are: how did he escape, and why did he come here?"

"He came here for Tanner. He wants revenge. Easy peasy, baby."

"Please don't call me baby. And I'm not sure it's that simple; he might want the drugs."

Jem opened his mouth to say something, but his phone vibrated. He pulled it out and saw Brigitte's name on the screen. Mommy Dearest's message was a reminder about the Pioneer Day party. *Can't wait for you to meet your brother and sister. Gerald is looking forward to getting to know you too.*

After clearing his throat, Jem said, "Let's try Jager while we wait for the Keystone Kops to clear out."

"Who was that?"

"My sex guru. He's worried I'm not having enough level-ten cosmic orgasms."

Tean muttered something that sounded like *dry spell*.

"What was that?"

"I said do you want to go back to the BLM building? Because I'm not ready for that. And honestly, I'm not sure you are either."

"No," Jem said. "If there was anything left there, Jager would have moved it. I'd really like to go through his jeep and his house."

Ahead on the left, a red, board-and-batten shed was painted with the words WICKED BREW. Jem pointed at it. Tean shook his head and kept driving.

"Where are you going?"

"To get you something real to eat while we figure out where he lives."

"Just park and let's do this."

"Jem, you pushed the eggs around your plate for half an hour this morning, and when I asked you if you were getting enough protein, you ignored me and chewed on your napkin. I don't know when you last had any decent sleep, and my usual wisp of air that has floated delicately between the leaves of a prickly pear isn't filling me up." Tapping the signal, Tean guided the truck across traffic and into the parking lot of a McDonald's—a reno job, with pale brick and crisp yellow paint, huge plate windows, and a green lawn shady with poplars and cottonwoods. "Please eat one million hash browns so I can stop worrying about you. I'll have half of one. No salt."

Jem stared at Tean as they sat in the drive-thru until the doc shifted in his seat, running his hands along the steering wheel, the soft sound of his thumbs bumping along the ridges of molded plastic filling the car.

"Will you cut it out?" Tean said.

"No. Come here."

"Oh my gosh."

"I'm going to kiss you."

"If you do, you can walk home."

"I'm going to kiss you exactly on the mouth."

"That's Scipio's job."

"Too bad," Jem said, unbuckling himself and climbing up onto the bench. "McDonald's talk always gets me going."

It was fun. It was easy. This, being silly, letting Tean push him away one-handed while laughing, pretending to fight until they both dropped back into their seats. The cab was too hot now with the sun pouring through the glass, even though the A/C was roaring. Sweat gathered under Jem's arms. Tean was still smiling, his cheeks flushed, the glasses crooked. Jem thought about touching his face the way he had last night, the way it fit in the hollow of his hand, and kissing him for real. *I think you're pretty as a book.*

When Tean buzzed down the window, a staticky voice asked for their order.

"A million hash browns," Jem shouted, plucking at his shirt to cool himself. "And one hash brown cut in half, no salt."

He grunted when Tean slapped his stomach. After Tean had placed their more reasonable order and picked it up at the next window, they pulled into a patch of shade. The bark on the poplar in front of the truck had pulled loose in places, waving in stray currents of air, so thin in places it was translucent. The heat hammered at the truck; it shimmered up from the asphalt.

While Jem demolished the breakfast sandwiches, Tean nibbled at a hash brown before sliding most of it back into its paper sleeve. He tapped on his phone. Jem was halfway through the second sandwich—a sausage, egg, and cheese biscuit—when Tean said, "Jager's not in any of the white page sites I've used."

"Anything—"

"I already checked Facebook; he doesn't have an account."

"God, I'm so proud of my morally bankrupt homosexual."

"Please finish chewing before you talk."

"My deviant genius."

Tean made a face and wiped invisible—and probably imaginary—flecks of food from his arm.

"My criminal mastermind."

"Sausage gristle." Tean tapped his own front teeth. "Right here."

"Finish this," Jem said, passing the remains of the sausage biscuit.

"I'm really not—"

"Eat it, and finish the hash brown that you desecrated by asking for no salt, or I'm shaving your head and painting a butt on it."

"You wouldn't."

Jem raised his eyebrows as he pulled out his phone.

After a moment, still watching Jem, Tean took a bite of biscuit. "Who are you calling?"

"Russell."

"Who's Russell?"

"The kid from the lodge." Jem held the phone to his ear.

"Pinyon-Pine Lodge. This is Linda."

"Yes, hi, I'm trying to get in touch with Russell."

"Well, I'm sorry. Russell's not working right now. He's on his video games, I bet."

"I bet I'm talking to Russell's mom," Jem said.

"That's right. And who's this?"

"I don't think you know me; my name's Jem. I'm one of Russell's friends—well, we met at the lodge, and he seems like a good guy. I wanted to invite him to go on a hike with me and my friends."

"Oh. Oh. Well, yes. Russell would absolutely love to do that. Yes, that would be fantastic. He's such a nice young man, but he just has trouble meeting the right kind of friends. They're all online. I think some of them might be foreign."

Jem struggled to keep his eyes from rolling out of his head. "Yes, he is a very nice young man."

"And a little sun would do him a world of good. It's the Vitamin D, you know."

"Yes, some sun would definitely do him some good."

"I'm so glad you hit it off. I think his sense of humor puts people off. He's such a jokester."

"Yes, he does have a very good sense of humor."

"Jim—" Nerves twisted her voice. "Jim, are there going to be any girls on this trip?"

"Well, I don't want to lie to you. But I promise we have a chaperone. Brother Jefferson will be there."

"Uh huh, uh huh, yes, well, I just worry about Russell and girls. He gets his heart smashed into a million pieces by blond girls. I don't know if the poor boy can take it anymore."

"Yes, I will make sure he doesn't get his heart broken by any blond girls." To Tean, he whispered, "Why blond girls?"

Tean scratched fingers through Jem's hair. "Because blonds are evil."

Slapping away Tean's hand, Jem scowled. He pulled down the visor and checked himself in the mirror as Linda said, "I'll get him right now."

"What the hell?" Jem whispered to Tean when the line went quiet. "You're a real jerk."

"I'm a morally bankrupt homosexual."

"Why can't you be the fun kind that just cares about ass play and bonking? Jesus, Tean, now I'm going to walk around all day looking like you and Scipio played beauty parlor with me."

With a tiny smile, Tean reached past Jem to open the glovebox. He held up a sandalwood comb. "Emergency comb. Just like you taught me."

"You're still a jerk," Jem said, snatching the comb.

"Hail Satan," Russell said on the phone.

"Russell, it's Jem."

"Who?"

Jem eyed the part in his hair, trying to repair the damage. "Your buddy from the other night. You wouldn't help me check in for my bachelor party, remember?"

"What the heaven?"

"Is this the part where I'm supposed to ask what that means, and you tell me that because you worship the Dark Lord, you use heaven and angels as swear words?"

After a moment, something scuffed across the mouthpiece on the other end of the call, and Russell mumbled, "We still say fuck too."

"Listen, I need to know where this guy Jager lives. He's local. He works for the BLM. Some sort of special-agent spooge."

"I'm hanging up," Russell said.

"I'll ask your mom to help me set you up on a blind date." Jem drew the comb smoothly through his hair and added, "With a brunette."

"God bless you."

"Thank you. What do you say?"

"I need to think about it."

"Great, stay on the line while you're doing your thinking. My friend wants to talk to you about this absurdist play where everybody is a giant cupcake and they cannibalize each other at the end."

"What in the world are you talking about?" Tean asked.

"No," Russell said, a little too quickly.

"Help me out here, Russell."

"He's got a cabin on BLM land. It's up past Porcupine Rim. That's where he lives."

"What does he drive?"

"He's got a jeep and a truck."

"Keep going."

"It's a BLM jeep; you can't miss it."

"And the truck?"

"A white one. Small. That's all I know."

"Thank you, Russell. Now, are you sure you don't want to go hiking?"

Russell was still ranting when Jem disconnected.

"Well?" Tean said.

"Something about dark angels and infernal masters and having my guts pulled out through my pucker."

"Sounds like a level-ten cosmic orgasm."

Jem had to fight to hide the smile.

The GPS showed Porcupine Rim and a forest service road. They headed out of Moab and into the pinyon-pine and juniper wilderness. By day, Jem had to admit, this corner of the world was impressive. He'd seen so much of it by night that he was shocked by the vibrant colors: rock red in places, orange, but also pink and tan. In one spot, grayish green. In another, a black that might have been blue. Scrubby shrubs and brush somehow found a way to live in this hard land. Dusty green bristled across buttes and mesas.

They drove up into the mountains, and the landscape shifted around them: more pines, fewer scrubby junipers. The road was dirt, and a plume of dust followed them. When they crossed a cattle guard, the bars singing out under the Ford, a wooden sign welcomed them to Manti-La Sal National Forest. North of them, a valley spread out below the mountain, a blanket of scrub running toward another line of red cliffs.

Jem glanced at Tean, about to say something, and then forgot whatever it was. Tean's eyes were wide and bright. His mouth was serious, but his eyes always gave him away—whatever it was out here that he touched or that touched him, whatever it was that transformed him, whatever it was that, once or twice, Jem had felt too. Jem had visited a grandmother once—his or someone else's, he wasn't sure because he'd been too young to really understand—and he remembered being left alone with a prism. He hadn't known the name for it then. He liked the way light played through it. The old woman had put *Barney* on TV, and the music had played in the background, and he'd turned the glass in his hand until it caught the sun. Then the glass and the sun became one, a piece of living fire, the whole world burning in a crystal vessel. And then he'd turned the prism again, and the fire was gone.

Jem tried to find it, but he saw only red rock, dust, the broken branches of an aspen.

"What is it?" Jem asked, voice sounding rough and too loud.

Tean shivered before he answered. "What do you—"

"Whatever it is you're seeing out here."

A long moment passed. "The light. The sky. The rock. Life, even though it seems impossible. And even more impossible, that it finds a way to be beautiful."

"Can you show me?"

Tean slowed the truck. Then they stopped altogether. "I don't know. I've never tried that before."

Jem licked his lips. His throat was suddenly very dry.

"Part of it's what you bring with you," Tean said slowly. "Inside you, I mean. Isaiah talks about the desert. He says God stretches out the line of confusion upon it, the stones of emptiness. It's the land of owls and ravens, dragons and ostriches, the bittern and the cormorant. It's some of that. The stones of emptiness." He was quiet for a moment and said, "There's something in that phrase that I understand, even if I can't put it into words."

More silence, broken only by the engine's rumble. Jem nodded.

Wiping the corners of his mouth, Tean seemed to struggle for the next part. "The Lakota believe that a spiritual landscape exists within the physical landscape. That the physical is, in a sense, the spiritual. That the divine or the transcendent, whatever we want to call it, is immanent, infused in the rock and the trees and the air. It's in the hoodoo stones, the spires, the sandstone fins, the quicksand washes, the goblins, the balancing rocks. Even the badlands. When we go somewhere physical, we go somewhere spiritual as well. And for me, out here, it's that the desert is so strange. It's alien. It might as well be Mars. And that strangeness helps me remember that the world is strange, that there's so much to wonder at, so many things we don't understand but that we come into contact with every day. It's good to be reminded of that, I think. We take the world for granted. We look past it and through it. The desert makes you stop and really look, really see." He hesitated. "And the strangeness of it is an analogue, I think. For me. I look at it, and I don't understand it, but somehow I'm part of it and not, all at the same time. That's what I mean about the spiritual landscape. The desert reminds me of how I feel around people: I can see them, touch them, be right up next to them, and I know I'm part of their world, but at the same time I'm not."

And for a moment, Jem glimpsed it: the talus, the striped sandstone, the scrub brush, the broken rimrock. He'd been staring at the same things for days, and now it was like seeing them afresh. It was more than that. It was like seeing a new world, everything for the first time. He remembered, once, getting high and saying the word *drawer* again and again, until the sounds had become something beyond a word. This was like that, only without the weed, and it made his heart thump in his chest and his eyes sting.

"I'm not explaining it very well," Tean said. "And I guess that sounds really weird."

Blinking rapidly, Jem heard the scratchiness in his own voice as he said, "It's not weird. Everyone feels that way, at least sometimes." He cleared his throat. "It's called being human."

Tean glanced over, and he must have seen some of it in Jem's face, because he smiled, and that was new and strange and wonderful too.

They found the cabin after trying several dead ends: trailheads, campsites, a defile that snaked between columns of stone. Then they came around a bend, the dust fanning out behind them, and spotted the small structure of logs and chinking. The chimney had a dangerous-looking tilt to it, and it was made of sandstone and shale that was the same color as the cliffs. Thin curtains hung in the windows. The jeep was parked under an aluminum awning—protection against the sun more than anything else.

"No truck," Jem said, scanning the land surrounding the cabin: rock, rock, rock, hey—scrub oak. "Why the hell would somebody live up here?"

"Lots of reasons, I think, but the top two are probably loving nature and wanting people to leave them alone."

"Don't even think about it."

"What?"

"I'm not going to let you move off into some weird cabin and grow a gross beard and raise my goddog in a place like this."

Tean smiled as he parked the truck and killed the engine. "Noted."

They got out of the truck. The heat and the dry air made Jem feel like a leaf caught in an updraft. They made their way to the cabin. Jem unfolded the tube sock from his pocket, filled it with rocks, and joined Tean on the porch. He took up position to one side of the door and nodded. Tean knocked.

The sound echoed over the valley and died into silence.

"What now?"

"What would a morally bankrupt homosexual do?"

Tean's eyes narrowed. "A morally bankrupt homosexual would be thinking about putting a gopher snake in someone else's bed. They look like rattlesnakes."

"You know what?"

A pair of crazy, bushy eyebrows rose into arches.

"I'm going to be very nice to you," Jem said.

"That would be a pleasant change."

Jem headed around the side of the cabin. The foundation was a cement slab that looked like it had been mixed, poured, leveled, and finished by hand. The building itself showed the same characteristics: logs cut with hand saws, raw-edged wood that had been sanded down by time, and unevenly applied adobe chinking. Even the windows looked ancient and custom glazed: thin, wavy glass that threw back funhouse reflections of the high desert, gaping maws of red stone and spears of blue sky.

"It'd be easy to get in through one of those."

"This place is practically an antique," Tean said. "We're not going to cause permanent damage." He hesitated. "Unless we have to."

Behind the cabin, a patch of dirt had been cleared of brush and scrub. Toward the trail, a scraggly pair of pines, their leaves tinged yellow, offered the illusion of privacy. Something that looked like a wooden trellis, but without anything growing on it, provided a patch of shade over a picnic table and two benches. Beyond that, dirt gave way to slickrock, and rock gave way to the sheer drop of a cliff.

"I'd love to have a ramada," Tean said, looking at the trellis thing. "I guess you have to have a yard first."

"Really?" Jem asked as he circled around, passing under the aluminum wing of the awning.

"Well, I can't put it in my living room."

"No." Jem peered into the jeep: polarized sunglasses on the dash, a fly-rod case and tackle box on the back seat, socks stuffed into boots in the passenger foot well, a half-unwrapped roll of Tums in the cup holder. "You'd like one of those things?"

"I think so." Tean moved around to the passenger side of the jeep, and he disappeared when he bent down to inspect something. His voice carried under the vehicle. "I like being outside, and you can be outside in Utah most of the year as long as you have decent shade. I could have a grill. I could read my books. I could throw a ball for Scipio. I could imagine heat death and the end of the universe."

"I can build you one. A ramada, I mean. Not a universe." Jem jiggled the jeep's handle. "I could probably build one of those too, I guess, but it'd be a lot of trouble."

Tean made a noise that sounded suspiciously like a laugh.

"Excuse me?"

"No, I was just remembering that I hadn't refilled the birdfeeder you made me."

"It's a good birdfeeder. It's supposed to have a lot of holes in the bottom. That's where the birds get their seeds."

"Jem."

"And the walls aren't supposed to meet exactly square because it's, um, abstract."

"Jem, come here."

When Jem rounded the jeep, Tean was on his knees, glasses balanced precariously on the tip of his nose as he inspected the passenger front tire. "Can you pull up those pictures of the tire impressions we saw by Blake's body?"

Jem pulled up the images and passed Tean the phone. After a moment's consideration, Tean passed it back. Rocking onto his heels, he pointed at a tread halfway down the tire, near the outer rim, and said, "What do you think?"

"It's definitely distinctive; cheap-ass tires, obviously, because a chunk of the rubber is just gone." Jem glanced at the pictures. "The tracks have the same defect. It's a match."

"Maybe," Tean said.

"It has to be. He had Blake's necklace. Now we have tire tracks that put him in the valley, within twenty yards of where we found Blake's body. It has to be him."

"I think so too," Tean said, snapping pictures of the tire with his phone. "But they'll need to do a full comparison. The good news is that tire impressions can be used fairly reliably to identify a specific vehicle. Can you send me the pictures from the creek?"

Jem did. As Tean tapped a few more times on his screen, Jem said, "Are you sending those to Ammon?"

"I will. Once we're finished here."

Nodding, Jem rose and gave Tean a hand up. They finished their circuit of the cabin, and Jem went up to the porch again. He knelt, fished out his picks, and eyed the ancient lock. "This should be easy unless he's got a bar or a deadbolt on the inside; if he does, we'll have to try the back door." But when Jem braced an arm against the wood, the door swung open before he even had a chance to set the picks in the lock.

Jem first, then Tean. Inside, the cabin consisted of two rooms: a large open space that combined kitchen, bedroom, and living area; and a bathroom barely big enough for a toilet, sink and shower stall. The sink hung over the toilet, and Jem figured Jager had cracked his elbow on it plenty of times. Jem didn't have a lot of firsthand experiences with cabins, but this place more or less fit what he'd imagined: a spindle-back bench draped with wool blankets that had been woven in brightly colored geometric designs; a bed with a sagging mattress, the sheets done with hospital corners; a porcelain sink webbed with orange cracks, two Corelle plates banded with an olive-green pattern resting against the side. The only item that looked relatively new was the wood stove in the corner. The heat was worse inside, and the trapped air smelled like mouse droppings and old leather.

Tean was still standing by the door. He shut it and pulled it open again, pointing. "Latch doesn't catch."

"Seems strange to leave his home unlocked."

"Not necessarily. This is a pretty remote part of the world, and the people who choose these places also tend to be lax about social conventions. As you pointed out, locking the door wouldn't have stopped anyone who really wanted to get in here; maybe Jager decided not to bother."

"Or you get the kind of people who go the other way and have tripwires and landmines and those holes with sharpened sticks at the bottom."

"Trapping pits." When Jem's head whipped around, Tean held up his hands. "I was helping."

"A little less help, please. Let's see what weird shit this guy has stashed."

But the answer, after a solid search, seemed to be nothing. Jem tried all of his tricks: light fixtures, pipes, toe kicks, false-bottomed drawers. He removed the wall plate from the lone switch and found nothing but a dead spider and knob-and-tube wiring. They tossed the bed. They pulled the two-burner range out from the wall. While Tean checked the propane tank and its hose, Jem went over every inch of the wood stove. By the time he'd finished, he'd turned up a few scraps of photographic paper, and he'd completely ruined his *Goosebumps* shirt. He knelt next to the stove, trying to decipher something in the crumbling fragments.

"You've got a bit of a crack situation," Tean said.

Jem pulled up his jeans and winced at the sooty fingerprints he left on the denim.

"Viewer, beware," Tean said. "You're in for a scare."

"Holy shit, you know *Goosebumps*?"

"Amos made me watch it when we were kids."

"Well, that's amazing, but first of all, don't ever misappropriate *Goosebumps*. Second, you like my ass." He would have added his third point about the viewer spending a significant amount of time viewing, but something, probably ash from the stove, got into Jem's eye. He blinked and wiped furiously, trying to clear it. "Come over here and take a look at this."

Tean sat crisscross next to Jem, examined the scraps of paper, and shrugged. "I can't make out anything."

"God damn it. I know this son of a bitch has something. He wouldn't have freaked out and tried to kill us otherwise."

"He had the necklace."

Jem didn't answer that. He kicked the wood stove, which rang hollowly and puffed ashes out of its open door. They snowed down on Jem, settling into his shirt and jeans. When he scrubbed at them, they left long, greasy smears.

Tean caught his wrist. "You're making it worse. Hold on." He left the cabin and came back a minute later with wipes, and he used them to clean Jem's hands first, then his face and neck. "I can't promise we'll be able to save the clothes, but we'll try."

The coolness of the cloths, the moisture on dry skin, and the light fragrance—they made Jem take a breath. It didn't hurt that the doc was so slow, so careful, so steady when he worked like this. Those crazy eyebrows were knitted together as he worked the cloth over the bridge of Jem's nose and then applied fresh bandages.

"You look like Scipio," Tean said with a soft smile. "After he's been trying to get a mole."

Jem rolled his eyes.

"It's a good thing."

"Of course it's a good thing. I'm not arguing that it's a good thing. Scipio and I are both fucking adorable."

"I hid my watch in a new spot."

Jem snorted.

"It's a really good one."

"Please, not this again. Every time you hide it, I find it in five seconds."

"Not this time."

"This time, we're not at your apartment, so I can't look for it."

"But you know where it is."

"Sure." Jem shrugged. "But you'll just cheat and tell me I'm wrong when I guess."

"Oh yeah?" Tean was cleaning Jem's fingers again, running another wipe between the digits. He had a little stubble on his cheeks. He smelled like sagebrush and the pomade Jem had used.

"No, I guess not. Because you're unbearably honest and when you try to lie, you do it for shit."

"So?"

Jem ran through the list of hiding spots; Tean had gotten surprisingly good at this game. Underwear drawer, inside a pair of shoes still in a shoebox, behind the books on his bookcase, in a baggie buried in the flour canister, in a baggie inside a carton of peanut-butter ripple. That one had been really good. Tean had somehow gotten the block of ice cream out of the container, sliced it down the center, carved out an open space, and placed the watch inside. Then he'd reformed the block of ice cream and returned it to the container. When Jem had opened it the first time, the ice cream had looked untouched; he almost missed it that time and lost the game. That was the secret to any good hiding spot—letting people convince themselves that whatever they saw was exactly the way it was supposed to be. In that case, the giveaway was the huge smile on Tean's face when Jem had started to put the peanut-butter ripple back in the freezer.

"Holy shit," Jem said, grabbing Tean's hand and squeezing it. "Holy shit, you're a genius."

"What?"

Grabbing the screwdriver from the pile of tools they'd brought in from the truck, Jem said, "Almost. He almost got me. He would have, if you hadn't helped me reboot my brain."

"I'm glad it worked, but if you're trying to get out of our game—"

"Somewhere on your balcony. Probably taped to the underside of the boards."

Shock painted Tean's face. "How in the hell—"

"Swear jar," Jem said as he jogged over to the front door. Squatting, he eyed the lock. Then he tapped the latch with the screwdriver.

"Seriously?"

"Only one way to find out." Jem undid the screws on the mounting plate, and immediately the lock and plate sagged free from the door. The reason was visible: a piece of paper, folded into a thick rectangle, was taking up free space. Jem jiggered the paper free. When he unfolded it, a flash drive slid out of the tight folds. Jem caught it before it could hit the ground.

The handwriting on the flash drive had been done with a fine point pen, and the spidery script made Jem's head throb. He passed it to Tean and said, "Please?"

"Dispatch log 7-19-18."

"That was Thursday." Smoothing the paper out against his knee, Jem studied it. It was a computer printout. A five-column table lined the page; the headings at the top were: DATE/TIME, INCIDENT #, LOCATION, TYPE, RESPONDER. Only six rows filled the columns.

"Here," Jem said, pushing the paper toward Tean.

Tean ignored it. Instead, he squatted next to Jem and brought Jem's hand down to where they could both see the page. "Let's look at location first, right?"

"Will you just do it, please?"

"Do you think we should start with location?"

"God, yes, obviously."

"Row one."

"472 E Kemper Lane."

"Row two."

"31 W High None Road."

"That's good, but it's noon. Two o's make that sound, and I know you know that, but I'm reminding you."

"For fuck's sake, Tean."

"What's our hurry?"

"I'd prefer not to be here when he gets back. I like my brains inside my skull."

"We'll hear him a long time before he gets here. Row three."

Jem made a noise in his throat.

"Row three," Tean said firmly.

"50 E Saxon Road."

"Row four."

"710 E Rocky River Street."

"Row five."

"850 E Wild Horse Ave."

"Great, but 'ave,' like avenue. Not 'ave' like fave."

"Fuck this."

"Row six."

"This isn't fair. This isn't supposed to be practice. I haven't even been working on my books this week."

"Excuse me?"

"Um, this weekend. I meant this weekend."

"Row six, Jem. You're almost done."

"Scipio gets a treat when he does a trick."

"You're not doing a trick, and you're not nearly as well behaved as Scipio. Row six."

"Onion Creek HMA." Jem's head came up. "Holy shit." He ran his finger along the row. "Date/Time: July 19th, 2018, 22:57:46. Incident number, who the fuck cares. Type just says, 'CHECK AREA.' Responder: Weckesser."

Tean ran his hands through his hair, pushing it back, messing up the neat lines of the comb. It was immediately bushy and wild again.

"I think," Jem said, "we just figured out who died in that canyon."

25

As Tean drove them down the mountain, with the Ford's A/C at full blast to combat the intense heat, Jem called the Grand County Sheriff's Department. The call was answered by a woman who was—he was pretty sure—sharpening pencils in the background.

"Arvinna speaking, Grand County Sheriff's Department, hold please."

But she didn't press hold, and hold music didn't come on the line. Instead, Jem heard the receiver on the other end clunk against something solid—the desk, he imagined—and the pencil sharpening went on. Then the pencil sharpening cut off, and Arvinna said something that sounded like, "Stop, Roy, stop," and then a high, nasally laugh with the same rat-tat-tat delivery of a machine gun.

"Hello?" Jem shouted. "Hello?"

The receiver scraped across the desk, and Arvinna said, "Arvinna speaking, Grand County Sheriff's Department, hold please."

"No! I mean, I promise I'll be really fast."

"Yes, sir. How can I help you?"

"I'm trying to deliver a package to Larry Weckesser. I've been to his house out on—" He held up the scrap of paper where he had scribbled the address they'd found on a white-page site. "—Pepperweed, but I can't catch him at home. I've got to have a signature, and he put this place down as his alternate delivery address. Do you have any idea how I can catch him?"

"Larry?" Arvinna said the name with disbelief. "Larry's at his folk's place in St. George. He left Friday and won't be back until a week from Monday. You're not going to catch up with Larry unless you drive to St. George." More rat-tat-tat laughter. "You bring that thing right in here, and I'll sign for him."

"Thank you," Jem said. "You're a lifesaver."

"Why are you making deliveries on a Sunday?"

Jem disconnected the call.

"That's the right address?" Tean asked.

"Not only is it the right address, but she told me Larry left for his parents' place on Friday. St. George. He's off for a week."

"Jeez. Ok, maybe it wasn't him in the canyon. Maybe we're jumping to conclusions."

"Maybe."

Tean frowned, but he didn't say anything, his gaze fixed on the uneven road that carried them back to juniper country, the land of prickly pears and tumbleweed and rattlesnakes. Once they were back in Moab, it was easy to find the deputy's house. Larry Weckesser lived alone by the look of things. The brick house was small and neat, well kept up without any frills or ornamentation. Like every house, it had a green lawn that looked ludicrous against the red rock walls and the high desert that stretched to the horizon. A row of white firs, their needles looking frosty even in the summer heat, marched along one line of the property. On the other side sat a nearly identical brick house, although this one's yard was littered with toys.

Tean drove up the street and back. They parked opposite Weckesser's house and watched it for twenty minutes. If he had curtains or blinds, they weren't in use; Jem could see into the darkened house and make out the shadowy shapes of furniture. Nothing moved; the street was quiet.

Tean was tapping quietly on his phone.

"Are you writing me a poem?

"I'm sending the pictures from Jager's cabin."

"Great. Ammon will be up our chutes in five seconds. You'll probably like it, but me on the other hand—ow! Jesus Christ, don't pinch me."

"You deserved it. And I'm using a burner address, so he won't know who the information came from."

"That'll fool him for five seconds." Jem was still rubbing his bicep. "You used your nails."

"Don't be such a baby. There. Done."

"Let's do this," Jem said, and they got out of the truck.

They were halfway up the driveway when a man came bustling out of the house with the toys in its yard. He was wearing a white dress shirt and tie with gym shorts, and he was one of those skinny men who managed to carry a lot of weight in his belly. Instead of shoes, he was wearing bunny socks with flip-flops.

"Excuse me," he called. "Excuse me, who are you? Larry's not home, so who are you?"

"Can you handle this?" Jem whispered.

"Absolutely not."

"Make it good. Something about bunnies."

"Jem, don't you dare."

"I believe in you. Dig deep and find your morally deviant homosexual."

"Don't—"

"That's not a sex thing either."

Tean looked like he was trying not to scream as Jem quickened his pace, leaving the doc behind to deal with the neighbor. "Teancum Leon," Tean said. "I'm with Utah's Division of Wildlife Resources. Thank you for stepping outside, sir. I needed to talk to you anyway."

"Larry's not home," the man called after Jem. "Excuse me, excuse me, where do you think you're going? Larry's not home!"

"Sir, this is a routine follow-up. We've had an outbreak of rabbit hemorrhagic disease, serotype two, and as I'm sure you know, the disease is often transmitted by humans carrying the virus on their shoes. Can you tell me the last time you were on Mr. Weckesser's property?"

"Oh my gosh," the man said. Jem looked back; the neighbor was clutching his tie with both hands, his face twisted up in anguish. "Did you say rabbits? Did you say rabbit disease?"

"Rabbit hemorrhagic disease, serotype two," Tean said. "As I'm sure you know, there's no treatment, and it's inevitably fatal."

"Oh no. Oh no. Oh my gosh, no."

"I'll just need to ask a few questions while my coworker looks for any sign that Deputy Weckesser carried the virus home with him."

By then Jem had rounded the back of the house. Weckesser's backyard was small, ending in a chain fence overgrown with some sort of thick brush. A detached garage, also brick, took up most of the space. Jem checked the window set into the garage door; no vehicle.

Then he went up the steps to the cement stoop and drew out a pair of disposable gloves he'd taken from the truck. He pulled them on and checked the door. Locked.

After a moment of inspecting the lock, Jem toed back the doormat. He ran his hands along the doorframe. Then he went down the steps again. He dug around for a few minutes in a planter that held a dead mum, and then he moved around to the other side of the stoop. A hardscape of loose stone followed the perimeter of the house. Jem found the fake rock, opened it, and drew out the spare key.

As he let himself into the house, he took a deep breath, and then he exhaled in relief. No stink of rot and decay. The air was warmer than he expected, although definitely cooler than the summer day. It had the faint mustiness of a closed-up space, with a note of something else. An old, fried-meat smell that had lingered. When he stepped into the kitchen and shut the door behind him, he spotted the source: a frying pan lying in the sink, with a blackened crust of burned food on the bottom of the pan.

He moved through the house quickly. Bed unmade, spare bedroom full of workout equipment, the fan in the bathroom droning endlessly. Downstairs, the basement was unfinished. When Jem lifted the lid of the washer, he smelled something foul. He pulled out mildewed clothes; in places, the fabric looked slimy. He lowered the lid and went back upstairs. In the living room, he found a tablet on the arm of a recliner. Jem picked up the tablet, tapped the screen, and let out a breath of relief when it didn't ask for a password. Nothing dramatically revealing in the emails, and a check of the browser's history only told Jem that this guy liked feet and didn't know how to use the browser's privacy feature. In the video chat app, though, was a series of missed calls from Mom. Jem turned off the screen and replaced the tablet. He glanced out the window. Tean was still talking to the neighbor, who was listening intently, nodding as Tean made some sort of gesture with his hands, obviously illustrating a point. Jem let out a sigh.

After locking up the house and returning the spare, Jem walked around to the front yard.

"—dandelions, willow leaves, that kind of thing."

"This is fantastic," the neighbor said. He paused to hitch up his socks. "You have no idea how amazing this is."

"We're all set," Jem said.

"Well?" the neighbor asked. "Did he bring it back with him? The virus, I mean. Should I be worried?"

"Right now, I want to say you're probably ok, but we may need to come back and run some more tests. For now, stay off Mr. Weckesser's property, just in case the virus is still present in the soil."

Tean nodded. "If you see anyone on the property, please give us a call. Contact tracing is the only way to contain this. Even if you can't give us a name, a description or a license plate will be helpful as well."

"Of course," the neighbor said. "Of course, absolutely."

"Have a good day, Mr. Lutz."

"Thank you again. Thank you so much. You're doing the Lord's work, you know."

When they climbed into the truck, Jem muttered, "The Lord's work. That son of a bitch would burn us both at the stake if he knew we were homos."

"He seemed nice," Tean said.

"And you're not supposed to actually help people when you're running a game on them. You should have asked for a cash donation to the Anti-Bunny-Sexualization League. Or you should have told him you could run a quick test on his rabbits for a small fee. Guys like that will pay a lot of money for peace of mind."

"I kept him from bothering you," Tean said. "And he's not suspicious of us. And he's going to tell us if anybody else shows up at the house. And I helped him with his rabbit constipation problem. I don't know why I can't do something helpful while also lying and aiding and abetting you as you commit misdemeanor trespass." He hesitated. "It is just a misdemeanor, right?"

"Who fucking knows?" Jem said, waving a hand wildly. "You're missing the whole point. It's the principle of the thing."

For some reason, that made Tean laugh softly. "Ok," he said. "What did you find?"

Jem told him and added, "I don't think he went anywhere. The clothes in the washer and the missed calls from Mom are the biggest signs."

"Mr. Lutz told me he normally hears Larry get home at the end of his shift. Thursday night, though, he didn't hear anything."

"He's at the end of his shift," Jem said. "A call comes in: somebody saw something weird out in Richardson Amphitheater. He's already changed out of his uniform, but he drives out there anyway and finds—what? Blake dead, and Tanner standing over him?"

"Something like that. Tanner might have been trying to retrieve the body from the ravine."

"So Tanner kills Weckesser, but now he's in even deeper shit because he's killed somebody local. He's killed a deputy, and people around here will notice that. Fast."

"Only they didn't."

"No, they didn't, but only because Larry was planning to go on vacation. That was Tanner's first lucky break in a while."

"We still don't know who was helping Tanner. It couldn't have been Larry; he couldn't help start the stampede, turn the herd, and at the same time already be dead and conveniently get trampled beyond recognition. Somebody else was out there, somebody who knew how to do what Tanner wanted to do."

"And how much do you want to bet that Jager destroyed the original callout logs? We've got the only proof that Weckesser ever went out to Richardson Amphitheater. I'd say that's a good clue as to who's helping Tanner cover up the murder."

As they turned onto Main Street, the squawk of a siren made Jem whip his head to the left. The black-and-white Highway Patrol car hung a U-turn, cutting across traffic to come back toward them. Its lights spun silently.

"Make a break for it," Jem said. "We'll lose them in the desert or die trying."

With a sigh, Tean pulled into the parking lot of the Big Horn Lodge.

26

Jem watched in the rearview mirror as the patrol car's door opened. Haggerty, the trooper who had been in the canyon the night they'd found the body, got out. He had his hands on his belt as he approached Tean's window. On his belt. Not on his gun, although that was a difference of about half an inch.

When Haggerty got to the window, Tean rolled it down. "Hello, Officer. Can I help you?"

"Were we speeding?" Jem leaned over Tean. "Six miles an hour in a five?"

Tean pushed him back into his seat.

Haggerty was young, handsome, his face sharp-edged and angular, and with a tight haircut. His eyes rested on Tean only for a moment before drifting to Jem, and Jem knew what that look meant. It had nothing to do with what Haggerty said next. "I understand you gentlemen have been asked to leave town."

"That's what we're doing," Jem said. "We've just got to pick up our dog, and we're leaving."

"Really? Because I just saw you come off a residential street."

"What's a Highway Patrol trooper doing in Moab on a Sunday? Shouldn't you be at home, dreaming up new speed traps and jerking off over your ticket book?" Jem faked a moan. "Failure to signal." Another moan. "Running a stop sign." An explosive moan, his hand coming open on the last stroke. "Violating railroad rules." He panted. "Was it as good for you as it was for me?"

"Will you cut it out?" Tean asked in a low voice.

"What were you gentlemen doing?"

"We're private citizens. Are we under arrest? We'd like to go."

"It's a simple question, Dr. Leon."

"Are we under arrest?"

"An honest man wouldn't have any trouble telling me what he was doing up that street."

Tean set his jaw; it was the same look he—and, for that matter, Scipio—wore when they played tug-of-war. "If we're not under arrest, we'd like to leave."

"I'll figure it out myself," Haggerty said. "It'll take me five seconds to drive up that street and figure out what you were doing. You can make things better for yourself and earn a little goodwill by saving me the trouble."

"We want to go."

"The way I hear it, you're going to need all the goodwill you can come up with."

"I think I should call my lawyer."

"You have a lawyer?" Jem asked.

Tean shot him a furious look, but all he said was, "I've only needed one since meeting you."

"There's no call for that," Haggerty said. "I'd like to talk to Mr. Berger for a minute. Please step out of the car." When Tean pulled on the latch, Haggerty braced the door with one hand and said, "Just Mr. Berger."

"No," Tean said.

"Stay in the car, Dr. Leon."

"I will not—"

"It's fine," Jem said, squeezing Tean's arm. He opened the door and got out. The sun and the heat were crushing; the smell of the Ford's exhaust and the hot asphalt spun up on invisible currents. The two-story Big Horn Lodge glowed, the stucco the color of an old lightbulb. Sweat sprang out across Jem's forehead, across his back. It was the middle of the day. It was Moab's busiest street. Everybody could see them. But the world shrank until it seemed to consist of nothing but hot air ruffling Jem's hair, the sun scorching the back of his neck, the rumble of the Ford idling and the whistle of cars shooting past.

"Mr. Berger?"

Jem moved to the back of the Ford, where Haggerty was waiting. The cop's eyes were hidden by the reflective aviators. He said nothing.

"I'm pretty good at mind reading," Jem said, "but it's a two-man job. All I get are images. My best friend has to interpret them. Right now, all I'm getting is an image of a massive, throbbing hard-on. Maybe you can help me. Does that mean you're a dick? Or am I missing something more obvious?"

"You think you're pretty funny, Mr. Berger."

"One time I made Tean shoot chocolate milk out of his nose. Well, it wasn't really chocolate milk. He just chopped up some almonds and put them in water and claimed it was almond milk, and then because it was so foul he put in cocoa powder. But, God, the man does try."

"Is he your boyfriend?"

"Who's asking?"

Haggerty let out a strained breath. Then he took a card out of his pocket and offered it to Jem.

"Is this for your dry cleaner? I love a personal recommendation."

"I'm up in Salt Lake a few times every month."

"To get your dry cleaning done."

"I have an aunt who lives in Sugar House."

Jem blinked. "Is she the one who does the dry cleaning?"

"Aw, hell," Haggerty snapped. Then, obviously trying to control himself: "Could you make this a little easier?"

Jem took the card and flicked it. Haggerty's first name, he saw, was Patrick. "Pretty bold, running us out of town, threatening us, and then asking if I'll meet up for a sneak-fuck."

"That's not what I'm—" Haggerty took off the aviators. His eyes were brown, so light they were almost yellow. "I'm asking if you'd like to have dinner with me."

"No, thanks. I don't like bullies."

"I wasn't threatening you. I'm telling you, it's in your own best interest to get out of town before you get charged with obstruction."

Jem thought about Prowler, about Tean's string of first dates, about the fact that everything came to an end. Eventually, Tean would meet the right guy. Eventually, he'd hit it off with someone who knew about elephant toenails or how to pluck a black swan or how to give a donkey an enema. And that'd be it, punto, the end.

He flicked the card again and turned back to the truck.

"What's that supposed to mean?" Haggerty called after him.

Jem glanced back, smiled, and kept walking.

When he got into the truck, Tean let out a shaky breath. "Are you ok?"

"Yes, let's get out of here."

"Did he hurt you?"

"No."

"Did he give you his business card?"

"Is that always your second guess? It seems oddly specific."

"Jem, why did he give you his card?"

As Jem tucked the card into his pocket, he said, "Because he wants to bone me. Or he wants me to bone him. We didn't work out the specifics. Come on, I want to drive past the Tafone again. Maybe they pulled the security detail and we can poke around."

Tean shifted into drive, and they left the Big Horn Lodge behind them. As they drove south and Main Street became US-191, the desert rolled out ahead of them: bluffs of red and gray and brown stone, pale stretches of soil, scrub and brush, a juniper tree twisted all around, branches pointing in every direction like it was Moe getting mixed up in a Three Stooges bit.

"Did he ask you on a date?" Tean said when they'd driven another mile.

"Oh boy. Here we go."

"He threatened us, Jem. He's running us out of town."

"Ok, well, Ammon threatens us all the time. Ammon's always trying to run us out of town."

"I'm not dating Ammon."

Jem snorted.

"What does that mean?"

"If we exclude all the men who want to kill us or threaten us or cause us bodily harm from the dating pool, we're not going to have many options left. I'm going to end up with Ernest, who braids his cats' hair and makes them sit perfectly still for tea parties, and you're going to end up with—"

"If you say Ammon, I'm going to shave your head while you're asleep."

"—George, who makes milk-carton dioramas of famous wedding disasters and has one of those fungal infections that no medicine can get rid of."

Tean was silent for another mile. "Why do you get Ernest?"

Jem had to cover his mouth.

"Did you—" Tean stopped and started again. "What did you say?"

"Well, I said, 'Ernest, I don't love plaits, but if you're—'"

"Jeremiah Berger."

"I didn't say anything. A big, macho guy like a trooper? You've got to chip away at all that power. I might text him in a few days, just to mess with his head."

"Do you like him?"

"I met him when we found a dead body, and then he just threatened my best friend."

"Normal friend. But do you like him?"

"He's hot." Jem shrugged. "But he's a cop. Can you imagine all the rules and ironing and spankings?"

"I think he's—wait." Tean's whole face turned red. With an effort, he cleared his throat and said, "I don't trust him."

"Like Nick."

"I don't trust him either."

"Yeah, great, message received. No normal guy would be interested in me. These guys are just pretending so they can seduce me and then murder us and cut us up into pieces and feed us to iguanas or turtles or whatever the fuck lives out here."

"That's not what I meant."

"Glasses."

Shoving them back into place, Tean said, "I think any guy would be lucky to have you. You know that, right?"

"Right."

"You're very sweet. And you're handsome. And you think you're funny, which isn't quite the same thing as actually being funny, but it's still nice. And back when we used to, you know—"

Jem made an O with his fingers, working the index finger of his other hand through the circle while he grunted.

"Ok, yes."

Jem kept going.

"Oh my gosh, you are so immature."

"Bump uglies."

Tean sighed.

"Make the beast with two backs."

"Are you done?"

"Lay pipe."

"That sounds oddly practical. Like a skilled laborer."

"Smash pissers."

"Ok, I'm pulling over."

"I'm done, I'm done," Jem said, laughing.

"Back then," Tean said, seemingly unaware that the glasses were dangling from his nose again, "you were a very considerate and gentle lover."

"Oh my God." Jem put his face in his hands. "Oh my fucking God."

"That's a wonderful thing. I felt very safe with you, and you were very attentive—"

"Stop. Please stop. You are actually, literally killing me right now."

"You're using those words wrong. And I don't know why being a sensitive partner—"

"Just stop," Jem moaned.

When he finally peeked through his fingers, he caught a glimpse of the smile on Tean's face. "You're an asshole."

Tean shrugged. "I learned from the best. For the record, though, I do think that it's suspicious that two men suddenly want to have sex with you, and they both happen to be involved in this case."

"Fine. Noted. Now let's never have anything remotely like this conversation again."

"And I do think Nick has a bad case of hemorrhoids that might need medical attention."

Jem sighed and clunked his head against the glass.

"And he needs to cut his hair."

"Look who's talking."

"And Haggerty isn't the right kind of personality for you at all."

"Yes, ok, please tell me how I can stop this conversation."

"You need someone you can take care of, but who's also aware of how much you need taking care of too. Because you won't tell people, and I think most people wouldn't realize, you know, that sometimes you need things, and you're not very good at asking for help yet."

Jem studied him: the crazy eyebrows, the pushed-back thundercloud of hair, the slight curve to his thin shoulders. He reached over and settled the glasses in place; the frames were tacky where the electrical tape held the broken pieces together.

"I need taking care of, huh?"

"I think so. Sometimes."

"Well, maybe you're not as dumb as you look."

Tean managed to get a really good punch in, and Jem spent the rest of the drive massaging his ribs and checking for a punctured lung.

When they got to Tafone, the hotel looked abandoned. The sheriff's department Jeep was gone, and the parking lot was empty. The wind had spun a tumbleweed up onto the porch, and now it was caught there, rolling back and forth and then settling down again when the wind died.

"Did they close it down?"

"That seems excessive," Tean said.

"Then where is everybody?"

"I imagine a shooting would clear out any guests."

Jem grunted.

"You don't agree?"

"I don't know. It just seems weird. You'd think somebody would be here."

"The crime scene must not have had a lot to process," Tean said. "Or they'd still be here. That makes me think that whatever happened here, it wasn't as . . . overblown as the news article made it sound."

Nodding slowly, Jem said, "They'd still be taking videos, snapping pictures, picking up casings, doing blood-spatter analysis or putting up those strings to show the path of the bullets."

"Bullet-trajectory analysis." Tean parked the Ford behind the hotel's main building, where it was out of sight from the main road, and turned off the engine. "I figure we can walk to the villa and hopefully keep anyone from noticing that we're here."

"God, it's really inspiring to know that people can change."

Tean rolled his eyes and got out of the truck.

"Just one year ago, you were this model citizen," Jem said as he jogged around the Ford to catch up. "You had a savings account—"

"I still have a savings account. What I used to have was privacy. In my entire life I'd never had someone who purposefully walked in on me in the shower. Every. Time."

"I like the view," Jem said with a shrug. "And I like how you scream and try to use the bar of soap like a fig leaf. Anyway, my point is, look at you now: this criminal reprobate who hides his vehicle and is already planning an escape route."

The only answer was the crunch of broken asphalt as they hiked toward Kalista and Nick's villa.

"Oh my God. You really are planning an escape route."

"I may have looked at some maps while you were sleeping."

"Please tell me you're thinking about hiding in a laundry cart."

"It never hurts to be prepared, Jem."

When they got to the villa, police DO NOT ENTER tape marked the door in yellow and black. Jem walked around the building once, taking his time to study it, even though the heat made him want to hurry. By the time they'd made their way back to the front door, he was frowning.

"Shooting makes it sound like bullets were spraying everywhere, but I don't see any broken windows, and the doors don't look like they've been forced."

With a nod, Tean said, "It could have been as simple as knocking and then showing them the gun. Kalista and Nick probably would have gone into panic mode at that point." Struggle showed on Tean's face, and he added, "Nick probably still would have been twirling his feather boa as he fainted."

"Yes, we get it: you're so much butcher than Nick. You don't need to make the point over and over again; anybody who looks at your clodhoppers can tell that much."

"I like these boots. They're comfortable on long hikes, and—"

"And don't shame him for his mannerisms. That's not cool. You're living in the 21st century; act like it."

"I wasn't—I wouldn't—obviously I support anyone who wants to act however—"

"Jesus Christ," Jem muttered. "It's so easy it's not even fun sometimes."

Jem picked the lock on the rear patio door for the second time, and they went into the villa. The table and chairs had been overturned. Fingerprint powder discolored the kitchen countertop, the refrigerator's handle, the stove, the sink, the door, even the window blinds.

"They really went to town," Jem said. "Guess they're making up for lost time, all those years when they didn't do anything except inspect rocks and make sure the scorpions were getting along."

Tean handed him a pair of disposable gloves and pulled on his own.

They moved through the villa slowly, repeating the search from their first visit. This time, Kalista's and Nick's luggage was gone, emphasizing the sterile, hotel-room décor, the pretense at domesticity. The beds had been flipped. The living room furniture lay on its side. Jem found a bullet hole in one of the walls in the front room; the longhorn cattle skull, which had also been dusted for prints, was staring down at the damaged drywall.

"He could have shot from the door," Jem said, trying to gauge the angle at which the bullet had entered the wall. "What the hell was he doing? Trying to scare them?"

Tean was toeing cushions near the overturned couch. "Why would Antonio come here?"

"Revenge."

"Right, I agree. Tanner killed Andi; now Antonio wants to get back at him. But why come here, to the villa?"

"Maybe he thought Tanner would be here. Maybe he thought he'd catch the three of them together."

Shaking his head, Tean said, "There are too many things I don't like about this."

"Like what?"

"Why is everything messed up? He only shot once. This looks like a search, not a fight."

"Good Lord, you sound like a genuine criminal. What have I created?"

"He didn't come here for Tanner, Jem. That's what feels wrong about this."

And it did; Jem's gut was twisting with it. What he said was "Then let's figure out what he was looking for."

Pushing back his hair with both hands, Tean sighed. Then he nodded.

They worked together, room by room. Tean wanted to be gentle at first, the way he was always gentle: turning the armchairs onto their sides, plumping the cushions, lifting the pictures by their frames. Once Jem showed him that this time, they weren't going to be nice about it, Tean took to the whole process with surprising enthusiasm. He was kicking out the spindles of a straight-back chair, checking to see if the legs had been hollowed out, when his glasses went flying. His expression was murderous as he finished stomping the chair to pieces.

When Jem passed over his glasses, Tean pushed back a sweat-heavy strand of hair and said thanks.

"You're really getting out some aggression, huh?"

"Just exercise," Tean said. He was breathing faster than normal, color in his cheeks.

"Like a beaver on Adderall."

"Title of your sex tape."

Jem gaped at him. The desert wind flung pebbles against the villa, the only sound the click of stone against stucco.

"Out of my way," Tean said, pushing Jem aside. "I'm going to smash that longhorn skull."

"I love you so fucking much right now."

"Save it for your tape."

"What in the world is going on?"

"I don't know," Tean said. "Maybe I swallowed one of Scipio's pills on accident."

They worked through the living room, turning over furniture, cutting and breaking, checking the walls and baseboards. Jem got tools from the truck and they removed the wall plates for switches and outlets. He even made Tean steady him while he inspected the light fixtures. He didn't bother trying to remount them; he just left them hanging by their wires.

Clockwise, they moved through the villa. In the bedrooms, they checked the dressers, the nightstands, the closets, the doors. They checked walls and baseboards again. In the bathrooms, Jem searched the caulking along the fiberglass shower stall, the drain, the caulking around the pan. He checked the toilet tank and under the sink. Tean didn't have the right tools to get the pipes loose, but Jem checked them by hand; nothing seemed loose, but that was the whole point. The medicine cabinet was in place again, so they lifted it out of the wall and checked the hollow space between the studs. Nothing.

"Somebody took the handcuffs," Tean said.

"The sex handcuffs," Jem corrected. "Maybe Kalista decided she liked them."

"Maybe Nick did."

"Ok."

"Maybe Nick's going to use them on you on your date," Tean clarified.

"Yeah, I figured it out."

"What? Oh my gosh, you're blushing."

"Nothing. Quit looking at me like that. I get why it's hot, I just—you're talking to a walking bundle of trust issues."

"Oh. I was just teasing."

Jem scanned the final bedroom, trying to figure out what they'd missed. "I know."

"I didn't mean—"

"This is actually worse than when you emotionally castrated me by telling me I was a gentle lover. You know that, right?"

"I don't know if I said gentle. I thought I said considerate. And attentive."

"Those are worse. Those are so much worse." He stalked toward the kitchen. Without looking back, he shouted, "And quit looking so goddamn smug."

"You just told me you loved me."

"I take it back. I take it all back."

"Even the part about your beaver?"

Jem was glad he was walking away because it was very hard not to smile at that one.

They broke apart the chairs in the kitchen. They took the legs off the table. They emptied the cabinets—which were mostly empty already. Tean smashed a few wineglasses.

"Did the prisoners refuse to talk?"

"I got a little caught up in the moment. I don't think I've ever actually broken anything before. On purpose, I mean."

"Great. This is the second time I've popped your cherry."

"I was not a virgin—" Tean cut himself off and crossed his arms. "No. I've got the upper hand right now. I'm not giving it up."

"Fine. Bring that upper hand over here and help me move this."

Together, they rocked the efficiency stove away from the wall. Behind it they found only a few dried elbows of macaroni and something very gray and very fuzzy that had obviously died a long time ago.

"Mouse," Tean said.

"Wake up your pet snake."

"You wake him up," Tean said, tugging on his waistband. "You already know how."

"What the hell is going on? Is it a full moon tonight? Did you take drugs? Were you bathing in tick medicine?"

Tean just shrugged and grinned. It looked so easy on him, so natural, that Jem got caught up looking. The tangle of wild hair pushed straight back. The thin face. The full lips. The hollow of his throat where the vee of his polo exposed pale brown skin and a tuft of dark hair. He realized too long had gone by when Tean cleared his throat.

"Right," Jem said. "The search."

After that, no more teasing.

They found the stash when they pulled out the refrigerator. Someone, presumably Nick or Kalista, had broken a hole in the drywall. Several ziplock baggies were stacked inside along with a flip phone. The baggies held blue crystals.

"Is that meth?" Tean said as Jem hefted one of the bags.

"It's not pool cleaner. Well, maybe it is, but I don't think so. There's at least a kilo in this bag. Times three," he gestured at the other bags, "this is probably worth more than ten thousand dollars."

27

Jem considered the stash of drugs again and tried to figure out what the hell was going on.

"Maybe Antonio needed money for his getaway," Tean said.

"Maybe." Jem returned the bags to the opening in the wall. Then he turned on the phone. It was relatively new-looking—the plastic wasn't scuffed or scratched, and the small screen was clear and bright. If you got a good deal, you could have bought it for as cheap as ten dollars. No outgoing calls. No incoming calls. A single text message from a number that Jem would have bet money came from another burner.

The message read: *replaces.broadly.shall 7/24/18.*

"I need your help," Jem said. "This doesn't make any sense to me."

"It's not you; it doesn't make any sense, period. 'Replaces broadly shall?' The syntax is off. I mean, the word order—"

"I know what syntax is. You practically whisper the word syntax into my ear at night when I'm sleeping."

"I would if I knew where you slept. If it were a normal sentence, it would be *shall replace broadly* or *shall broadly replace*. The way it's written doesn't mean anything to me. And I don't know why they're separated by periods."

"Maybe they're not a sentence. Maybe they're a code."

"If they are, I have no idea what it means."

"Or—" A rush of excitement hit Jem. "Or they're passwords."

Tean's eyebrows revealed his skepticism.

"Think about it," Jem said. "They've got the phone. They've got a date. They obviously prearranged the location. But whoever they're dealing with, they haven't met face to face before, so they need a password to make sure this is the right person for the handoff."

Tean hesitated. "This type of country would be ideal for moving that kind of thing without having to risk cops. Nobody would look twice at someone with a heavy pack—a strong guy could carry twenty or twenty-five kilos. Heck, nobody would look twice at someone with a pack horse. It would explain why Nick, Kalista, and Tanner have been hanging around Moab. The date in that message is Tuesday, still two days away."

"Are they handing off this shit?" Jem gestured at the stashed drugs. "Or are they getting more?"

"I don't know. And please don't be mad, but I've got to tell Ammon."

"Can you tell him after we're gone? Preferably once we're well away from here so we won't get charged with trespass, breaking and entering, vandalism, possession with intent to distribute, criminal teasing, that kind of thing."

"It's not criminal if it's deserved."

"I'm going to remind you that you said that."

They let themselves out, drove fifteen minutes back to town, and pulled into the City Market Fuel Center. In the convenience store restroom, they ditched the gloves that were now covered in fingerprint powder and washed up. Jem combed his hair, careful of the stitches.

When they got back to the truck, the cab was already cooking, even in the shade. They ran the A/C, and Tean sent another anonymous email with pictures of the drugs and the phone and the hiding place in the villa's wall. Tean had missed a smudge on his jawline, and Jem took him by the chin to wipe it away. The second day's stubble tickled his palm.

"You're looking like a regular mountain man these days."

Tean made a noise, still staring at his phone.

"Like a grizzled trapper working the wilderness of Minnesota."

"Uh huh."

"I bet Proton or whatever his name is, I bet he'd like you with stubble."

"Ragnar," Tean said. Then he looked up. "Why isn't Ammon yelling at me?"

"The fact that you're worried about that explains a great deal of your relationship."

"Jem, you were right. I sent him that stuff from Jager's cabin, but that wouldn't have fooled him. I just sent him a picture of drugs. Why isn't he on the phone screaming at me right now?"

"Because you blocked him?" Jem said.

"No, I didn't."

"Damn. I don't know. He's busy. He's in a meeting."

Tean shook his head.

"Please don't tell me you're worried about him. Please don't tell me you've got some sort of premonition that something bad happened to him."

"What? No."

"Then what is it?"

"I think he's lying to me."

"Shocker."

"Excuse me?"

Jem bared his teeth in what he hoped passed for a smile. "Nothing. You were saying?"

"He's hiding something. And he's doing it to protect me."

"I don't know about that," Jem muttered.

"Excuse me?"

"I said," Jem said, and for one final moment, he tried to stop himself. Then the dam broke. "I said I don't know about that. And please hold all of your shouting until the end. Ammon has lied to you a lot. For a lot of reasons. Mostly selfish ones. Actually, from what I can tell, exclusively selfish ones. And I know you don't agree with me, and I know you think I'm—I'm missing out on this great guy, that somehow I'm not seeing him. But I want to go on the record that he's not a great guy. He's possessive. He's manipulative. He's abusive. He cheated on you—"

"We were never actually a couple."

"Bullshit, Tean. That's bullshit. Don't do that. Don't—don't let him spin things around so that you're in this upside-down world where all his fuckups have an explanation."

"I want to drop this."

"Too bad."

"I said drop it, Jem."

"No. You're worth a million of Ammon. He's dogshit, and you're the best thing on this planet. But somehow he crawled inside your head, and now he doesn't even have to try. You do all the work for him. You've got this whole fantasy spun out about—"

"Shut up."

"This whole fantasy about how great he is, how kind he is, how much he loves you. I don't think he does love you. I don't know if he loves anyone except maybe himself. He's a bully. He's a thug, actually. He's obsessed with you, and he's a narcissist, and he's cruel. If you'd heard him at the hospital, hell, if you'd heard him any of the times he goes pissing all over to mark you as his property—"

"Shut your fucking mouth!"

In the silence that followed, Jem could hear quite clearly the VW bus, powder blue, that rolled past them on a squeaky axle. The driver, an old man in a rainbow serape, tapped the horn, and the bus played "La Cucaracha."

"I've told you before that you don't understand. I've asked you not to talk about it. Why can't you respect that?"

"Because I love you. Because I want you to be happy."

"He makes me happy. Ammon does. I've been in love with him since I was fourteen years old, before I even knew what I was feeling. He was the first person I was ever with, and he made me feel safe and cared for and protected. He made me feel worth something. He makes me laugh. He's my whole past—my family, my friends, everything I came from. Ammon is all of that." Tean's voice softened. "And yes, we've had some rough patches lately. We've both made mistakes."

Jem snorted because the alternative was bursting into hot, stinging tears.

"But I'm not going to walk away from everything just because Ammon had a rough time coming out. I don't know if I'll end up with him romantically. But he's this huge part of my life, and I can't just cut him out and pretend he never existed."

"Too fucking bad," Jem said, his eyes cutting past Tean's shoulder to stare at the cars stopped at the light on Main Street.

Tean's hand was warm. It smelled like the convenience store soap and, faintly, like pine, and he turned Jem's head carefully until Jem was looking into those soft brown eyes. "I love you too, Jem.

You're my best friend. Honestly, you might be my only friend. And I'm sorry I yelled at you."

"Yeah." Jem couldn't help it; the sniffle escaped him. He popped open the door, hocked a wad of spit and snot onto the cement pad, and then slammed the door shut.

"I just wish you could understand—"

"Right, right. We've done this bit. Fast forward." He made the noise of a tape screeching. "If you think Ammon is hiding something, what do you want to do?"

"Jem, please. Can we talk about this?"

"I think we should follow him."

"I don't want you to be mad at me. I hate when you're mad at me."

"You've got about ten seconds to decide. That's his shitty silver Impala sitting in traffic out there."

Tean's eyes narrowed, but he glanced over his shoulder.

"Well?" Jem said. "Want to see what your boyfriend is protecting you from?"

The look Tean shot him was a mix of pain and a fair amount of anger, but all he did was shift into gear and guide the truck out onto Main Street.

28

It was easy to follow Ammon; even in summer, the height of tourist season, Moab was a small town, and Jem had no trouble keeping an eye on the Impala ahead of them. After they had gone a quarter mile south on Main Street, in the direction they had just come, Tean shifted in his seat and glanced over.

In what he obviously hoped was a normal voice, he said, "That's kind of a strange coincidence, right? Seeing him there, I mean."

"This place is dime sized. You're lucky you two aren't bumping ass cracks every time you turn around, although you'd probably enjoy that."

"This is a very mature way to handle being upset with me."

"I'm feeling my fucking feelings, Tean. You're lucky I'm not pulling your hair and stuffing grass down your shirt."

"I hadn't thought of it that way. I'm really proud of the progress you've made." And for some reason, he looked incredibly satisfied with himself.

Jem clunked his head against the door, trying to knock himself out.

They kept going south on US-191. They left behind the frame houses with their bleached siding and patched stucco, the wire fences, the obnoxiously green rectangles of lawn that looked like they'd been dragged here from New England. The desert sprawled ahead of them, rippling with its own heat. Jem had never been interested in camping, but he'd loved escaping to the Jensens' ranch in Tooele, and sometimes Mr. Jensen would build fires in the fall and winter, and they'd sit on logs and roast what Mr. Jensen called wienies, which made Benny and Jem giggle and Mrs. Jensen blush. He remembered at the end of those nights, sometimes Benny would drag a section of log closer and fall asleep on Jem's shoulder, smelling like the fire and, usually, clothes that needed washing. The coals in the bonfire would be the same red as the rock here, pulsing like the heat in the air. He reached over, squeezed Tean's neck, and left his hand there.

Ammon passed the Tafone without slowing, and that made Tean glance over at Jem. Jem shrugged. They drove until the highway split, and then they cut east on US-46. They passed miles and miles of scrub and dirt. More wire fencing, more brownish-green scrub, more dirt that could be pinkish-brown or whitish-brown or reddish-brown. An aluminum trailer that was so bright in the sun it left a purple-white afterimage in Jem's vision. A pole barn with rolled bales of hay visible through an open door. A saltbox house, one wall completely gone to expose a kitchen, a bathroom, a living room. The curtains were flapping in the breeze.

A sign marked the next stretch of desolate waste as La Sal, population 339. Tean had stayed far enough back until now that the Impala was just a silver dot ahead of them, but now that dot grew.

"What are you doing?"

"He's slowing down."

"So slow down."

"I am slowing down, Jem. He's slowing down more."

A green Chevy whipped around them, and a moment later, it passed Ammon's Impala as well. Jem watched the silver car; it wasn't getting any closer for the moment, which meant Ammon had found his new cruising speed.

Five minutes later, though, when a low clump of buildings appeared on the south side of the highway, Ammon slowed again.

"Just pass him," Jem said.

"What if he looks over?"

"I'm going to move the visor and duck down. Pass him. He's going to that place, whatever it is."

"What if he—"

"Christ fuck Jesus God damn, Tean. Just do it. Please."

"Only because you said please."

Jem pulled the visor so that it blocked the upper stretch of the passenger door window. Then he slid down into the Ford's footwell. It wasn't big enough for him; it wouldn't have been big enough for Scipio.

"Don't get any ideas."

"Head down a little more."

"That sounded very objectifying. I'm not here to provide you with your first sexual experience in a car."

"Head down, Jem. Oh shit, here we go." Tean's hand bore down on the back of Jem's head, forcing him against the seat, and the Ford accelerated. Ten seconds, Jem counted. Twenty. Thirty. Then Tean's hand released Jem, and he stroked the short bristles of hair and said, "Ok. You're good." As Jem eased back into the seat and belted himself in, Tean kept glancing in the mirror. "He's turning in at that place."

"Did you see what it was?"

"The La Sal Rooms-4-Rent."

"Flip around."

Tean slowed, pulling onto the shoulder so a tractor-trailer could pass them, and then a purple Cutlass, its paint peeling, shot past them as well. When the road was clear, Tean swung around and headed west. They came even with the motel: two stucco buildings that formed a loose L, with a flashing neon sign advertising LA SAL ROOMS-4-RENT and VACANCY - VACANCY - VACANCY. Three vehicles were parked in the lot: Ammon's Impala, with his silhouette behind the wheel; a small white truck; and some sort of Toyota minivan with a handful of bumper stickers. It was too hard for Jem to read most of them, but he recognized the elephant logo of the Hogle Zoo.

When Tean signaled to turn, Jem said, "No, keep going."

"I thought—"

"He's sitting in his car watching the place. Antonio's there. Jager too."

"What?"

"Russell told us Jager drives a small white truck. I'm betting that's his. And the minivan is whatever Antonio stole when he escaped."

"It might belong to another tourist. Or to the motel clerk. And a small white truck could belong to just about anybody."

"But Ammon's here, and he's waiting. Park on the shoulder."

When the truck came to a stop, Jem grabbed the handle.

"Where are you going?"

"To see what Jager and Antonio are doing. Maybe ask them a few questions. My guess is that Tanner sent Jager to finish off Antonio, but I've been wrong before."

"No. No way. Jem, do not get out of this truck. Those guys are dangerous; Jager has killed before, and Antonio is a fugitive and has very little to lose. Ammon's here—"

"Sitting in the parking lot with a limp dick."

"—and he'll take care of it. He'll notify the sheriff or the police or the highway patrol or whoever needs to know—"

"The same crew of assholes that has independently threatened to jail us if we don't stop asking questions? You still think they want to know what really happened? They just want this to go away, Tean. They'll do anything they can to get it off their plates, and that means they'll let Tanner walk away."

"—so please," Tean said, breathing deeply as he tried to continue, "let's just sit here and let Ammon handle this?"

"Ammon couldn't turn shit with a stick properly."

"And you can? Is that what this is about?"

"Of course. I'm a natural shit-stirrer. Keep the engine running, and make sure you don't let anybody walk up to the window. Pull away and drive all the way back to Moab if anybody approaches you."

Jem slid out of the truck and shut the door. He was jogging across the highway when he heard the Ford's engine cut off. A door opened and slammed shut. Steps came after him. Tean was swearing under his breath, a steady stream of "Damn, damn, damn, damn." Then they reached the other side of the road, clumps of brittle brown grass and scrub scratching at Jem's jeans.

"I think we should do Magic Teacups first."

"Be quiet. Do not talk to me about that stupid swear jar." Then, "Damn hell shit fuck damn bastard."

"You missed bitch."

"I don't like that one."

"You missed—"

"God damn it, Jem. This does not need to be a pissing match between you and Ammon. Let's just do the smart thing and wait."

"Also, I don't want to get your hopes up too much, but I've heard they have these things that are called Dole Whips, and they're the best thing anybody's ever had. Now, please go back to the truck and be a good boy and wait."

Wiping sweat from his forehead, Tean said, "I honestly don't know if you're serious right now, but if you are, you can shove it."

They climbed over the wire fence, Tean holding out a hand to steady Jem when he landed, and then they set off through the sage. A swell in the ground put the motel above them, the parking lot out of sight—which, Jem hoped, meant that they were out of sight of anybody sitting in the lot as well.

"Shove it where?"

"Up there."

Jem glanced over, letting his eyes grow wide and blank. "Where?"

"Up there. You know. Your butt."

Jem bit the inside of his cheek and nodded.

They rounded the back of the motel. The white truck and the minivan had been parked on the east side, where the long leg of the L ended. They hurried past a window A/C unit that chugged steadily. A bead of condensation fell as they passed, swallowed up immediately by the thirsty dirt. A few gnats spun in the air here, drawn by the faint moisture. Jem didn't blame them; he was already baking again; the skin on the back of his neck felt ultrasensitive, and he figured he was due for a sunburn.

The sound of music grew steadily as they moved along the long leg of the L: screaming, thrashing metal. It was coming from a unit in the middle of the motel, and it was loud enough to cover the sound of their footsteps as they approached. When they reached the final unit, Jem considered the small window. The glass was frosted, but he could tell that a light was on inside. He pressed his ear to the glass and heard nothing; the shriek of the music next door swallowed everything else. For a full two minutes, he watched the frosted glass, hoping for any hint of movement on the other side. Nothing.

"Can we go back now? This is pointless."

Jem shook his head. He took out the folding slim jim he carried in a pocket, and he worked it between the sashes. The lock was stuck. Probably painted shut, he guessed, although who the fuck knew in a place like this. Grunting, he applied more pressure.

"Ok, we tried. Now let's go back."

"Tean," Jem said between grunts, "I've had a really bad week. I've had a really bad day. Right now, I could use some support or some quiet; you get to pick."

Tean was silent. Then he said, "You can do this. I know you can. You're very, very good at breaking into places and doing what you're not supposed to do."

The sash lock turned, and Jem let out a hiss of relief as he withdrew the slim jim. He shook out his hand, which had started to cramp around the tool, and said, "That was very nice. A little stilted, but your heart was there, and that's what counts."

"It was my first try; I've never had to provide emotional support to someone committing a misdemeanor before."

"You'll get better."

"Gosh, I really hope not."

Jem slid the window up; flakes of paint fell, dusting his hands and the sill. He managed to raise it three inches before he saw the dead body: Antonio lay naked across the shower pan, paler than he'd ever been in life, an ugly red hole drilled into his head. A spray of blood and bone and brain covered the tile behind him. Next to the shower pan, where the water looked pink on the linoleum, was a pistol. Jem swore under his breath. The second man had fallen in the bathroom doorway; the weight of his body held the door open. Jager had been shot twice: in the chest and in the belly. On the other side of the door, in the motel room proper, scattered bullet holes marked one wall, and Jem stared at them because they made no sense at all.

Then Jager's chest rose and fell; pink foam outlined the wounds and frothed at his lips.

"Go get Ammon," Jem said. "He's alive."

29

To Tean's surprise, Ammon's response to all of it—seeing them here, hearing about the shooting, Jager's condition—was calm and direct. Shaking his head, he half-smiled as he said, "The shitbird made a collect call to his mom; I was waiting for him to poke his head out. Get back to Moab right now. I don't even want to think about what's going to happen if you get dragged into this."

"But if they ask how you found them—"

"Tean, sweetheart, go. I'll handle this."

And then, squeezing Tean's hand through the window, Ammon pulled out his phone and placed the call.

Tean and Jem rode back to Moab in silence. When the town appeared ahead of them, a bramble outline of stucco and brick against the striated rocks, Jem said, "What the fuck was that?"

"It's like you said: Tanner sent Jager to get rid of Antonio, but Antonio got him too. If he pulls through, it'll be interesting to hear the story he comes up with to explain this mess."

"No."

"What do you mean, no?"

"No. That's not what happened. I don't even know where to start; it's all wrong."

When Tean glanced over, Jem was staring straight ahead, his jaw rigid.

"I think you need to eat."

Jem shook his head.

But one Big Mac, two fries, two handheld apple pies, and three Cokes later, he was propping his head in one hand, elbow resting on the laminate tabletop of the McDonald's booth. A pair of kids ran past, screaming.

"I want Mario, I want Mario, I want Mario," a little boy with chubby legs kept screaming.

An older boy wearing plastic dog tags ran just fast enough to stay ahead, laughing.

"What a little shit," Jem mumbled. "That's the kind of thing Tanner would get off on. He'd pretend to give you something and hold it just out of reach."

"Cigarettes? Junk food?"

"Whatever he knew you wanted," Jem said. He folded one of the apple pie cardboard sleeves. Then he released it, and the cardboard unfolded, slapping against the plastic tray that had held their food. "A devil dog from dinner. A full night's sleep. Freedom."

"What do you mean, sleep? Freedom?"

Jem shook his head. He went to take a drink, but the Coke was empty, and the straw sputtered.

"Do you want to talk about it? About Decker. About—" What they did to you, Tean almost said. "About what happened?"

"There were bullet holes in the wall."

Tean sat back in the booth. A light film, something greasy, coated the back of the seat; when he rested his hand there, his fingers came away slick. The kids made another pass; the chubby boy was crying now. Tean watched as Jem's eyes followed them.

"Ok," Tean said, fighting the urge to push his hair back. "Tell me about the bullet holes."

"They were in the wrong place."

"I'm assuming that's not an attempt at a joke."

"Unfortunately, no. They were literally wrong. Well, that's not right either."

"Maybe next time, you should have a salad. I'm worried these hamburgers are starting to clog up your brain. You realize that trans fats and saturated fats adversely affect memory and—"

"Stop, stop, just stop before you say something you regret." Jem took a deep breath, and then he offered a weary smile. "Ok. Thank you. That helped; this," he gestured at the food, "helps." After another deep breath, he said, "Antonio was killed in the shower."

"Ok.

"The water was off."

"Ok."

"Jager was lying in the doorway. I couldn't see blood on the floor, and the wounds looked pretty bad, so I don't think he got shot somewhere else and then dragged himself into the bathroom."

Tean made a considering noise. "Ok. But the bullet holes in the wall are in the wrong part of the room."

"Exactly. There are a lot of ways to make a story out of some of the details, but all together, they don't add up. For example, let's say those holes in the wall, that's from Antonio shooting at Jager when he came into the room. They both miss, which explains the holes in the wall, and Antonio retreats to the bathroom."

"And takes a shower," Tean said.

"Yup."

"Maybe Antonio was already in the shower. He came out for something right when Jager was breaking in, they exchanged shots, and Antonio retreated."

"Nope. No water on the bathroom floor except right near the shower."

"Maybe he hadn't gotten in the shower yet. He's naked, he's dry, he comes out of the bathroom for something, Jager is there, shots fired, he retreats."

For the first time since leaving the motel, a real, true Jem smile flashed out. "You're surprisingly good at imagining murder scenarios."

"We have to do this with poaching and animal attacks, figure out how everything happened."

"And I've corrupted you."

Tean sighed and nodded.

"It's a good theory, but it doesn't make sense because who turned off the shower? It couldn't have been Jager because he got shot when he came through the bathroom door." When Tean opened his mouth, Jem added, "And there aren't bloodstains on the floor, so he didn't drag himself to the shower and turn it off and then drag himself back to the doorway."

"Antonio hit the faucet handle when he fell. A weird, tiny probability."

"Nope. It's the old-fashioned kind: two knobs that are so rusty you probably have to crank them to turn off the water."

From a table on the other side of the dining room came shouting: "Broderick, give Sage your toy right this minute!" Both boys exploded into outraged wailing. Someone on staff must have had a low threshold for that kind of thing because the next minute, the volume of the TV mounted overhead increased. A man who looked like the human equivalent of saddle leather was bellowing golf scores.

"Someone else was in that motel room," Tean said reluctantly.

"Tanner," Jem said, leaning forward and drilling a finger into the tabletop. "Tanner was in that fucking motel room. I know he was. He was cleaning house. He killed Andi. He killed Blake. He killed that deputy—Jager helped him cover it up—and now he's got Antonio and Jager out of the way. All he's got to do is pick up that shipment on Tuesday, cap Kalista and Nick, and he can ride off into the sunset with a few million dollars."

Tean was silent.

"What?" Jem said. "You think I'm wrong?"

"I think we shouldn't make any final decisions yet."

"Jesus Christ."

"I'm not saying you're wrong, I'm just saying—"

"I know what you're saying. Let's ask Ammon. Then you can nod and smile and be his little fucking puppet as he tells us what he thinks is going on."

Tean slid the tray toward him and began gathering their trash. His movements were mechanical. He fumbled the Big Mac box, and it slid off the table. When it hit the floor, the top popped open, and a few watery strands of shaved lettuce fell on the floor. Tean grabbed a napkin and bent, but Jem caught his arm.

"I'll get it."

"No, I'm doing it."

"No, I'm a piece of shit, and it was my Big Mac. You just had a few wisps of desert air, parboiled, plated with the powdered scale of an iguana."

Before Tean had any idea how to respond to that, Jem had wiped up the lettuce and special sauce. As he was straightening in the seat, his hand clenched tight around the napkin, and he muttered, "Fuck my life."

"I thought I'd find you two here," Ammon said. Dark circles ringed his eyes, which Tean hadn't noticed at the motel. His shoulders slumped as he came to a stop at their table.

"You did?" Tean said.

"Well, there's only one white truck in town with the DWR logo."

"How bad is it? Sit down."

"Bad," Ammon said, sliding into the booth next to Tean. "Come on. We've got to pick up Scipio and leave."

"No," Jem said.

"Why?" Tean said.

Ammon threw a glance at the door. His partner, Kat, stood near the entrance, hands on her hips, watching them. The politest term that could be used for her expression was murderous.

"The sheriff and Chief Nobles didn't exactly believe my story about an anonymous source. Even that highway patrol trooper got pretty heated. I believe his exact words were, 'I told those shit-birds to get out of town.' So the general consensus is that the first one who sees you gets the pleasure of arresting you for obstruction."

"No," Jem said, leaning back in the booth. "We're not going."

"What's going on with Jager?" Tean asked. "Do they have any idea what happened?"

"Sure," Ammon said. "It's all tied up with a neat little bow: Tanner, Blake, and Antonio had something going with Kalista and Nick, something with drugs. Then things fell apart. Some kind of internal disagreement. Tanner killed Andi and tried to kill Antonio, but Antonio got away. He came back here and killed Blake, left him in that gully. Jager was involved at some level. Tanner must have tried to eliminate him too, only Jager got the upper hand, and Tanner ended up dead in the canyon, trampled to death. When Antonio showed up, Jager went after the missing piece. Now they're all dead and Jager is being transported by air to Vegas's University Medical, and nobody knows if he'll live long enough for them to hang it all around his neck. Frankly, they'll probably be relieved if he doesn't."

"Vegas?"

"It was supposed to be Denver, but there's a storm over the mountains. Then it was supposed to be Albuquerque, but something happened, and their trauma center is overloaded. After that it was a toss-up between Phoenix and Vegas; I guess Vegas answered first."

"But that's bullshit." Jem flattened his hands on the table as he broke into the conversation. His fingertips blanched from the pressure. "That's all bullshit. Tanner's not dead. Tanner did this. Tanner is still out there, and in two days, he's going to walk away with enough money to live comfortably for the rest of his life in Venezuela or Thailand or God knows where."

"What about Nick and Kalista?" Tean asked. "When you got the information about the drugs, what did they say?"

"They're gone, Tean. No one has seen them since the hotel called in the gunshot. I don't think we'll see them again anytime soon, and if we do, what are they going to tell us? They were trafficking meth, and they asked the wrong guy to help them score an unprotected shipment? They hooked Tanner, only he ended up turning the tables on them?"

"They'll be able to tell us where the drop is going to happen. They could give us Tanner."

Ammon grunted. "It's a moot point; they're gone, and we will be too."

"No," Jem said.

"What about Weckesser? Somebody's got to be asking questions."

"Yeah, McEneany freaked out when I told him about what you'd found. You should have seen how fast that kid got on the phone; I think he was so panicked he actually sprouted his first pube. He talked to the parents right there in front of me; Weckesser's camping in Yosemite. Good luck getting through to him on a call until he's back at the end of the week."

"For fuck's sake," Jem said. "You don't see how convenient that is?"

"Am I supposed to believe his eighty-year-old parents are involved in this conspiracy too?"

"What about the dispatch log we found? Why would Jager care about that if Weckesser was still alive?"

"The current theory is that Jager altered the log and took those copies because he wanted to make sure that nobody ever remembered anything strange about that night—including the callout asking for a check on the Richardson Amphitheater."

Jem was clenching his teeth so hard that the cords of his neck stood out. "This is bullshit. I've got things to do."

"You're going to get arrested."

"Yeah, thanks, I heard you the first time."

"You're going to get Tean arrested."

Jem hesitated.

"And he's going to lose his job," Ammon said.

"Don't do that," Tean said. "That's not fair to him."

"When word gets out about the trouble you two have been in down here, when his supervisor learns he was using his job to interrogate potential witnesses."

"He didn't—"

"The neighbor," Ammon said. "Weckesser's neighbor. And if I figured it out, somebody else will too."

Bright spots burned in Jem's cheeks. He was taking shallow, rapid breaths.

"Jem, don't worry about that right now. Ammon, I told you not to do this. Drop it. Right now."

"Then he can go," Jem said, staring at Ammon. "He can go with you."

Ammon snorted. "That would be the day." Glancing at Tean, he said, "You're not going to leave him, are you?"

Tean swallowed, his throat so dry he was amazed he managed it, and shook his head.

"There you go. So, you get to be selfish and play vigilante and ruin his life."

"Tean, go home. Go back with him."

Tean was silent.

Jem finally looked at him. "Go back with him. You're done here. Don't be stupid."

The sound of a dozen conversations filled the dining room. The fountain machine hissed and gurgled. Little feet slapped the tile floor.

"I don't think I should do that," Tean finally said.

"God damn it." Jem put a hand over his eyes for a moment and then dropped it. "God damn it, Tean. Will you please just do what I'm telling you to do?"

"I don't think I should."

"For fuck's sake," Jem shouted, and he turned and kicked an empty chair. It squeaked along the tile and fell over with a clatter. A shocked silence cut through the dining room.

From the door, Tean could hear Kat say very quiet, "This is a shitshow."

"Everything's all right, folks," Ammon said his voice calm and full of authority as it carried through the dining room. "Police business. Nothing to worry about." Then, more quietly, he said,

"Maybe I can offer an alternative to pitching a hissy fit in a fast-food restaurant and getting yourself arrested that much faster."

"I need to go," Jem said, his gaze swinging wildly. "I've got to get out of here."

"Jem," Tean said, "hold on. Please. Just wait."

"We go to Vegas," Ammon said. "And we talk to Jager."

Jem plucked his *Goosebumps* shirt, which was filthy from the ash in Jager's wood-burning stove, as though trying to cool himself. His eyes were wide, his pupils dilated. Tean wondered, again, what had happened? What had these men done to Jem so that the hurt ran so deep?

"You said he might not survive," Tean said.

"He might not."

"And he'll be in police custody."

"He's tied up in my case now; he killed the man I arrested for murder, the one who escaped custody. I've got a right to question him."

But his voice held a note of doubt.

"What happened?" Tean said.

"Nothing."

"Don't do that. Tell me what happened."

"It's all going to blow over, but McEneany, Nobles, and Haggerty have all complained to my lieutenant. He wants me to quit, in his way of putting it, fucking him over like the rent boys I pick up."

"That's sexual harassment."

Ammon gave a tired grin. "I'll make sure he understands that. He wants Kat and me back in Salt Lake today. And Kat agrees with him; she doesn't like how things went down here."

"Based on how she's glaring at you," Jem said, his voice sounding a few degrees closer to normal, "she blames you."

"She does. And she's not wrong. I let the two of you get away with a lot that I wouldn't have put up with from someone else."

"That's cute," Jem said. "You think you were letting us."

"Look, if you're right about Tanner and this drug shipment, he's not going anywhere for two days."

"Two days I could be looking for him. Two days I could use to find him."

"Two days that you'll spend sitting in a jail cell. Maybe longer. They can hold you for seventy-two hours before they even have to file charges, and then you'll sit around some more while you wait to either be arraigned or make bail. Or both. You might still be sitting in a cell when Tanner steps onto a plane for Argentina. If we go to Vegas, though, we don't lose anything. Tanner will still be here in two days, and maybe we'll get something out of Jager we can use."

"Jem," Tean said quietly, "it's not a bad plan."

"Then you go. Go to Vegas. I'll be careful. I'll—I'll stay out of sight."

"I thought you said he was smart," Ammon said.

"He is smart. Ammon, will you give us a minute?"

"Don't take too long; your family wants to have dinner tonight. In Vegas, I mean."

"What?"

Ammon shrugged. "Amos has been calling me for two days straight, asking me to find a way to get you down there." To Tean's surprise, scarlet dusted Ammon's cheeks. "He invited me too, actually. I didn't say anything because I assumed you didn't want me to go."

"Amos invited you?"

"He said you wouldn't come without moral support. Kat's already volunteered to take Scipio to your sister's place."

"This is unbelievable."

"Ok, she didn't actually volunteer, but she did agree to do it."

Tean pushed his hair back. "This is—ok, let me talk to Jem, please."

Squeezing Tean's knee, Ammon slid out of the booth and joined Kat by the door. Tean took a few deep breaths, wondering if smashing Amos's face with a rock would fall under the guidelines of brotherly love, and then raised his head. Jem was looking at him, his face a sickly white, expressionless.

"I'll do whatever you want," Tean said. "But I think Ammon's right."

"Of course you do." Jem took a shuddering breath, like he was on the verge of breaking into sobs, but his eyes remained dry. "Ok. Fine. Let's go."

30

It wasn't quite as easy as that.

Jem went insane when Kat tried to load Scipio into the back seat of the Impala.

"He's not a criminal. He's not a fucking criminal. He should get to ride up front with you."

It went on and on like that. Scipio, completely unaware that he was the object of contention, was climbing around inside the car, investigating every inch of upholstery with thorough sniffing. Tean finally had to drag Jem back to the truck. The look on Kat's face could have fried both of them.

"Jem, you're freaking me out. What is going on? Did you—" Tean hesitated and then took the plunge. "What have you been taking?"

Jem just kept shaking his head. "He's not a criminal. She shouldn't be putting him in the back seat because he's not a criminal."

"What the hell is his deal?" Ammon asked when he joined them. He was carrying a roller bag, which Tean tied down in the Ford's bed. Jem was pacing by the side of the truck, muttering, gesticulating, the word *criminal* carrying on the desert air.

"Can you drive?" Tean asked, fishing out the keys. "He hasn't slept, not real sleep, in days, and he's having some sort of panic attack or anxiety attack. I don't know. I just need you to help me right now."

Ammon nodded and accepted the keys, but the look on his face spoke volumes. Tean took two Xanax from his bag and forced Jem to take them. They climbed into the cab, Tean in the middle, and Ammon guided the Ford north toward I-70. They were three miles outside Moab when Jem fell asleep. It was so abrupt and complete that for a moment Tean worried. But Jem was breathing softly and evenly, and he let Tean adjust him until he was slumped against Tean, sleeping on his shoulder.

When Jem was finally settled, Tean risked a look at Ammon.

"He's lucky he has you," Ammon said.

Tean watched the rolling miles of ephedra and bitterbrush and sage, rock the color of coral, rock the color of sun-bleached straw, rock the blue-black of the bottom of the ocean. Fissures spread through the white clay hardpan.

"I don't think he's the lucky one," Tean finally said.

Ammon's hand settled on his leg, warm and heavy. "Don't rev yourself up," Ammon said with a soft smile, his fingers flexing once around Tean's leg. "I just—I just need this, ok? I'm not going to make any attempts on your virtue."

"Thank goodness," Tean said.

Laughing softly, Ammon squeezed his leg again.

After that, they drove in silence, except for two stops to get gas and use the restrooms. The drive was longer than Tean had expected, and by the time they reached Vegas, night was settling in: a band of amethyst haze along the rim of the world, shadows pouring in like a flood, the sodium lights and fluorescents and neons of the Strip violent after so many days in the quiet and emptiness of the high desert.

Caesar's Palace had a parking garage that was like every other parking garage Tean had ever seen: rough cement, the sound of brakes squeaking, the smell of urine and motor oil. When Tean's phone made a yowling noise, Jem woke from his third nap. He glanced over, eyes puffy, and said, "Prowler."

Tean jammed buttons on his phone, trying to silence it.

Jem gave a lopsided smile and tried to fix his hair in the mirror; his color looked better.

"Come on, pretty boy," Ammon said. "You can fix your hair in your room."

"Nobody's going to see me in my room. I need to fix it now."

Tean's phone yowled again.

"Really?" Ammon said.

"I'm trying to turn it off," Tean said, tapping frantically through a maze of options.

Tean had never been to a Vegas casino before; five feet into the building, he knew why. It was fake. It was all fake. The pseudo-classical architecture: columns and friezes and painted domes; murals and tilework and mosaics; fountains and statues. Replicas, imitations, thefts from another place and another time. The light was fake; there were no windows, only the intense artificial brilliance of the lobbies that contrasted with the dim labyrinths of the casinos, where screens flashed and alarms rang out. The sounds were fake; ringing bells, chimes, and the jingle of coins competed with laughter, shouts, and drunken cries. Even the air was fake, a mélange of smoke and perfume and pure oxygen forced through the vents to keep gamblers alert and active.

At the reception desk, they got their keys. Tean already had a room reserved, courtesy of Amos. Ammon booked one for himself, although he was so slow about it and threw so many questioning looks at Tean that Tean just about lost his mind. Jem wandered off. When he came back, the grease- and ash-stained *Goosebumps* shirt was turned inside out, and dark smudges of something—some of the ash, Tean guessed—hollowed out Jem's eyes like exotic makeup. A puppy-eyed young man was following him. His name tag said Victor, and below that, it said Concierge.

"Miranda," Victor said as he trotted up. "These gentlemen have been upgraded, and we need to process Mr. Berger's complimentary suite."

"What the frick?" Ammon muttered.

Miranda, who had an Audrey-Hepburn neck and a lot of fake gold jewelry, was smiling and typing like she'd polished off a bottle of Adderall. She couldn't have been happier about the upgrades. She couldn't have been more pleased about the complimentary suite.

"No need for a suite," Jem said with a laugh that made Victor vibrate like a plucked string. "Just a room on the same floor as these guys, thanks."

"Did you blow him in the bathroom?" Ammon asked when Victor and Miranda stepped away to talk.

"Do you hear how he talks to me?" Jem asked Tean, hitching a thumb at Ammon. "Do you like guys with dirty mouths? You ought to scrub that out with soap."

"So you did blow him."

"I didn't give him oral pleasure, Ammon. I'm a gentleman. I like someone to buy me a nice dinner first. Remember?"

Ammon's face colored. Tean felt his own face heating; he had tried to forget that Ammon had once cruised Jem—or maybe it had been the other way around—at a Salt Lake bar.

"Right," Ammon said. "I forgot it takes a six-piece nugget to get you to go down."

Jem just smiled, and Ammon's face got redder.

"Seriously," Tean whispered as they rode up the elevator of the Augustus tower, "what did you do?"

Jem moved his tongue against the inside of his cheek to create an obscene bulge.

"I hate you," Tean whispered.

Jem worked his tongue back and forth.

"Gosh, I hate you so much sometimes."

"I might have convinced him I work for a famous street magician," Jem whispered. "Maybe. Just possibly."

"What are you two talking about?"

"Blowing each other," Jem said.

"Nothing," Tean snapped.

Then his phone betrayed him, yowling again.

"You can delete that app, you know," Ammon said, fixing Tean with a flat stare.

"Leave him alone," Jem said. "Hot boys want to rip his clothes off; it's his God-given right as an American to be informed when they're nearby."

"Do you ever know what he's talking about?" Ammon said to Tean.

"Not really."

The phone yowled twice more as Tean was letting himself into his room.

"Is that number five or number six?" Jem called from where he was opening the door to the next room.

Tean hurried inside, shut the door behind him, and threw his phone under the bed. The hotel room was like so many others he'd been in: geometric patterns on the carpet; innocuous watercolors on the walls; a big bed with crisp, white sheets. The air conditioner was set to Arctic Blast, circulating the smell of hotel laundry, and Tean shivered as he adjusted the temperature. He washed up in the bathroom to the sound of three more yowls. Then he crawled under the bed to retrieve his phone, stared at the stream of 'claws' that guys had sent him on Prowler, and dismissed all of them.

Next, he did some exploratory searching, looking for Kalista Sweet and Nick Reddick. He pulled the last names from the pictures of their luggage tags that he'd taken the first time he and Jem had broken into the villa. He got results on a Nick who was a lawyer and possibly a politician, but the picture didn't match the man with the swishy hips whom Tean had met in the Tafone's villa. There were other Nick Reddicks, and Tean got through ten pages of results before giving up. Kalista Sweet was also a dead end: results on Facebook, Pinterest, Instagram, and more, but none of the pictures matched the woman he had met. Then he tried their names together, using various search limiters. One combination finally turned up a result: a short article about a charitable relief organization in St. George, Utah, from a newspaper called the *St. George Mercury*. The story only had a single photo of Kalista and Nick in formal wear; presumably whatever charitable work they were doing required a tuxedo and an evening gown. Nick's hair was still in the ridiculous low bun, which was probably because he was trying to hide elf ears, Tean decided. After that, Tean checked several of the links on the page, which all dead-ended in 404s.

The phone buzzed with an incoming call from Amos.

"Are you here?" Amos asked.

"Just checked in."

"Great, great. Guys, let's wrap it up. Tean's here."

"No," Tean said, flopping back onto the bed. "No, don't come back just for my sake. I'm exhausted. I'll see you guys in the morning."

"I don't care if you haven't had your turn yet, Cor. Tean's just checked in. Let's go!"

"No," Tean said. "Don't. What are you guys doing, anyway?"

"Zipline. It's this adventure park. I know we're only halfway through it, Seth. It was only forty bucks. Suck it up."

"You guys stay. Have fun. We'll get breakfast tomorrow; trust me, I'm not going to be good company." A knock came at the door. "I've got to go."

When he answered the door, Ammon stood there barefoot in mesh shorts and a thin, athletic-fabric gray tee. It hugged his body, tracing his pecs and abs. He'd lost weight. A lot, Tean realized now, and he'd added definition and tone to the muscle he already carried. He looked more than ever like the man Tean had fallen in love with. His hair was wet, his cheeks ruddy, and he smelled sweet. Verbena, Tean thought. And lemon.

"Eyes up here," Ammon said with another of those soft laughs. "Can I come in?"

Tean stepped back. Down the hall, the elevators dinged, and two women traded tips on the slots. Ammon followed him into the room and shut the door.

"I called the hospital. Jager is still in surgery. Unofficially, they say he'll pull through, but I guess we have to wait and see. The earliest we can see him is tomorrow afternoon."

"The perfect reason to get away from my family. I looked up Kalista and Nick, by the way. I think those were fake names."

"That sounds about right. Too bad; wherever they went, I don't think we'll see them again."

There didn't seem to be anything to say to that; the silence made Tean's skin prickle.

Ammon smiled. He stepped forward. Tean stepped back and bumped into the desk behind him. The plastic phone clicked in its cradle. Distantly, the elevators dinged again. Ammon stepped forward again, and this time, Tean didn't have anywhere to go. Ammon's arms slid around him, pulling him tight. Tean remembered this: the hard lines and planes of Ammon's body, the way they fit together. He remembered how it felt to stand like this naked, with only Ammon's arms between him and the world, and to feel safe.

Ammon tried to kiss him, and Tean buried his face in Ammon's shoulder. If it bothered Ammon, he didn't give any sign. He laughed, running one hand down Tean's spine. "I've wanted to do this for so long." He kissed just below Tean's ear. "When I thought I'd lost you." He kissed his neck. "When I thought I'd never see you again." He kissed his shoulder. "When I thought I'd never get to be with you again, I wanted to die. I'd rather die than lose you. Do you understand that? I will die before I lose you. I'm not going to make the same mistake twice."

"I'm all sweaty," Tean whispered, raising his head. "And I don't know if—I think we should slow down."

"I don't want to slow down. You're everything to me. You're my whole life. And I don't care if you're sweaty. You're the sexiest man I've ever met. Everything about you turns me on."

The words popped out before Tean could stop them: "Even my toenail gunk?"

Ammon stopped moving. Then he chuckled. "I forget how you like to ruin a moment." He released Tean, but he kept him penned against the desk. He got down on his knees. One hand hooked the waistband of Tean's chinos. With the other, he palmed Tean's erection. Tean let out a shaky breath, and Ammon smiled up at him, blue eyes bright and surprisingly boyish. "We never got to take our time, did we? I never got to show you how good I can make you feel. I want to make you feel so good, Tean. I want to show you how special you are." He was still massaging through the chino's thick cotton, still smiling up at Tean. His fingers slid along the waistband, and one-handed, he undid the button. He yanked the zipper down in two tries and folded back the chinos. Then he leaned forward, kissing the hard line of Tean's dick through the boxers. "I never got to do this for you," Ammon said, his voice husky. "But will you believe me when I tell you I jerk off to it? I want you to pull my hair." He guided Tean's hands to his head. The strands were silky and soft, and he moaned when Tean buried his fingers in it and gave a soft tug. Ammon leaned forward in response. This time, he licked the cotton boxers, the heat and texture of his tongue making Tean gasp.

A knock came at the door.

"Oh shit," Tean whispered.

"Ignore it."

The knock came again, longer and louder.

Tean let go of Ammon's hair.

"Ignore it," Ammon said, catching his wrists. "They'll go away."

"No." Tean let out a long, unsteady breath. "No, I think we need to slow down. This is too fast for me."

For an instant, Ammon's eyes were flat. Then he shifted his hands to Tean's waist, his mouth hot and wet as it closed around the head of his dick, pasting the cotton against sensitive skin. He sucked for five seconds, maybe ten, and pulled away. Wiping the back of his mouth with his hand, he got to his feet. His erection bulged behind the gray mesh of his shorts. With a wry grin, he dropped onto the bed, which helped. A little.

Tean adjusted himself, zipped up the chinos, and swore when he saw how he looked in the mirror: face flushed, strands of hair stuck to his forehead, and, as Jem probably would have put it, a boner as big as King Kong and just as hard to miss.

"Tean? Have you fallen in the shower and can't get up? Press your Life Alert bracelet if you need me, Tean. Tean, tap out in Morse code the lyrics for 'Yankee Doodle Dandy' if you're being held hostage. Tean, are you trying to take a nap, are you—"

"Just a minute," Tean said.

"Are you going to smashtown? If you're going to smashtown, make that fake orgasm noise that I taught you, and I'll come back in thirty seconds when you guys are finished."

"Jem, just a minute."

Panic went a long way to killing the buzz of hormones, and after adjusting himself one last time, Tean opened the door.

When Tean opened the door, Jem was standing there, hair wet and perfectly combed, wearing a *Saved by the Bell* t-shirt that said ZACK MORRIS IS MY BABY DADDY. Grinning, he pushed into the room. "Seriously, is it porksville in here? What are you—oh."

"You're in a better mood," Tean said.

"Meaning," Ammon said, "you don't seem batshit crazy. What the heck was going on with you earlier?"

"Bad case of the grumps," Jem said, moving to the dresser, where he did something with Tean's room keycards before drifting to the window. He rolled up the blinds; the Vegas lights wove a quilt of green and red and blue haze over the city. "Aren't these rooms fucking ace?"

"If I were a World War II fighter pilot, sure."

"Oh my God, did Ammon Young just make a joke? Did you accidentally fall off a cliff? Maybe you knocked that stick out of your ass."

"I certainly feel like I hit my head."

"Ammon was just telling me that he's already checked with the hospital," Tean said. "Jager's still in surgery. We'll have to see if we can talk to him tomorrow."

"Great," Jem said. "Let's go."

"Go where?"

"Umm, first to get food and drinks. Lots of drinks. And then to Omnia. That's the club here. And then to get pounded or to do some pounding—gentleman's choice."

Tean glanced over at Ammon.

"Seriously?" Jem said. "Your phone has been blowing up since we got here. Have you even looked at the guys who have clawed you on Prowler?"

"Well—"

"Oh my God. You're extremely hot. You're smart. You're a new guy in a town that's always flooded with tourists. Let's find you a rich, greasy sleazeball who will let you fuck him until he calls you daddy. You'll feel a million times better in the morning."

Tean glanced at Ammon again. Those blue eyes were as flat and shiny as mirrors.

"Yeah," Ammon said. "Let's see who's been hitting you up."

"Fuck yeah," Jem said.

"No," Tean said. "No way."

"Give me one good reason."

"I'm tired. No, I'm exhausted. I'm filthy. I'm hungry. I'm going to get roofied and have my kidneys stolen. I just gave you five good reasons."

"You gave me four shitty reasons. You said tired and exhausted; that's the same thing. Let's see who's trying to throw your little doggy a bone."

"What does that mean?"

"It means," Jem moved faster than Tean expected, snatching the phone from the bed, "let's find you a hot piece of ass."

"Give that back," Tean said, surging up from the bed. Jem fended him off with one hand while he tapped the screen. "Jem, don't you dare!"

"Here's Billy, from Missouri. He's an actor, and he's in an open relationship. He—"

Tean knocked Jem's arm out of the way and lunged.

Jem was faster. He tossed the phone to Ammon, who still had an athlete's reflexes and caught it.

"Or," Ammon said, swiping at the phone's screen, "there's Nottingham. He's from Utah, big surprise with that name, and he works in musical theater. His favorite place to get coffee is," Ammon made a face, "out of a bowl on your kitchen floor while you use him as a human footstool."

"See?" Jem said. "Dick shopping and furniture shopping all at the same time! Vegas is magical."

"Hippos attract mates by peeing," Tean said. A little too loudly, maybe, because Ammon lowered the phone and Jem covered his mouth. "And male white-front parrots vomit on the females they want to mate with."

"Thank God you're gay," Jem whispered.

"And male peacocks make fake mating noises to attract mates." Tean's face was hot, and he was sweating. He picked at the polo bunched under his arms. "It makes them sound more popular, um, you know."

"With lady peacocks."

"They're called peahens."

"No, that's stupid."

"This whole thing is stupid," Ammon said, standing and tossing the phone on the bed.

"Jesus Christ. Are you saying that my fake orgasm noise that I taught you is a legit, Animal-Planet sex move?"

"Ok, I'm out," Ammon said. "You can do whatever you want."

"He doesn't need your permission to date." To Tean, Jem added, "You don't need his permission to date."

"Tean, I'd really like to finish our conversation from earlier."

Tean couldn't bring himself to meet Ammon's eyes. He looked at a spot over Ammon's shoulder. "Maybe not tonight. I really am tired."

"Yeah. Of course you are." Ammon stomped toward the door. He tried to slam it shut behind him, but the door closer interfered, and eventually he let out a frustrated breath and marched down the hall.

When the door finally clicked shut, Tean said, "Please don't say anything."

"One thing."

"No. Zero things."

"One tiny thing."

Tean couldn't help himself: he made a high-pitched noise and fell face-first onto the bed. The mattress dipped as Jem dropped down next to him. "Even if you end up with Ammon," Jem said, "don't you want to make sure you're doing it for the right reason?"

"I don't want to do this."

"Tough titties. This is really, really important. For you, I mean. And you need to do it even though it's hard. You told me Ammon is your whole life. Ok. But you broke things off with him for a reason, and I think you owe it to yourself to see what else is out there before you decide to spend the rest of your life with someone who treated you like a cum rag for ten years."

Tean raised himself up enough to glare at Jem.

"Yeah," Jem said with a tiny smile. "I knew that'd get you mad enough to stop sulking. Let's look at some hot guys."

"No."

But five minutes later, he and Jem were lying shoulder to shoulder on the bed, staring at the screen as Tean tried to decide.

"He's smart," Jem said. "He's an anesthesiologist."

"He's giving his mom a piggy-back ride."

Swipe left.

"This guy brings his own bag of anal training cones. Look!"

Tean couldn't close his eyes fast enough.

Swipe left.

"Ricardo has a nice penis."

"It's not that nice. And he's got a bull tattoo, which means he's compensating for something."

Swipe left.

"This is pointless," Tean said. "Did you know that on average, ten percent of dating accounts are created by scammers?"

Jem flopped onto his side, his head pillowed on Tean's shoulder.

"And only thirty-three percent of online daters ever form a relationship. An equal number finally just give up."

"Giving up is underrated. I like giving up."

"It's a one-point-eight billion-dollar industry, and it's all pointless because no matter how much time and effort you put into those online profiles, it doesn't mean anything. Research has shown that people decide whether or not they're attracted to someone within three seconds of meeting in person."

"Three seconds seems like a long time. It doesn't take me that long."

"When they survey women about dating fears, women mostly fear that they'll date a psychopath who will hurt or kill them. Men, on the other hand, in a charming example of how fucked up the entire male gender is, are afraid of a lot of things: they're afraid a woman will come between them and their friends, they're afraid a woman won't allow him to have free time, they're afraid she'll be a stalker or high maintenance. But mostly—I'm not even joking here—they're afraid she'll be fat."

"Tean?"

Tean refused to look. He stared at the ceiling, where the paint was imperfect around one of the overhead fixtures.

"I know it's scary. But you're very brave. And more importantly, you deserve to be happy, and that means taking some risks. It means trying new things. Sometimes, it means letting old things go."

"Ammon—"

"I'm not talking about Ammon. I'm talking about a lot of stuff, I guess. But mostly I mean, it's ok to let things come to an end. You've had some bad dating experiences. That's not your fault. But you need to stop letting that stuff haunt you."

In the room next door, Ammon was blasting *SportsCenter*.

Tean squirmed until his head was resting against Jem's.

"All right."

"You'll look at some more?"

"Please don't tell anyone you gave me a motivational speech."

"I won't. I'll tell everyone you gave me a demotivational speech."

"That would be perfect," Tean murmured.

Fifteen guys later, it was a match. Jem passed off the phone so Tean could type, but he insisted on Tean reading every new message to him.

"This is perfect," Jem said, bouncing on the bed hard enough to shake Tean. "This is perfect. He wants to have dinner tonight. He wants to have drinks tonight. Say yes!"

"It seems—"

"If you say too fast, I will go borrow that other guy's bag of anal cones and shove them all up your butt at once. Say yes. This guy is cute. He's got a nice smile. He writes polite messages. And the whole point is to try something while we're here. If you don't like him, you don't have to smush. Just pay for your half of the meal and get out of there."

Tean hesitated. Then he typed: *Yes, I'd love that.*

"Yes, yes, yes, yes, yes," Jem screamed, grabbing Tean in a bear hug and rolling across the mattress. They hit the floor in a tangle. Jem burst out laughing. Tean, to his own surprise, burst out laughing too. Then, slapping Jem's chest, he tried to work his way free.

"What the heck is wrong with you?"

"God," Jem said, still laughing, "I don't even know."

31

When Tean left for his date—freshly showered, hair combed and styled courtesy of Jem, and wearing a powder-blue button-up that made him so gorgeous Jem wanted to cry—Jem made a big show of going back to his room. He wished Tean goodnight, loudly. He walked to his room, loudly. He shut the door as loudly as he could, although the door closer made it difficult. Then he pressed an ear to the door and waited.

The elevator dinged.

Thirty seconds.

Ammon's door opened.

Jem counted to fifteen, checked that he had his own room key as well as Tean's spare, which he had stolen on his earlier visit, and let himself out into the hall. Ammon had changed into jeans and a short-sleeve gray henley, and he stood at the bank of elevators, pressing the down button.

"Hey stranger," Jem said as he joined him. He flashed a hard smile. "Fancy meeting you here."

Ammon's face was expressionless.

"You wouldn't happen to be following your boytoy, would you? Because that would be some shady, scary, stalker-level psychopathy, and you've already given that poor guy enough mental scars for a lifetime."

"Jem, I've been civil to you because that's what Tean wants, but fuck off."

"See, I thought it was really strange how none of those guys wanted a second date with Tean. He's a great guy. He's actually the best guy. Ever. In the whole universe. And so I started thinking something didn't add up."

Ammon pressed the down button again.

"How long have you been doing this?"

"I'm going to tell you one more time, nicely, to fuck off."

"That's not very nice, actually. Did you see me when I followed you?"

The tightening at Ammon's jaw was the only answer.

"So, here's what we're going to do. We're going back to one of our rooms—you can decide, yours or mine—and we're going to watch *SportsCenter* or *BroBang* or *DoucheNet* or whatever you want to watch. And if Tean comes back and we hear him getting pounded like a three-dollar chuck roast, we'll turn up the volume and smile and pretend we don't know what's going on. But what we're not going to do is go downstairs and continue to fuck up his life. Both of us have done enough of that. Let's give him a chance to be happy."

The elevator door opened; Ammon didn't step into the car, but he caught the door with one hand to hold it open. "Do you have any idea how seriously I could jam you up?"

Jem cocked his head. "I remember you wanted to take a drive to Vegas once. Here we are, Ammon. What now?"

"I wouldn't have to do anything illegal. That's the best part. You're your own worst enemy when it comes to this kind of stuff. An ordinary guy, I can make his life hell with all the bullshit laws out there that nobody knows about. I could make his life hell with a million inconveniences, all of them perfectly legal. But you? Jeez, you make it a walk in the park. All the cons you run, the petty thefts, the shenanigans, the drugs. There's a million ways I could make your life hell, and you're such a mess, I'd probably get a commendation for doing it."

"Let's go find somewhere quiet," Jem said. "If we're not going to watch TV, let's have this conversation once and for all."

Ammon gave a chilly smile. "I've seen your alley-rat toys. Put your hand on one, and it's assault with a deadly weapon. Come at me, and I'll put four slugs in your chest. It'll be self-defense. Justified use of force."

Jem put his hand in his pocket, hand closing around the length of paracord.

Ammon's cold smile had spread. "Come on, you little pussy faggot," he whispered. "Are you just going to stand there playing pocket pool?"

Jem's knuckles ached around the cord.

"That's what I thought," Ammon said. "You're not just a thief and a conman and an addict. You're a coward. And Tean deserves a hell of lot better than you."

"He does," Jem managed, his voice patchy. "But he deserves better than you too."

"Maybe. But I'm smart enough not to let him realize that."

Shrieking children emerged from a room down the hall, and they raced toward the elevator: a potbellied little black girl in a flamingo swimsuit, and a ropey boy in Transformers swim shorts who must have been her older brother. They pushed past Jem and Ammon onto the elevator, talking excitedly about which pools they were going to try, how long they could hold their breath, who could make the biggest splash. The parents came next, a young couple with approximately a hundred tote bags. They smiled at Jem and Ammon, then hesitated when they must have caught the energy between the two men.

"Go ahead," Ammon said with a smile, stepping onto the elevator. "He'll take the next one."

With sidelong glances at Jem, the couple slid past him. The elevator door closed, and Jem let out a shaky breath. He pried stiff fingers from the paracord, tented his hands over his nose, and took a few deep breaths. Then he pressed the Down button.

When he got to the lobby, the crowds were even worse. He made his way along the wide, brightly lit hallways, moving through the pockets that appeared in the ebb and flow of bodies. He'd lost sight of Ammon, but he knew where the other man was going, and he knew what was going to happen if he didn't intervene. He passed mosaics and fountains and statues. Tean would have known the names of the originals, Jem guessed. He got turned around in something called the Appian Way; a statue of a twunk with a tiny prong was staring off into the distance, and that didn't help. Finally Jem asked a girl named Maria at the FedEx store for directions. After that, he made it to the Old Homestead Steakhouse easily.

It was about what he expected: dark wood, low lighting, leather banquettes tufted with dull brass upholstery nails. Decorative wine displays tempted people into drinking more and, therefore, spending more. The smell of seared meat filled the air. Ammon was sitting at the bar. Jem made a beeline across the restaurant, waved off a hostess who looked like she might want to help, and dropped onto the stool next to Ammon.

"Oh boy," Ammon said. He was holding a lowball, and he rocked it side to side, the cocktail slopping against the cut crystal. "You're really determined to fuck yourself over, aren't you?"

"Normally, I prefer to do the fucking." Jem flagged the bartender, a trim older woman with a mane of silvery hair. "But we'll see how the night goes."

"Yes, sir?" the woman asked. Her name tag said Luz.

"Do you want to order for me again?" Jem asked. "For old time's sake?"

Ammon grunted.

"Do you have a local whiskey?" Jem said.

"Several, actually. Nevada whiskey, which is from the Las Vegas Distillery, Seven Troughs bourbon, and Silver Corn from The Depot."

"Your choice, neat, with a water back. And another for my friend." When Luz had moved off, Jem said, "This is like old times, isn't it?"

"Jem, this isn't going to end well for you. Tean cares about you; that means I'm willing to cut you some slack. You'd be smart to use it."

"Do you hate me because of how we met? It wasn't ideal, granted, but we both got what we wanted that night. Doesn't this remind you of it? A couple of out-of-towners who happen to run into each other at the bar, they drink, they eat, they go upstairs together. We could play it all out again. I remember some of the stuff you like."

"You're really messed up."

"Why not? Tean doesn't want either of us, and you and I both know that sex doesn't mean anything. You get your rocks off. I get to let off a little steam."

"You're screwed up. You really are."

Jem shrugged and accepted the drink from Luz.

"Was it really such an ego blow that I wasn't that innocent boy from Montana? Did it really mean that much to you, giving me my sexual awakening with a power fuck?"

Ammon's knuckles were white as he clutched the lowball. "Keep talking, Jem."

Sipping his whiskey, Jem glanced around the restaurant. He couldn't see Tean, and he wondered why Ammon had picked this spot. Then he checked the mirror behind the bar. Bingo bongo. Tean looked fabulous, and his date wasn't too bad either: late thirties, built, a polo that had probably cost a couple hundred bucks for the little alligator on it.

"Frat boy gone to seed," Jem said.

Ammon grunted again. He threw back the rest of his drink; Luz had placed another in front of him, and he slid it closer now.

"That could be a new porno series."

"Who's going to watch that?"

"There's an audience for everything."

"Jeez," Ammon muttered into his drink.

In the mirror, Tean was smiling, nodding, laughing. Some of the hair had fallen out of place, but the strands were still glossy, finely separated by the pomade Jem had worked through them. It looked better this way, Jem realized. Not the crazy, wild, pushed-back mess that Tean normally wore. But not the perfectly combed style that Jem had imposed on it either. Something in between, softening his thin face, accenting the full lips. The broken glasses had slid to the end of his nose, and the date—Logan? Parker? Chase?—reached across to steady them. Tean blushed and laughed some more, and Logan/Parker/Chase laughed too. Jem put back the rest of the whiskey and gestured for another.

"Can't you just let him be happy?" Jem asked.

"He isn't happy. If you can't see that, you're blind."

"But he's trying. He's getting there."

Ammon spun the lowball between his hands, staring down into the cocktail. It was only half-drunk; when he exhaled slowly, Jem could smell the booze on his breath. He spoke into the glass. "What do you think matters most to Tean?"

Jem took a moment. He was lost in the mirror world, where Tean had a tiny, embarrassed smile and was blushing, where Logan/Parker/Chase was reaching across the table to squeeze his hand. "His family, I guess. He's put up with so much shit from them, and he keeps going back for more, so he must love them pretty fiercely. His friends. He's very loyal. He wants to be a good person. He cares about the truth. He's given up just about everything to be honest about who he is and how he sees the world, even though it terrifies him."

Tean's laughter carried to the bar, and then his voice saying, "Oh my gosh, you've got to be kidding."

"Why do you think he puts up with them?" Ammon asked when Tean's voice had faded.

The question sounded like a trap, so Jem stayed silent and sipped his drink.

"Why," Ammon said, "does he still have a box full of Hollister calendars in his closet?"

"He likes blonds." Jem fought to work up a smirk. "Obviously."

"Why does he wear those same awful glasses?"

"He's been giving his parents money. He hasn't been able to afford things for himself."

"Why do you think he put up with all my shit for almost twenty years? The lying, the sneaking around, being treated like dirt."

Jem shook his head; his eyes stung, and he closed them. "Because he loves you."

"Maybe. He did at one point, but I think I might have fucked that up beyond repair." After a moment, Ammon said, "Well? Why does he hold on to all this stuff?"

"This is a trick."

"It's not a trick. Answer the question."

Opening his eyes, Jem was surprised to find Ammon looking directly at him. The blues eyes were frank and, for perhaps the first time since they had encountered each other in Tean's apartment, empty of hostility. "Whatever I say will be wrong. That's why this is a trick."

"What are you going to give him?" Ammon asked. "You've got no job, you've got no life, you've got no healthy relationships. You lie about everything. Tean might be able to look past that, but here's the sinker: his family hates you. Do you really think he's going to give them up for you?"

The clink of cutlery on china, the chime of glass against glass, the murmur of voices. Jem wanted to close his eyes again. Instead, he said, "We're just friends."

"Same old song and dance," Ammon said. He downed his drink, wiped his mouth, and shrugged. "It's going to hurt worse if you force him to make the decision. If you haven't learned this about Tean, let me fill you in: he can't let go. Not of his old pretty-boy calendars, not of the glasses he wore on his mission, not of me, not of his family.

Not of anything that meant something to him, even if it was years and years ago. Do yourself a favor and spare yourself a lot of time and a lot of grief. You'll be doing Tean a favor too: you'll be letting him have his family, his life, me. The things he's been holding on to almost as long as I've known him." Then he got up and left.

Jem didn't watch him go. He had to close his eyes for a while until he could pack everything away, until he was ok again. And then he was fine, everything under lock and key, the taste of blood in his mouth from where he had bitten open the inside of his cheek.

His phone buzzed with a text from Mommy Dearest. He could hear Brigitte's voice in his head, the thin, high nervousness of it: *I am so sorry, Jeremiah, but Gerald thinks it's best if we wait a while longer before you meet your brother and sister. I'm afraid you can't come on Tuesday. Please let me know about the checks. If you need more, I can talk to Gerald.*

Jem deleted the message. Then he deleted Brigitte's contact. He wiped his mouth, his fingers trembling, and found himself on the brink of something, some noise he couldn't even name. When Luz threw him a worried look, Jem waved her off.

He watched the mirror, watched Tean lean back in his chair, watched him snort with laughter and barely catch the glasses when they fell, watched him get that look of hyperfocused interest. He was still watching when Tean excused himself, pushing away from the table, and headed to the back of the restaurant. He was still watching when the date leaned across the table and put something in Tean's drink.

Jem was out of his seat before he knew what he was doing. He was vaguely aware of Luz saying something to him, but the words buzzed at the edge of his hearing. One of the display cases for the wine was in his path, and he had to cut around it. Then he was standing at the two-top, staring at Logan/Parker/Chase, who was poking at a piece of potato and looking bored. Before the frat boy-gone-to-seed could react, Jem had pulled Tean's chair around the table and set it next to him. Jem dropped into it. He grabbed the steak knife from the table, caught Logan/Parker/Chase by the collar, and set the tip of the knife against his side. Logan/Parker/Chase had gone stiff.

"What did you put in his drink?" Jem said.

"What the fuck?" Logan/Parker/Chase said. His eyes were set too close together, Jem saw now that he was closer, and he smelled like a drugstore beauty counter.

"What did you put in his drink, motherfucker? You have five seconds to tell me before I put this between your ribs."

"I—I—I—"

Jem released his collar, slapped him on the back of the head, and patted him down. He found the small, stoppered vial in Logan/Parker/Chase's front pocket. It was unmarked.

"What is it?"

Logan/Parker/Chase was hyperventilating.

Jabbing him with the knife, Jem said again, "What is it?"

"G, it's G. I wasn't going to—"

"Get the fuck out of here."

Logan/Parker/Chase pushed back his chair so fast that it fell over. The crash silenced the room, and then low, excited murmurs filled the room while Logan/Parker/Chase sprinted away. Jem reached down to pick up the chair. When he straightened, Tean was standing there, staring at him.

"What are you doing?"

"He was—"

"Where's Bradley?"

"Tean, this guy—"

"Is that a knife in your hand? Are you kidding me right now?" The color had leached out of Tean's face; his dark eyes looked huge against his sudden pallor. He grabbed the table. "I cannot believe this."

"You don't understand. If you'll just let me explain—"

"I saw you follow me to Stanza. I saw you, and I thought it was just a coincidence. I thought it was a misunderstanding. But then Ragnar wouldn't respond to any of my messages, and I thought—" He couldn't seem to catch his breath, and Jem was worried he was on the brink of passing out. "How many others?"

"I didn't do that."

"How many others? How long has this been going on?"

"Tean, please sit down. Take a breath. I can explain—"

"All you ever do is explain. All you ever do is explain and explain and explain. This is what you did with Ammon, too—the lying, the hiding, the manipulating. And with Ragnar. And now with Bradley. So answer my question: how many others?"

His shouts echoed through the stillness of the dining room; every eye was fixed on them.

"Let's go upstairs," Jem said, rising to take Tean's arm. "I'll tell you what happened, but you've got to calm down first."

Tean yanked his arm free. "All of them? All the guys that wouldn't go on a second date? Is that what's been going on?"

"Ammon—"

"Don't fucking talk to me about Ammon."

"He put something in your drink, shit-for-brains," Jem shouted. "Will you shut up and listen to me?"

Tean got even paler if that were possible. He was taking thin, whispery breaths, and his hand was clutching the table so tightly that it looked like a claw. "Here we go again," Tean said. "Another story. Another game. Bradley's conveniently gone, and I have to take your word for it."

"What the fuck is wrong with you? When have I ever lied to you?" Then, face heating, Jem said, "Recently, I mean."

"You lie all the time. All you do is lie. You lie about where you're living, what you're doing, how you're doing, whether or not you're ok. You lie about why the fuck we've spent the last few days in the middle of nowhere. You lie about why you haven't been sleeping and why you've been acting like a lunatic lately. You lie about so many things I can't even keep them straight anymore."

"We're going upstairs. We're going to talk about this—"

When he tried to take Tean's arm again, Tean shoved him. Jem staggered back. He caught up against the chair, stumbled, and almost went down. Someone whispered, and Jem was suddenly aware again of their audience. He was shaking. Somehow, he got clear of the chair without falling.

"Go away."

"No, I want—"

"I don't care what you want. I don't fucking care. Go away, Jem. Just go away."

Clutching the vial in one hand, Jem turned for the exit. He walked. Then he broke into a run, the hub of voices chasing after him.

32

Tean didn't sleep. He lay in bed, staring up at the ghost of the ceiling, replaying the scene over and over again. He waited for Jem to call or text or knock at the door. He turned his phone off and turned it on again. Once, he began pulling on clothes, planning on marching to Jem's room. But then he remembered looking out the windows at Stanza and seeing Jem on his motorcycle and knowing, even though he hadn't wanted to admit it, that Jem was following him.

The next day was a blur for Tean. His dad and brothers showed up at his door at the crack of dawn. Less than an hour later, he was downstairs with them at the buffet, moving scrambled eggs and a croissant around his plate without eating anything. Ammon was there too, laughing as he talked to Tean's brothers and dad.

"The girls have a whole day planned out," Amos said. "They let us off the leash, so we get to do whatever we want."

"And we've got lots of stuff to do," Timothy said. "Plenty of stuff to do."

Tean smiled and nodded as they listed out the day's itinerary. When the conversation shifted, and Tean's dad began expounding on the history of the mob in Las Vegas, Ammon leaned over and said quietly into Tean's ear, "Are you ok?"

Tean wanted to shake his head. Instead, he nodded and forced another smile.

"You're not eating."

"I'm not hungry."

"Are you sure?"

Another nod. Another smile.

"I just want you to know," Ammon said, "that I talked to your dad and brothers. I told them they had to include Jem. But we knocked on his door, and he didn't answer. Do you want to call him?"

Tean shook his head. "He's doing his own thing today. He's probably stealing the pearls off widows' necks and taking candy from babies and torching Shriners hospitals."

"Ok," Ammon said slowly.

Tean had to close his eyes, but a few tears leaked out.

"Hey," Ammon whispered. "What's going on? Are you all right?"

Tean opened his eyes, wiped his cheeks, and nodded again. Smiled. "Yes. Yeah. I'm fine."

"Tean—"

"Please don't do this right now."

Instead, Ammon squeezed his hand, and after a moment, Tean squeezed back. Hard. He was holding on for dear life, a part of him realized, and Ammon didn't let go.

"The gals are going shopping," Tean's dad announced, drawing Ammon and Tean's attention back to the conversation. "So the boys have the day to themselves."

Tean waited for the comment. *Somehow, Tean switched groups*. Or, *I guess Tean already had enough shoes.* Or, *Tean promised to keep an eye on us for them.*

Instead, though, his father only said, "And we're very happy to have Tean's . . . friend with us."

Ammon slung an arm around Tean's shoulders. Amos looked back at them, beaming like he'd orchestrated this whole thing masterfully. Seth gave a quick glance, an indulgent smile, before turning back to their dad. Tim and Cor didn't even look, which was its own kind of message.

"Everything's ok," Ammon whispered. "Try to relax. We're going to have fun."

And they did have fun. Tean couldn't believe it: even though he was miserable, a part of him had a great time. It wasn't the events themselves that were enjoyable, although he'd have been lying if he said he didn't like Madame Tussauds. Not the wax figures, because he had no idea who most of them were, but they played a VR game that involved searching for a way to escape a locked room, and he liked the puzzle-solving aspect of it. Ammon was the one who solved the final puzzle, of course, and when they were all pulling off headsets, Timothy said, "Not fair. You guys had a real detective on your team. Next time, we get Ammon."

"You had Tean," Ammon said with a laugh, sliding an arm around Tean's waist. "He's solved a couple of murders himself."

"Tean spent fifteen minutes trying to climb through the mirror," Seth said, giving him a playful shove as he went past.

"It looked like a secret passage," Tean protested.

As they were heading out of the VR room, Amos caught Tean's arm and whispered, "Dude, don't screw this up."

"What? I didn't even say anything when Dad made that big speech about the evils of sex work!"

"No, dummy. Don't screw this up with Ammon. He's a stud, or whatever I'm supposed to say."

"Well, you aren't supposed to say, 'whatever I'm supposed to say,' because that sounds really alienating."

"Don't screw this up," Amos growled, jabbing his finger into Tean's chest.

"What was that about?" Ammon asked as Tean rejoined him. His arm settled comfortably around Tean's shoulders.

Tean had absolutely no idea, so he just shrugged and said, "You know Amos."

And the weird thing was, it was true: Ammon did know Amos. He knew all of them, and they knew him, and more importantly, they liked Ammon. They didn't know all of it, of course. They didn't know what a lot of those years had been like, the really bad ones, when Tean didn't know if he could keep living the half-life Ammon had offered him. They knew Ammon from when he'd been a three-sport athlete, a star, the golden boy at church and school. And they all obviously had big-boy crushes on him. Still.

Even, in some weird way that Tean didn't understand, his father. When Ammon ordered a beer at lunch—they ate at Gordon Ramsay's Hell's Kitchen, which was apparently a restaurant based on a TV show based on a game, from what Tean could tell—Tean's dad gave a twenty-minute, rambling speech about the Israelites drinking beer and the importance of alcohol in providing safe drinking water and sufficient calorie intake.

"I'm starting to remember where you get it from," Ammon whispered, his breath yeasty and warm when it tickled Tean's ear. He grunted when Tean elbowed him, but Tean didn't bother hiding the smile.

They stopped to see the Bellagio fountains, but by then it was mid-afternoon, and the heat shimmered in the city's trapped air. They went inside the Bellagio instead, wandering the halls, listening to the electronic chings of the games. Seth stopped at a quarter slot machine and said, "What do you think, Ammon? Should I do it?"

"Do it," Ammon said.

Seth dropped the quarter, pulled the arm, and burst out laughing when he got a horseshoe, a heart, and a bell.

"Am I exclusively related to twelve-year-olds?" Tean asked as his brothers moved away.

"Maybe just primarily," Ammon said. He stopped, stopping Tean with him, and kissed his cheek. "Sorry. Maybe that's crossing a line, but you're so beautiful when you're happy."

From ahead came whoops and laughter.

"Kiss, kiss, kiss," Timothy and Cor shouted.

"I guess they don't object," Ammon said with a smirk. "And it is a pretty good suggestion."

"It's a terrible suggestion," Tean said, pushing Ammon's face away and slipping free of his arm. "You're all jerks," he shouted up to his brothers.

For some reason, all of them, including Ammon, thought that was the funniest thing Tean had ever said.

Their next stop was Sin City Smash.

"But what's the point?" Tean asked as they waited in the lobby.

"That is the point," Cor said. "You smash things."

"Why?"

"Because it's fun. Oh my gosh, Ammon, please help."

"It is kind of fun to destroy things."

"See?"

"But we're paying to do it," Tean said. "Why not just destroy things you already own? Or when it's already part of the process. I kind of had fun breaking things when Jem and I were searching—"

The brothers traded glances, and Tean cut off.

"It's just a guy thing," Ammon said into the silence. "Don't worry about it."

"Yeah, it's a guy thing," Cor said. Then he yelped when Amos swatted him across the back of the head. "What the heck? Ammon said it, but I can't?"

Their rage room had plenty of things to smash: hardwood chairs, particleboard tables, an Ikea bookshelf with ceramic figurines of lambs and dairy maids and what Tean imagined were probably meant to be Swiss villages. It had clocks, computers, brick cell phones. It had a mirror, with a warning that seemed to be completely unironic: WARNING - PIECES WILL BE SHARP.

The guys went to town: smashing, stomping, bashing, kicking. When Ammon picked up one of the hardwood chairs and hit it against the wall, it exploded into pieces, and Cor, Tim, and Seth actually cheered. Tean and his dad stayed off to one side. Neither of them spoke, and Tean waited for a comment about the sanctity of the family, about the trials of the flesh, maybe just something truly banal like how disgusting it must be for two men to do such things to each other. Instead, Robert Leon, who had spent the cab ride over lecturing their driver, who was from Ethiopia, about the current situation in Ethiopia, said nothing.

When time was up, Cor grabbed Ammon's arm. "You're a beast, dude. What have you been doing?"

"Just changing things up at the gym," Ammon said. He was flushed. Sweat trapped fine blond hairs on his forehead, and his chest rose and fell rapidly. His arms were ropey with veins.

"Is it a website? A book?" Cor patted his stomach, where a little pouch had formed. "I'm in the worst shape of my life."

"Sure, I'll send you the link. Or we can meet up, and I'll coach you through it the first few times."

"Seriously?"

"Why not?"

"Jeez, maybe I'll actually get to have sex again this side of eternity."

"Oh my gosh," Tean muttered, putting his head in his hands.

"You try having four kids," Cor snapped, but he was grinning. "See what that does to your libido and your diet."

"We'll get you back into fighting shape," Ammon said with a laugh as they headed for the door.

"Ammon," Tean's dad said, his voice cutting through the conversation.

This was it, Tean realized. This was the speech or the lecture or the confrontation, although why his father had chosen this moment, he didn't know.

But what his dad said was "I've been thinking about buying a new rifle, and I've been having a hard time deciding between a Seekins and a Browning."

Ammon nodded. "Good guns."

"I have to admit," Robert Leon said, "I'm leaning toward Browning because he was a man of the church." That sentence opened the floodgates, and Tean's dad was talking a mile a minute as he walked Ammon out of the room.

"Holy crap," Timothy said, grabbing Tean's collar, "did you see that?"

"See Dad turn a question into a lecture? Yes, I'm very familiar with it."

"Maybe you forgot, but Dad doesn't ever ask questions. Never. And he just asked Ammon one."

"Not really. He didn't even phrase it as a question. He mostly wanted to prove—"

"Ammon is awesome, and he's into your scrawny butt and your chicken legs. Don't screw this up."

"Why does everyone—"

"Don't screw it up," Seth said, pointing a finger at him.

"There's not even anything to screw up because—"

"I already tried to tell him," Amos said, arms crossed, his expression supremely satisfied.

"Look, you guys don't know—"

From the other side of the room, where he was smashing a few final ceramic figurines, Cor shouted, "Don't screw it up, Teancum!"

"Frick," Tean muttered, knocking Tim's hand from his collar. He looked around, saw all four brothers staring at him like he was planning on immediately going out and screwing things up, and said, "Frick," again.

They ate dinner at the Rainforest Café, which seemed to sum up everything about Vegas: a manmade tropical illusion, with plastic macaws and machine-generated humidity and artificial waterfalls all manufactured in a desert city. An animatronic capuchin monkey seemed to be touching himself in a way that wasn't acceptable in polite society, and Tean spent a good part of the meal trying to figure out who had programmed that behavior and why.

After dinner, dusk settled across the city. The disc of the world burned red to the west, throwing the miles and miles of suburban homes into a sharp contrast of glare and shadow. To the east, though, blue haze settled over the desert, deepening to purple, then black at its farthest point. The heat was still tremendous, crushing, made worse by the unending parade of taxis and the billowing clouds of exhaust. When the Strip's lights came on, flooding the street with neon blues and fluorescent reds, Vegas could have passed for beautiful: the dappled shadows hid the flyers for titty bars that papered the sidewalk; the inelegant bumps and swells of industrial air-conditioning units and construction scaffolding softened in the shadows; dramatic lighting raked the facades of the Venetian, Caesar's Palace, Paris Las Vegas, and none of it seemed quite so preposterous.

For whatever reason, Robert Leon wanted to do the Eiffel Tower Experience, which consisted of riding up to the observation deck of a half-sized Eiffel Tower replica. In the elevator, Amos poked Tean in the back, hard, and whispered, "Hold his hand, dummy."

Everyone in the elevator heard. A tiny smile played around Ammon's mouth before he got it under control.

When they got off the elevator, Tean took a deep breath. The air was cooler up here. The breeze coming in smelled like fried food and what he guessed was a pumped-in cinnamon fragrance to entice people into buying something sugary and fattening. People moved around the observation deck singly, in pairs and in small groups. In suspicious silence, Tean's brothers and dad hustled away, leaving Ammon and Tean alone.

Ammon laughed quietly.

"I'm going to murder all of them," Tean said. "There's not a single court in this country that will find me guilty."

"Teancum, may I please hold your hand?"

Tean nodded, and Ammon's fingers laced with his.

They strolled around the observation deck. The city was bright, fierce, insistent against the darkness dropping steadily over the desert. A pre-recorded accordion track played in the background. Tean vaguely recognized it as the music often associated with Venice and gondolas; he wondered if it was carelessness or intentional.

Perhaps whoever had chosen the music hadn't realized that Venice wasn't in France and had nothing to do with the Eiffel Tower, but Tean doubted it. Everything else in this city was designed to take you by the throat and make you do what it wanted; why not this?

When they stopped at the rail, looking out over starbursts of artificial pinks and blues and red, Ammon stood shoulder to shoulder with him. His body painted a line of heat down Tean. His hand bumped along the knobs of Tean's spine and came to rest at the small of his back. His thumb moved in a small circle there. Tean remembered that gesture. After the first time they had made love, horny teenagers in a shower in Lima, they had climbed into bed together, and Ammon had held him and made the same slow circles with his thumb. Tean's brain made lists: Vegas, the city where you could have Venice and Rome and Egypt and Paris all within a half mile. Vegas, the city where you could have romance and adventure, shopping and gambling, dinner and dancing. Vegas, the city where you could have it all.

Tean's face was hot. His eyes stung, and the lights swam in his vision. He took a deep breath, and then another.

"Are you ok?"

Tean nodded.

"Tean—"

"I'm ok." His voice was wet and broken.

"Talk to me. What's wrong?"

"Nothing." But what he wanted to say was, *Everything*. "Today has been wonderful. Thank you for being wonderful."

"You're upset. What did I do?"

"Nothing. You've been amazing. I'm sorry, I'm just being weird. As usual."

Ammon cupped his face and kissed his cheek. Then he kissed him on the lips. Softly, just a brush. And then once more.

"This isn't the right place to do this," Ammon whispered, "because you deserve everything to be perfect, but I want to tell you that I love you."

"I love you too," Tean said, and he didn't know why, but he started to sob.

For some reason, that seemed to make things easier for Ammon. He told Tean to wait, and then he left. Tean's crying turned into racking, hitching gasps that he managed to choke back only barely.

The men and women around him took a few steps back. One woman removed a tissue from her purse, clutching it in her hand, staring at him but not willing to approach. When Ammon came back, he put an arm around Tean and led him to the elevator.

"My—my—my—" Tean tried to say.

"I told them you need to go back to the hotel. They're fine."

Tean cried the whole ride down. He cried the whole walk back. He couldn't say why, and he couldn't stop. He cried on the elevator ride up to the Augustus tower. He was crying harder than ever when Ammon removed the wallet from Tean's pocket, found the card key, and let them both into the room.

Ammon helped Tean lie down. He lowered the blinds and turned on a single lamp. He got water from the sink in a thin plastic cup that crinkled when he set it on the nightstand. Then he removed Tean's shoes.

"I'm sorry," Tean said. Or tried to say. "I'm really sorry."

"It's ok. You don't need to be sorry. It's been a lot; you've been through a lot lately." Ammon's hand was hot on Tean's leg. "Do you want me to stay? Go?"

Tean put an arm over his eyes.

"I'd like to stay," Ammon said.

After a moment, face still hidden in his elbow, Tean nodded.

Ammon stretched out next to him, his hand gliding up to rest on Tean's belly. His breathing evened out and became an anchor, and eventually Tean's breathing slowed too. His face was still hot and puffy; when he peeled his arm away, the dried salt of tear tracks pulled at his skin.

Ammon's hand came up, his fingers combing slowly through Tean's hair. "Have some water."

Tean propped himself on his side. The plastic was cool and flexed in his grip. He managed a swallow, coughed, and drank again. When he lay down again, he rolled to face Ammon, who was still running one hand through Tean's hair. A tiny furrow marked the skin between Ammon's eyebrows. His mouth was a thin, hard blade.

"I'm sorry I made a scene," Tean said.

"I don't care about that."

"I'm not going to go crazy again. I just—I was feeling a lot of things, and they were overwhelming."

Ammon hummed something, a song Tean didn't know, and his fingers continued their rhythmic pull and glide. "What were you feeling?"

"I don't know."

"It's been a long time since you lied to me about what you were feeling."

Tean swallowed. His throat was thick; his nose was stuffy with snot.

"I want to show you something." Ammon lay on his belly, drew out his phone, and unlocked it. He tapped through a series of screens and then held the phone to Tean.

The display showed a scanned document. Pages and pages with text and signatures. Tean pinched and zoomed, blinking because his eyes were still hot and itchy. Then he pulled in a deep breath.

"Ammon, why didn't you tell me?"

"I am telling you, dingbat. I'm telling you right now." He chucked Tean under the chin, forcing his eyes up. He wore a nervous smile. "I am officially a single man."

"I didn't—I don't know what you want—"

"I want to kiss you," Ammon said. He shifted, supporting himself on his elbows, his leg moving between Tean's. He smelled like the beer from dinner, like sweat, like Ammon. He kissed Tean, and he tasted like beer and Ammon. He shifted again, and his hand slid under Tean's shirt, pawing at his chest. When he broke the kiss, he whispered, "I want this to be our first time. This is our real first time."

Over the tattoo of blood in his ears, Tean could hear the ice machine rattling. He nodded, and he sat up to help Ammon strip off his shirt. Then he arched his back so Ammon could tug his chinos down to his ankles. And then Ammon pulled them off completely, kissing the inside of Tean's calves, kissing up to the knobby knees, kissing over the thick dark hair on the inside of Tean's thighs. He pulled down the black briefs and took Tean in his mouth, and Tean gasped. Ammon looked up at him, eyes hooded, irises so dark they were almost purple.

When he pulled off Tean's dick, Ammon licked his lips and said, "Tell me what you want."

Tean's breath whistled in his throat.

"I only want to do what you want. Please tell me what you want." From the hall came a thunk as something hit the floor, then drunken laughter. Ammon kissed Tean's stomach, turning his face so that Tean's dick left a wet mark along his cheek. His eyes slid toward the minibar with its airplane-sized bottles. "If you need help."

"I don't want to do that anymore."

"Ok. That's ok. I only want what you want; I just thought it made it easier for you."

And it did. It always made it easier. Everclear or schnapps or vodka or gin. Whatever could go through his brain like a battering ram, knocking down everything that tried to stand up to this. And for the first time in his life, Tean wondered why it had become so difficult with Ammon, at what point in all their years of doing this, things had changed between them. He wondered why something that should have been easy had only gotten harder and harder.

"Ammon."

His mouth took Tean again.

"Ammon, stop."

His big hands gripped Tean, spreading his legs, exposing him.

"Ammon, I don't want to do this."

Ammon pulled off with another wet pop. "Let's get you something to drink."

"No, I don't want to do this. I don't want to do this anymore."

"What does that mean?"

Over Ammon's shoulder, Tean could see them both in the window, glass specters. "You know what I mean."

"No, I don't. I don't know what the fuck you think you mean." His lips were full. A hint of saliva glistened at the corner of his mouth. "Let's calm down and talk about this."

Ghosts in the glass. Maybe in the flux of quantum possibilities, that was the real Ammon, the real Tean, the real world.

Shouts erupted in the hall. No words, just a bellowing rage.

"Jem," Tean said, sliding out from under Ammon.

"We're not done talking." Ammon caught his arm.

But Tean twisted free. He pulled his briefs into place, grabbed his shirt, and looked around for where Ammon had tossed his chinos. Ammon was getting off the bed, trying to grab Tean's arm again, so

Tean decided to forego the pants. He hurried to the door and threw it open.

A dark-haired man was backing down the hall, naked except for one sock, holding balled-up clothing to his chest. His lip was split, and blood ran down his chin. "You're out of your fucking mind," he shouted.

Jem stood in the doorway of the next room, naked and clutching the jamb. He roared something back at the man, and the sound was frightening because it resembled words without making any sense.

"I'm calling the cops. You're a fucking lunatic."

"He's sick," Tean said, moving toward Jem. "He didn't mean to hurt you."

"The fuck he didn't. I'm calling the cops."

"He's not well. Can't you see that?"

Jem made more of those horrible, slurred noises.

"What the fuck is going on out here?" Ammon said from behind Tean.

"That maniac attacked me!"

Jem lunged, or tried to. As soon as he released the door jamb, he began to fall. Tean caught him, grunted at the other man's weight, and then swore when Jem clubbed the side of his head.

"Stop it." The second blow knocked the glasses from Tean's face. "Stop, Jem. Stop. It's me. Stop it! Ammon, can you help."

By then, though, Jem had gone still, slumped against Tean. His face was hot against Tean's shoulder. His breathing was unnaturally slow, and drool soaked through the cotton of Tean's polo.

Ammon scooped up the fallen glasses.

"He's really heavy."

"So dump him in his room and close the door."

"No, I want to get him to the bed and make sure he's ok. I don't like how he's breathing."

"Then call an ambulance."

"He doesn't like that. He doesn't like hospitals."

Ammon didn't say anything.

"A little help?"

"I'll help you get him in bed. Then I want to talk to you."

"I don't think tonight is the right time for this."

Ammon crossed his arms. It was hard, without the glasses, to make out his expression, but Tean had known him long enough that he recognized the stiff posture.

"Fine," Tean said. "Just give me my glasses. I'll take care of him myself."

"No."

"What do you mean, no? Give me my glasses."

"No. I'm tired of this. You need to stop acting like a crazy person. We'll put him to bed, and then we're going to talk like adults."

"They're my glasses, Ammon. Give them to me. Right now."

"Sure. As soon as we're back in your room. Talking."

"This is extortion."

"Don't be so dramatic."

"I'm not going to ask you again, Ammon. Give me my glasses. We're not having this conversation tonight. Frankly, the way I'm feeling right now, maybe we never need to have it."

The whole world was a blur to Tean's impaired vision, but he heard the crack of plastic breaking, and then the soft thumps of something hitting the carpet.

"There you go," Ammon said. "There are your glasses."

Tean stared at the out-of-focus shape. Then he said, "Goodnight, Ammon."

"Fuck your goodnight. You don't have any fucking idea what I've put up with from you. I'm sick of it. When you're thinking clearly again, I'll be waiting for your apology. And trust me, Tean, you're going to spend a long time convincing me you deserve to have me back."

Tean waited to see if there was more. Then he shouldered open the door to Jem's room, got Jem into a fireman's carry, and staggered to the bed. The room was pitch black and smelled like sex. After easing Jem onto the mattress, Tean made his way back to the hall. Ammon was gone. He crawled around on the floor, picking up as many pieces of the frames as he could find. Then he let himself back into Jem's room and set the swing bar.

He left the broken glasses on the black plateau of the entertainment center. He found a lamp and switched it on. Jem lay on his side, his breathing still artificially slow, his eyes cracked open, glassy and vacant. Faint, blush-colored marks on his thighs would be bruises in the morning; the pink print of a hand marked one butt cheek. Tean rolled him onto his stomach, finished his inspection, and found nothing else external. Then he made a wall of pillows and rolled Jem onto his side again, with the pillows as a backstop. Jem was still watching him from the other side of those empty eyes.

In polo and briefs, Tean climbed up onto the bed and lay next to Jem.

"So you don't slide onto your back, vomit, and asphyxiate," Tean told him.

Jem didn't even blink.

"Can you tell me what you took?"

The A/C came to life; it was like the whole room sucked in a breath. On the entertainment center, an empty glass vial stood next to a three-pack of condoms. If they had to go to the hospital, Tean would take the vial with him; maybe they could test it.

With another of those protoverbal moans, Jem pushed on Tean.

"Cut it out."

Jem mumbled something again; whatever he'd taken had left him sedated almost to the point of unconsciousness, but he was still trying to force Tean off the bed.

"I said cut it out; I'm not going anywhere." And then, the words coming out of nowhere, Tean snapped, "Zebras can't sleep alone. They won't sleep unless a member of the herd is with them, standing guard. Tonight, you're a zebra."

This time, the words sounded dangerously close to *not a zebra*.

"You goddamn are. And you've got the stripes on your ass to prove it. Now go to sleep."

Tean wasn't sure, but Jem might have mumbled *swear jar*. But he settled down, his head coming to rest on Tean's belly. Goosebumps covered his pale skin, so Tean drew up the covers. Then, under the comforter, he found Jem's hand.

Jem stirred again.

"Oh, be quiet," Tean said. "All you ever want is to touch. So be quiet. Don't make me tell you about otters holding hands."

"Not an otter."

"I said be quiet."

"Not a zebra."

"Jeez, you are a serious pain in my butt. That's what you are."

Jem's breathing continued to be slow, tidally deep. Tean closed his eyes and rested against the headboard. He kept playing it out, over and over again: the day with his brothers; Ammon kissing him; the tears that wouldn't stop. Sleep took his brain out of focus, and other thoughts drifted in.

He'd been twelve, spending Christmas break at his grandparents' house in northern Utah. They'd had a dog named Straw, a Golden Retriever mix, who'd been twelve too. That had seemed very important at the time. Straw had cancer; now, in the bizarre clarity that came sometimes at the threshold of sleep, Tean knew even the most rigorous treatments couldn't have saved her. The same end came to everything, no matter how hard you fought, and it could be a mercy. But he had been twelve, growing into himself, uncertain of everything and wanting to be certain about something. When Straw had become incontinent, his grandfather had gotten out his .22.

Tean had begged. He had argued. Finally, he had defied. He had made a bed for Straw in the barn: a Chiquita banana box—the big kind, the size of shipping pallet—and he'd put down horse blankets. He'd carried Straw out, ignoring his grandfather's shouts and the way he strutted around, his turkey neck jiggling as he called orders. He'd spent two days in the barn, giving Straw water, combing snarls and burrs out of her fur, the smell of the kerosene heater mixing with the smell of the banana box, and under it all, Straw's sickness and incontinence. He'd cried for two days, or that's how it seemed now. Two days drinking from the same spigot as Straw. Two days with a horse blanket around his shoulders, huddled next to the kerosene heater, not sleeping for fear Straw would die if he did. He'd woken to the sound of the .22 and the banana box empty. After that, he hadn't cried for a long time.

He touched the back of his hand to his face, surprised to find his eyes dry. Then he combed Jem's hair with his fingers. The blinds were up. The city eventually snuffed out. Dawn came on like an infection. He slept.

33

When Jem woke, the room was peach-colored, and he thought he was still doped. Then he realized it was sunrise, and he was curled up around Tean, the doc half-propped against the headboard. The light softened his face, took out so many of the lines of worry, protectiveness (another kind of worry, Jem guessed), fear and hope and care (more worry, it seemed to Jem right then). The G had wiped out pretty much everything from the last twenty-four hours, but Jem had a strange half-memory of zebras.

He peeled himself away from Tean, stumbled to the bathroom, and threw up for a long time. Then he cleaned himself up and brushed his teeth, his head pounding so badly that it made his eyes water. In the mirror, one side of his face was red and stippled with the texture from Tean's polo. The lacerations and their stitches itched. He tried to drink water and gave up. When he got back to the bed, he hooked one arm around Tean's shoulders and the other under his knees. The doc's eyes came open.

Jem shushed him as he slid Tean down to lie on the mattress and placed a pillow under his head. "Your neck is going to thank me later."

Tean just stared at him, his eyes dark and bottomless, and then went back to sleep.

Jem lowered the blinds, crawled into bed, and curled up around Tean.

When he woke the next time, the room was no longer peach-colored, and Tean was lying on his side, watching him.

"Heidegger says death is what gives life meaning."

"No," Jem said, burying his face in Tean's chest, smelling the city on the polo, missing the scents of pine and sage and the wide-open range. "It's too early." Tean laughed softly. His fingers tickled the back of Jem's neck. After a while, Jem mumbled, "Ok. Ready, set, go."

"No, it's nothing. I don't even know why I said it."

"Dear God, I am a fucking wreck from taking G, and I just spent the last day and a half thinking you'd never talk to me again, so please have pity on me and don't make me beg you to talk to me about weird old German men."

"What's G?"

"Liquid X. GHB. Gamma hydroxy-something-with-a-B acid."

"Hydroxybutyric."

"Of course you know the actual name." Jem snuggled into Tean's chest.

"Is that what that guy tried to put into my drink?"

"How do I answer that without getting yelled at?"

"I should have listened to you, Jem. I'm sorry. I'd had this weird feeling that someone had been following me, and nobody would ever talk to me after a first date, and I took all that insecurity out on you. I'm really sorry. And I'm even sorrier that I didn't trust you."

"I'm going to say this, and then you can do whatever you want except make loud noises because my head might actually fall apart, but did you think about the fact that maybe you weren't completely wrong?"

Jem felt the hitch in Tean's breath when he understood. Then Tean said quietly, "Ammon."

"He always wanted to know where you were going. I followed Ammon when you went out with Ragnarok—"

"Just Ragnar."

"—and he was keeping an eye on you."

Tean punched the mattress. "I am such an idiot."

"Ok, ok, but less noise, please. My head."

After a few labored breaths, Tean managed to ask, "Do you need to go to the hospital?"

"No, I just need you to talk quietly and maybe play with my hair."

"How about some ibuprofen?"

"God, yes."

Tean left and came back. This time, it was easier to drink some water and get the pills down. They found a more comfortable position, with Jem wrapped around Tean, Tean's hand lazily working its way through Jem's hair.

"Tell me about death," Jem said.

"Oh my gosh. No."

"Teannabelle Mahjong Leon, when I am feeling better, I will tie your ball sack into a knot if you don't talk to me about whatever you need to talk about. You're the one who's always going on and on about feeling your feelings."

Out in the hall, kids were laughing, then one of them shrieked so loudly and shrilly that Jem winced. Whatever the cause, the noise cut off after another moment, and peals of laughter followed.

"Goddamn kids," Jem whispered.

"So much of my life, I believed—I was supposed to believe—that what happened in this life didn't matter. What mattered was the life to come. This was . . . a stepping-stone, I guess. Your chance to prove that you were worthy of eternal bliss. And looking at life like that, it was easy not to be too bothered by much. I mean, part of that was because I was relatively comfortable in a functioning, middle-class family."

"I've met your family. Functioning is a stretch."

"But when you're told over and over again that this life doesn't matter, then you can convince yourself that suffering doesn't matter either. Sure, it's a little bit sad. And you've got your Christian duty to help other people. But it's easy not to let it have any claim on you. Other people's suffering, but also your own. And the same goes for joy and pleasure. Why stop and seize a moment now when you've got an eternity of perfect moments waiting for you? It strips everything out of life until it might as well be a standardized test."

"I liked to make patterns. B, B, B, A, A, A, C, C, C."

Tean laughed again, his fingers scratching Jem's scalp pleasantly. "Heidegger, Nietzsche, Kierkegaard, Sartre, Camus—for them, confronting the inescapability of death is at the heart of being authentic, of finding meaning in existence. When you see death, when you understand its finality, when you know that it's coming for you and that nothing you can do or say will change that, you have two options: you can recognize your total potential for living and being, or you can retreat into comfortable illusions where you feel safe. It's our anxiety and dread of death, maybe even our despair, that makes real, authentic existence possible."

Jem raised his head, blinking to clear his vision, and fixed Tean with a look. "What happened yesterday?"

"I had a good day with Ammon and my family."

Groaning, Jem let his head fall again. "I can't do this. Not this hungover. I honestly can't."

"That was a big change for me, when I finally understood that life wasn't limitless, that eternity wasn't waiting just around the corner. Everything we do means something now, here. Dying is real. And killing someone or something, ending their existence, that's real. Suffering is real. Victimhood is real. For some people, it's the only thing they ever know—or close enough." His hand was shaky as he gathered the hair from Jem's forehead and brushed it back. "Pleasure is real, joy too, and it's only now, right now, when we can have them, so we have to fight for them. Fight for ourselves. Fight for other people. Fight for justice and peace and happiness and safety right now, instead of waiting for a perfect world that we'll all get sometime later. Later isn't worth anything; we only have right now. And how we choose to use this moment, how we choose to spend the precious little time we have alive, that's the most serious ethical responsibility we have."

"Please don't tell me you're going to make me stop watching Saturday-morning cartoons. I ask for very little." Jem raised his head and asked again, "Tean, what happened yesterday?"

"I realized it was time for a few things to end. Ammon was right: I need to recognize that I can't have everything. I need to choose what I want the most and let the rest go."

Closing his eyes against the sudden sting, Jem lowered his head again. "Well, it sounded awful when Ammon said it, and it still sounds awful even when you say it. So thank you, for, you know. Making sure I didn't die or whatever. That means a lot to me. And I'm always going to love you because we're rover buddies and—"

He cut off when Tean put a hand over his mouth.

"I have spent my entire life trying not to lose anything," Tean said, his voice choked. "I've lost a lot, and it hurts too much, and I'm tired of hurting. I felt like I lost my family when I came out. I felt like I lost my sense of self, my identity, my purpose, my place in the universe. And then I met you, and I realized how happy I could be, but I still couldn't . . . I still couldn't let it go, this fantasy that if I was good enough, patient enough, if I swallowed enough crap and wrote enough checks, if I found the right guy, somehow I could be me again, the old me, and I could have it all: I could have my old life with my family, and I could have this new life with a man I loved, and I wouldn't have to lose anything."

Peeling Tean's fingers away, Jem said, "I get it. I'm happy for you, I really am. I'm going to be a total bitch about it, but I really am happy for you. I'm glad Ammon makes you happy, and I'm glad your family loves him, and I'm—I'm—" He couldn't seem to finish, and even with his eyes closed, tears spilled out. Tean's thumb ran across his cheek, wiping them away.

"For someone who might be the smartest man I've ever met," Tean said, "you are very dumb sometimes. I'm trying to tell you I love you."

Sniffles. Then Jem wiped his eyes and tried to open them, but they burned with fresh tears. He wiped those away too. Then he slapped Tean's ass and said, "Well you're doing a fucking terrible job of it."

An unsteady grin wobbled on Tean's face. "I love you, Jem. I want to spend the rest of my life with you. I don't know if you want that after how I've—"

Jem grabbed his mane of wild hair, pulled him down, and kissed him. When he broke away, the pounding in his head had gotten significantly better. It might have had something to do with the ibuprofen, but he didn't think so.

"Don't you dare choose me over your family, Teancum Leon. I love you, and we'll figure out a way to be together, but I don't want you cutting things off with your family. Even if they are a bunch of manipulative, selfish assholes."

"I'm not cutting them off. And they're not what you said. Not exactly. I'm just letting go of something that died a long time ago. And that's ok; it's time for that part of my life to be over."

Jem sat up. He touched Tean's face; the skin was fever hot. "I don't want you to have to lose something again. I don't want you to ever have to hurt. Not ever."

"Everything ends, Jem." He turned into Jem's touch. "That's what allows things to be beautiful. That's what gives things meaning."

Tean moved to kiss him again, and Jem drew back.

"What?" Tean said. "Did I—"

Blowing out a shaky breath, Jem said, "I have to tell you something."

Tean watched him. Those soft, dark eyes held Jem's reflection. "You don't have to tell me anything. Not if you're not ready."

"No, I have to. I have to because if I don't now, I might not ever do it, and I need you to know. You deserve to know." Jem drew a thick, wet breath. "Tanner, Antonio, and Blake, they took turns. Hurting me. They'd get me alone, and two of them would hold me down, and they'd take off my clothes and—" He'd reached the end. His throat seized. Then, swallowing, he shook his head.

"It's ok," Tean whispered. "You don't have to say it."

Jem cleared his throat, but his voice was still rough when he spoke again. "They fucked me. So, there. Now you know. It's not a big deal. It's not like it means anything. But I hate them for it, and that's why I've been acting so weird, and—and—" His eyes were hot and stinging. His chest hitched. He couldn't seem to make his tongue work correctly, and the words came out broken. "They did it to me again and again, and I couldn't make them stop."

That was all. As far as he got. And then he sobbed while Tean held him.

Tean rubbed his back, stroked his hair, murmured soft, soothing things the way he spoke to Scipio when the wind got too loud. And after a while, Jem peeled himself away from Tean, wiping his face.

"Jem—"

"I'm fine. I'm sorry about that. I'm totally fine."

Tean shook his head. "What if you aren't fine? What if you let yourself not be fine for a while?"

"I just need to pee."

Without waiting for a reply, Jem rolled off the bed and padded into the bathroom. He washed his face, cried some more, and washed his face again. When he stepped through the door again, Tean was sitting on the edge of the bed, arms wrapped around himself. He had been crying too, the tracks still staining his cheeks.

Jem picked up his phone and tapped his way through several screens. Music started to play. He tried a smile. "Am I going to have to go over there? Or are you coming over here?"

Tean looked like he wanted to talk more, but after a moment, he said, "We could meet in the middle."

"I like that idea."

When they reached each other, Jem wrapped his arms around Tean, and the doc settled his hands on Jem's waist. They rocked together, Tean guiding Jem into the music's rhythm. Jem's eyes were hot again, and he rested his head on Tean's shoulder, trying to pretend his tears weren't soaking Tean's shirt.

"Emmylou Harris," Jem said, his voice still hoarse. "This is 'Orphan Girl.'"

Tean's hand ran up and down Jem's back, smooth and slow. Emmylou told them about God's highway, about God's table. She told them about friendships pure and golden.

"You're not an orphan, Jem," Tean said quietly, his mouth at Jem's ear. "And you're not alone."

Jem kissed him. His hands were shaking as he reached for the buttons on Tean's polo, then he stopped. "Is this ok?"

Tean nodded, but he said, "But you don't feel well."

"I'm hungover," Jem growled, yanking on the placket as he worked the buttons free. "Not dead."

Then the polo slipped up and over Tean's shoulders, exposing the delicate lines of his neck, his shoulders, his chest. They fell together, tangled on the bed. He was the way Jem remembered: the thin stripe of fur running down the center of his chest, the skin tight over his ribs, the slight bump of his sternum. Too thin. Deep breaths made his belly rise and fall; the trail of hair disappeared under the waistband of his briefs. Jem let his hands wander over Tean, tracing his clavicle, his chest, teasing a nipple, tugging at the furry strip. He was exactly the way Jem remembered, back when they had tried this the first time.

But he was different too. More confident as he took Jem in hand, his smile playful instead of shy when Jem made a pleased noise. He arched his head, exposing his neck, where Jem took advantage of the sensitive skin and scraped his beard back and forth until Tean moaned. Tean remembered what Jem liked too: the spot between his shoulder blades, the weight of his hands on Jem's ass, his mouth everywhere he could reach. Jem loved his mouth, couldn't get enough of it.

"I want you to fuck me."

Tean cupped the side of Jem's face. His breathing was ragged, his lips swollen from kissing.

"I want you to," Jem said. "I want you to fuck me."

"I don't think that's a good idea."

"I love you, and I want you to."

"Jem, you just told me—"

"It's not like I haven't done it before, Tean. Lots of guys want to top. And I want this. I want it with you. For my entire life, I haven't been in control, no matter how hard I tried. I'm tired of trying to be in control. There's never been anybody else to take care of me, and—and now there's you. And I trust you. And I want you like this."

To Jem's surprise, something shifted in Tean's face, and he didn't argue again. He kissed Jem tenderly, his hands tracing every inch of Jem's body. His mouth followed his hands. Part of Jem itched for Tean to get on with it, and part of him was coiled with dread.

"Take some deep breaths," Tean said, "and let's see if I can give you something else to think about."

He took Jem in his mouth, and then Jem definitely had something else to think about. Jem tensed again when he felt a fingertip slick with lube, but Tean was slow and careful. Jem gasped when Tean finally pressed in, but he was shocked to realize it hadn't hurt and then he felt dizzy with relief and endorphins.

"Ok," Jem said, the word guttural. "Ok, I'm ready."

But Tean went slowly. One finger, curling, searching, and then a pop of pleasure like a flashbulb going off behind Jem's eyes.

"There it is," Tean pulled off Jem long enough to say.

"Oh God," Jem muttered. "Oh God."

Tean kept it up, Jem spewing a stream of pleas and praise. Then two fingers, that same spot, the same flashbulb bliss. Jem arched his back, head thrashing from side to side.

"Ok," he panted. "Ok, ok, ok. Please." The word came out in a long whine.

Tean was merciless. Tean was relentless. Jem gathered fistfuls of the sheets and bellowed.

He was barely aware when Tean slid into him, and then it had already happened, and Tean was rocking gently, adjusting Jem's hips. When another of those lightning bolts of pleasure struck, Jem let out a shocked, "Holy fuck," and Tean grinned, the expression surprisingly wicked.

"Oh," Tean said, the grin getting bigger. "There it is."

After that, neither of them could hold himself together for long. Jem came apart first, shaking in his own fist, as Tean held his hips with slick hands. Tean followed a few moments later, shuddering as he drooped over Jem. And then they were lying together, Tean's sweat-covered body like a furnace against Jem.

When Jem felt like his brain wasn't in a million pieces anymore, he brought his mouth to Tean's ear and whispered, "Teancum Leon, I love you."

"Holy God," Tean mumbled.

Jem laughed.

Rolling onto his side, Tean reached out, and he ran his hand along Jem's belly. He kissed Jem's shoulder. He smiled, vulnerable, almost shy now that they were past the sex.

"Thank you," Jem said, blushing at the rush of emotion. He buried his face in the mattress again. "I wanted to give you something so you'd know how much I love you."

"I love you too," Tean whispered, tugging on Jem's hair until Jem looked at him again. Jem's face got even hotter for some reason he couldn't explain. He'd never known he could blush this hard. Then a smile cracked Tean's expression. "But if you think I'm going to be doing all the work from now on, you're out of your mind."

Jem smoothed the wild, brushed-back hair and smirked. "It's your own fault. You're just too damn good."

34

The next morning, Jem was trying to fix Tean's glasses when the knock came at the door. He'd purchased tape at the FedEx store inside the hotel, and he'd torn off pieces and stuck them to his fingers, ready to use as he tried to reassemble the glasses again. Another knock came, hard and furious. Jem glanced over at Tean, who was on the bed, squinting at the TV.

"I'm going to handle this," Jem said. "Call a funeral home."

Tean got up from the bed, pulled on the briefs and polo that were the only clothes he had in the room, and forced Jem to sit down at the desk again. Another knock came.

"Tean, open this goddamn door right now."

"Forget the funeral home," Jem said, starting to get up again. "Call the zoo. See if they'll accept anonymous donations of bodies that have been ripped limb from limb."

Tean sighed and pushed him back into the seat again.

When Tean answered the door, his body blocked Jem's line of sight. Jem had to settle for listening.

"Give it to me," Ammon said.

"What?"

"The necklace you took from Jager's desk. Give it to me right now."

"Try that again, motherfucker," Jem shouted. "Politely."

"Good morning, Ammon. Is Jager awake?"

"Don't worry about that. You're not going. Neither of you is going. You're in possession of evidence, and I'm taking it into police custody now. You've got sixty seconds to turn it over before I arrest you two."

"Let us get ready, and we'll head over to the hospital with you."

Ammon's laugh was bitter and choppy. "You're out of your mind. This is an official investigation. My investigation. I'm going to talk to Jager. You're going to turn over that evidence, or I'm going to have two Vegas police officers up here tossing your rooms until we find it."

"Fifteen minutes," Tean said, starting to close the door.

Even from where Jem sat, he could hear Ammon's labored breathing. Tean flinched when Ammon slapped the door, and Jem jolted out of his seat. He froze at Tean's outstretched hand.

"Did you scare off my dates? The guys who never called me back? Was that you?"

Some of the color bled from Ammon's face.

"When I saw you a few days ago and you had those bruises on your face," Tean said, his voice steady, "was that really your father who hit you? Or was that Ragnar, who threw a punch when you tried to run him off?"

"I don't know what you're talking about."

"We're going with you to the hospital. That's not up for debate; you owe me."

Fury struggled with another, indefinable emotion in Ammon's face. Finally he spat out, "Word of advice, Teancum: if you're going to moan like a whore, get a hotel room with better soundproofing."

"We'll meet you in the lobby, Ammon."

Then Tean shut the door. Ammon hit it again, and it rattled in the frame. Tean let out a slow breath, his shoulders curving, and he put a hand over his face.

"I wanted to handle that," Jem said, crossing the distance to take Tean in his arms.

"No, it's fine. I need to deal with him."

"But I wanted to cut him up and make monkey soup out of him."

"Maybe next time." Tean patted Jem's back and then tried to wriggle free. "I need to get ready."

Jem tightened his arms.

"Jem, stop, I need to shower."

"Next time," Jem whispered, kissing Tean lightly between the words, "a guy asks you if you're out of your mind, you tell him, yes, my very handsome boyfriend fucked my brains out."

"I don't remember saying you were my boyfriend."

Jem kissed him on the mouth.

"It's very presumptuous of you to—"

Jem kissed him on the jaw.

"We should start things slow," Tean said, his breathing uneven, "and see—"

Jem kissed the side of his neck and nipped twice.

"Oh." Tean said. "Fuck."

"Go get in the shower so your handsome boyfriend can do wonderful, life-altering, slippery things to you."

"My very handsome boyfriend."

"You've got a side piece?" Jem said, eyebrows arching. "Where is the son of a bitch? I'm going to kill him."

Bathrooms, with all that tile and porcelain and glass, carried sound pretty damn well, and Jem was proud of himself, even if his knees were killing him by the time they finished.

Tean went to change, but he came back when he realized he had locked himself out of his room the night before. He was grateful (and surprisingly unsurprised) when Jem revealed that he had palmed the spare key to Tean's room. He left again, and Jem dressed. He was wearing his Smith Fieldhouse tee, jeans, and fire-engine red ROOS when he knocked on Tean's door. When Tean answered the door, Jem closed his eyes and said, "No. I will die before I let this happen. I thought we threw away all your carpenter jeans."

"Ross had a sale," Tean protested as Jem hustled him back into the room. "Jem, we're—no, I just bought these."

By that point, though, Jem had finished stripping him out of the jeans. He wadded them up and held them over the trash can. "We talked about this."

"They were $1.99. For two!"

"Where is the other pair?"

Tean didn't answer, but he threw one guilty look at his suitcase.

Jem found them, ignoring Tean's protests, and threw both pairs away. He stood over the trash can, stabbed a finger at the jeans, and said, "A lot of great things came out of the 90s. And a few evil things. Let the evil things go."

"That's what you say when you don't like the things I like."

"Those jeans are an offense against God."

"You're dodging the issue. You just pick my things you don't like and claim they were the only bad thing from the 90s."

"Bullshit."

"Name one other thing out of the 90s you don't like."

Jem put his hands on his hips. "It's not like I keep a list."

"That's my whole point."

"I mean, the crack epidemic wasn't good."

"I'm getting my clothes out of the trash now."

"Don't you fucking dare. I'll be right back."

Jem darted next door and came back with a plastic bag. Tean was studying himself in the mirror, adjusting the repaired glasses. They sat cockeyed, and no matter what Tean tried, he couldn't get them level.

"I'm sorry," Jem said. "I need more tape."

"More tape is definitely not the problem."

"What was that?"

Tean smiled from under the crooked glasses. "What's in the bag?"

Jem pulled out a pair of khaki-colored pants and a green t-shirt. "Pants first," he said, tossing them to Tean.

"What are these?" Tean asked.

"They're pants. You're currently not wearing any, and we need to go, remember? Your legs go inside. First one, then the other, unless you want to show me a new trick."

"They're . . . soft," Tean said as he pulled them on.

"They're outrageously fucking comfortable is what they are."

"But—" Tean buttoned the waistband and scratched the fabric. "This feels like canvas."

"They're tech pants, some sort of blend of materials that's tougher than work pants and feels like you're wearing sweatpants. Plus they're stylish while still being simple, and that's a good look for you."

"How did you know my size?"

Jem snorted. "I've picked through enough clearance racks with you by this point. Change shirts. More green. Less brown."

"I like brown," Tean said as he wiggled into the shirt.

"I know."

"Brown goes with everything."

"Oh my God, this is the whole problem."

Tean looked down at the tee and smiled. It had a retro graphic with the National Park Service logo and the words JUNIOR RANGER.

"I don't know if that shirt is a legally binding contract," Jem said. "You might be obligated to perform various junior ranger services now."

"I love it. Jem, when did you buy this stuff? And how much did it cost? I'll pay you—"

"The only payment I need is to never have to see carpenter jeans again." Then, flushing, Jem said, "I got them yesterday; I had this great game running. I was a tourist who'd had his luggage stolen, and this old lady—" Something on Tean's face made him talk faster as he said, "—gave me some words of advice and I decided to straighten up and fly right. Then I got an hourly job and bought that stuff with my hard-earned money."

"I can't wear this."

"It looks so good on you. Please don't take it off. I like clothes, and you're so handsome, and I like finding things that make you look even more handsome. And sometimes when you wear those plaid shorts, I feel like I'm witnessing a human rights violation, so if you think about it, I'm the real victim here."

Tean stared at himself in the mirror. He touched the shirt.

"I promise I'll only buy you presents with money I've earned from now on. Please. This is one of the three things I'm good at, and I want to do it for you. It's fun, and it makes me happy, and I think it makes you happy because I will never believe in my heart that anyone can be happy wearing all brown."

"It makes me very happy." Tean zipped in for a kiss, pulling back immediately. "Thank you."

Jem smiled.

"Just on general principles, though, please don't steal from old women in the future."

"She was loaded, and she was happy to—ok, ok, stop grinding your teeth. I have learned my lesson."

After a moment of waffling, Tean kissed him again.

"A little slower," Jem said, hooking one arm around Tean's waist. "You're my state-licensed boyfriend now. You can kiss me whenever you want. Wherever you want. Maybe not at the dentist, I guess, when they have all those tools in my mouth."

So Tean did.

"Thank God you're a good kisser," Jem said through heavy breaths. "If I had to deal with those hiking boots every day and a bad kisser—"

He cut off when Tean kissed him again. Thoroughly.

"What?" Tean said when he pulled back.

Jem managed a bleary "Huh?"

"What were you saying?"

Jem shook his head, blinking.

"About my boots?"

"Boots?"

With a tiny smile, Tean said, "Let's go find Ammon. Please try to be cool about things today. It's going to be very hard for him."

"Really? It's going to be hard for an obsessive, controlling, manipulative—ok, ok, God, you're going to crack a molar."

They met Ammon downstairs; Jem expected an argument, but the detective seemed to have changed his mind about them accompanying him. Except for short, necessary fragments of interaction, he ignored them, although he insisted on having the window seat when they got the truck out of the self-park garage. They drove to the University Medical Center. Like so many desert cities, much of Vegas had built out instead of up. The hospital complex was no exception, a compound of sand-colored brick and cement broken by the bright blue logo. A few scrubby pines wilted in the heat that was already shimmering above the asphalt, but most of the property was hardscaped, a concession to the environment that was very different from the Strip. Inside, the hospital reminded Tean of every hospital he'd ever been in: the chill snap of air conditioning laced with the smell of cleaner; the murmur of conversation bracketed by prerecorded announcements that repeated over the hospital speakers; a bulletin board near the elevators where someone advertised FOUND: FROZEN WEDDING CAKE - SEE PICTURE BELOW - PLEASE CLAIM BY FRIDAY OR CAKE WILL BE EATEN - TOPPER WILL BE RECYCLED.

"Thank God they've got a conscience," Jem murmured.

Being a detective apparently meant knowing all sorts of magic words, which resulted in Ammon guiding them through the maze of halls and desks, nurses and administrators, until they found themselves talking to an officer wearing the Las Vegas Metropolitan Police patch on her uniform. Apparently this had all been cleared ahead of time because she only asked to see his badge, recorded the number on a clipboard, and then glanced at Jem and Tean.

"Consultants," Ammon said.

"I don't have them—"

Ammon pushed open the door and went into the secure hospital room. Tean followed, and Jem gave the officer a shrug and an apologetic smile.

It was a small room, and it had obviously been set aside for intensive-care treatment of people who needed to be either kept safe or kept secured: the window was reinforced, and the bathroom door had been removed, although Jem guessed that most of the patients who came to this room weren't making it to the bathroom on their own. The air smelled like body odor, sweat, and something astringent and medicinal that made Jem queasy. Jager lay in a hospital bed, the morning sunlight raking across his legs. He looked gray and greasy, his thinning hair matted, his eyes soft and dopey from the good stuff they were giving him. He was breathing on his own, but it sounded like it took a lot of effort.

"Damn it," Ammon said. "There's no way we're going to get anything out of him."

"I'm not sure about that," Tean said. "Agent Jager? Can you hear me?"

Jager released a spittle-choked cough.

Giving Tean's neck a soft squeeze as he passed, Jem made his way to the bed. He dropped into one of the tubular chairs. For a moment, he considered Jager. Then he leaned forward, elbows on knees.

"Hi, there," Jem said. "How's it hanging?

"Good fucking Lord," Ammon said.

Jager stared into the middle distance. Something moved across the sky—a bird, a plane, Superman—and its shadow flitted over the white hospital bedding.

"Guess you're pretty far gone," Jem said to Jager. "Guess we wasted our time."

A rivulet of drool escaped the corner of the agent's mouth.

Jem leaned forward and snatched the plastic control for the morphine pump from Jager's hand. Jager reacted, but too slowly, his fingers twitching around empty air. Leaning back in the seat, Jem twirled the pump's control.

"Do you know what this is?" Jem asked. "Or are you too far off in la la land?"

Jager didn't move, but Jem thought he saw fresh tension in his face: a tightening around the eyes and mouth.

"Dr. Teancum Leon is a specialist in little plastic things with buttons." For some reason, that made Tean blush, so Jem clarified, "Not just fun, sexy-time things either. All sorts of things. Dr. Teancum Leon, what is this plastic thing with a button that I'm twirling?"

"It's a patient-controlled analgesia pump."

"Huh. I always called it a morphine pump."

"That's inaccurate in two ways."

"Boyfriends," Jem said, rolling his eyes at Jager. He didn't miss the way Ammon's posture stiffened. "Am I right?"

"First," Tean said, reddening even more, "because there are analgesic pumps that are activated by someone other than the patient, and second because while morphine is often the pain medicine used in the pumps, it's not the exclusive choice."

"So," Jem said, twirling the control by its cord, "you have to call it something different if the patient isn't controlling it."

"That's right."

"In this case, for example, we couldn't call it a patient-controlled analgesia pump."

"I suppose not."

"What would a better name be?"

"A fucktard-controlled pump," Ammon muttered.

"That's got a nice ring to it," Jem said, "but I was thinking a Jem-controlled analgesia pump. Does that sound accurate?"

"You're in control of it," Tean said. "I'd say that's accurate."

"Well, that's very interesting." On the next twirl, Jem let the control slap into his hand. "How about it, Jager? Are you feeling the pinch? Want me to press your little button for you? Again, not a sex thing."

This time, the shift in Jager's face was visible: a rush of blood darkened his cheeks, and his eyes cut to the emergency call button.

"Go ahead," Jem said. "Then everybody will know you're wide awake. We'll make sure the docs know we need to dial back the meds so you can have a nice, lucid conversation. And then we'll take our time. We might get hung up at the coffee machine. We might run into an old friend. And you'll be up here, and the pinch will be getting worse and worse. We might get turned around. The elevator might break. God, it could take us hours before we finally make it back."

Panic lit up Jager's eyes.

"Why don't we wait a few minutes?" Jem said. "So you see what the pinch feels like."

"Jem," Tean said.

Jem waved him to silence.

"Ammon," Tean said, "you're not going to let him do this, are you? This is torture."

Ammon's gaze was surprisingly cool as it flicked to Tean and then came to rest on Jem. "It's not torture. We're trying to find the right balance between lucidity and pain management; it's trial and error."

"Jem," Tean said again.

Jem shot him a look; Tean's mouth thinned out into a frown, but he didn't say anything else.

It took ten minutes.

"Jesus Christ," Jager moaned. "Give it back."

"Feel it?" Jem said. "That's the pinch."

"I got shot. Jesus, I feel like I'm on fire." He licked his lips, which looked as gray as the rest of his face. "Please."

"How about this?" Jem said. "I ask a question. You give me an answer. I push this button. If you suddenly get dozy, well, I stop pushing the button, and we'll let the pinch catch up to you again."

"Aren't you worried about this?" Tean said. "No court is going to let you enter this as evidence."

"You and your boyfriend fucked my case up from the beginning. This interview isn't about evidence; this is about figuring out what the fuck is going on."

"Well?" Jem said.

A sheen of flop sweat covered Jager's forehead. He gave a shaky nod.

"Did you shoot Antonio Hidalgo?"

"No."

Jem pressed the button, and Jager let out a quiet breath. The relief in his face was transparent.

"Who did?"

"The rodeo kid," Jager said. "The wonder-boy sheriff."

For a moment, the only sound was the beep of the heart monitor. Then Ammon said, "McEneany?"

Jager gave a weary nod as he slumped against his pillow.

"Why?" Tean asked.

"He got in too deep. I tried to tell him. The minute you start this job, they already got you in the chute, don't matter how you kick. I tried to tell him you can start this job however you want, but we all end up the same. Just running cattle down the same chute."

Jem glanced over; Tean's brow was wrinkled, but Ammon's expression was strangely intense.

"How was he in too deep?" Jem asked. "What was he doing?"

"Drugs. Girls. Money. They ran him down the chute. Good guys, they start off thinking they're doing the job. You don't see it until it's too late."

"Go back," Ammon said. "Start from the beginning."

"Followed him over there. Knew he was in with them. When they started turning up dead . . . sheriff let him smash Weckesser's face in with a rock. He was a good guy. Good deputy. Then they got the horses running."

"You saw someone kill Deputy Weckesser?"

"Smashed his face in and dragged him up the canyon. Had to get the log before McEneany altered it."

"But you didn't report the death. You didn't provide the log as evidence that Weckesser had responded to a callout and been murdered to cover up another killing."

"McEneany. Stupid rodeo kid. Pay for what he did. Pay for it. I wasn't going to . . . wasn't going to let anyone else have the satisfaction. Log was proof. For after."

Jem hesitated and then asked, "And what happened when you got to the motel?"

"McEneany was inside. I went in after him. Out of my mind by that point. TV on. Shower on. Music next door. He didn't hear me. Found them in the bathroom. The Mexican, dead. Bleeding out on the shower. McEneany looking like he pissed himself. Reached for my gun." Jager gave a wet-sounding cough. "Shot by the goddamn rodeo kid."

Jem remembered the strangeness of the scene, the evidence of a third person. Although light on the details, Jager's version sounded possible. More than that, it sounded plausible.

"What is McEneany helping them do?" Tean asked.

"Gotta press it again," Jager mumbled, licking chapped lips. "Promised."

Jabbing the button, Jem said, "What is he helping them do?"

A comber of narcotics washed in, burying Jager for a moment. When he spoke, his voice had dissolved into wisps. "Drugs. Blake told me."

"What did Blake tell you?" Jem asked. "Why was he helping you?"

Jager lay very still. His eyes were mostly closed now. His drool darkened the pillow.

"Jager, wake up." Jem threw another glance over at Tean and Ammon, but neither of them said anything. After a moment, Jem asked, "Why did you have Blake's necklace?"

Jager's face twisted; he looked like he was on the brink of tears.

"Why did you have it?" Jem said. "Why was he helping you? Were you blackmailing him for information? Was it evidence you collected at a scene? Did Blake find out and he killed him?" Jem's voice slipped into a shout. "Why the fuck did you have his necklace? What the fuck were those sons of bitches doing down here? Why'd you help Tanner cover up Blake's death? Where's that son of a bitch hiding?"

Tean's hand settled on Jem's shoulder; Jem hadn't heard him cross the room. "Take a breath."

It was hard, but Jem took a breath.

"Let's step outside for a minute."

Jem shook his head.

Tean's fingers tightened once in a silent question.

"I'm all right," Jem whispered. But he wasn't all right. They had come this far. He was so close to finding Tanner. And now it was slipping away. Antonio was dead; he'd never pay for what he'd done to Jem or who knew how many others. Blake was dead; he'd never pay either. And now Tanner would walk off with millions of dollars. He'd never pay for Andi. He'd never pay for Weckesser. He'd never pay for the days and nights in Decker, when he'd broken something in Jem over and over again.

Tean rubbed his shoulder, and after a moment, Jem opened his eyes.

Jager was staring at them, his gaze surprisingly clear, hate and fear skinned back by the drugs. Jem understood.

"You were in love with him," Jem said quietly.

Jager started to cry. "I found him after they'd already done him. Tossed him in that ravine like he was garbage. Knew I shouldn't touch him; they'd be all over that area eventually. Had to. He was mine." His tears slowed; the tracks on his cheeks glistened when he rolled his head. He seemed to be struggling up from somewhere impossibly deep. "Wait my whole life, hating who I am, and there he was. Smiled when I told him about the stars. Made him a ricegrass bracelet."

"So you took the necklace."

"He wanted to be a chef. He made me scrambled eggs and told me all about all the folds on a chef's hat." After that burst of clarity, Jager's voice grew muzzy again. "Kissed him in a stand of box elder. Pressed me against the wall. I could feel the sun trapped in the sandstone." Then Jager started to cry again. "I was going to kill them. The night I found you in my office. Was going to kill them. Kept his gun and his necklace so I could kill them. When I came across you in the office that night, I was going to kill them, but you'd already found the gun, and everything went wrong."

Jem was silent for a long time; he could feel the strain in Tean's body, his fingers hooked like iron in Jem's shoulder. Ammon was frozen on the other side of the room.

"He told me about the drugs." Jager broke the silence in a surprisingly steady voice. "He knew they were going to kill him, so he told me."

"He knew who was going to kill him? What did he tell you about the drugs?"

"Floating them in on the Dolores River. Two million dollars. Maybe three."

"Who was going to kill Blake?"

"That one. Tanner. He saw Blake talking to me. Walked right up to the Jeep because he wanted the rifle. Liked it. Thought it was a toy, cause of the darts. I was supposed to dart the mares that day; Ronnie called in sick. He heard us. Saw us. They both tried to play it cool, but Blake knew Tanner wanted to kill him after that, so he told me all of it."

Jem traded looks with Tean, but Ammon spoke first. "As best you can, why don't you walk us through the whole thing."

"Somebody was cooking meth in Gateway."

"Colorado?" Jem asked.

"DEA raid coming. Got a tip." Jager's eyes fluttered, and he whined, "You promised."

Jem held up the pump's control and pressed the button; he wasn't sure it was doing anything at this point because it probably had some sort of limit, but he didn't mind making a show out of it.

"Managed to get some of their stuff out. Floating down the Dolores because feds are watching the roads. Tanner and them—they're supposed to meet the mule Tuesday, take the shipment."

"Today," Tean said.

"What guy?"

Jager shook his head.

"Where does Kalista fit into this?" Jem asked. "And Nick? What about them?"

"Dating the guy who got raided. Supposed to meet the mule and provide a vehicle, but she just wants money. She said . . . she said Tanner could have half. He was supposed to be the muscle, kill the mule, take the meth. Blake said he'd kill her when he got the drugs."

"And Nick?" Ammon said.

"Her friend. Gay best friend." Jager gave a very un-special-agent-like giggle. "Cute ass."

"Not that cute," Tean muttered.

Jem and Ammon each shot him a look, and Tean blushed.

"No," Jager mumbled. "Got all those scars. Ears fucked up. Not that cute."

"How many times did you press that thing?" Ammon said.

Jem ignored him. "Tanner stole the injection rifle from your truck and saw Blake talking to you; that's what you said. Is that why Tanner killed him? He thought Blake was ratting him out?"

"Told him . . . careful." Jager's eyes screwed shut. "Whole life being careful. Went back to the lodge for his stuff. I told him no. Forget it. Went back anyway. When I found him, they already done him. Dropped him in that ravine like old garbage."

"Where's Tanner?" Jem asked. "Where's he been holed up?

Jager shook his head.

"Don't hold out on me, Jager. You're not going to like it."

"Don't know. Gone."

"Gone where?"

But Jager just dry swallowed and squeezed his eyes shut.

"Where the fuck could he be hiding? Where is he? Where is he?" Jem realized he was shouting again; he couldn't seem to rein it in, but the pain in his shoulder, where Tean was clutching him, helped ground him again.

"Something wrong in here?" The Vegas officer poked her head in from the hall.

"Still figuring out our rhythm," Ammon said. "We're good."

She studied each of them again, rubbing her tight fade, and then nodded and shut the door. As soon as she did, Ammon drew out his phone. "I've got to call Nobles."

Jager made low, moaning noise.

After pressing the button a few more times, Jem tossed the pump's control on the bed. "This was useless. We got nothing except McEneany out of him."

Ammon was talking quietly in the background.

"That's not quite true," Tean said. "We not only got McEneany and a reason for why he's involved—the drugs—but we also got confirmation that Tanner killed Blake and Weckesser, and that McEneany helped cover it up. Jager verified our suspicion that Kalista and Nick are trying to steal a shipment of drugs, and that somehow they got Tanner to agree to help them kill the mule. At the very least, now we know why everything has happened."

"But we don't know where Tanner's hiding. And we don't know where the handoff is supposed to take place. Sometime today, Tanner's going to grab several million dollars' worth of drugs, put a bullet in Kalista and Nick, and leave their bodies in the desert while he spends the rest of his life getting hand jobs in Ibiza."

"Ibiza is too expensive," Tean said, "not to mention environmentally—oh. That was just a figure of speech."

Jem smiled wearily and squeezed Tean's hand.

"I don't care if he's out of the station," Ammon snapped. "Get him up on the radio. I'm a detective with the Salt Lake City PD, and I'm telling you this is an emergency." The steady beep of the heart monitor made counterpoint. "What the fuck is that supposed to mean?" Ammon swung around, pacing toward the window. "Then get somebody on the phone who can."

"Maybe you should call Haggerty," Tean said to Jem.

"My hot cop boyfriend? But what is my hot vet boyfriend going to think?"

"Your hot vet boyfriend is going to downgrade you to dogwalker with occasional sexual benefits if you ever mention your hot cop boyfriend again."

"Wait, you'd seriously pay me to walk Scipio? And I'd get sexual benefits? Ok, don't make that face. I'm calling, I'm calling."

Haggerty picked up on the third ring. When Jem identified himself, his voice warmed and he said, "Hey. I was hoping I'd hear from you."

"Sorry, I don't want to give you the wrong idea. I just got hired to be a sexual dogwalker, so I'm basically spoken for."

"He didn't," Tean said, "and he's not."

Faint static rustled on the call. "What's going on?"

Jem talked him through their conversation with Jager. When he'd finished, he waited for questions, but all he got was more of that static.

Finally, Haggerty said, "I've got to make some calls about this. It's way above my pay grade. Keep your very fine ass away from Moab. Do you understand?"

"You're breaking up," Jem said.

"I'm not joking. I will put both of you in the city jail if I see you—"

Jem disconnected. The heart monitor was still beeping. From the next room, he could hear *The Price is Right*'s theme song.

"I think Haggerty is right," Tean said. "I think we should—"

"Fuck," Ammon said. "All right. Thank you. Goodbye."

Jem turned in his seat to look at the other man. Ammon was pushing the fine blond hair away from his forehead; his face was red, and when he looked up at them, he shook his head.

"Last time anybody heard from Noble was yesterday afternoon. He was going fishing with McEneany."

35

Jager couldn't give them anything else, so they returned to Caesar's Palace long enough to collect their belongings. Tean shook his head when Jem asked if he wanted to say goodbye to his family; Tean knew it would only precipitate more drama, and he preferred to handle that by phone. Half an hour after they left the hospital, they were driving north on I-15, headed back to Moab. Mile after mile of subdivisions with stucco homes and Astroturf lawns and nacreous swimming pools gave way to the true outskirts of the city, where the old bones of ranch houses and barns and unroofed silos told the story of Vegas before it became Vegas. Then they were past even the bones, driving along dusty valleys of prickly pear, tumbleweed, and fishhook cacti. The hardpan glowed like a tungsten filament.

Jem had offered to drive so that Tean and Ammon could make phone calls, and Tean had offered to sit in the middle to prevent any incidental murders. Ammon was on the phone, talking to a supervisor—Tean thought he had heard Ammon say lieutenant—explaining their conversation with Jager. Judging by the blistering shouts from the other end of the call, the lieutenant was not pleased with how Ammon had handled things.

The conversation registered only at the edge of Tean's consciousness, though. In his mind, he kept turning over something that had been bothering him for the last two days.

"How was Tanner supposed to find the mule?"

"Kalista and Nick told him," Jem said. "Actually, if they're smart, they won't tell him until it's time to pick up the drugs."

"That just begs the question, though. How did Kalista and Nick know where to meet him?"

"She's a drug dealer's girlfriend. He told her before she came to Moab."

"I don't think so."

"That's what I would have done."

"But," Tean said, "that's not what this guy did."

"You don't know that."

"Actually, I do. We both do. Someone sent a burner text with the date for the meeting and that string of words."

Jem was silent for almost a full minute. When he spoke again, his words were slow. "He gave a date."

"Right."

"And if he gave a date, that means they hadn't arranged the meet in advance." Jem grimaced. "I see your point: they were communicating about the meet. But they still could have arranged the location ahead of time."

"But what do those words mean? 'Replaces, broadly, shall.' That's what was in the text. And today's date: Pioneer Day. Two pieces of information. That's what you need for a meet: time and place."

"Ok, I'm not saying you're wrong. But what does 'replaces, broadly, shall' mean?"

Ammon's conversation seemed to have become completely one-sided. He was leaning against the window, head bouncing with the truck's vibrations, his expression washed out. Covering the phone's mic, he whispered, "Code."

"Oh really?" Jem said. "It's a code?"

"Jem."

"I'm just saying it's awesome that we have a paid, professional detective who's so brilliant he can figure out that three random words in a drug dealer's text message are probably a code. Thank God. I don't know what we would have done without Ammon Young here to crack the case."

Ammon shot him the finger before saying into the phone, "No, sir, nobody else is here. But if I could explain—"

Shouting cut him off.

"Now that somebody with a college degree and fifty years of professional experience has helped us figure out that we're dealing with a code—"

"Stop antagonizing him," Tean said quietly.

Pulling a face, Jem said, "So how do you crack a code?"

"Let's see what the internet has to say." Tean opened his phone and began doing a search. He skimmed several articles, picked two to read more in depth, and realized he had quickly gotten into something well beyond his expertise. When he glanced up, Jem was smiling.

"What?"

"Normally you'd tell me about how the Nevada slot rat, *slotmachinicus rodentis*—"

"Not a real animal."

"—leaves secret, coded messages in its droppings, or about how the greater Lake Mead lazy bass, *douchicus partyboaticus*—"

"Again, not real."

"—transmits its location in Morse code by blowing bubbles."

"Well, I'm sorry that I'm not an expert on classical or modern cryptography."

"So am I," Jem said. "This is a real disappointment."

"It's not my fault that my specialization—"

"Will you two cut it out?" Ammon said. At some point during Tean's reading, the phone call had ended. Ammon's voice was rough, and he was still slumped against the window, eyes closed. "I didn't sleep five minutes last night."

More quietly, Tean said, "Well, according to this stuff, modern cryptography, in public-key algorithms, relies on computationally expensive mathematical problems to encrypt information."

"We're talking about three words on a burner phone. I don't think there was anything computationally expensive about it."

"Right." Tean thought for a moment. "The whole idea of cryptography is that you want to send a message to someone else without a third party understanding the contents. In order to do that, the receiver has to know a couple of things."

"They have to know it's a code," Jem said.

"Right."

"And they have to know how to decode the message."

"Exactly right. Why did you let me do all this reading if you already knew?"

Jem's cheeks reddened slightly. "I just—it just made sense once you started saying that stuff."

"I'm going to take this opportunity to beg you one more time to take the GED test—"

"So, for example, if the code is to write words backward, then they have to know that to decode it, all they have to do is flip it around. TAC becomes CAT. Like that, right?"

"Yep. That's a transposition cipher, moving the letters around. A substitution cipher is another option, when you switch one letter for another."

"So the way to decode something, they have to agree on it in advance, right?"

"Or it's transmitted separately."

"Three words: replaces, broadly, shall. None of those can be flipped."

"No, it's not a transposition or substitution cipher because that kind of text looks meaningless when it's encrypted."

"So maybe we're talking about a key. Maybe they had a list of possible places, each one with a code word. Like, 'replaces' means Grand County, and 'broadly' means the Twins, and 'shall' means the north side."

"That's entirely possible."

"You sound like you don't like it."

"Well, if it's a key, then we don't have any chance at cracking it because the associations are arbitrary. We don't have enough samples to try to figure out if there's a pattern."

"What else might it be?" Jem asked.

"Well, typically you either needed to know something or to have something in order to decrypt a message."

"Like that two-factor thing on your phone."

"Yeah, more or less. I can't log into my email account without both the password, something I know, and a unique code generated on my phone, something I have. An encryption method could rely on one or the other or both. For example, the Spartans used something called the Scytale cipher, which involved winding a piece of paper or papyrus around a staff. They'd write the message, filling in a bunch of nonsense, and then take the paper off the staff. If the enemy captured the messenger, they couldn't make the letters line up correctly without the right size of staff. Another common method is to use a shared book or text and to reference page numbers and word numbers to spell out a message. The Enigma machine that the Nazis used is an example of a very complicated system, with daily local settings that were reinforced by unique settings used for each message. If you didn't have both the Enigma machine and the daily settings and the unique setting for the message, you wouldn't be able to unscramble it even if you did have an Enigma machine. Well, that's not quite true because the Allies did eventually crack Enigma, but—"

"Ok, ok, ok." Jem slumped over the wheel. "Message received. This is hopeless."

"That's not what I was saying."

"We don't know what they were using to send this message, and we don't know what someone would have needed to decode it, and we're never going to figure out where he is. He's going to run off with millions of dollars and live the rest of his life drinking Mai Tais out of a girl's bellybutton. He'll probably become some sort of international drug lord and slaughter millions of innocent people and smoke Cuban cigars that he puts out in his enemies' eyes and—"

"Don't stop," Tean whispered.

"Oh my God," Jem said.

"No, you were doing so well. Keep going!"

"Oh my God, what is happening to me?" Jem smacked his head against the steering wheel. "You're in my head now. This is so messed up."

"That was possibly the best thing I've ever heard you say. More importantly, Tanner might be clever, but he's also greedy. He stayed near Moab because he wants to take over this drug shipment, even though it would have been smarter to run. That means he's greedy enough to be stupid sometimes. And that's to our advantage."

"Ok, fine, but we're still not going to find him."

"Don't be so dramatic," Tean said. "Let's think about this for a moment. The code was sent to Nick and Kalista so they could meet the mule. That means they had to have a way of decoding it. Did you see anything in the villa they might have used?"

"Like a list of secret code words? No, Tean. No, I didn't."

"Maybe you would have if you hadn't been so busy handcuffing yourself to the bed."

"First of all, they were sex handcuffs, so I was sex handcuffing myself to the bed. Second of all—"

"Jesus Christ," Ammon barked. He lifted his head from the glass to stare at them blearily. "You two are unbearable. Do you realize that?"

"I'm sorry," Tean said. "We'll be quiet."

Ammon muttered something and laid his head against the window again.

"We went through that whole place. We didn't see anything. That means it has to be a code that they knew how to decipher without a physical object."

"They might have destroyed whatever they needed," Jem said. "Just to be safe."

"They might have, but then why keep the phone? Why keep the message? Why not destroy all of it if they're trying to be safe?"

Jem chewed his lip. The only sound was the wind whistling along the truck's frame. "It couldn't be a very complicated list of keywords if they memorized it."

"I don't think it's a list at all. And I don't think they're keywords."

"Then it has to be something they could have decoded without special resources, because we went through their stuff and they didn't have anything."

"Why don't you google it?" Ammon said.

"I understand that you're upset," Tean began, "but you don't need to—"

"Actually," Jem said, "that's a good idea."

So Tean typed *replaces, broadly, shall* into a search engine. He got results on blockchain analysis, robot overlords, and a replacement manual for some obscure Medicare policy. "Nothing."

"What if you add something like 'code' or 'decrypt'?"

"More blockchain. More of California's civil code."

"Maybe," Ammon said without opening his eyes, "you should try typing in 'google please help me decode replaces, broadly, shall.'"

"Look, dickhole," Jem said, "if you don't have anything constructive to say, keep your mouth shut."

"I'm a big enough person that I'm not enjoying watching you two get outsmarted by a pair of meth heads, but I'd be lying if I said it wasn't a little satisfying."

"You haven't been able to decode it either."

"I'm not trying to." After a moment, though, Ammon asked, "What about giving each number a letter and adding them up?"

"Coordinates are always given in pairs," Tean said. "A set of three doesn't make sense." Then, doubtfully, he said, "Unless they included elevation."

"It was just an idea. Too bad we can't do what Jem always does and make someone else solve the problem for us."

"Next time we stop," Jem said, "I'm going to knock his teeth out."

Tean squeezed Jem's arm.

"With your jerkoff sock you carry around in your pocket?" Ammon said, eyes still closed.

"And I'm going to break his nose," Jem said.

"Enough," Tean said.

"Tean's pretty good at playing nurse," Ammon said. "You'll probably get some decent sex out of him for once if he's taking care of you. Tean, tell him about when I hurt my ankle. Tell him about some of the stuff we tried."

"All right." Jem guided the truck toward the highway's shoulder. "I guess we're doing this right now."

"Ammon, stop being a jerk." Tean grabbed the wheel. "Jem, stop letting him bait you so easily."

"I—" Ammon said.

"He—" Jem said.

"No. Both of you shut up. I'm tired of it." Taking out his phone, Tean placed a call on speakerphone. It rang several times.

"Who are you calling?"

"Ammon was right. We're not using all our resources; maybe this requires local knowledge, just like the Enigma machine."

The ringing cut off, and a young man answered. "Pinyon-Pine Lodge. This is Russell. How may I help you?"

"Russell, this is Tean. Remember me? We were talking about *Dasein* and Kierkegaard's views on the cross as symbol of—"

"I remember," Russell cut in. "Things are really busy here, so I can't talk right now. Sorry, gotta go. Bye."

"Hold on," Jem said. "Hi, Russell. It's Jem."

"Oh." Then, his voice muffled as though he'd cupped a hand around the phone's receiver, "Hail Satan."

"Uh huh. Listen, we've just got a couple of questions for you. And, I suppose, for the Prince of Everlasting Suffering. If he's available."

"That's not funny," Russell said in a furious whisper. "And you shouldn't take His name in vain. When the Earth's festering corpse is writhing with maggots and the rest of humanity is slowly fed to the great serpent in the pit, we, the chosen and the unsanctified, will frolic in the eternals flames—"

"Frolic?" Ammon said. "Who the hell is this guy?"

"Who the heaven is this guy?" Jem corrected. "Russell, I need to ask you a question."

"—under the dark, necrotic gaze of the High Lord of Air and Shadow—"

"If you don't stop, I'm going to make Tean talk to you about why everything we do is meaningless."

"No!" Russell squeaked. He was silent for a moment. Probably, Jem guessed, trying to bring his voice down to sound like he'd been through puberty. Then he said, "I mean, I don't have a lot of time, so you have to be fast."

"What do these words mean to you? 'Replaces, broadly, shall.'"

"Nothing. No, Mom, don't come over here! Stop it! I'm not talking to anybody." A few moments passed, and he whispered. "You got me in trouble."

"You're sure? You've never heard them before? It's not something local."

"Mom, they're my friends! And they're asking me something really important. I can't unclog the shower right now!"

"Russell, I need you to focus."

"I don't know. It sounds like what hikers and climbers do. Mom, I told you I'd do it later! It's my room. I can leave it messy if I want to. No, don't touch my stuff!"

"Russell! What about hikers and climbers?"

"They use this website to change coordinates into words."

When Jem glanced over, Tean grabbed his phone, pulled a browser, and began searching.

Russell was still talking. "They leave each other clues. It's so stupid. They think they're so cool because they can get on a dumb, stupid rock. I bet they won't feel so cool when the Great Beast is sucking the marrow from their bones—"

"Got it," Tean whispered. He held up the screen. A pair of coordinates were displayed. Tean tapped the phone a few more times, and when he showed Jem the phone again, a pin on a map marked a location northeast of Moab.

"Thanks, Russell. Say hi to the Prince of Fabric Softeners for us."

"Wait, wait, wait. Is this about your friend?"

"What friend?"

"The one who was around here yesterday, asking about you."

"Who was asking about us?" Tean said.

"He didn't tell me his name. He had long hair. He was kind of, um, gay. Oh, and he had that really messed up ear he was trying to hide. He got pretty mad when I couldn't tell him where you were. Shit—I mean, shoot. Mom, I said shoot! I've got to go."

The call disconnected.

"Nick was looking for us at the lodge?" Tean said.

"The same day the sheriff and the chief of police disappeared," Ammon said, finally sitting up, his blue eyes cold and alert. "Sounds like someone is tying up loose ends."

36

They drove for another ten miles of scrub and bone-bright hardpan before Jem looked over at Ammon and said, "You think he was trying to kill us?"

"I think he was going to kill you if he found you. You and Tean showed up at his and Kalista's door, asking questions about Tanner. They already knew you might be trouble. Then you found the drugs—"

"We don't know that," Tean said.

"They weren't going to walk away from their stash of drugs, Tean. They had that place under observation; they were waiting until night to retrieve them."

When Tean glanced over, Jem shrugged and said, "He's probably not wrong."

"So," Tean said, the mangled glasses balanced on the tip of his nose, "Antonio shows up. They're not expecting that. They're certainly not expecting Antonio to turn on them. Somehow, they get out of that situation alive."

"Probably by running like hell."

"By that point, they had to leave town. But they didn't go far." Tean frowned. "They couldn't go far; they had to be back by Tuesday for the pickup."

"And in the meantime, they need to start cleaning up after themselves." Ammon stretched, taking up way more of the cab than he needed to. "The sheriff's compromised; sooner or later, people are going to wonder what happened to Weckesser, and that kid doesn't seem smart enough to keep his own neck out of the noose. He needs the drugs so he can get out of town and set himself up somewhere else. Tanner needs the drugs for the same reason; he's got multiple murder charges hanging over his head."

"I don't understand Kalista and Nick," Tean said. The taped-up glasses had already fallen halfway off his face again.

"You heard Jager: she's stabbing her boyfriend in the back, and she's going to run off with his drugs."

"If she doesn't get a bullet in the head courtesy of Tanner," Jem said. "Which she will."

"No, it's something else. Something that keeps nagging at me."

"His ear," Jem said.

Tean nodded. "That's what I was thinking too. Russell's the second person to mention that; Jager pointed it out too. I didn't notice anything about his ear when we met him. Did you?"

Jem shook his head. "He had his hair covering his ears."

"His ear?" Ammon waved one hand in front of Tean's eyes. "Hello? What are you two talking about? I've seen his ear. He's got a nasty scar; it makes one ear stick out a little bit, and it's ugly, but it's not exactly a red flag."

"You've seen it?" Tean said.

"I walked in on him in the restroom at Tafone; I went over to check them out after you called me the other night. He was standing in front of the mirror, fixing his hair."

"Men's Room Confessionals," Jem said, "the Ammon Young story."

"It's not exactly a secret; his ear is hard to miss—I'm surprised he hasn't had plastic surgery to make it less noticeable."

"What did the scar look like?" Tean said.

"Have you ever seen a scar? It looked like that."

"Ammon, what did it look like?"

"It looked like somebody tried to cut his ear off."

Jem felt his jaw slacken. He managed to say, "No fucking way."

Tean was already tapping frantically on his phone. Jem tried to read over his shoulder until they hit the rumble strip, and then Ammon said, "Eyes on the road."

"Is it—" Jem asked.

"Hold on." Tean was still typing. "I think so, but hold on."

A fire had burned through this part of the world. Everything south of the interstate had been scorched: a black crust, shining where it caught the sun, covered the ground, and the skeletons of scrub and sage looked brittle enough to flake apart on the next strong wind. It was hard to tell when it happened. A part of Jem remembered the hand between his shoulder blades, the pain between his legs, Tanner's jumpy breathing, the smell of jalapeño Cheetos. A part of him knew Tean would say that fires cleared out undergrowth, dead brush, made way for new vegetation. A part of him knew about seeds that only opened after the passage of tremendous heat. But he looked out at the scorched deadlands and thought that sometimes, fire just burned the hell out of a place, and nothing could grow there again. He remembered the first time Tanner had thought of choking him, and how the older boy had gotten so excited that he'd come in two stuttering thrusts.

"It's him," Tean whispered. More loudly, "Holy shit, it's him."

Tean turned the phone to show Ammon. Then he showed Jem. Jem barely had time to process the Facebook page that he was seeing, and then his eyes narrowed in on the primary photograph. There he was: the man who had called himself Nick, maybe five years ago, long hair hiding his ears. But the name on the page was Nathaniel Dayton.

"How'd you find him?" Jem asked.

"I went back to the article I told you about. The story of Tanner assaulting that girl, and the boy who tried to stop him. He's not named in the story itself, but plenty of people seemed to know who he was in the comments." Tean turned the phone back toward himself, tapped a few more times, and held it up again. Jem was looking at the woman who had called herself Kalista, only now, the name below her picture said Kristine Colin-Bowman. "She's even friends with Nick online."

Ammon was already on the phone again, reciting the names and pausing to listen. "I heard you, Kat. And I'm saying they've got no leadership and, from what I can tell, no fucking clue that they've got a shitstorm blowing in. Get Highway Patrol down here. Light a fire under them." He listened again for what felt like several minutes. "Ok. Email it over. Yes, I said please." When he disconnected, his hand tightened around the phone until his knuckles were white. "Nathaniel Dayton has a string of misdemeanor charges for prostitution. He's spent time in the county jail—most of last year, in fact. The last time he got picked up, a patrol car found him lying in the street. A john had used a knife on him. He was in the hospital for a long time; they didn't think he'd make it."

"What about Kalista, Kristine, whatever we want to call her?" Jem asked.

"No criminal record."

Tean was scrolling through photos on social media. "Skiing in Aspen. Drinks on the beach in Maui. Shopping in Madrid. Ok, either she's very good at faking this stuff, or she's legitimately got money."

"The money angle makes sense," Jem said. "Tanner came from money too, so it makes sense that Kristine is from that same crew."

"She looks like she's had a pretty normal life. She was on the rifle team at the University of Utah."

"Makes sense too; she told us she's an excellent shot, and she's obviously got good reflexes and great hand-eye coordination. Remember how she caught that tumbler Nathaniel whipped at her head?"

"Nathaniel, on the other hand," Tean tapped the phone a few times, "mostly has local pictures, and his page is pretty scanty."

"So let's play this out," Ammon said. "He and Kristine are kids. Tanner, this nascent psychopath, tricks them into making themselves vulnerable and then tries to rape Kristine. When Nathaniel intervenes, he gets his ear ripped halfway off. Then nothing. Kristine goes off to live her life, presumably enjoying the benefit of Daddy's money. Nathaniel, on the other hand, falls apart. He's gay. He's traumatized. Somehow, he ends up doing sex work, skating in and out of jail. And then, one day, they decide, what? They're going to ask this asshole from their childhood to help them steal a shipment of drugs?"

"What if there are no drugs?" Jem said slowly, staring out at the charred slope of the valley. "What if the whole thing is a setup?"

Tean was already nodding. "Nathaniel is already on the brink, psychologically. He's had this horrible life, and he blames it on Tanner, the attack, and never really being able to come back from it. Then a john nearly kills him. It takes him back to Tanner, where his life went wrong. That's the trigger. That's what makes him snap. He wants revenge, so he plans this whole thing to murder Tanner."

"And so he calls up his childhood gal pal, and she agrees to go along with this?" Ammon shook his head. "No way."

"Maybe not like that," Tean said. "They may have stayed in touch. They were both traumatized by Tanner. This could have been something they talked about before. This could be something that's been building for years."

"Could have. May have. Maybe."

"What's your competing theory?" Tean asked.

Ammon shifted in his seat. "Here's another thing—"

"That means he doesn't have one," Jem said.

"—why wait? I mean, let's say I agree with you. Let's say Nathaniel snaps, and he and Kristine agree that they're going to kill Tanner. Why not figure out where he lives, wait for him to come home late one night, and put a bullet in his head? Why not run him down with a car? Why not burn down his house? This whole thing, it's . . . elaborate. It's over the top. They come down here, they hang around. She pretends to be someone else, and she lures him into this drug deal scenario. I mean, Jesus, Tean, could it be any more complicated?"

"I still haven't heard a competing theory," Jem said. "Just want to note that."

"It's complicated, but maybe not as complicated as you're making it sound," Tean said. "And I really don't think it would be that hard to get Tanner interested in a big score. How would you do it, Jem, if you were running a con like this?"

"They're all the same when you get down to it." Jem shrugged. "People believe you because they want something to be true or because they're afraid it is. They want to believe that they can get rich quick—that they're smart enough, savvy enough, connected enough, whatever, to seize an opportunity that other people are going to miss. They're afraid, at the same time, that they'll miss out on a chance to make a ton of money. Boil any game down, and that's what you get."

"Where would Kristine and Nathaniel have to start?"

Jem frowned. "You do the legwork in advance—in this case, getting enough drugs to make your story convincing, like the stash we found in the villa. You have to set it all up first. The only really tricky part is the next one: you have to meet the mark, and you have to do it in a way that doesn't make them suspicious. The best thing is if you can get them to come to you; if you have to approach them, you've already given up some of the power. With Tanner, she probably just tracked him until she knew his patterns and then hung out at the clubs he visited, waiting for her opportunity. If you have time, you wait until the connection happens naturally. Then you make them work for it: they ask about your job, you give just enough to set the hook, and then you wait until they ask another question."

"It sounds like it takes a lot of time," Ammon said.

"It can, but that depends on a lot of factors. You can do all of this in fifteen minutes if you're in the right setting. Or it can take weeks or months. Eventually, they've got the scent of money—you've laid down just enough bait about who you are, about something big about to go down. If you're lucky, they come right out and ask if they can get in on it, and that's when you try to turn them down. It makes them want it even more badly. If you're not lucky, you have to fake an emergency. In this case, the story about a DEA bust and an unprotected shipment of drugs. Sometimes the marks jump in because they like feeling like the savior. Sometimes, you have to make it look like you're going under and they can take advantage of your moment of weakness; some people only slip up when they think they've got a chance to cut your throat. I think we can guess where Tanner falls."

"Jeez," Tean said. "And you think I'm dark."

"Once Kristine and Nathaniel had Tanner on the hook, they must have been hoping he'd slip up. Drop his guard. But then shit went sideways with Blake and Jager, and Tanner went berserk and went into hiding, and now they have to wait for him to pop his head up again when the delivery is supposed to happen."

"But why?" Ammon said. "You still haven't answered that part. Why not just put a knife in his back, drag him out into the desert, and leave him for somebody to find in fifteen years?"

"Because." Jem's jaw cracked. "Because when someone hurts you like that, you don't want to kill them. You want to do it to them. You want to do it a hundred times worse to them. It's not about smushing them out like a bug. It's about power. It's about getting back the power they took from you." The A/C from the vents was a hiss of white noise in Jem's ears. He worked his jaw from side to side; it popped one, two, three times, and the sound made him think of juniper branches exploding in a blaze. "And it's about humiliating them, debasing them, the way they did to you. It's not just about killing Tanner. It's about showing they're smarter than he is, tricking him, and then it's about taking their time with him, making him pay.

That's what Nathaniel wants. That's why we found those handcuffs under Kristine's bed. Tanner didn't put them there to blackmail Kristine; Kristine and Nathaniel put them there for Tanner so they could . . ." It was hard to swallow. "Get even. And record the whole thing. They would have wanted it to go on for days. For weeks. Months. You don't ever want it to end because it's the only way to feel better." He cleared his throat. "But time is limited, so a recording is the next best thing."

A stronger blast of wind hit the truck, forcing the truck onto the rumble strip again. Jem swore, jerked the wheel, and overcorrected. A Mack truck's horn blared. He yanked the wheel again and brought them back into their lane.

Tean's hand came to rest on his arm. Jem shook him off, his gaze still fixed on the road.

"Scientifically," Tean said, turning so that he was speaking into the dead space ahead of them, "revenge is biologically programmed into us because it's evolutionarily advantageous. They've done studies, and even fantasizing about revenge triggers the brain's reward centers, primarily with the release of dopamine. It's a mechanism for ensuring survival; revenge means making sure that the costs of acting against someone outweigh the gains. It's nonspecific, in fact. Other mammals display revenge behaviors—elephants, apes, chimpanzees. Some fish and snakes show this retaliatory behavior. Birds. Crows are so smart and have such high visual acuity that they can connect imposed costs with a specific human face; they can recognize individual humans who have done them wrong, and they'll try to retaliate, as Jem learned firsthand."

"Really fascinating stuff," Ammon said. "Too bad revenge means the total breakdown of law and order. The whole reason we have a civil society, laws, a justice system, all of it, is to keep the world from descending into tribal eye-for-an-eye bullshit."

"I'm not saying it's the right course of action. I'm saying it's biological, it's functional in terms of group and individual evolutionary advantages, and it's also something that we can understand at a personal level. I sympathize with Nathaniel. There are people who have hurt me, and I've wanted to hurt them back twice as badly."

"But you didn't."

Tean's mouth thinned into a line.

"You didn't, Tean. Am I right?"

"We're getting off topic."

"Answer my question."

"No, I didn't, Ammon."

"No, you didn't. Because you're a good person. You chose to take the high road. If it had been significant enough, you might have gone for legal compensation, but you didn't take matters into your own hands."

"Who was Nathaniel supposed to go to?" Jem said. "The cops? You're a joke. All you do is scratch each other's backs. You get away with murder—look at McEneany."

"Yeah," Ammon said. "There are some bad guys. But you don't know what it's like: the stress, the uncertainty, never knowing if someone's going to put a bullet in you when you turn your back on them. It gets in your head."

"Boo hoo," Jem said. "Tell that to Antonio. Oh, you can't. McEneany murdered him and walked away from it."

"And yeah, sometimes cops get away with bad things. McEneany isn't going to be one of them; you can bet your ass that the FBI will rip the sheriff's department apart looking for anybody who helped McEneany get away with this shit, because you can bet he wasn't working alone. But the point is that revenge isn't the answer. Vendettas aren't the answer. Legal recourse, law and justice. That's what you're supposed to do."

"Nathaniel didn't have that option," Tean said. "Years had passed since Tanner had hurt him. He'd been failed by the system before, failed by the people who should have helped him and protected him and kept him safe. He made decisions while suffering from the shock of another life-threatening assault, and—"

"Do you think revenge is right?"

"We're not talking about me."

"I'm asking you. Teancum Leon, who thinks he's so fucking moral because he's an existentialist and he gets to sulk and wallow and pretend his life is meaningless. Do you think revenge is ok?"

"Is that really how you think of me?"

"Is it moral?"

"Is that what you've thought of me all these years?"

"Answer me."

"No." Tean's narrow shoulders were drawn up. "No, I don't. But that doesn't mean I don't understand it. And it doesn't mean I don't sympathize with it."

"You're just saying this to make your boyfriend feel better," Ammon said. "And it's pretty fucking amusing watching you twist yourself into knots so you can tell him what he wants to hear without compromising your precious moral integrity."

"Talk to him like that again," Jem said. "Talk to him like that one more fucking time, and I'll pull this truck over and murder you. And that has nothing to do with revenge, motherfucker."

"Jem, please let me handle this." Tean turned at the waist to face Ammon. Tufts of wild dark hair stuck up along the back of his head, which Jem wanted to flatten, and the tension visible in his shoulders made Jem want to squeeze his nape and promise him it would be ok. But he couldn't do any of that. Not right then. "I didn't realize you thought so little of me."

"Grow up, Tean."

"I'm very sorry that I hurt you, Ammon. That's not—"

"Don't flatter yourself."

Tean let a beat pass. "That's not what I wanted. What I ever wanted. I'm always going to love you. And I'm going to want what's best for you. And when we've both had some time, I'd like to be your friend and be a part of your life in a way that's healthy for both of us. But I held on to you for a long time, Ammon, waiting and hoping that somehow you could make my life perfect. That's very common for gay men. Did you know that? They tend to hold on to their first relationship much longer than is healthy because they've often lost so much in the process of coming out."

Ammon was staring straight ahead, the muscles in his jaw standing out.

"Holding on to you, that wasn't fair to either of us," Tean said quietly. "And it wasn't a good way to live for either of us, and we both did things we shouldn't have. I'm sorry for my part in that." On a hill ahead of them, in the shade of a squat cedar, a bony horse whipped its head around. "This is for the best."

"Yeah. Well." His voice was thick, and his jaw moved soundlessly a few times. "I'm a sex addict, Teancum. Let's not pretend it was anything else." He covered his eyes. He was frozen, lacquered where the sun touched the side of his face.

"Ammon—"

"Leave him alone," Jem said.

Tean looked over his shoulder, his face twisted with indecision.

"Leave him alone right now. You're only making it harder for him."

After scrubbing furiously at his eyes, Tean nodded. Jem slid an arm around him, and Tean scooted closer, resting his head on Jem's shoulder. They drove that way for hours, Tean's tears hot where they fell on the thin poly-cotton of Jem's tee.

The sun moved behind them. They left the blackened valley behind them. The rock walls took on bands of color: gray-green, brown, pink, red. Fins and spines of sandstone corkscrewed in seemingly impossible ways. They passed redrock goblins, huge stone heads balanced on tiny bodies. Stone needles rose toward the sky. A bridge crossed a dry wash, where a sign hand-lettered with oil paint read: QUIKSAND!!!! Prickly pear, pinyon pine, juniper. Sage—a million kinds of sage that Tean probably would have known the names of. A slickrock path snaking up a bluff. A dugway crumbling on its north face. In places, the exposed rock was covered with something black, as though kids had gotten wild with the spray paint.

"Desert varnish," Tean whispered.

Jem smiled and squeezed him closer.

They were half an hour outside Moab when a cruiser appeared in the rearview mirror, lights flashing. It must have been going well over a hundred because it gained rapidly on them. When it was close enough, they could hear the sirens.

"What the hell did you do?" Ammon said scratchily. He wiped his face, smearing the salt tracks there, and looked around. "Jesus. How fast were you going?"

"I wasn't speeding."

"What the fuck did you do?"

"I didn't do anything!"

"He's passing us," Tean said. "He doesn't even care about us."

"What kind of shit are we walking into?" Ammon said.

As the cruiser drew even with them, though, it slowed. It kept pace for five seconds before Jem glanced over. STATE TROOPER was printed above the wheel wells—easy enough for Jem to read those words—and the Utah Highway Patrol logo, with the state beehive, marked the front door panel. Officer Haggerty shot them a quick look. Jem raised a hand in greeting. Haggerty smiled.

Then he cut hard to the right, clipping the Ford's rear wheel, and sending them spinning off the highway.

37

Jem's surprise only lasted half a second, but it was long enough for him to lose control of the truck completely. Haggerty was determined and a fuck-ton bolder than Jem would have guessed. He drove hard into the side of the Ford, keeping contact until the truck went off the road. The shriek of metal, which had been the only sound that Jem could hear, ended abruptly. Jem had just long enough to feel strangely relieved. He pulled hard on the steering wheel, trying to keep the truck on the shoulder. Then the first tire went out over empty air. Haggerty hit the truck again with another crunch and squeal. There was a loud pop—the tire, Jem guessed—and the smell of burning rubber. Then the truck was rolling, and Jem had a long enough to think, *Oh shit,* before the first impact.

Glass shattering. Metal crumpling. Shouting. The sudden suspension of gravity. Then impact, the seat belt biting into Jem's neck. Then it all happened again. And again.

When the truck came to a stop, Jem was hanging upside down. Every inch of him hurt. The world spun, settled, spun again. Blood ran along the side of his face, hot, stinging when it got into his eye. He fumbled with the seat belt, realized he'd done something stupid, and fell. He landed badly, on his shoulder and neck, driving a spike of pain to the base of his skull. The weight of his body drove some of the pebbles of tempered glass into bare skin, but he barely felt them. The smell of gasoline made him lightheaded.

Tean groaned.

Jem got onto his knees, twisting to inspect the other man. Tean's seat belt had held, and now the doc hung suspended from his seat, the belt cutting into his thighs and shoulder as it kept him from falling. His glasses were gone, and he looked like he was trying to focus.

"Are you ok?" Jem asked, his hands moving to the seat belt clip. "Can you understand me? Did you hit your head?"

Tean tried to nod and then must have understood the ridiculousness of it. "Yes, I'm fine." He tried to turn. "Ammon?"

"In a minute. Hold still." Jem depressed the seat belt's release, but the clip didn't come free. A wave of nausea was flooding him, and he breathed through his mouth as he yanked on the belt. "God damn it, God damn it, God damn it, God—"

The clip slid free, and Tean fell. He tried to catch himself, but mostly he landed on Jem, flattening the two of them against the cab's ceiling. By the time Jem got them sorted out, the nausea was worse, and he had to close his eyes and swallow against the urge to be sick. Sweat stung as it broke out across his face and chest.

"Jem?"

He nodded.

"Jem, I can't see anything."

The wave crested, and more sweat broke out, hot little spats of it like grease burns. Then Jem was ok, or close enough. He opened his eyes, found the twisted, taped-together frames, and pressed them into Tean's hand. Outside the truck, boots clapped against the hard-baked soil.

"Shit," Jem whispered. "He's here, and he's going to kill us if we don't get away from here. We've got to try to run."

"Ammon's not moving."

A quick glance confirmed that Tean was right: Ammon still hung upside down, his eyes closed. A starburst in the passenger window showed where his head had hit the glass, and as Jem watched, blood dripped from the other side of Ammon's head.

"Get him out of the belt," Jem said.

"We can't carry him."

"Do you want to leave him?"

Tean bit his lip as he shoved the glasses into place.

"I didn't think so. Get him out of the belt. We've got to take care of things one at a time."

The sound of footsteps was louder. Jem reached past Tean, his hand following Ammon's waistband until he touched the leather holster. He unsnapped the pistol there, fumbled, and recovered.

Then Jem tried the handle on the driver door. The latch released, and when he pushed there was only a moment of resistance before the door opened. It scraped across the hardpan, raising tiny whorls of dust. Jem had to crab out of the cramped space.

He had only a heartbeat to try to adjust his gaze to the intense brightness of the afternoon sun. Then a boot caught the side of his head, and the world scrambled. Instinct made him keep moving, long years of living when being cornered, being trapped, meant bad things would happen. So instead of collapsing and trying to retreat into the Ford's cab, he stumbled clear of the truck. The kick had messed up his horizon, though. The blue sky tilted precariously. He landed on hands and knees, the pistol slipping in his grip. His finger ached where the trigger guard twisted the knuckle.

The next kick caught him in the same spot Jager had gotten him, and the world exploded. It was all white fire—huge, shifting billows of it. When he came back, his eyes were watering with the blueness of the sky, and the pistol was gone.

"Stay down," Haggerty said. "You're cute, and I don't want to hurt you any more than I have to."

Blue, blue, blue. Jem could barely keep his eyes open, the sky was so blue. When his lids drifted down, the relative darkness was a mercy.

"Good boy."

Jem opened his eyes; the light made them water, so he let his head roll. He stared at a huge barrel cactus. He was thirsty, he realized. In a movie, once, he'd seen a guy lop off the top of a cactus and drink out of it. Now its shape reminded him of a camel's hump. He wondered if that was science, if there was an explanation for why camels and cacti both stored water in humps; Tean would know. He reached into the pocket where he kept the paracord with its hex nut, the barrette with the sharpened clip, the tube sock.

Haggerty made an annoyed noise. The kick caught Jem in the ribs, and he felt something snap in his chest. The force of it propelled Jem onto his side. He managed to drag out the barrette. The next kick caught him in the back, driving the breath from his lungs and forcing him onto his stomach. Strong hands caught his wrists, and then metal closed around them. Haggerty pried the barrette from his hand. It clicked softly when it hit the ground twenty yards away.

"Now, hold still so I don't have to seriously fuck you up."

The sound of the gunshot hammered against Jem's ears. He flinched. He felt Haggerty move, heard the trooper stand and spin.

"Get away from him," Tean said shakily. "I'll kill you if you don't get away from him."

The air was still. Jem's ragged breathing was the only thing he could hear, and every breath stoked the fire inside his chest. Broken ribs at the minimum.

Then Haggerty took a step.

"No," Tean said. "Over there. I said over there."

"I heard you," Haggerty said, his steps still moving toward the sound of Tean's voice.

"I'll shoot you."

Haggerty laughed quietly and kept walking.

Gritting his teeth, Jem managed to roll onto his side again. It cost him a shout of pain that he only partially managed to suppress. When he blinked his eyes clear, he could see Haggerty advancing on Tean. The glasses hung on the tip of Tean's nose, and sweat ran down his face in rivers. He was holding Jager's throwdown piece, the revolver with the American-flag grip that they'd discovered in Jager's locked filing cabinet. Tean must have kept it, the little miscreant. Jem had never been prouder.

"Stop right there," Tean said. "I'll kill you. I mean it. I'll—"

Haggerty kept the same steady pace. When he was close enough, he slapped the gun out of Tean's hand. Then he slapped Tean—great, openhanded blows that drove him backward until he had blood streaming down his face and was slumped against the Ford's chassis.

Jem didn't understand the pain in his chest until he realized he was screaming, struggling against the handcuffs, trying to get to his feet.

Haggerty grabbed Tean by the hair, spun around with the doc in front of him, and buried the muzzle of Ammon's pistol in Tean's side. The trooper's light brown eyes, almost yellow, were cool.

"Be quiet."

Jem swallowed his howls. He tried to catch Tean's gaze, but Tean had lost his glasses again. Blood masked his features, most of it from his nose and a split lip. Nothing serious, Jem told himself. Nothing really serious. Then he heard his own thoughts, and he wanted to laugh.

"Where's the pickup happening?" Haggerty dug the muzzle deeper into Tean's side. "I want the coordinates, and I want whatever instructions you were able to decode."

"We don't—" Jem tried.

Faster than Jem could believe, Haggerty pointed the pistol off at an angle and fired. The clap of the shot echoed across the valley. Then Haggerty returned the pistol to Tean's ribs. Tean squirmed, trying to pull away from the hot metal, but Haggerty had a tight grip.

"Next one goes into your boy's knee. And after that, his ankle. Then his other knee. Then his other ankle. Then his wrists. Then I start blowing off fingers. I've got a box of ammo in my trunk. I've got all day, and the best part is, your boy will still be alive. He'll live a long life, remembering every day how you pissed me off."

"You don't have time," Jem said. "And you have a witness."

Haggerty grimaced. Then, after a cautionary jab with the muzzle, he glanced over his shoulder. A blue Prius was parked on the shoulder behind his cruiser, and a heavyset woman was trudging toward them. She was carrying a first-aid kit and, from a distance, appeared to be wearing a pith helmet, although Jem was willing to admit that he might have been imagining it from all the blows to the head.

After letting out a sigh, Haggerty squeezed off two shots in the woman's direction. She turned around and sprinted back to the car.

"Guess we'll do this hard and fast," Haggerty said, shaking Tean by the hair and then shoving him to the ground. "For fuck's sake, why can't one thing be easy about this?"

"We can show you," Jem said.

Haggerty hesitated. He drew a bead on Tean, who was on his hands and knees.

"We know where the pickup is going to be. It's happening just after sunset, so you still have time. We don't have coordinates, but we can show you."

Haggerty's mouth was a thin line. He shifted his weight. His hand and the gun were coated with fine red grit like powdered blood.

"All right, boys. We're going for a ride."

"He needs his glasses," Jem said.

"Go on, Dr. Leon. Get your glasses."

"By the truck," Jem said. The tide of adrenaline was pulling out, and he was shaking and about to be sick. "No, farther back."

Tean's hand closed around the taped frames, and he settled them on his face. His face screwed up with worry when he glanced at the truck, and Jem willed him to stay silent.

"Ready?" Haggerty scooped up the revolver, Jager's throwaway piece, and shoved it behind his waistband at the small of his back. He kept Ammon's pistol in his other hand. His own service weapon was still holstered at his side; he hadn't even needed to draw it. "Here we go."

38

The cruiser rumbled along a dirt BLM road, heading northeast up the canyon. They were half an hour on the other side of Moab now, heading toward the Dolores River and the coordinates that had been encoded in the burner phone. The desert was a boneyard at the cusp of evening: the twisted, ossified outlines of ocotillo, jackpine, juniper, and scrub oak; the bristling, dead-man's-hair of locoweed, quinine, sage, and panic grass; the sun licking its way along rimrock like wood catching fire, old stone burned by an even older flame.

Tean had stripped off his shirt, and in the back seat of the cruiser, he wadded it against the side of Jem's head. Haggerty had reopened the nasty laceration that Jager had given Jem, and Jem definitely had at least one broken rib. He was leaning against Tean, the position allowing him some relief and enabling him to breathe more easily.

"He needs these cuffs off," Tean said.

"I heard you the first five times, Dr. Leon."

"He can't breathe."

Haggerty sighed. That had been his attitude through this whole thing: tired and mildly frustrated, as though he'd been forced to give up his Saturday morning to help an elderly aunt.

"I'm sorry," Tean whispered to Jem for what felt like the millionth time. "I'm sorry I couldn't do it. I'm sorry I let you down."

Jem just shook his head.

"Let me see your eyes again," Tean said. "I don't think you have a concussion, but I want to check."

Groaning, Jem let Tean maneuver him until Tean could check his pupils.

He's going to kill us, Jem mouthed. His color was terrible, and he'd already been sick once, forcing Haggerty to stop the car so that Jem could puke on the side of the road.

Tean nodded.

For a moment, emotions battled in Jem's face; Tean ignored them. Instead, he helped Jem recline against him again, adjusted the improvised bandage, and laced his fingers with Jem's good hand. His skin was textured with the desert's red dust, and his grip was strong.

"At this point," Tean said, speaking loudly to be heard over their rumbling passage along the dirt road, "there's still a way you can walk away from this. Jager is convinced that the sheriff killed Antonio, so you don't have to worry about him. Jem and I are the only ones who know you're involved, and we're good at keeping secrets. You can take the cuffs off Jem, leave us right here by the side of the road, and nobody has to know anything."

Haggerty laughed. "I don't think you're as smart as you think you are."

"What am I missing?"

"The whole thing is fucked to hell now. Too bad, really. We had a good thing going."

"You were all in on it," Tean said. "All of you."

"Like I said: we had a good thing going. Everybody had their part. Moab's a nice, safe place. Tourists come and spend their money, but you can raise a family here too. I grew up here. We make sure we don't have any problems."

"Sure," Jem croaked. "You keep the drugs moving safely, and they stay out of your little bubble. Oh, and you fellows get rich off it."

"Well," Haggerty said, flashing a smile in the rearview mirror. "I've got to retire sometime. The rodeo kid bought his horses. Nobles was smart; lived off the cash, invested most of what he earned as chief. Bet you didn't know he was a bona fide millionaire. Too bad the rodeo kid turned out to be the little twat I predicted he'd be. I watched that kid grow up, and he thought he was the biggest thing since Jesus because he could get cheerleaders to give him a zinger in the back of his truck, and the only reason he got elected to sheriff was because he won that championship. Good riddance."

"You killed him," Tean said quietly.

"Jeez, you really think the worst of me. The kid had a crisis of conscience. It started when your friend Tanner got his hooks in McEneany: pictures of McEneany with girls, with drugs, McEneany out of his head on crystal. When he sobered up and realized Tanner had his balls in a vise, the kid wanted to be done with everything. Tanner kept riding him, though—made him go out and help him clean up the mess with Weckesser. That's when McEneany told me and Nobles how stupid he'd been. I don't know what he was expecting, but we told him he had to play out the rest of it. That was the first we'd heard about drugs moving in on the Dolores, and we didn't like the idea that somebody was trying to run something through our territory without paying the toll. McEneany threw a fit, of course, but it got even worse after he killed that fellow in the motel, the one he shot in the shower. You should have seen the kid after, crying, praying, begging for help. Nobles told him to come over, and they'd talk it out. Figure a way to deal the rodeo kid out of the game. Nobles already had everything set up: plastic drop cloths covering everything. One tap to the back of the head. Then he drove him into the Maze."

"And you shot Nobles in the back," Jem said. His breathing had a whooshing noise to it that worried Tean a great deal. "Is that it?"

Haggerty shrugged. "By then, I knew we were fucked. Time to close up shop. Like you said, nobody else can put this on me. I'll find a way to unload the pickup, and that'll be the last of it."

Jem's hand tightened again around Tean's, and Tean nodded. Haggerty didn't know that the pickup was fake. Haggerty didn't know that Kristine and Nathaniel had cooked up the whole thing as bait to draw out Tanner.

They drove into the narrowing canyon, and Tean played out every possibility he could imagine until the future blurred. When the dirt road ended, Haggerty stomped the brakes and glanced over his shoulder. Through the security partition, his gaze was hard as slickrock.

"You haven't been playing games with me, have you, Dr. Leon?"

Tean visualized the map he had pulled up. Then he scanned the ground ahead of them. Clumps of antelope brush were broken and sagging, and something had snapped a Russian olive's branch, which now hung from strips of bark. Tean pointed. "You should have brought a vehicle with higher clearance. We have to go off-road from here."

Haggerty spun in his seat and considered the faint trail. Then, shoulders drooping, he shifted into gear. The Charger nosed up onto the uneven slope; the clumps of antelope brush crackled under the chassis like Black Cats. When the tires rolled over a clump of snakeweed, the dry stalks hissed like their namesake. They limped forward, the Charger rocking from side to side, dipping abruptly when the ground dropped away, Jem groaning as the movement jostled his injuries.

When they reached the edge of the bluff, the western sky had purpled, and shadows thickened in the canyon below them. The last light traced the Dolores with silver, outlining the flat, rust-colored water. Tamarisks and cottonwoods grew thick along the bank, and in one clump of salt cedar, Tean spotted the outline of a ranger's cabin. An inflatable raft had been dragged up onto a gravelly strip of shore.

"Well," Haggerty said, his smile flickering in the rearview mirror. "Fuck me."

"Now let us go," Tean said. "We'll walk."

"Not just yet. I don't see any cargo."

"They probably moved it inside the cabin."

"That seems like a lot of extra work," Haggerty said slowly. "Just to turn around and load it again."

"There's a comment box," Jem said. "Make sure you leave them a suggestion."

"And how the hell are they going to get a couple hundred kilos of meth up here? They're sure as fuck not going to carry it."

"I don't know, man. They didn't write out their master plan for us."

"There's probably a trail that leads down there," Tean said. "A dugway. Or a switchback. Something big enough for an ATV so they could shuttle it up here."

Haggerty was quiet for a long time. The silence stretched out, broken only by the engine's rumble and the hiss of the A/C. In spite of the cold air, Tean was sweating, and he could smell his own fear. Then Haggerty seemed to reach a decision, squaring his shoulders and reaching for the door handle.

"We can check the cabin," Tean said, the words coming out so fast they were a jumble. "You need more information. They might have hidden the shipment inside the cabin. Or it might be nearby. Jem can find it."

Haggerty craned his head, glancing at them over one shoulder. Then he shook his head. "I think this is the end of your road, guys. I'm going to open your door, and you get out nice and quiet." The car rocked, adjusting for the loss of Haggerty's weight as the trooper stood. His door slammed shut. When he got to the rear door, he had Ammon's gun in his hand again. He rapped on the glass with the barrel, three times, and repeated, "Nice and quiet."

Tean's breath caught in his throat.

"It's ok," Jem whispered, squeezing Tean's hand. "Let me go first. Maybe I can surprise him."

"No." Tean resettled his glasses and put a hand on Jem's shoulder to keep him in place. "No, Jem."

When Haggerty opened the door, Tean scooted along the seat. The vinyl upholstery stuck to the bare skin of his arm and shoulder. He suddenly wanted his shirt, but it was a crumpled, bloody mess in the footwell, and it was too late anyway. He planted his feet on sun-hot ground and stood.

"Officer Haggerty, you won't be able to find it on your own."

Haggerty's yellow eyes were steady. "I'm not so sure about that. They left the boat just sitting out in the open. I figure I'll walk through the cabin door and find that stash just fine."

"Do you want to take the risk? You've got a lot riding on this. It's your last score. Do you want to lose it because you—" Tean had to stop to swallow here; the desert had sucked the moisture from his throat. "Because you were hasty?"

"I prefer the term cautious."

"You're not being very cautious. Someone muled the cargo down the Dolores. Where is he? Waiting inside that cabin? Hoping someone stupid walks through that door? And you can't wait him out, either. Kristine and Nathaniel, or whatever you want to call them, they'll be here soon. They're not going to miss this pickup, and they're not going to be happy if they find you here."

Shifting his weight, Haggerty hooked one thumb in his utility belt. His eyes cut past Tean to the road they had followed. After a moment, he said, "I'd better hurry up, then."

"You won't be able to find it. I wouldn't be able to find it either. The only person who's going to be able to find it is Jem, and you need me to help him down there."

"Not necessarily. I could get him down there; I think I can motivate him."

"The only thing that motivates me," Jem said from inside the car, "is McDonald's. Do you have McDonald's? Fries would be ideal. Tean, get out of the way. This motherfucker is dead set on being stupid, and we're holding him up."

But Tean held his spot, blocking Jem's exit, the cruiser's door between him and Haggerty. "And how are you going to get it all back up the bluff? That was your question. How are you going to move it up here before Kristine and Nathaniel arrive?"

"Your busted-up boytoy isn't going to be good for carrying anything."

"He's going to find the drugs. I'll move them."

"Tean's stronger than he looks," Jem said. "He's like one of those old, broken-down mules that can still carry hundreds of pounds."

"Quit helping," Tean whispered. To Haggerty, he said, "You don't lose anything by letting us go down there."

"You guys are determined to make this more complicated than it needs to be," Haggerty said. His gaze moved back to the dirt road, west, where the swollen sun was sinking behind the goblins and hoodoos and sandstone fins. "Let's get this over with. We're running out of day."

It took Tean a few minutes to find a switchback hiking trail that led them down from the bluff. No matter what Tean argued, Haggerty refused to remove Jem's cuffs, and so Tean had to balance both of them on the steep, slickrock path. Jem did his best, but his injured ribs made everything more difficult, and he was gasping and making sharp pained cries that only got worse as they made their way down. After the third time Jem stumbled, almost pitching all three of them off the slope, Haggerty ordered them to go ahead.

"I'm sorry," Tean whispered, steadying Jem as they rounded another switch. "I know this is really painful, and I'm so sorry."

Jem rolled his eyes.

Tean moved on autopilot for the next five steps. Then he whispered, "Oh my gosh."

"Don't act so surprised," Jem whispered back.

"Oh my gosh."

"You really ought to know better by now."

"But I saw him kick you. I saw—" Tean tightened his grip, nails digging into Jem's arm. "I've been scared sick."

"Ow, ow, ow. Does it make you feel better that I really do think I have broken ribs?"

Tean thought about this and relaxed his grip. "A little."

"Were you always this evil? Or is it just my influence? Ow, ow, ow. Stop it, I was just kidding."

Their conversation paused so that Jem could do more moaning and whimpering. After the next switch, Tean whispered, "Jem, what if I'm right? Somebody might be waiting in the cabin."

"Your imaginary drug courier?"

"No, dummy. Tanner."

"Good. I hope he is. I've got a lot of catching up to do with that fuckstick."

"You won't feel that way when he shoots both of us as we walk through the door."

"I might. You don't know how I feel."

"Jem!"

"Tanner won't shoot to kill. He likes to play with his food, remember? And he's probably pissed, seriously pissed about the missing drugs. He's going to want answers before he kills Kristine and Nathaniel. On top of that, he's going to be disoriented when he sees us instead of those two. It's going to give us a few seconds to work."

"What are we going to do?"

"I've got a plan."

"What's your plan?"

"I can't tell you. It's a secret."

"You don't have a plan. You never have plans. You always want to riff or whatever you call it when you pull the whole thing out of your butt."

Jem smirked. "First of all, it really loses something when you say butt instead of ass. And second, I'm fucking fantastic at riffing. Watch this. When I go down, put as many rocks as you can in my pocket."

"What—"

Scree on the slickrock worked like ball bearings, and on Tean's next step, Jem stumbled into him. Tean's foot slid on several loose stones. He tried to catch himself on the branch of a dead yellowleaf, but he was moving too fast, and it ripped out of his hand. The bark scraped his palm raw, and he landed hard on his butt. Jem stumbled against the scrubby slope, let out a pained wheeze, and dropped to the ground.

On his knees, Tean scrambled closer and bent over Jem. He followed Jem's instructions, filling his pocket with rocks while pretending to check him for injuries and help him sit up. By the time Jem was upright again, Jem's face was green, and he stumbled to the edge of the trail and puked downhill. Haggerty watched from the switch above them.

"That was a fucking terrible idea," Jem whispered as Tean urged him down the trail again. "Why did I let you talk me into it?"

"It was your idea. And you said you were going to fall, not that we both were."

"That was part of the riffing," Jem said. "Fuck, my ribs. I really should have thought that through."

In spite of everything that was going on around them, Tean was remarkably proud of himself for managing not to say anything to that.

Night came quickly on dark wings, brooding over the lower canyon. Shadow swallowed the pinyon and juniper, the tamarisk and cottonwood, the sedge and reeds and sego lilies along the Dolores's banks. The cabin, in its tangle of salt cedar, looked like a burned-out thing as night took it: an afterimage of char, and then nothing. The redrock walls, banded with pale tan and gray green and ocher, turned blue. Then purple. Then dusklight robbed them of any color at all, just a silvery wash that clung to everything like desert varnish.

Something exploded when they set foot on the lower canyon floor.

Tean jerked to a stop. Jem laughed, and after a moment, behind them, Haggerty chuckled too. Then Tean saw above the rimrock: trailing sparks of red and green. Another explosion, and then the pop and crackle of silver and blue flowering overhead.

"Fucking Pioneer Day fireworks," Haggerty said, his voice so relieved that Tean suddenly understood how tense the man had been.

"They're going to start a fire," Tean said.

Jem nudged him forward. "Maybe Officer Haggerty will write them a ticket. Come on, let's get this over with."

Sand sage bristled and crackled when they pushed through it. Wiregrass, when they stomped a path through it, sounded like a bonfire. Drawn by the river, gnats clouded together in the air, and bats swooped and looped over the water for their evening meal. Along the bank, a scraggly patch of cattails quivered, and then golden eyes blinked out at Tean. He remembered the last time he had seen a coyote, how Jem's face had lit up. He said nothing, and the trickster eyes winked out.

The cabin was built on a raised foundation of irregular sandstone slabs. The logs looked like cottonwood that had been harvested in the canyon, probably along the river, and the adobe chinking was chipped and gone in many places, exposing holes into the darkened interior. Tean steadied Jem as they went up to the porch. Jem tilted his head, and they moved to one side. Haggerty waited below.

"Knock," Jem whispered.

Tean stretched around him and knocked.

No answer. The Dolores was a white hiss in Tean's ears.

"Push it open," Jem whispered. "If you can."

Tean sidled past Jem, tested the handle, and felt it turn. Jem tensed behind him. Drawing a breath, Tean shoved the door open. It flew inwards, crashed against the wall, and wobbled back.

Silence inside. Darkness.

"So much for that," Jem said in a normal voice. "Do you have a flashlight?"

Haggerty's answer was to click on a penlight. He played it across their feet and through the half-open door. The light picked out the uneven boards, tracks in the dust, a riverstone hearth.

"Where the fuck is the cargo?"

"Let's go inside," Jem said. "Look around."

Jem went first. Tean followed. The cabin smelled closed up, like dry rot and the faintest hint of juniper smoke. Enough ambient light allowed Tean to make out the shapes in the single room. Several empty bunks. A wood-burning stove full of ash. A ceramic basin with a cracked pitcher next to it. A back door that led out toward the salt cedar tangle and the river. Just the essentials, built decades ago for a ranger who might spend the night. Campers might be able to rent the place now; many of the cabins had been repurposed that way.

Steps rang out on the porch, and Tean turned. Haggerty moved into the doorway. The penlight swept the room; Ammon's gun was the shadow that followed. In the darkness, the only clear part of Haggerty's face were his eyes.

A red dot moved across the jamb behind Haggerty.

Tean had just enough time to think that it looked like a laser pointer.

Then Haggerty's head exploded.

39

Weight bore Tean down, pinning him to the floor, and he struggled to get free. Then he heard Jem's pained grunt and stopped moving. The gunshot rang out across the valley, sounding not much different than the distant pop of the fireworks. Then another noise: a soft, wet sound. Dripping. Tean felt himself start to shake.

"Stay right here," Jem breathed into his ear. "You're safe, but I need you to stay right here."

After a moment, Tean jerked his head in a nod.

Jem crabbed away on his knees, twisting around to try to drag Haggerty's body farther into the cabin. The pain must have been intense because he swore softly, then loudly, and then he gave up. With his hands cuffed behind him, and with his injured ribs, he couldn't manage to move the body. Swearing, Jem contorted himself again.

Haggerty lay only a few feet away, his ruined head in Tean's line of sight. Brain and bone and blood made an arc across the floor, the walls, even the beams and rafters above them. The smell of violated body cavities filled the air.

Jem was making a long, despairing noise as he tried again to move the body.

Tean rolled onto hands and knees, crawled across the cabin, and touched Jem's shoulder. Jem panted and shook his head. Tean nodded, and after a moment, Jem crabbed away from the body. Tean watched the doorway, waiting for the red dot of the laser sight to drift into view again, but everything was a dark. Then he grabbed Haggerty's utility belt and hauled the dead man into the room.

"Keys," Jem whispered.

It took Tean a few fumbling tries to free them from the belt and unlock the cuffs. Jem wrung his wrists and let out a shaky breath. He reached for Ammon's gun, which had fallen from Haggerty's hand and was now halfway under one of the bunks, spotlighted by the small flashlight.

The back door flew open, and a tall, well-built man stepped into the cabin. In the weak glow from the penlight, Tean could make out a few details: he had dark hair and dark eyes, and he looked like he'd been living rough for a while. Dirt smudged his face, his eyes were hollow, and several days' scruff covered his cheeks. Rage flooded Jem's face, and Tean knew this was Tanner Kimball.

Jem lunged for Ammon's gun. Tanner was faster, firing his own gun first. The gunshot was louder than a thunderclap inside the small cabin, and Tean's ears rang with it. Jem cried out and fell to the ground, a hand over his arm where blood ran thick and dark between his fingers. Tanner took two more quick steps into the room, bent, and grabbed Ammon's gun in his free hand. Then ripped Haggerty's from its holster and retreated until he stood at the back door, which he braced open with one foot. The smell of the river flowed into the cabin.

"Who the fuck are you two?"

Jem was hyperventilating. He'd taken the bullet high in his arm, and there was a lot of blood, but Tean needed to see the wound before he could decide how bad it was. Not the brachial artery. Not enough blood for that. But it could still be bad, very bad.

"Who the fuck are we?" Jem roared. He was trying to sit up, but he couldn't seem to do it. "Who the fuck are we, motherfucker?"

Tean shifted his weight to crawl forward, but Tanner swung Ammon's gun in his direction. The other gun, Tanner's gun, was still trained on Jem.

"He needs medical attention," Tean said as calmly as he could. His brain was cycling up, trying to process the immediate chain of events: Haggerty shot and killed, the back door opening, Tanner's appearance. "I'm going to take a look."

"Stay right where you are."

"I'm just going to take a look. You're going to need help getting out of this, so you can't afford to kill us. How long has Kristine had you pinned down?"

Tanner's eyes looked dead as they fixed on Tean. "Who the fuck is Kristine?"

"How long?"

"About six hours. Christ, the dump I've got to take."

Curled up on the floor, Jem started to laugh. "He's got to take a dump. This gaping cumhole has been inconvenienced because he needs to drop a deuce. Holy fucking shit."

"Where's the meth?"

"There are no drugs, you fucking imbecile. Jesus Christ, somebody give this guy a clue."

Tean crawled over to Jem. Some of the blood on Jem's fingers was already sticky, but mostly it was slick and hot. Tean pulled Jem's hand away from the wound, ignoring how Jem swore at him. A graze. Nothing bad. Tean's eyes stung, and he had to fight hard to keep from dissolving into tears. Just a graze. Jem could have done worse to himself falling off his motorcycle. Tean's hands shook as he gathered a handful of Jem's tee and used his teeth to start a small tear.

"Who's Kristine?" Tanner said. He took a nervous step toward the cabin's front door and then retreated again. "Who the fuck is out there, and what the fuck is going on?"

Once Tean had the tear started, it was easy to rip the shirt into two pieces. He helped Jem sit up, aware of how hard Jem was shaking, and peeled them off. He left bloody handprints across the soft blond hairs of Jem's chest, along his shoulder, his belly. He used the pieces of the shirt to improvise a bandage, and he yanked hard as he tied the knot.

"Jesus fucking Christ, Tean," Jem shouted. He hammered on the floor with his free hand. "What in the seven fucking hells?"

"Don't be a baby."

"All right, he's going to live. Good job, Dr. Quinn." Tanner took another of those prancing steps forward and then back again. "Now who the fuck is Kristine? You'd better start talking before I blow your head off."

"He doesn't remember," Jem said, closing his eyes. His head fell back against the bunk. "He doesn't even remember."

Tean didn't know if Jem meant Kristine or himself. Part of him didn't want to know. He caught Tanner's eye and said, "Kristine Colin-Bowman."

Tanner had the look of a kid lost in algebra class.

"What about Nathaniel Dayton?"

Rolling a shoulder, Tanner shook his head.

"You tried to cut his ear off," Jem said, eyes still closed. "In case that jogs your memory."

Tanner's thumbs played nervously on the grips of the guns. "You're kidding. The faggot?"

"Jesus Christ," Jem muttered.

"And who's the cunt?"

"It must be hard," Jem said, eyes opening. He turned to look at Tanner. "Keeping a list of all the people you've fucked up, all the lives you've ruined. That must get time consuming after a while for a guy like you."

Tanner's smile was vividly white in the darkness, almost luminescent. "Holy shit. Am I supposed to know you too?"

"It must be hard, keeping track. No reason you ought to remember a girl you tried to rape when you were a kid, just getting started."

"Every bitch wants it right up until she doesn't," Tanner said. "It's the same song and dance once it's over."

Jem was taking uncontrolled gulps of air. He shifted his weight as though he meant to stand.

"Not right now," Tean said. "Jem, this isn't the time."

"But she was smarter than you," Jem said. "They were both smarter than you. And now they've got you where they want you. And you're going to get what you deserve. I'm going to stand here and watch as they cut your balls off and feed them to you. I'm going to give them a few ideas myself. I'm going to start by sticking a knife up your asshole and letting you sit on it while they work on you. Then I'm going to get really creative."

If anything, Tanner's smile got bigger. "Fuck me, I am supposed to know you. Who are you? You've got to at least give me a clue."

"They don't lock the laundry doors at night," Jem said, and the words had the sound of a quote, although Tean didn't understand the reference. "You can walk right out."

The transformation in Tanner's face was instantaneous: shock, then laughter. "No fucking way. Jeremy?"

"It's Jeremiah, shit-for-brains."

"God damn. No fucking way." Tanner glanced at Haggerty, then out into the emptiness of sage and night. "What is this, some kind of reunion party? You all had sore titties, so you decided it was time for payback?"

"I'm here, you sperm-sample reject, because of Andi. Because you killed Andi. I'm here to make sure you pay for that."

With another laugh, Tanner shook his head. "Jesus. The party cunt? There's millions of dollars on the line—"

"There are no drugs," Tean shouted over him. "None. How do you not understand that? If you want to make it out of here alive, you're going to need help. Kristine is up there, and she's apparently a really good shot. Judging by how easily she got Haggerty, I think it's safe to say she's got the right gear to keep us here all night. We're miles from anyone who might stumble onto us, and nobody's going to hear the gunshots because of the fireworks. So shut up, stop pointing those guns at us, and let's find a way out of here."

The guns dipped an inch. To Jem, Tanner said, "Who's he? Your pussyboy?"

"I'm his boyfriend," Tean snapped, catching the glasses as they threatened to slide free. "Now tell us how you got down here, and maybe we can figure out a way to leave."

Tanner shrugged. "I was camping up the Dolores. I stole a truck from this old guy, right out of his barn; I bet he doesn't even know it's missing. After everything with Antonio's party cunt and Blake getting . . . talkative, I decided I better lie low for a while. Besides, it's not like I needed Kristine and her fag anymore. They'd left the phone out on the table, right where I could see it. I picked it up. I knew climbers liked to use those codes. Why the fuck should I split that money with those two when I was doing all the work? I figured I could float down here the day of the pickup, take the cargo, and float everything a couple miles farther downriver before that bitch showed up. Then I could take my time unloading it. I've got a guy in West Valley who could move this shit for me. Once I had the money, I could go wherever I wanted." A little furrow appeared between his eyebrows. "Why didn't the bitch just shoot me?"

"What?"

"You're talking about Kalista, right?"

"Her name is Kristine," Jem said.

"Why didn't she just pop me one?"

"Because she wants to take her time with you. She and Nathaniel want to make you pay. Can't say I blame them." Jem's face had whitened, waxy in the weak illumination from Haggerty's penlight. "They had a pretty sweet setup at the villa you rented for them. Cuffs and chains. I bet they would have spent a long time taking you apart."

"No wonder that bitch was always ordering me drinks and trying to get me alone. Rule fucking number one: if you didn't mix it yourself, don't drink it." Tanner smiled, and for a moment, in the shadows, Tean could see the superficial charm, the guile that had carried him this far. "Too bad for the bitch that this was business. If there hadn't been money on the table, I would have had a lot of fun with her. She's my type."

"Jesus," Jem said. "He really does not understand."

"I know there aren't any drugs," Tanner barked. "I'm talking, you know, how I was thinking at the time."

"And you didn't find it strange at all that this girl wanted to bring you in on a multi-million-dollar drug heist? For fuck's sake. You're honestly beyond helping."

"I forgot little Jeremy always had a mouth on him." The guns dipped again. "I forgot we had to find other ways to keep Jeremy's mouth busy."

Red blotched Jem's face, making the waxiness even worse.

"Does he still moan when you bottom out in him?" Tanner asked Tean. "He likes it rough. You got to give it to him rough or he won't get off on it."

"I'm going to kill you, you son of a bitch," Jem whispered. He tried to stand, but Tean caught his uninjured arm and held him down. "I'm going to kill you." This time, it was a scream, and Jem thrashed, trying to get free of Tean's grip.

Grinning, Tanner gestured at Tean with Ammon's gun. "Back up, pussyboy. Put on those cuffs. Christ, I wish we had time for a round right now. You know what the best part was? The best part was when he'd be sobbing, face covered in snot, and he'd start making these little noises. Uh. Uh. Uh. He just couldn't help himself; he liked having his hole tapped, no matter how much he pretended he didn't. I said back up."

But Jem was still trying to get up, making a wild, uncontrollable growling noise. His eyes were huge and empty, and Tean realized that, bullet wound or not, Jem was going to get free.

"Stop," Tean whispered, yanking him back toward the floor. "Stop, Jem. He's trying to make you mad so you'll do something stupid. Stop, or he'll kill both of us."

"I said back—" Tanner began. He never finished.

A shadow detached itself from the open doorway behind Tanner, darting into the cabin. The penlight's narrow beam only gave a haze of light to the rest of the cabin, but it was enough for Tean to glimpse the man he had met as Nick, whose real name was Nathaniel: the wide, dark eyes, the too-red lips, the long hair pulled back to expose his mutilated ear. Tanner turned toward the movement. He was too slow. Nathaniel grabbed Tanner's ear and sliced it off with two savage hacks from a knife that was almost as long as his forearm. The blade was too big for the job, and it looked cumbersome; the long, wide blade opened furrows along Tanner's temple and cheek.

Tanner screamed. He was still turning, but now the instinctive reaction to pull away made him stumble back. The guns came up. Tanner fired. Muzzle flashes gave popcorn bursts of light. The clap of the shots rocked Tean. One bullet hit a bunkbed, and part of the frame exploded into a cloud of splinters.

Nathaniel's knife went into Tanner's belly, and Tanner screamed again.

Jem was on his knees, doing something—Tean couldn't process it. Tean was only aware of this opportunity. He launched himself up from the ground. Tanner was still caught in the movement of turning, still stumbling back as he reacted to Nathaniel's attack. He fired again. The muzzle flashes painted Nathaniel in gold, outlining where a mist of blood had beaded on the bridge of his nose. One of the bullets slammed into a window, knocking open the shutter.

Nathaniel lunged, following Tanner with the knife, and the second bullet caught him in the head. The bullet tore away the side of his skull and his scarred ear. He dropped. The noise from the gunshots had deafened Tean, but his brain supplied the clink of metal when the knife hit the floor.

By then, Tean had closed the distance. He was behind Tanner, who had turned to face Nathaniel. He grabbed Tanner's left arm, which was holding Ammon's gun, and twisted. Tanner screamed. Tean wrested the gun from Tanner's grip, but the metal was slick and oily with sweat, and Tean almost fumbled it.

"Down, down," Tean shouted.

But Tanner was already spinning around, and he clubbed Tean with the side of his own pistol. The blow was hard enough to scramble Tean's vision. He was vaguely aware of stepping back, his foot coming down on something soft but unyielding, and tripping. He landed on his back, his legs across Haggerty's corpse. Under one calf, he felt a hard, familiar outline. Something hidden under Haggerty's shirt.

Tean didn't have time to consider it; when his hand hit the old boards, pain sparked along the nerves, and his fingers extended automatically. Ammon's gun flew out of his hand. Tean flipped over, reaching for it, but he was too late. The gun disappeared through the cabin's front door. It was gone.

A crunch and a horrible scream made Tean scramble around. He had a mental vision of Jem being pistol-whipped. Instead, though, he saw Jem on his feet, swinging the tube sock in lazy circle. He had loaded it with the rocks that Tean had hidden in his pockets on the switchback; a few of the smaller stones lay on the boards where he had been kneeling. Tanner had backed up to the cabin's wall, cradling an arm to his chest. The arm was obviously broken, part of the forearm sagging grotesquely. Blood streamed down his face from the stump of his ear. It soaked his shirt. More blood stained the bottom of his shirt and his jeans where Nathaniel had driven the blade into his gut. It was a miracle that he was still standing, but Tean was starting to understand that Tanner was a survivor in more ways than one. He was breathing in rapid bursts, his eyes roving back and forth. His gun lay in the corner near the back door, where it must have fallen after Jem had broken his arm with the improvised sap.

"Say something again," Jem said. The words were muffled to Tean's damaged hearing. He swung the loaded sock faster. It made a soft, humming noise. "Say something again about what you did to me. Laugh about it."

"Jem," Tean said, sitting up. The movement brought his leg in contact with that hard shape under Haggerty's shirt again. "Jem, you're ok. You—"

"I'm not ok," Jem shouted; his eyes remained fixed on Tanner. "I'm not ok. He did . . . that to me. He did it again and again. It was a game for him. He'd play with me like it was a fucking game. He'd let me run, let me think I could get away. He'd tell me he'd make it nice. Once, he staged this whole scene so I'd overhear him talking about the laundry, about a way to escape. I thought I was finally free. When I tried, he was waiting there with Blake and Antonio. They took turns, Tean. When they'd finished, he shoved a . . . a sheet up there, and he made me thank him for putting in my tampon. Because I was bleeding. Because that's what he did to me every time. He couldn't get hard unless there was blood." He managed a few gasping breaths. "You want to know how I learned that people will believe anything if they want it to be true? LouElla might have taught me that, but you're looking at the guy who drove it home."

Even cradling his broken arm, Tanner managed a smile. "I bet you're so loose now I could drive a Mack truck up there. You wouldn't be any fun."

Jem howled and swung. The sock caught Tanner on the side of the face. The rocks crunched, and Tean thought he heard bone break. Tanner stumbled, caught up against the wall again, and slid to the floor, sprawling almost to the back door. Jem hit him again, bringing down the improvised sap across Tanner's ribs. And then again, twice in a row, on Tanner's leg.

"Jem, stop!" Tean wasn't sure how long he'd been screaming the words. He wasn't sure how many times he'd already said them. He only knew that his throat was raw from it.

Panting, hunched over from the pain in his own ribs, Jem finally slowed. He was crying, Tean realized. Silently, the tears running down his face. When he spoke, though, his voice had only the faintest hoarseness. "Tell me again about animals, Tean. Tell me about the biological imperative of revenge. And then I'm going to beat this motherfucker to death for what he did to me. What he took from me."

On the floor, Tanner's eyes were half closed, and from the shape and position of his jaw, Tean guessed it was dislocated, probably broken. Tean thought of a lonely, frightened, kindhearted boy who had never had a home, who had been tortured and abused. And for a single, frightening moment, Tean wanted to kill Tanner himself.

"Jem, if you do this, you're going to regret it. You're going to do something because of all the pain inside you, not because you want to. And you're going to have to carry it for the rest of your life, and you'll never be free of it. You can't do this."

"I can." He laughed, the sound thick. "I really can, Tean. Maybe you should wait outside. I don't want you to see this."

Tean shook his head.

"Go outside. I don't want you to see this."

"No. If you're going to do it, I'll stay. But you don't have to do this." Tean took a deep breath. "You want me to talk about animals, but I don't know anything about animals and forgiveness. I don't know if they can forgive. But you're not an animal, Jem, no matter how hard the world tried to make you one. You're a human, and you're the most wonderful human I know. And if there's anything that's purely human, it's forgiveness. You can stop. You can let go of all the hurt and the pain. I know it's not that easy, but you can start right now. You can start to let go."

For a few moments, the only sound was Jem's hitching breaths. Then, in a broken voice, he said, "He hurt me. And he kept hurting me. And sometimes it felt good, and that was the worst part because he'd hurt me so many times and I didn't understand how it could feel good. Then he'd hurt me more. And nobody would help me. I was alone. I was a kid, and nobody would help me, and I was all alone."

"You're not alone now."

For a terrible moment, nothing. Then Jem let out a sob. Still pulled crooked by the pain in his side, he let the sock drop and turned away from Tanner.

Tanner's eyes shot open. He sat up, and in his good hand, he held the gun that had fallen into the corner of the room. "Big fucking mistake, faggot."

Jem froze.

"Fuck," Tanner said, the word distorted by his broken jaw. His hand hovered over the wound in his belly. "Fuck me if that little cunt didn't fuck me up."

Tean moved very slowly, finding the hem of Haggerty's shirt, sliding his fingers underneath it.

"I guess I've gotta—" Tanner's voice was muzzy. "Oh fuck. Can't leave you two hanging around."

At the small of Haggerty's back, where the flesh was already cooling, Tean closed his hand around Jager's throwdown piece. He worked it free slowly. Tanner's gaze was fixed on Jem's back.

"Wish I had time to enjoy—" Tanner started to say.

"Put it down," Tean said. The grip, with its American-flag design, was smooth to the touch. His hand trembled.

"Tean," Jem said.

"I said put it down."

"Oh man," Tanner said in the fuzzy voice. "You just don't have the look. Sorry. Jeremy here might have the balls for it, but I know a loser when I—"

Tanner's hand came up, the gun moving toward Jem with a speed and certainty that belied his earlier performance.

Tean fired.

40

The bullet tore out part of Tanner's throat. Blood sprayed out in an arc. Tanner fell backward, blood still fountaining from the ruptured artery. His heels drummed against the boards. He arched his back. And then the bursts of blood stopped, and he was still.

Dropping the gun, Tean scooted away from the weapon. He couldn't take his eyes off Tanner. An ocean of blood rolled across the floor. Even with his damaged hearing, Tean thought he could make out the sound of drops falling between the boards to hit the ground below.

Jem's hand was warm and firm, turning Tean's face into his shoulder. "You don't need to look at it." His other hand clutched Tean's back. The intensity of his grip was confusing to Tean; Tean wasn't really sure what the big deal was.

"I killed him," Tean said. It was like talking into a tin-can phone.

"Oh my God," Jem whispered, shuddering as he pulled Tean against him even tighter.

"I killed him, Jem. He's dead."

"I know. Oh my God, I know. I never wanted you to do that. I never wanted you to have to do that. I'm sorry. I'm so sorry. But I need you to hold it together for just a little bit longer."

"Yes, of course." The words were easy down the tin-can line. "I'm fine." Then, because it seemed the thing to say: "I killed him."

Jem made a noise that sounded like a sob. His voice was strangled as he said, "I know, Tean. I know." Pushing back Tean's hair, he kissed him on the temple and said, "Can you help me get outside? Through the back door and down into the trees? The only thing I can think of is to take the raft. Kristine won't let us hole up in here forever; she's got to wrap this up and get gone."

"The raft."

Letting out a shaky breath, Jem kissed Tean on the temple again. "We're going to stand up, and you're going to look into my eyes. Ok?"

"Ok."

They got up, Jem grunting with pain, and then he allowed Tean to pull away from his shoulder. His fingers, tacky with dried blood, found Tean's chin and turned his head up. "Right here. Look right here. You don't need to see any more of that."

It was like dancing, Tean thought. Moving like this, their bodies in sync, it could have been a waltz. Except for the splash of their footsteps.

"No," Jem said, redirecting his face. "Up here."

The stairs were harder. Jem backed down them, grimacing as he lowered himself. His hand stayed steady, though, on Tean's face. The coppery smell of blood on his fingers made Tean think of pennies in the fountains at Caesar's Palace. The sun had been very bright. A desert sun. Refracted by the water, it had smeared long, red-gold flashes of light against the painted-blue cement.

"Yes," Jem was saying, "the fountains were very nice. We'll go back sometime and see more fountains. Keep talking about that."

Tean hadn't known he'd been talking.

"I need you to stay here. Are you going to be all right?"

When Tean nodded, Jem hauled himself back up to the cabin, swearing explosively as he handled the steps again. Footsteps made the boards groan. Under it all was the steadily slowing drip-drip-drip. A light breeze stirred the tangle of salt cedar that hung inches from Tean's face, and he breathed in the smell of its dusty leaves and gray-green bark. The bullet had torn a hole the size of a quarter in Tanner's throat before passing through the open doorway, and that meant flecks of shredded flesh and microdroplets of blood now stippled the salt cedars.

Tean startled at the proximity of Jem's voice: "I need you back here with me."

A hand closed over his. "Yes," Tean said. "Ok."

"It's not ok. I know it's not. But you can do this for a little bit longer, right?"

"Of course."

Jem squeezed once, hard, and then said, "I'm going to distract Kristine. As soon as I come running back this way, I need you to run with me. We're going to get to the raft, and then we're going to push off and float downriver and hope she doesn't spot us."

"You can't run. With your ribs, you can barely walk."

"Then we'll hobble to the raft." Tean opened his mouth to argue, but Jem spoke over him. "You'll help me, right?"

Tean nodded.

"Then we'll be fine."

One hand pressed to his side, Jem limped toward the far side of the cabin. He became a shadow, drifting like smoke through a valley lit up by a haze of starlight. A measure of clarity was coming back to Tean, and he walled away what had happened in the cabin. He'd deal with it another time. Jem could barely walk, let alone run, and to make it to the raft, they'd need all the speed they could get.

Tean pushed himself away from the cabin wall, the logs rough under his hand, and sprinted after Jem. He kept his eyes straight ahead, even though the cabin was dark, so he wouldn't have to see.

"What are you—"

"Whatever you're going to do, I'll do it. Jem, you can't. You can barely walk. If we're going to make it to the raft before she realizes it's a distraction, you need to be as close as possible."

Frustration twisted Jem's face. Fireworks bloomed in the distance.

"Tell me how to do it."

"She has to know something went wrong," Jem said. "Otherwise Nathaniel would have contacted her. The whole plan was probably for her to pin down Tanner, and then Nathaniel would come up behind him, disable him, and then they could spend a few days in this cabin torturing him. We screwed that up for them. Now she's up there, wondering if Tanner pulled one over on Nathaniel, if we're still in the picture—wondering who's still on their feet, in other words."

"And?"

Jem gestured with Haggerty's penlight, still dark, which Tean now realized he had gone back into the cabin to retrieve. Ahead of them, a break in the salt cedar created a narrow, open passage along the side of the cabin. "I go out there, click the flashlight a few times, and hope she takes a shot."

Staring at him, Tean felt his jaw unhinge. The movement of air carried the desert perfume of water on stone, mud, and humidity from the Dolores. He finally managed to say, "You're kidding."

"Well, I'm going to throw the flashlight eventually."

"Jem!"

"Do you have a better idea for how to deal with a lunatic sniper who has some sort of night-vision gear and is excited to blow our heads off?"

"Pretty much any idea is better than that."

"Oh, I'm sorry. She's up there, and she's waiting for the first person who isn't Nathaniel to show himself. What we need is a decoy, but unfortunately, I don't normally carry those in my pockets."

After another glance around them, Tean let out a slow breath. He grabbed a salt cedar's branch, pulled it down, and released it. It snapped back into place, and then it continued to bob up and down for a few seconds.

"God, I love you," Jem said.

Taking Jem's arm, Tean began unwinding the bracelet of paracord that he wore there. "It has less impact when you also say it every time I buy you McDonald's. Go get as close to the raft as you can. We're going to have to be fast."

"It's important that you know how I feel."

"Jem."

"And Big Macs are a part of that."

"Jem!"

With a tiny smile, Jem squeezed Tean's arm and limped back the way they'd come, moving deeper into the thick growth along the river. Tean waited until the sound of movement through the cedar branches stopped. Then, drawing a breath, he inched out from behind the cabin's cover and began to move down the side. The salt cedars were thinner here, leaving Tean exposed, but he needed the light to be visible from the western rim of the canyon. That meant getting past the cabin's bulk. Even though the rational part of his brain knew that the chance of Kristine spotting him, let alone successfully shooting him, was very small, the rest of him kept replaying the scene in the cabin: Tanner's arm coming up, the certain knowledge that he was about to shoot Jem in the back, the moment of dilemma—of wanting two incompatible things, for Jem to be safe and for Tean not to have to hurt, not to have to kill. And then the dilemma passed because there was only one real choice. The throwdown revolver had bucked in Tean's hands, and a bullet had torn away Tanner's throat and his life.

Tean's hands were shaking as he lashed the penlight to a long, slender branch. Depressing the branch, he counted silently to three and then turned on the flashlight. He released the branch and ran back along the side of the cabin. A shot came almost immediately, and splinters of bark and pulp exploded from the trunk of a salt cedar ahead of him, stinging the side of Tean's face. Another shot rang out. Branches whipped against each other in the force of its passage.

The third shot came as Tean rounded the back of the cabin. His breath burned in his chest. His heart pounded inside his head. He had to fight his way through the next thicket, branches slapping him in the face, leaves in his mouth, then the tang of blood. It seemed to go on forever, and then he was clear, stumbling into the powdery starlight that coated everything in the canyon without really letting him see. The sound of the Dolores guided him, and after a few more yards, gravel crunched underfoot. Either Kristine was still shooting, or the fireworks were reaching a crescendo; maybe both. Jem had already gotten the raft into the water, and he hunched there, the river already up to his ankles.

"Get in," Tean called, trying to keep his voice as quiet as possible.

Grimacing, Jem swung one leg into the raft, still holding it in place.

"Just get in!"

With a bewildered look, Jem climbed onto the raft. Even over the water's rushing noise, Tean could hear Jem swearing in pain. The raft wobbled, turned, and began to float. Tean splashed into the Dolores, the water at his ankles, then at his shins, the force of his movement throwing droplets up to sprinkle his chest and face and glasses. The water made his jump awkward, but he landed halfway in the raft. The rubber side threatened to fold under him.

Then a hand caught the waist of his tech pants and hauled him in. Jem was still swearing as he dragged Tean down next to him, where they lay in the silty, chilly water at the bottom of the raft, keeping flat in hopes that either Kristine wouldn't see them or, at worst, wouldn't be able to hit them.

Jem's swearing reached a muttering crescendo when he finally managed to ask, "And just what the fuck was that?"

"We needed to move, and I figured I was close enough to catch up."

"You figured?"

"Plus it looked like something those dumb, butch het guys always do in the movies you like."

The sound of the water against stone made counterpoint with the sound of water against the raft.

"Oh my God," Jem whispered. "What have I created?"

They shifted around until Tean was snuggled up against Jem, who was pleasantly warm in contrast to the water puddled on the bottom of the raft. Jem held him close, although he winced whenever Tean moved abruptly.

After a while, the rush of adrenaline faded, and Tean started to shake. Jem grunted as he reached across to stroke Tean's hair. The feel of the gun bucking in his hands was very real. That instant of seeing the raw, torn edges of Tanner's throat. The blood, and the sound of their footsteps splashing, and the way it dripped between the boards. He remembered being very young, the smell of his grandfather's cognac-dipped cigarillos, the bright, stiff November morning they had gone out to hunt.

Jem didn't try to quiet him. He held him, and he ran his fingers through Tean's hair as the sobs grew more and more intense, shaking Tean until water sloshed over the raft's side. Eventually, the crying stopped, and Tean wiped his hot, puffy eyes against Jem's chest.

Overhead, the stars were a river too, channeled by the high stone walls of the canyon. Maybe heaven was a place, Tean thought. A planet. A star. Enough rocket fuel and enough time, and anybody could get there. Maybe it was like the ocean, and all rivers flowed to it, carrying souls along. Maybe it was the end of a flat world, and when you reached it, you dropped off into nothing and nowhere.

"Do you want to talk about it?" Jem asked quietly.

Tean shook his head, his eyes stinging again. "No."

Jem tightened his hold around Tean, and they floated. A nighthawk floated too, above them, drifting on the river of stars. Jerusalem crickets made soft, hissing noises when the raft disturbed them: the sound of pages rustling in a great book. Where seeps opened in the high walls, garlands of columbine and borage and maidenhair ferns hung down, living tapestries with their colors muted by night. Once, where a thin strip of muddy bank allowed sedge and a sad cattail to grow, a firefly winked at them.

Then the sound of the water changed, and ahead, a ravine cut up and away toward the canyon's rim. A man stood there, shoulders slumped, but he held up one hand when he saw them. Farther back, huddled figures cut silhouettes out of the flashing lights of emergency vehicles.

"Fuck me," Jem groaned.

When they drew even with the rocky shore at the bottom of the ravine, Tean climbed out of the raft, and Ammon helped him pull it to shore.

41

First, the paramedics had to look at them. Then Jem and Tean had to ride in the ambulance to the hospital, with Officer Tebbs accompanying them. The woman Tean remembered from his first visit to the Moab police station, the woman who had looked after Scipio for a few hours, was gone. Exhaustion made her look ill, hollowing out her face, leaching the color from her skin until she looked jaundiced. She didn't speak until they got to the hospital, and then all she said was, "Detective Young led us straight to her. To Kristine Colin-Bowman." Then, after swallowing, she added, "Suicide by cop."

Jem and Tean were separated, and they had to deal with nurses and doctors and paperwork. The worst of the injuries seemed to be the laceration on the side of Jem's head, which Jager had given him and Haggerty had reopened, and his broken ribs. The doctor who examined him touched the still-healing cut on Jem's throat, the one that Jager's knife had opened.

"Who did these sutures?"

"A friend."

"Looks like your friend actually knew what he was doing; you're lucky."

"Lucky doesn't come close to describing it," Jem said.

The whole time Jem was being suitably stitched and bandaged and wrapped, his arm fitted in a sling, he was riding a nice little cloud of Vicodin. Then the questions started. Officer Tebbs did most of the talking, but a sheriff's deputy Jem hadn't met before was there too, and she asked a few questions as well. With Chief Nobles and Sheriff McEneany gone, both departments were struggling to deal with the slaughter that had unfolded in the canyon outside Moab. Jem ran them through the whole thing: Kristine and Nathaniel's plan and the fabricated story about the shipment of drugs, Blake's betrayal, Andi's murder, Weckesser's callout and the subsequent killing and coverup that McEneany had assisted with. Jem explained the conspiracy among the three law-enforcement officers that had fractured after McEneany killed Antonio and shot Jager, and how it had dissolved completely when Haggerty took matters into his own hands to clean house. He told them about Jager's confession in the Vegas hospital, and then about Haggerty's attack after they had decoded the pickup location.

Tebbs looked punch-drunk through the series of revelations. The deputy, with her frizzy hair and her attempt at a hard face, said, "I don't get it. There were never any drugs?"

Jem sighed and walked them through it again.

The only hard part was the question at the end.

"And who killed Tanner Kimball?"

"Nathaniel whatever his name. Dayton. They killed each other."

Tebbs and the deputy exchanged looks.

"You need to work on your tells," Jem said. "You're never going to win any money in poker like that."

"Don't gamble," Tebbs said.

"Only bingo nights," the deputy said. "Now quit bullshitting us and tell us who killed Tanner. We know it wasn't Dayton; there's no way that adds up with what you two left behind in that cabin."

"Nathaniel did," Jem said.

Another long look was exchanged.

"That's interesting," the deputy said. She ought to be wearing a name tag, Jem thought. "Because your buddy tells us he killed Mr. Kimball."

"He's not my buddy. He's my boyfriend."

"Actually, he told us," she checked a notepad, "'If Jem says I'm his boyfriend, remind him that I only said that to make a point in the heat of the moment, and probably a better term would be romantic interest, but the kind where you've only been on one Prowler date, and you still have to pretend to find everything the other one says really interesting, and you do that weird thing where you both try to kiss each other on the cheek at the end of the night, and immediately after that you think maybe it would be better if you died alone and your dog ate your face before anyone found you.' Is that about right?"

"He's like a Valentine's card," Jem said. "He can't turn it off."

"Who killed Tanner Kimball?"

"Nathaniel did."

They went at it like that for a while. It was past two in the morning when they finally let him go. Jem asked for directions to wherever they had stashed Tean, and he found himself wandering past examination cubicles, where thin plastic curtains stirred in his wake. Ahead, he heard familiar voices, and he slowed. A row of molded-plastic chairs lined the opposite wall; on one of them, a paper pharmacy bag sat next to a Ziploc holding a familiar-looking watch and wallet. Ammon's shit. When Jem dug through the pharmacy bag, he found two brown vials with Ammon's name on them. It took him a minute to decode the labels; he was tired, and he hadn't been practicing. He didn't recognize one of them—eszopiclone—but he recognized his old buddy codeine with acetaminophen.

Ammon's voice rose sharply on the other side of the curtain. "I'm not trying to talk about us. I'm saying I want to take care of you. Please let me take care of you right now. Why won't you listen to me? Can you even hear what I'm saying?"

"I am listening," Tean said. "Everything you say is about us. That's the only thing we can talk about anymore, and I don't want to talk right now."

"Everything I say is about us? Bullcrap. We're talking about you right now."

Tean sighed.

"You're scaring me, and I'm worried about you. I want to help you—"

"You can't!"

Jem opened the first vial and shook out a handful of pills. He stashed them in his pocket.

"You can't, Ammon," Tean said more softly. "Go away, please."

Jem replaced the first vial and drew out the second. He helped himself to a generous pour of his old buddies.

"Please go away. Please. I can't do this right now. I can't do any of this right now."

Jem replaced the second vial.

He was pocketing the pills when the curtain was flung back and Ammon stormed into the hall. His gaze settled on Jem. His eyes were red, his cheeks flushed, his chest rising and falling rapidly. He drew the back of a hand across his face and cleared his throat. Then he took two steps and grabbed Jem's good arm.

"Let go of me."

"We're going to have a talk," Ammon said. "Give me one second of trouble about it, and I'll beat you to death with my bare hands. Understand?"

Before Jem could answer, he was being dragged down the hall, his ribs screaming as he stumbled to keep up.

They stopped at the next intersection, where Ammon released him with a shove that sent Jem back into the opposite wall. The thrum of the fluorescents filled Jem's ears. Down the hall, an older man wheeled a squeaky mop bucket along the linoleum. He wore ancient headphones, the foam pads covering his ears, and his gaze was fixed on the arc of his mop. So much for a witness.

"We're doing this right now?" Jem said, one hand sliding into the pocket where he kept the length of paracord with the hex nut. "Right here? All right. Tell me about how he belongs to you. Tell me about that trip to Vegas you want me to take, how you're going to make sure I never show up in his life again. How'd that go for you last time?"

Ammon's fingers curled into fists, and he held his arms stiff at his sides. "Do you know what that did to him? What it's still doing to him?"

"Of course I—"

"Shut your goddamn mouth!"

The shout echoed up and down the hall. The old man paused, slid the foam pad off one ear, and glanced around. The tinny sound of rock played through the headphones. The Ramones, Jem thought. I'm going to kill a man or possibly be killed myself, and I've got The Ramones as my fucking killtrack.

"This is on you," Ammon said, stabbing a finger at Jem. "You dragged him into this. You ruined his life. And now you let him get hurt, and he's not going to get better from it. Not by himself. He can't. Do you hear what I'm saying?"

Jem gave a jerky nod.

"If I ever run into you, just the two of us, I'm going to do something I'll regret. Do you hear what I'm saying?"

Another jerk of his head.

Ammon loosed a shuddering breath, the tension melting out of him, and he looked tired and empty. "Go clean up your fucking mess."

42

Days turned into weeks. Weeks turned into months. After a period of unrelenting clarity, juggling the broken-glass memories as they cut deeper and deeper, Tean felt something give way inside him. His daily life became a blur of half-sleeping and half-waking, liminal spaces that he could barely distinguish. He went to work. He came home. He walked Scipio. He talked to his parents and his siblings—short, fractured calls that left Tean relieved for the silence that came after them. Ammon had vanished from the apartment building. Once, Tean made the mistake of checking Facebook and saw a picture of Ammon with Lucy and the kids; the caption described their family trip to Lake Powell.

When various law enforcement branches came back again and again, wanting to hear the details from those days in Moab, he talked through it all again. He shared his bed with Jem, and more than once, in the labyrinth of those threshold places, when he bolted upright because he could feel the gun in his hands and see the hole in Tanner's throat, he realized Jem was awake too. He knew Jem needed something, and he knew he couldn't give it to him. He was aware, at the edge of consciousness, of Jem trying very, very hard to fix him.

One November day, it was a food-mat puzzle for Scipio. Tean had come home from another of those featureless days at the DWR office, unable to remember a single specific event, and heard laughter inside the apartment.

"No, no, no," Jem said. "You're cheating. You have to wait until I say go."

Tean pushed through the door. The puzzle was enormous, three feet by five feet, with toys attached to it at a couple dozen locations. Tean had seen this kind of toy before, and the premise was simple:

food was hidden in various toys and pockets, and the dog was supposed to spend time searching out the treats. It was supposed to be both a way to keep the dog busy and a form of mental exercise.

Jem was kneeling on the mat, hiding treats and using his shoulder to edge out Scipio. Scipio, undeterred, was trying to get around him to the treats.

"Uh uh," Jem said. "Sit."

Scipio sat. Then he licked a long stripe behind Jem's ear.

"God, now I have to shower. Stay. Good boy."

As soon as Jem turned to stow more of the treats in their hiding spots, Scipio lay down and began nosing through the hidden pockets, eating the treats Jem had already hidden one by one.

"No," Jem said, "I told you—" When he caught sight of Tean, his smile faltered and then came back twice as bright. "Hi. How was work?"

"It was good."

"Your son is a cheater."

Scipio currently had his nose halfway inside a pocket designed to look like a squirrel. He met Tean's eyes with a surprisingly guilty expression.

Tean smiled. "He's just doing what he's best at."

It was like watching a cloud move across Jem's face—the disappointment that whatever he had hoped for, Tean wasn't giving him. The smile stayed where it was, but it dimmed.

"Show me how this works," Tean said, bending down to unlace his Keens. "Maybe between the two of us, we can manage to keep him away long enough to set it all up."

"You're tired. We'll do it another time."

A few months before, Tean would have insisted. Now he just nodded.

"We could go on a walk," Jem said.

"Twenty minutes? I'm just going to lie down."

"Ok," Jem said. He didn't even stir when Scipio ran a tongue over his hand. "Sure."

Once, it was clothes. Tean came home to voices through the apartment door again.

"For Christ's sake, your father does not have the coloring for that. Are you out of your damn mind?"

When Tean pushed into the apartment, Jem and Scipio were standing in the middle of the living room, surrounded by clothes: t-shirts, button-ups, sweaters, cardigans, crew-neck sweatshirts and zip-up hoodies. Jeans. Tech pants. Sweatpants. Scipio was sitting on an orange tee.

"It looks like a Kohl's truck got hijacked," Tean said. "Or a Ross exploded."

"We're picking out clothes for you," Jem said with another of those huge smiles. "How was work?"

"It was good," Tean said as he unlaced the Keens.

"Your son inherited your sense of style."

Fondling Scipio's ears as the Lab pressed into him, Tean smiled and studied the spread of clothes. "Lots of green and blue."

"You look good in green and blue."

"More green," Tean said with a smile.

"That's right. Come on, you can try on some of this stuff. Don't listen to Scipio; he's a bitch when it comes to the runway, but I promise I'll be honest."

So Tean tried on a flannel shirt in blue plaid. Jem's fingers were shaking as he did up the buttons, and Tean had to take over and finish the job himself.

"There," Jem said, tugging on the shirttail. "You look so handsome. What do you think?"

"I like it."

And that's how it was with the sweater, with the corduroys, with the long-sleeved tee.

"That's enough for right now," Jem said. He had red spots in his cheeks, and he tried twice to refold the tee before he gave up and dropped it on a pile of more shirts.

"I'm ok. We can keep going."

"No, no. That's enough. I know this isn't your thing."

Tean nodded.

"Excuse me," Jem said, and he hurried into the bathroom with stilted movements.

The water ran for a long time. Tean made sure Scipio had dinner, and then he lay down on the bed. It was like an airport, your flight delayed, he thought as his thoughts got looser, hazier. Everybody around you going somewhere fast, fast, fast, and all you could do was sit there and watch.

Only one time did Jem try sex; since coming back from Moab, they'd used the bed for sleeping and nothing else. He undressed Tean slowly, trailing kisses everywhere he could reach. His hands were like worn-out flint, raising tiny flashes of heat where they used to start fires. Or maybe Tean was the one who was worn-out. The kissing and the touching went on for a long time, through it all Jem murmuring, "I love you. God, you have no idea how much I love you."

"I love you too," Tean whispered, mussing Jem's perfect hair with clumsy caresses.

The kissing and the touching went on too long. Jem settled back on his haunches, his well-developed chest and shoulders and arms on display, his dick hard and wet. "I want you to fuck me."

"Jem—"

"Please. I've never—I mean, not since, you know. But I love you, and I trust you, and I want not to feel so fucked up about it."

Propping himself on his elbows, Tean said, "Thank you. I know what that means for you. But—"

"Tean, I'm ready. I want this."

Tean shook his head. "No, that's not what I was going to say. I'm not—I don't think I'm going to get hard."

Jem bit his lip. The only light came from the moon, filtering through the window, and it made the tears shine in his eyes.

"I still want to . . . be with you tonight," Tean said quietly. He touched Jem, and a noise caught in Jem's throat. "Please?"

Jem nodded, and the movement made the tears spill over and leave platinum tracks down his cheeks. They went slowly, even at the end, Jem's arms curled protectively around Tean as he finished. Then he put his face on Tean's bare shoulder. He felt to Tean like he had a fever; the salt made his skin sticky.

"Please tell me what I can do," Jem mumbled. "Please tell me how to make it better."

"You don't need to do anything," Tean whispered, stroking the short blond hair at Jem's nape, his fingers running lower into the beads of sweat along Jem's upper back. "Everything's fine."

It was the Saturday before Thanksgiving when Jem came into the apartment apple-cheeked, wearing his winter coat: heavy, undyed wool with broad colored bands across the chest in red, yellow, blue, and green. He had on one of Tean's old scarves, which he had declared *retro as fuck* when he'd found it in the closet. Tean and Scipio were on the couch—Tean reading, Scipio snoozing. Scipio jumped down, shook himself, and padded over to greet Jem. Jem kissed his muzzle, crossed the room, and kissed Tean's muzzle too. Then he took the book.

"*A History of Circus Fires*?"

"Don't worry," Tean said. "None of the animals got hurt."

With a small smile, Jem closed it and put it aside.

"I was reading that," Tean said.

"Your sweatshirt is ok, but you need either jeans or tech pants with long underwear. Heavy socks, your Keens, and your winter coat. Like we're going on a hike."

"What's happening?"

Jem grinned, exposing the crooked front teeth. "We're going on a hike."

"I'm not sure I'm up to—"

"We're going on a hike, Tean."

"No, I didn't sleep much last night, so I'm going to lie down and—"

"Teancum Leon, either you get ready yourself, or I get you dressed, and the whole time I'll be singing the full musical score from *Man of La Mancha*."

Tean's eyes narrowed.

"To dream—"

"You're a monster."

"I'm just getting warmed up. I memorized that whole one about Dulcinea."

Twenty minutes later, they were in Tean's new truck, Jem behind the wheel. Scipio was in the back seat, snuffling at Jem's hair and occasionally licking it. Tean was worried that Jem didn't even seem to notice. He was even more worried when he saw the cooler, tent, sleeping bags, and various other pieces of gear strapped down in the bed of the truck.

"Did you raid my storage unit?"

"Yes."

"Why?"

"Because I'm kidnapping you."

Tean sighed and let his head fall against the window.

"We're not going back until this is better. It doesn't have to be a hundred percent better. It doesn't even have to be one percent better. But I can't do this, watch you die by inches. I'm not going to do it."

"So, your plan is to kidnap me, hold me captive, and wait for me to somehow get better, even though there's nothing wrong with me—"

"That, right there. That's the first thing that's going to stop."

They were heading south, cutting through the Wasatch Mountains. The scrub oak on the slopes was an autumn blaze, rippling in the wind, the whole world come alive in one last gasp before winter.

"And we're going to camp?"

"That's right."

"You're going to camp?"

"I resent that tone. Well, only a little."

"So I guess it's safe to assume you packed the insulated sleeping mats because it's so cold, and you got the mess kits, and the cookware, and you remembered vegetable oil for the cast iron, and you got extra fuel for the stove."

"First of all, rude. Very rude. Your whole demeanor."

"So you didn't grab our pillows, the lantern, new mantles for the lantern, a multitool, my hatchet, biodegradable soap—"

"For your information," Jem said, his chin coming up, "I got all of it. Including the manterns."

"Mantles. And lanterns. Two separate things."

"That's not even what I was trying to say. I said manterns."

"Right. You meant to say manterns."

"It's a lantern shaped like a man."

"Uh huh."

"It's a sex thing. And before you get on your high horse again . . ." Jem drew a big breath. "I asked Maddie."

It took Tean a moment. "Maddie Beck? My conservation officer?"

"Well, she's not your property, but—ow! Don't pinch me!"

Scipio barked a warning that was clearly directed at both of them.

Massaging his arm, Jem shot a glare at Tean and said, "She made a list."

"You just happened to keep in touch with her?"

"No, dumdum. I went to your office to spy on you because I've been so scared, and I bumped into her."

"Hold on. You've been spying on me?"

"Yes, obviously, because I love you." Jem made a frustrated noise. "What are you not understanding about this?"

Tean honestly didn't know what to say to any of that, so he settled for taking his boyfriend's hand and lacing their fingers together.

The drive was easy. They stopped a few times for Scipio to stretch his legs. They left behind the mountains and the steppes and moved into the high desert: the rolling ground of bitterbrush and quinine, dockweed and ephedra, rabbitbrush with its tiny brown leaves. As they went south, prickly pear and barrel cactus began to appear, and yucca, and datura—the witch's weed, the angel's trumpet, its flower persisting until first frost, tiny white bells that opened the door to another world.

A part of Tean had known where they were going when Jem headed south out of Salt Lake. Now, as they turned onto a dirt BLM road and headed northeast into a canyon, he felt a fist close around his chest. Part of him knew he was holding Jem's hand too tightly; he could see where the skin of Jem's fingers whitened from the pressure. But Jem just looked over at him, expression steady, and Tean nodded and let out a breath.

When they reached the end of the road, Tean got Scipio out of the back, fitted him with the harness, and took Jem's hand again. They made their way down the switchbacks. Beneath them, the lower canyon was vibrant in a way it hadn't been in the summer: the orange and red of the scrub oak; the white, rose-shaped autumn blossoms of Apache plumes, their lavender styles barely visible at a distance; the final blush of pink feathers that clung to the tamarisks—the last of the fall bloom. A dead place could come alive. Even at the end of the year, even with winter creeping closer, a dead place could come alive again.

When his gaze rested on the cabin, Tean took deep breaths to steady himself. Instead of gunpowder, he smelled sage and salt cedar and pinyon pine, the dust on the pepperwort. Instead of the clap of a shot, he heard the river's song, the song it sang to itself. Instead of that terrible pounding of hate and fear, he felt something else. The echoes of that hate and fear, yes. But something else too. Something Tean couldn't name yet.

They followed the switches to the canyon's floor. Jem waited for Tean to take the lead, and after a full minute, Tean started walking. He kept his grip on Jem's hand. The cabin loomed in his vision.

For Augustine, eternity was singular, not chronological: a single, perfect moment. For Bill Murray, hell was the same frozen day, again and again. Tean remembered the gun bucking in his hand, Tanner with the hole torn in his throat, still sitting up, his face confused like he didn't understand.

The desert on the cusp of winter made something move inside Tean, something that came unmoored by the hard land around him. His mind searched for a reason, for an answer. How could a place be more than a place, inside you as well as outside? How could geography become a map for the soul, and the soul an index for the world? He knew some of it. He'd read. For the ancients, deserts had been the edge of the world, the limit of civilization. The end. To walk into the desert was to step outside the realm of men and enter the domain of owls and dragons, demons and angels. To walk into the desert was to find a god in a burning bush, to be tempted by a devil. In the desert, apocalypse. An end. An unveiling.

Beyond the rimrock, hoodoos and goblins and spires looked down into the canyon. Beyond them, the sky was purple, Tyrian and limitless. The last of the sun followed the striped sandstone; bands of peach and pink darkened to hematite red. Tean understood, as they walked deeper into the shadows, the desert's claim on prophets and madmen: the alienness of stone, the vast, open spaces, life driven back to the cracks of existence but persisting, the bones of the world laid bare, tissue peeled back in a dissection of eternity.

At the cabin, Tean let go of Jem's hand. He took the steps up to the porch, tested the handle, and found that it turned. He pushed it open. It was much as he remembered it: the old, ash-choked stove; the bunks with their bare slats; the ceramic basin. Different, too. The boards were darker now in places, and one of the bunks was gone—the one that Tanner had shot, damaging the frame. A ranger, or possibly a volunteer, had whitewashed the cabin's interior walls, hiding the stains that must have marred the logs. He knew he was imagining it, but he thought he could smell the lime in the wash, mineral, not unpleasant. His steps clicked crisply against the boards as he crossed the cabin, and he opened the door and went out the back. He took the steps down and turned; Scipio scrambled past him.

Jem stood in the doorway. The last of the light picked out the gold and silver in his beard, and the hair, dirty blond, was in its usual part and fade. The collagen ripple of the scar on the side of his head was one more reminder. Tean waited for the declarations: if you hadn't acted, on and on like that. Maybe the insistence: I'd be dead, do you understand that, dead, and he was a monster, and he deserved to die. If Jem said any of that, what would happen? Tean would wade into the river and let the Dolores drown him against the rocks. Or maybe he'd just climb up to the truck and ask to go home.

But all Jem said was, "Beep beep boop?"

Tean's eyes stung with the rush of it all: Jem's pillow hair, Jem's crooked front teeth, the way Jem had spent hours untangling Christmas lights and insisting he could find the bad bulb, the way his beard tickled when they kissed, the shape of his shoulders when he curled up on the couch to watch TV with Scipio. What is the universe, he wanted to ask, except a desert? And what is a desert except a place where life holds on?

He played it out once more in his head: Jem broken, trying so hard to be good, and turning away from Tanner. Tanner lifting the gun.

Tean's hand came up, floating the way the gun had floated, and he helped Jem down the steps. "Beep," he said softly as Jem came to him. "And a little boop."

They pushed through the brake of salt cedar. Dusty pink plumes tickled Tean's neck, and he smelled the river, and then they were free, moving out into the canyon again. Something had relaxed inside him, a muscle contracted like a held breath. No, no, that wasn't right. It was like stepping through a door, from one room to another. The same house of grief, but a different room. A little bigger, a little brighter, the sense of relief like he could stand a little straighter, ease cramped muscles. And there would be a room after that, and a room after that.

They climbed the switches, letting Scipio stop to mark the turns and sniff a clump of mule's ears. The Lab sneezed, his whole body shaking with the force of it, and for some reason that made Jem laugh. Jem clapped a hand over his mouth, shooting a worried look at Tean, but Tean just smiled and squeezed his hand.

When they got to the top, Tean scouted the rim until he found a safe spot, and then they sat with their legs hanging out over empty air. Jem scooted closer, put his arm around Tean, and drew him against his shoulder.

"I don't know if I can be who I was," Tean said. "I'll try, but I just don't know."

Jem pushed back his hair. "I don't want you to be who you were. I just want you to get better. And I want to be with you." He ran his hand through Tean's hair again, and Tean wondered how it looked. Impossibly wild, he guessed, after the long day and the hike and Jem messing with it. Then Jem said, "Can I give you something?"

Tean nodded.

From a coat pocket, Jem withdrew an oblong black vinyl case. He opened it and withdrew a pair of glasses: simple black frames, slightly more fashionable than what Tean probably would have picked out for himself, although he couldn't say how exactly they were different. The way Jem held the new glasses was a question.

Tean nodded, and Jem eased the taped, broken frames from his face and replaced them with the new glasses. Tean was surprised at the difference. The glasses didn't just fit better; he could see much more clearly.

"I guess I didn't know how badly scratched the old lenses were."

"You like them?"

Tean tested the fit. "I love them."

Jem kissed him, and then they sat, the sun burning out behind them.

"Is it weird that I might miss my old ones, though?" Tean asked after a while.

"We'll keep them. They'll be your backups." Jem made a funny noise in his chest, and then he said, "I brought one other thing. I don't—I don't want to scare you, but I've thought about it a lot, and I figured if things went well today, if it felt right, maybe . . ."

Tean shifted around; he was surprised to see Jem's face blotchy with color, Jem blinking rapidly as he drew something else from his pocket. A packet of papers, Tean realized when Jem pressed it into his hands. Tean unfolded it slowly, trying to make sense of the pictures and numbers. It was a real estate listing. A house. A brick bungalow in Federal Heights that had been on the market for months.

"We can afford it." Jem cleared his throat. "Tinajas helped me run the numbers on it. And it has a yard for Scipio. It's not far from your work."

"It's lovely. But I'm still saving up for a down payment, and—"

"Actually, you don't need to. My mom, my birth mom, Brigitte, whatever I'm supposed to call her—she's been sending me checks. I don't want them, and I didn't ask for them, but then I thought, fuck, I might as well use them."

"A down payment for this house would be—"

"Tean, she's been sending a lot of checks."

Tean tried to choose his next words carefully. "I love you. A lot. So much, actually, that it scares me. And I want to say yes to this. But ending things with Ammon, Jem, it almost killed me. And I can't help thinking that it might happen with you. You'll get tired of how weird I am, or you'll realize how much better you can do, or you'll decide you need space, and if that happens, Jem, it really will kill me. And I don't know how I can say yes when I'm so afraid of how things are going to end."

A breeze ran through the canyon, stirring the dwarf junipers so that the branches creaked and the leaves rustled. Then the breeze died, and the canyon held its breath.

"You know how you told me that everything ends?" Jem said quietly. "How death is what gives life meaning, and how our anxiety over death, our fear of it, propels us to live life truly and authentically? How everything has to have an end, and how looking into the face of that reality is so terrifying that most people will choose something safer, something easier, rather than coexist with their fear?"

"You must have heard that on *Darkwing Duck*. Ow, ow, ow, jeez! You're ripping my hair out."

"Oops," Jem said, smoothing the locks he had just pulled. "Did that jog your memory?"

"Yes," Tean growled as he snuggled into Jem's shoulder again. "I remember something that might have sounded something like that."

The first nighthawk sped across the sky, and over the Dolores's murmur, a coyote howled. The breeze lifted again, carrying the fragrance of wild sage. On the far rim of the canyon, a tumbleweed spun into the thickening shadows. As Tean watched, the last of the daylight thinned, limning the redrock walls in gold.

Jem tilted Tean's head up. "Maybe you're right about all that. Maybe everything does end. Maybe that's the only way things have meaning."

Tean swallowed against the knot in his throat.

"But this isn't the end," Jem said, and then he kissed him. "It's the beginning."

INDIRECTION

Keep reading for a sneak preview of *Indirection,* book one of Borealis: Without a Compass.

Chapter 1

"STAKEOUTS DON'T REQUIRE CHEESE," SHAW SAID to his partner, boyfriend, and best friend since college, North McKinney. They were sitting in a Ford sedan on a quiet block of Kingshighway. On one side of them, Forest Park opened up, where puddles of safety lights illuminated February-bare branches. On the other side stood businesses, churches, Barnes-Jewish Hospital, condominium buildings, and the glowing façade of The Luxemburg. Still nothing.

"It's not cheese." North's voice was low and deep, with the heat of a fire about to catch. He rattled the can for emphasis.

"It's got cheese in the name."

"No, it's got cheez in the name." North traced the letters with one finger. "See? That's so they can't get sued for false advertising."

"That makes it even worse. You understand that, right? It's probably full of benzoates and carrageenan and that's not even getting started on what dairy does to your body."

"It's not—"

"Because of your dairy allergy."

North's jaw tightened before he spoke again. "That's what I'm trying to tell you: I'm ninety-nine percent sure there's no dairy in this. None. It has cheez, Shaw. Not cheese. So I'm totally safe."

"I really think—"

"No."

"I'm just going to—"

"No," North rumbled, and when Shaw reached for the can, North planted a hand against Shaw's head and shoved him against the driver's window.

"It's killing you," Shaw said, trying to knock North's arm away. "By 2038, I won't have a boyfriend anymore."

"It's going to take that long? God, I need to start buying this in bulk."

"North, I absolutely forbid you to—"

The can's hiss interrupted Shaw. One-handed, North sprayed a mound of the artificial cheez onto a cracker balanced on his knee. The mound got bigger. And bigger. North didn't stop until the pyramid of cheez started to topple, and then he scooped up the cracker and shoved it in his mouth. He grinned, displaying the cheez foam between his teeth, and crunched loudly. Then he coughed.

Shaw watched him for a minute as the coughing continued and tears ran down North's face. North was getting plenty of air. He was also white-knuckling the can of cheez spray as though he thought Shaw might take advantage of this moment of weakness.

"Don't worry," Shaw said, putting his fingers to his temples. "Master Hermes just recognized that I'm now a level-five psychic. I'll dissolve the cracker with my mind, and while I'm in there, I'll fix that acid reflux you've been—"

"Don't you fucking dare," North croaked, swatting Shaw's hands away from his temples. He managed to swallow, cleared his throat, and in a raspy but more normal voice continued, "First of all, that psychic stuff is bullshit Master Hermes sells you when he has to pay the vig to those Bosnian guys he borrowed from."

"Oh, he didn't borrow it. The spirit of George Gershwin showed him where—"

"And second of all, even though I know it's not real, don't you ever fucking dare use that juju to mess around inside me."

"A lesser man would point out that a couple of nights ago you were begging me to mess around inside you."

"And third of all, I don't have acid reflux. I got food poisoning from that fucking toxic nacho cheese—"

"Dairy allergy," Shaw murmured.

Whatever North had been about to say, he didn't finish because instead he screamed with what sounded like frustration. Softly.

Movement at The Luxemburg's front door drew Shaw's attention. In the flood of lights illuminating the building's exterior, Chris Hobson might as well have been standing on a stage. He was in his late twenties, close to North and Shaw's age, cute but on the verge of being rat-faced. He was an investment wunderkind at Aldrich Acquisitions, the company owned and run by Shaw's father, and he'd been responsible for helping Aldrich Acquisitions become a principal investor in several highly valued biotech startups. He was also, Shaw and North were pretty sure, a thief.

"He's moving," Shaw said, taking out his phone. He sent the same message to Pari, their assistant, and to her nonbinary datemate, Truck.

Kingshighway was a busy road during the day, but late on Saturday, the flow of cars was irregular. Twice that night an ambulance had pulled into Barnes-Jewish, sirens screaming, and once a Silverado had pulled to the curb ahead of Shaw and North, breaking the crust of old snow so that a troop of frat boys could pile out and piss on the sidewalk. Chouteau boys, undoubtedly—the same college, just up the road, where North and Shaw had met. Other than that, though, the night's entertainment had consisted of Shaw trying to tap into his past lives and North trying to see how many crackers he could sandwich together with spray cheez.

Now, though, Hobson had emerged, and it was time to work.

Hobson turned up the street, walking toward the portion of St. Louis known as the Central West End. It was a ritzy area, with Chouteau College, Washington University, and the hospital creating anchor points for people with way too much money. It had trendy bars and coffee shops, fancy restaurants, and even a handful of clubs. If Hobson stuck to his usual routine, he'd be going to the Jumping Pig, a hipsterish bar that offered pork infusions and bacon-themed everything. If Shaw had to guess, he'd say it would be closed in a couple of months, but for now, it was Hobson's go-to.

As though on cue, Hobson went east at the end of the block.

Shaw and North waited a tense ten minutes; the only sounds were their breathing and the cars whipping past, the whisper of slush churned by tires. Then a message came from Pari: an image of Hobson backing through a men's room door, his hands on Truck's waist.

HE'S TOUCHING MY DATEMATE!!!!!!

"You're never going to hear the end of that," North said, grabbing the door handle. "You know that, right?"

Shaw sighed, nodded, and got out of the car.

At the next break in traffic, they jogged across Kingshighway, cutting at an angle so they reached the sidewalk at the end of the block. Pari was coming towards them along the cross street. Her long, dark hair was bundled up under a ski cap, and she wore a quilted down coat that came to her knees. The bindi today was raspberry colored.

"He's touching my datemate!" was her first, screeching announcement.

"I think it's sweet," Shaw said. "Having a bisexual villain. I think that's really kind of nice. And progressive. Don't you think, North?"

Pari's head swiveled toward him.

"I mean—" Shaw tried again.

North groaned.

"You think it's sweet? You should have seen Truck's face. That…that new-money prick was groping Truck through hir jeans. Truck was so scared!"

"Truck offered to spank my monkey—those were hir words, by the way—this week, Pari. Twice. Ze's not exactly a sexual shrinking violet."

"We're getting into the weeds here," North said.

"I'm sorry," Pari said. "I'm sorry, did I hear you correctly? Are you slut-shaming my datemate? Ze's level of sexual activity is none of your business."

"Well, it's kind of my business when we're talking about my monkey."

"Let's not—" North tried.

"Truck is an unbelievably generous lover," Pari said, shaking the set of keys she'd lifted from Hobson.

"So is North!"

"That's really not—" North said.

"And Truck is extremely well endowed."

"So is—"

"Ok," North said, grabbing the keys from Pari's hands. He caught Shaw's arm and dragged him down the block toward The Luxemburg. Over his shoulder, he called back, "Let us know if we need to hurry."

"I've seen North when he wears those cutoff gray sweatpants," Pari screamed after them. "He might as well have been holding a measuring tape for me."

"Jesus Christ," North muttered.

"It's very difficult to have a conversation with her because she's so—"

North growled and shook Shaw by the arm. "Don't. Start. You two were fucking made for each other."

By then, they were getting close to The Luxemburg. North released Shaw's arm, and Shaw stumbled a few steps before catching himself. He set off toward the condo building, glanced back, and said, "I don't want you to feel bad, so I just think I should tell you that I think you look really good in those gray cutoffs. They make your whole, you know, business area look very impressive."

"I'm going to murder you," North stage-whispered. "Get the fuck in there so I can be done with this nightmare."

"Very bulge-y."

North packed a snowball faster than Shaw expected, and it caught him in the back of the head as he ran toward the condo building. He was still shaking snow out of his hair, the snowmelt trickling down his nape, when he stepped into the lobby.

It was about what he had expected from The Luxemburg's outside: tile and wainscotting, coffered ceilings, lots of white paint. A mural of the 1904 World's Fair covered one wall; in the bottom-right corner, a young lady looked like she was having an indecent relationship with a waffle cone, although Shaw would have to inspect further to be certain. On the other side of the lobby, a security desk marked the midpoint between the front doors and the elevators.

Two women stood behind the desk: one was white, in a security uniform, a hint of a pink-dyed curl slipping out from under the peaked cap. The other was black and wore scrubs. An ID clipped to the waistband identified her as Dr. Holloway. The women had been looking at something on a phone, and now they both turned their attention to Shaw.

"Hi," Shaw said, wiggling out of his sherpa cloak. "I'm—" He'd gotten his arm stuck, and it took him a moment to get it free. "I'm Max. I'm here to see my cousin. Oh, I like your nails!"

The women exchanged a look as Shaw approached the desk. "Sir," the woman in the security uniform said. Her nametag, now that Shaw was closer, read Weigel. "You said you're here to see your cousin? What's the name and unit number?"

"I told my boyfriend I wanted to get rainbow-painted cat claws for Pride," Shaw said wistfully, staring at Weigel's nails, "and he told me no. Oh, you've got a tattoo! Is it a rose?"

"It's a carnation," Weigel said, rotating her arm to display the underside of her wrist.

"For purity," Holloway said and started to laugh until Weigel slapped her leg.

"My boyfriend won't let me get any tattoos. Or piercings. I told him I wanted to get my nipples pierced, and he said he'd break up with me. He said he's the only one allowed to touch my body."

"Boy," Weigel said, drawing out the word. "What'd you tell him?"

"Oh, I know he just wants what's best for me. Davey's so sweet. He picks out what I'm supposed to wear—well, not my cloak. He told me I couldn't have this, but I bought it anyway. But he made me wear this stuff." He gestured at the long-sleeved tee and jeans. "And I have to hide the cloak at Mom's. But I can't tell her about Davey because when I said something about the diet Davey put me on, she just about lost her mind."

Holloway narrowed her eyes at him; she was picking at her weave with one hand. "You ain't nothing but skin and bones. Why're you on a diet?"

"Davey likes it when he can count my ribs. He says that's when I look best for him. Oh, Coca-Cola. That's my favorite! I don't know when the last time was that Davey let me have one."

"Like a giant, white baby," Holloway murmured to herself.

Weigel held out an unopened can of Coke, but instead of taking it, Shaw moved around the desk. "Hey, you've got all sorts of cool stuff back here. Do you really watch all those screens?"

"You know you shouldn't be back here," Weigel said.

"Leave him alone," Holloway said. She reached out and caught some of Shaw's hair. "Now don't tell me Davey makes you wear your hair like this?"

"Oh." Shaw let his expression fall. "I was, um, really bad. One time. And Davey cut my hair. It was for my own good. You know, he had to teach me a lesson."

"Child," Weigel said. "Why don't you call Davey and tell him to come down here?"

"Do you want to see what my hair used to look like? It was really long. Oh, that's a picture of a mole on Davey's back that I think might be cancerous. And that's a carousel horse, but the carousel's gone, so I guess maybe it's just a regular horse now. But out of wood. And that's—"

"Just a giant baby," Holloway said to herself again, both women turning away from the lobby to face Shaw, leaning closer to look at the pictures on his phone. He glanced up just once, over their heads, as North sprinted silently across the tile. Then he went back to the patter, dragging it out until North rode the elevator up and Shaw guessed that several minutes had passed.

"Anyway," Shaw said, "I guess I'd better go see Chris. Chris Hobson. He's my cousin; he lives in 8A."

"Sweety pie," Holloway said, "you got to get this Davey out of your life. He's got some bad energy."

"I say call him," Weigel said. "Get him down here and let the two of us talk to him for a few minutes. That boy won't ever trouble you again."

"And drink that Coke," Holloway said. "I think I've got a Kind bar in my purse. You're too thin; don't listen to that boy."

"Drink that Coke right up," Weigel said as she grabbed the desk phone. "What's your cousin know about all this?"

"Oh, he and Davey don't get along at all. That's the whole reason I came over tonight; Chris wants to talk about it."

The women exchanged knowing looks.

"Uh huh," Holloway said, fluffing Shaw's hair again. "Listen to your cousin, Max. You're too pretty to waste on a jerk like Davey."

"Mr. Hobson? Yes, I've got your cousin Max—yes, sir. I'll send him right up."

It took a little longer, but Shaw finally managed to extricate himself and ride the elevator up. He found the door to 8A unlocked, and when he stepped inside, North was waiting near the landline phone where he'd answered the call from the security desk and told them to let Shaw into the building.

"What the absolute fuck was all that fuckery?"

"I got a Coke!"

"You've got an abusive boyfriend named Davey? Jesus fucking Christ, Shaw. I didn't say you couldn't buy that stupid fucking cloak. My exact words were, 'I don't think you'll wear it very much, so I don't think it's worth the money.' And I didn't say you couldn't get tattoos or have your nipples pierced. I said maybe you should think about the fact that you don't like needles and having the script of *Memento* tattooed over every inch of your body might be a decision you regret in a few months."

"I—"

"And if you say one fucking word about that Coke, I'm going to lose my fucking shit."

North's shit looked pretty lost already, so Shaw just sipped the cola and nodded. "It's been a hard night. Your penis. Those cutoffs."

North's fists clenched at his sides. Then he turned slowly and stalked down the hall.

The condo looked like it had come straight out of a CB2 catalogue: sinuously modern furniture, glass and teak, the occasional bleached wicker and white-varnished rattan piece. It even smelled store-bought, like all-purpose cleaner and artificial lavender. Sliding glass doors opened onto a balcony overlooking the park: asphalt ribbons, the arched backs of stone bridges, winter-brown grass rippling like water.

Shaw and North pulled on disposable gloves and moved quickly through the unit. They couldn't toss the place the way they normally would have, but they still managed to work efficiently, dividing the rooms without speaking, each man methodical in his search.

North found the safe hidden on the bookshelf. It had a cover designed to look like a row of books, and it was surprisingly good—from a distance. With the cover pulled back, a keypad and lock were visible. They tested keys on the lock until one of them turned, and the safe's door swung open.

"Computer," North said as he drew several external hard drives from the safe.

"Got it," Shaw said, already powering up the laptop. A login screen appeared, and Shaw typed in the Aldrich Acquisitions administrator password—provided courtesy of his father, who also happened to be their most valuable client. After an uncertain flicker, the screen changed, and Shaw had access to Chris Hobson's computer.

After scrolling quickly through the files, Shaw said, "Nothing obvious."

"It's corporate espionage," North said as he plugged in the first external hard drive. "He's been smart enough so far not to leave a trail of bread crumbs. That's why we're here."

"So far," Shaw said with a smirk. A new window popped up, showing the contents of the hard drive that North had just connected. "Porn."

"Tentacle porn," North corrected.

"You really shouldn't judge—oh." Shaw cut off when North double-clicked one of the files. He covered his eyes and then peeked between two fingers. "I didn't know he could fit so many inside him."

North was already disconnecting the drive. He plugged in the next one.

"This is it," Shaw said as he looked at the files.

"Make a nice, obvious folder to stash it all. Something like 'Chris's Secret Stuff - DO NOT TOUCH.'"

Instead, Shaw burrowed into the computer's main drive, created an unnamed folder, altered the properties so that it was hidden, and copied over the contents of the hard drive. It was a lot of data, and it took several minutes. While they waited, he sent a text to their contact at Aldrich Acquisitions—a woman named Haw Ryeo.

Everything uploaded.

Haw didn't respond, but Shaw knew how things would go: Hobson's computer, which was technically company property, would be inspected immediately. The stolen files and documents would be found, providing grounds for a warrant. In their search of the condo, the police would find the hard drives. Hobson would go to prison, and Aldrich Acquisitions would maintain control of millions of dollars' worth of intellectual property.

"Done?" North asked.

Shaw nodded.

While North disconnected the cables and returned the hard drives to the safe, Shaw powered down the computer. They locked up the condo, took the fire stairs, and let themselves out through a service door. Shaw sent another text, and Pari met them on the same street corner.

"He touched Truck's butt," Pari informed them as she accepted Hobson's keys.

"Get back there and claw his eyes out," North said. "Just make sure you put the keys in his pocket while you do."

Pari's grin was vicious; she practically ran toward the Jumping Pig.

Shaw followed North across Kingshighway again. This side of the street was dark, and the air from the park smelled like wet wood and mulched leaves. In the distance, a few artificial lights looked like silver brads fixing the trees against the night sky.

"Is this how you thought things were going to be?" Shaw asked as they approached the Ford.

"I thought it went pretty smoothly."

"No, I mean—corporate work, planting evidence, tracking down the mistresses of high-level executives."

"Is this a morals thing? Are you feeling guilty?"

"What? No. He stole that stuff; we just gave them a way to prove it. No, it's just—I don't know, I didn't think this is what we'd be doing."

"It's work, Shaw. And we're good at it." North opened the door and rested one arm on the roof of the car. "We're fucking fantastic at it."

"Right."

"And Borealis is doing great."

"Right."

"So?"

After a moment, Shaw shrugged and got into the car.

Chapter 2

WHEN THEY PULLED UP in front of North's Southampton duplex, Shaw had one thing in mind.

"Huh?" North said. And then he grunted and spread his legs. "Oh."

The borrowed Ford rumbled quietly beneath them. The inside of the car smelled like the air freshener—shaped like a cluster of cherries, although smelling more like Laffy Taffy than anything else Shaw could name—and like the American Crew gel North still wore in his textured thatch of blond hair. He was hardening rapidly under Shaw's touch, and he leaned back in the seat, eyes hooded as he watched Shaw impassively. Normally his eyes were a remarkably light blue, the predawn color of fresh snowfall, or like light caught on the rim of a sheet of ice. Tonight, in the darkened interior of the Ford, with his pupils blown wide, they might as well have been black.

He made a sound in his throat and tried to spread his legs farther. His knee thumped the door panel.

"This is when you invite your beautiful, sexually prodigious, unbelievably generous boyfriend inside," Shaw whispered, his fingers tracing the length of North's dick through the denim.

North made another of those noises, but he was still relaxed against the seat. With one hand, barely more than a flick of his fingers, he beckoned Shaw closer.

Grinning, Shaw leaned over the center console. North's movement was minimal, only a few inches, making Shaw come to him. He moved toward North's mouth for a kiss.

At the last moment, though, North veered, his mouth coming to Shaw's ear, and at a normal volume he said, "What about Davey?"

"Ow!" Shaw reared back so fast that he hit the car's headliner. "North, what the hell?"

"I just remembered your crazy, abusive, controlling boyfriend Davey. I just wanted to make sure he was ok with us messing around."

"You are really taking that the wrong way."

North just watched him through hooded eyes. His erection was still visible through the jeans.

"I just took a few details and, you know, made something else up."

"Uh huh."

"You and Davey have absolutely nothing in common."

"Uh huh."

"He was a total figment of my imagination."

"Uh huh." North reached down, pretending to adjust himself, although his hand lingered long enough to suggest something else. "Except those details that you took from real life."

"North, come on!"

"Night, Shaw."

"Hey, hold on." Shaw caught his wrist, drawing North's hand to the bulge in his own jeans. He let out a satisfied noise and rutted softly against North's palm. "It's been almost a week," Shaw whispered. "And last time, we didn't even get to do a sleepover."

"We're not ten, Shaw." But his fingers curled possessively, rubbing slow and hard against Shaw's dick.

Shaw made another of those appreciative noises; he didn't miss the flush speckling North's throat. Leaning over the console again, he stroked North and found him, if anything, even harder than before. "Please? I want you to fuck me."

The rumble in North's throat was almost a growl. "Is that what you need, baby?"

Shaw nodded.

"Say it," North ordered.

"I need it. I need you to fuck me."

North's grin was sharp and sudden. "Then ask Davey."

"North!"

North's grin got bigger.

Shaw slapped his erection.

"Holy Christ, Shaw!" North folded, covering himself. "What the fuck?"

"You're being a brat."

"Did you just fucking spank my cock? And not even in the fun way, I might add?"

"Quit being so mouthy," Shaw said, "and take me inside and fuck me."

"You're a fucking monster."

Shaw turned off the car and withdrew the keys from the ignition. "Now, North."

North grumbled the whole way to the front door. He let them inside, and the puppy—North's puppy—was there, waiting for them. He immediately started yipping, dancing around their heels, clawing at North's legs.

"Hello," North cooed. "Gotta take care of him first."

"He's a fucking cockblock," Shaw called after him. "This is worse than having children. Children you can just lock in their rooms when daddy needs some dick."

North pointed at the ceiling and glanced back long enough to reply softly, "Keep shouting; I'm sure Mr. Winns is interested in what daddy needs."

Face hot, Shaw locked the door behind him and headed into North's bedroom. He left the sherpa cloak on a chair, kicked off the engineer boots, and climbed onto the bed. A few minutes later, North was there too, toeing off his Redwings, rucking up the sweatshirt he'd worn. He peeled it off, exposing the dense slabs of muscle, the old scar on his side, his chest and belly covered by thick blond fur. He crawled between Shaw's legs, ran his hands up Shaw's thighs, and kissed him. Then he pulled back, palming Shaw through his jeans, a smirk plastered on his face.

"Why are you being so mean to me tonight?"

"Keep whining," North said, eyebrows shooting up, "and you're going to find out how mean I can be."

Huffing a breath, Shaw reached for North's waistband. He unbuttoned the jeans, worked the fly down, and pulled out North's dick. North shivered and let out a breath. Shaw stroked him slowly, watching North's eyes glaze.

Then Shaw's gut twisted.

North was tugging on Shaw's shirt, trying to turn him out of it, his fingers warm and rough.

"Just a second," Shaw said.

"What?"

"Just a second. I've got to, um, clean up first."

North studied him, kissed him, and fell onto his side. Swatting Shaw's thigh, he said, "Hurry, mister. Now who's being mean?"

Shaw did what he needed to do. Perched on the toilet, he suddenly felt hyperaware that none of the guys in the books he liked ever had to deal with this situation. When he'd finished, he opened the door and called to North, "Just gonna take a quick shower." He stepped under the hot water, found the bar of hemp-milk soap he'd stashed so that he didn't have to use the chemical-laden Irish Springs stuff that North bought in bulk, and cleaned himself up. His hair looked like a cumulus cloud after he toweled it, but North seemed to like his hair more the longer and wilder it got, so he left it the way it was and padded into the bedroom naked.

North was asleep on the bed, jeans still around his thighs, the puppy curled up in the crook of one arm. He yapped at Shaw once.

"I don't know what you're complaining about," Shaw muttered as he walked around to North's side of the bed. "You got exactly what you wanted."

"Shaw?" North mumbled.

"Let's get you out of these," Shaw said, helping North free of the jeans.

"Just give me five minutes. Gonna fuck you…" He made a sleepy noise. "…can't walk."

Sliding under the covers, Shaw found North's hand and squeezed it. Then he kissed him. By the time he was reaching to turn off the lamp, North was asleep again. And in the morning, when Shaw woke, North had already left for work.

Chapter 3

"SHE DOESN'T LOOK like a romance author," Shaw said, studying the picture on the website. It showed a woman still on the young side of middle age, trim, her hair in a severe black bob. She had a cigarette holder in one hand, a wisp of smoke artfully photoshopped into the image, and she wore elbow-length gloves. "If anything, she looks like Audrey Hepburn. Or a flapper. Or Audrey Hepburn playing a flapper."

It was Wednesday, and although Shaw had taken Sunday off (North hadn't), Monday and Tuesday had been nonstop with the work Aldrich Acquisitions sent their way. It wasn't just the investigations that kept North and Shaw busy; it was the paperwork. Shaw's father had mostly kept out of the arrangement, at Shaw's insistence, and although Haw was a reasonable woman, corporations still apparently required massive amounts of paperwork, documentation, and evidence—all of it carefully organized and presented. After their first job, North had insisted on doing the paperwork himself.

Today was a paperwork day. The Borealis offices occupied the main floor of the house Shaw owned in Benton Park, and they consisted of two main areas: the outer office, where Pari pretended to be an administrative assistant and where Truck and Zion occasionally completed reports for the part-time jobs they did for Borealis; and the inner office, where North and Shaw worked. The inner office had seating for clients and two desks, placed side by side in the center of the room. North's was immaculate: a large, high-definition computer monitor, a lamp, and a stacked chrome inbox-outbox combo that looked like something Don Draper might have used. Shaw's desk did not quite reach the level of immaculate, although it was definitely cleaner than it had been. It currently held a series of four Twinkies that had been dissected to various degrees and pinned open against their cardboard sleeves; volumes one, three, and six of the *Encyclopedia of Environmental Analysis and Remediation*, a Vitruvian Man coffee mug full of water and green onions, and the LP for *The Best of Gallagher*, which was currently being used as a plate for a piece of a child's birthday cake. Shaw didn't remember who the child had been, but the cake still looked edible.

"North?"

North was typing something in a spreadsheet, checking figures against a page he held.

"North, I think she might be lying."

"Hmm."

"I think she might be lying, the woman who called us. She doesn't look like a romance author at all."

"Uh huh." North pecked at the keyboard.

"North!"

"Look at this. It's the middle of February, and we've already billed more than we did in the whole first quarter of 2018. And that's not even counting jobs like last night."

"North, I'm trying to tell you something."

After one last, lingering glance at the spreadsheet, North looked over. "That's her?"

"That's what I'm trying to tell you: I think this is a ruse."

"A ruse."

"A con."

"A con."

"A scam."

North sighed. "Ok. Let's hear it."

"She doesn't look like a romance author at all."

"And just because I feel like my life won't be complete until I hear this: what is a romance author supposed to look like?"

"Well, you know." Shaw gestured vaguely. "A corset. Fishnet stockings. Stiletto heels. Would it kill her to wear a bustier?"

"I don't—"

"Or one of those vinyl bodysuits. And maybe a whip!"

"I think you're thinking of a prostitute—"

"Sex worker."

"—or dominatrix." North pointed to the screen. "This lady just looks like she has too much time on her hands, and maybe she likes playing dress-up."

"Says the man who just ordered an adult Naruto costume—" Shaw cut off at the noise North was making. "I mean, right, yes, whatever you were saying."

A knock came at the door, and a moment later, it opened.

"Ms. Maldonado is here to see you," Pari said, all sweetness and light with a prospective client standing behind her.

"Thank you, Pari."

"And Truck asked me to tell you that hir job is taking hir to East St. Louis."

North nodded; he was obviously trying not to make a face. "Please remind hir that we only reimburse legitimate expenses."

"Ze knows," Pari said, her smile turning brittle.

"That means—"

"Ze knows. We all know."

"All right," Shaw said. "Great. Thank you, Pari. Thanks so much. Ms. Maldonado?"

A soft voice answered, "Yasmin," and then the woman and Pari traded places, and Yasmin Maldonado moved into the office. She had a skunk stripe of gray roots where her hair was parted, and she looked thinner than she had in the picture. She wore a MICHIGAN IS FOR LOVER'S sweatshirt, snow pants that crinkled every time she took a step, and ratty Reeboks. The only thing consistent with the picture was the smell of cigarette smoke that moved with her.

They took a few minutes getting her settled, exchanging introductions, and her eyes roved around the office before settling on the LP with its slice of birthday cake. With what looked like a great deal of effort, she dragged her gaze up to look at North and Shaw.

"I know you're going to think I'm fangirling, but I just can't believe you're willing to take this case. The gay detectives! This is so exciting!"

"Well," North said with a sidelong glance at Shaw, "there might have been a miscommunication. I'm interested in hearing about the job you want us to do, but I have to be honest and tell you we're very—"

"Very interested," Shaw said. "Very excited about a chance to do some work with the LGBTQ community."

Yasmin nodded. Then her mouth widened into an O. "You mean us! Oh, right. Yes, that would be great. I mean, you're gay! It would be fantastic."

"Right," North said with another of those sidelong looks. "We're definitely gay."

"And you're boyfriends," Yasmin said, clasping her hands.

Another of those sidelong looks. Shaw discreetly rolled his chair back a few inches and kicked North in the ankle. "Why don't you tell us," Shaw said, ignoring North's murderous glare, "what's going on? You mentioned death threats. Against you, in particular? What's been happening?"

"Well, I don't care what anyone says: we can't cancel the con. We can't. I won't. I'm not going to let some pathetic nobody terrorize us into ruining a wonderful time for hundreds of people."

"You're talking about the…" Shaw checked his notes, which he now saw were written on the back of a Jack in the Box receipt. "Queer Expectations Convention? Is that right?"

"Yes. The premiere gay romance literature convention in the world."

"The only," North coughed into his fist.

But Yasmin had heard him, and she shook her head. "Oh no, there's another. Gay Romance Literature. Very…hoity toity. Noses in the air. Not like us; we just want to have fun."

"And this con, Queer Expectations, it's being held in St. Louis this year?"

"That's right." Yasmin squirmed to the edge of her seat, snow pants crinkling. "A few weeks ago, I started getting emails. 'I'm going to get my revenge.' 'You're all going to pay.' That kind of thing. Then the physical letters started showing up. They had the words cut out of magazines, you know. They said the same kind of things. I brought them, in case you want to see them." She gestured to a folder on her lap. "And I checked in at the hotel Monday; Tuesday morning, I had another one. Someone had slipped it under the door while I was asleep. It's crazy. The whole business is insane. And of course, someone leaked it, and our guests are going wild. We already have a lot of people who suffer from anxiety, and this is going to put them in the ground. It really will."

"I'm not sure," North said slowly, "what you want us to do. This sounds like something you need to take to the police."

"I tried! They're not interested. Actually, if I'm being frank, they looked at me like I'm crazy. Very homophobic. It's probably because we're in Missouri."

"The Metropolitan Police aren't always my favorite people, but they wouldn't ignore a credible threat."

"But they did. I mean, they are. They talked on and on about being careful and keeping an eye out for anyone strange or unfamiliar. It's a romance convention! We're all strange! And we love it that way. I tried to explain to them that something horrible is going to happen, but they just won't listen."

"Did the messages you received have any specifics?" Shaw asked.

"Like what?"

"Well, anything, really. Any details."

Yasmin made a face, opened the folder, and spread a half dozen pages on the desk. They were all as she had described them: cut-out words pasted onto copy paper, spelling out a variety of threats: *I'm going to get you, No one is safe, Watch your back*. Shaw sighed and looked at North.

"Oh no," North said. "You're the one who opened this particular door to Batshit Land."

"The problem," Shaw said, "is that even if the police wanted to help, there's nowhere for them to start. You might be the intended target, but you might not—this one says, 'I'm watching all of you.' There's no sign of when or how someone might be in danger. We're even making the assumption that this is connected to the con. You're giving the police a black hole of possibilities, and they'd need limitless resources in order to even try to make a difference."

"But they can't do this. You're not allowed to threaten people."

"You're right; harassment is against the law, but it's a misdemeanor. Unless you can give them a viable suspect, they just don't have the resources to run down something like this."

Yasmin stared at them, mouth agape, her breath stirring invisible eddies with the smell of cigarette smoke. "Fine. Fine. That's why I'm here, isn't it? I'm going to hire you: private detectives. Gay private detectives."

"If I have to hear about how gay I am one more time," North said to Shaw, "I'm going to shit a unicorn."

"We're not gay detectives," Shaw said to Yasmin. "We're detectives who happen to be gay. And this isn't a gay detective agency. It's a detective agency that helps the LGBTQ community."

"Or anyone who can pay."

"Well," Yasmin said, "I fit both those criteria. I can pay, and I'm part of the LGBTQ community. I mean, I'm straight, but I write about gay men. I'm an ally."

"We know," Shaw said. "And we're really grateful. And we're looking forward to reading your books."

North cleared his throat.

"We really are," Shaw said. "I think North got a little chub just looking at the cover for *Spankin' Angels*, and I really liked the description of *Marcus the Marquis*, especially the part about the Prince Albert—"

"What Shaw is trying to say, in perhaps the most backassward way possible, is that we can't take this case. We'd like to help you, and I'm sorry this is upsetting for you, but you're asking us to do something impossible. We don't have the resources to provide security for an entire convention. Your best bet is to do what the police recommended: remind people to be vigilant, keep hotel staff and security in the loop, and immediately inform the police if anything suspicious happens."

"What if I have a suspect?"

"You just said you have no idea—"

"We had to ban a convention-goer last year. She was way too aggressive with the men who attended. Objectifying. Sexualizing. She hired a young man, a hustler, to seduce a very well-known author, and then the police got involved because it was a vice sting. It was awful. We had to tell her she was never welcome back at Queer Expectations."

"Why didn't you mention this to the police?" Shaw said.

"Because...because I didn't think of it at the time."

"Very convenient," North said.

"I didn't! A friend just told me that Leslie—she's the woman I'm talking about—Leslie is planning on crashing the con. And sitting here, listening to you, it all suddenly clicked."

"What a wonderful coincidence," North said.

"Exactly," Yasmin said, straightening in her seat with excitement.

"No," Shaw said. "He's being sarcastic."

"Oh." Yasmin's expression fell, then she brightened again. "I can pay you to see if Leslie really is in the area. That's something you can do, right? You can just try to find her. Come to the convention. See if she's hanging around. And if she's not, if she's safely back in Utah or wherever she normally is, your job is done, and you get paid. Although I really hope you'll attend the whole convention because you'll be our local celebrities."

"Would you give us a moment?"

"What? Oh, yes. Of course. We can even pay you for your time at the convention. Your hourly rate. You really don't understand—everyone will be so excited."

When the door shut behind her, North spun in his chair to face Shaw. "No."

"Hold on."

"No way, Shaw. This is amateur hour. We might as well be investigating a high-school mean girls club. Samantha told Sarah who told Megan that the boys' swim team stuffs their speedos."

"First of all, you would know, because I remember freshman year you bragging about that water polo player and telling me, quote, 'Turns out I like the taste of chlorinated balls.'"

North made a disgusted noise. "Shaw, we've got four open jobs from Aldrich right now. Four. I honestly don't know the last time I slept more than six hours in a night, the paperwork keeps piling up, and on top of that, we've got independent clients who are willing to pay obscene hourly rates for us to take pictures of cheating spouses. This is a fan convention for romance readers. Gay romance readers. How are they going to pay us? In poppers?"

"Actually, that's not a bad—"

"This is what we've worked incredibly hard for, Shaw. This. What we've got right now. We built Borealis from nothing, and it's finally paying off. Why can't we just enjoy that things are good right now?"

"We didn't start Borealis to get rich," Shaw said quietly.

"Speak for yourself, you fucking trust-fund baby."

With a shrug, Shaw waited, holding North's gaze.

Outside, a diesel truck lumbered past the house, engine grumbling as the driver struggled to shift up.

North let out a wild growl. "Fine. Fine. Just shut the fuck up. If you say one more fucking word, I'm going to lose my mind."

"All I said was that you like chlorinated balls and that you might want our clients to pay us in poppers."

"You got what you fucking wanted, Shaw, like you always do."

"You—"

North stabbed a finger at Shaw. "Not one. more. fucking. word."

Shaw shrugged again.

Wiping his face, North stood. He bent, caught Shaw's hair, and kissed him. Then he gently tugged on the hair, turning Shaw's head, and whispered, "If you ever tell anyone how easily you just made that happen, you're going to need a truckload of poppers to handle what I'll do to you."

"Is that a bad thing or a good thing? It kind of sounds like a good thing."

North scowled, released Shaw, and headed for the door. As he pulled it open, he said, "Ms. Maldonado? We'll take the job. The contract is standard, and we do require a retainer—" North cut off, and when he spoke again, his voice was tight and hard. "I'm with a client."

A man's voice, familiar, carried back to where Shaw sat: "North, North, North. Is that any way to greet your uncle?"

Acknowledgments

My deepest thanks go out to the following people (in alphabetical order):

Austin Gwin, for helping me think more carefully about Nick's situation in this book and how to make him more believable, for urging me to think about how to make characters distinct and memorable, and for appreciating my 'low booze bitch mode' t-shirt.

Anne Justice-Allen, for providing (as always) her expert advice generously and enthusiastically, for thinking about crazy things like what an immunocontraceptive might do in a human body, and for helping me figure out exactly where a dart tip might break.

Steve Leonard, for catching so many little thing (a crumpled ball of foil), for keeping track of open windows and missing texts, and for pointing out how the final chapter might be revised to match better with the other books.

Cheryl Oakley, for urging me to think more carefully about Jager and Blake's relationship, for working on the convoluted plot and how we could make it simpler, and drawing my attention to inconsistencies and continuity errors (like Tean using the paracord!).

Tray Stephenson, for laughing with me about the palliative measures for hemorrhoids, for teaching me the origins of the Dopp kit (even if I stuck with my lowercase d), and for nudging me toward clarity when I let my prose get too vague.

Dianne Thies, for always offering the perfect blend of feedback and encouragement, for pointing out that Jem's naked (and it's not a problem), and for helping me brainstorm how in the world to get a hotel key to Tean.

Jo Wegstein, for her usual incisiveness in suggesting clarity in prose, for making me rethink how much text Jem could easily read (especially in a short period of time), and for pushing back against the version of Ammon (even though we may not have agreed completely, I appreciate so much the thoughtful dissent).

Wendy Wickett, for her gentle suggestions that I use more italics, for reminding me that Ammon and Jem have had physical altercations before, and for not cutting off communication when she realized how deeply I'd researched confidence scams.

About the Author

Learn more about Gregory Ashe and forthcoming works at **www.gregoryashe.com**.

For advanced access, exclusive content, limited-time promotions, and insider information, please sign up for my mailing list at **http://bit.ly/ashemailinglist**.

Made in United States
Orlando, FL
27 November 2022